Praise for Deb Kastner
and her novels

"A slight twist to the usual romantic formula is most welcome in this tender love story by Deb Kastner."
—*RT Book Reviews* on *The Christmas Groom*

"An entertaining story of changing plans, moving forward and learning to lean on God."
—*RT Book Reviews* on *Phoebe's Groom*

"Kastner's latest will grab the reader with familiar characters and engaging dialogue."
—*RT Book Reviews* on *Yuletide Baby*

Praise for Virginia Carmichael
and her novels

"Readers will especially connect with Calista as her character grows and learns to love."
—*RT Book Reviews* on *Season of Joy*

"Carmichael crafts strong, honorable characters who try to do what is right."
—*RT Book Reviews* on *Season of Hope*

"Having a female mechanic as a heroine is a welcome twist."
—*RT Book Reviews* on *A Home for Her Family*

Publishers Weekly bestselling and award-winning author **Deb Kastner** writes stories of faith, family and community in small-town Western settings. She lives in Colorado with her husband and a pack of miscreant mutts, and is blessed with three daughters and two grandchildren. She enjoys spoiling her grandkids, movies, music (The Texas Tenors!), singing in the church choir and exploring Colorado on horseback.

Virginia Carmichael was born near the Rocky Mountains, and although she has traveled around the world, the wilds of Colorado run in her veins. A big fan of the wide-open sky and all four seasons, she believes in embracing the small moments of everyday life. She's a homeschooling mom of six young children who rarely wear shoes, so those moments usually involve a lot of noise, a lot of mess or a whole bunch of warm cookies. Virginia holds degrees in linguistics and religious studies from the University of Oregon. She lives with her habanero-eating husband, Crusberto, who is her polar opposite in all things except faith. They've learned to speak in shorthand code and look forward to the day they can actually finish a sentence. In the meantime, Virginia thanks God for the laughter and abundance of hugs that fill her day as she plots her next book.

The Christmas Groom

Deb Kastner

&

Season of Joy

Virginia Carmichael

H HARLEQUIN® LOVE INSPIRED®

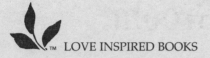 LOVE INSPIRED BOOKS

PLEASE RECYCLE · THIS PRODUCT IS RECYCLABLE

Recycling programs for this product may not exist in your area.

ISBN-13: 978-1-335-19998-0

The Christmas Groom and Season of Joy

Copyright © 2017 by Harlequin Books S.A.

The publisher acknowledges the copyright holders of the individual works as follows:

The Christmas Groom
Copyright © 2002 by Debra Kastner

Season of Joy
Copyright © 2012 by Virginia Munoz

www.Harlequin.com

Printed in U.S.A.

CONTENTS

THE CHRISTMAS GROOM

Deb Kastner

To the Lord, my God,
with grateful thanks.

Therefore if the Son makes you free,
you shall be free indeed.
—*John* 8:36

Chapter One

Colin Brockman was late to his first day of school. More accurately, his first day *back* in school.

He crept as casually and quietly as his big, squeaky-tennis-shoed feet would let him into the muted twilight tones of his Child Psych auditorium classroom. Gym shoes were far more comfortable than navy dress shoes, but Colin found that, for a moment, he missed the familiarity of the spit and polish, the recognizable click of the heels as he walked.

At least he knew what to expect from navy issue. He hadn't a clue what to expect from this day.

With a relieved huff, he slid into a seat that, while made with an adult in mind, certainly didn't take into account his considerably large frame. He shifted backward and forward, left to right, knocking his knees against the bottom of the desk, raking his elbows against the steel hardware and knowing that with every movement he continued to draw unwanted attention to himself and his dilemma.

Didn't these desks adjust for height somehow? Or had he just picked one meant for a third-grade kid?

When no bolts loosened under his fingers, he changed tactics, turning, stretching and curving himself as smoothly as possible into the seat, mentally comparing himself to a piece of artist's molding clay.

Mashed, rolled and squished into the creation of the Master's form.

Despite his discomfort, Colin grinned at the mental picture he'd created of God pounding and kneading him into shape, and knew he wasn't so very far off. He was a work in progress, potter's clay in the Master's hands. He trusted God could make more of him than he could of himself—he'd gone that route already, and anyone with an eye could see where that had taken him.

He continued his slow, steady movements until he was certain he could breathe and stretch his long legs, which appeared to be his two greatest problems at the moment. That, and maybe the ability to actually reach the desk with his hand in case he wanted to take notes on a class that was rapidly moving along without him.

Pushing the hood of his oversize gray sweatshirt off his head with both palms, he used his fingers to scrub through the tips of his fine blond hair. It had been years since he'd grown his hair above a military buzz cut, and no one had mentioned how terribly it would itch and bother him.

Still, he thought he might live through it if he could grow it past the Chia Pet stage.

He smothered another grin. He didn't mind, not really. In the big scheme of things, it was a pretty small annoyance. At least he had the choice of whether or not to grow his hair out, to make his own decision about something even as minimal as that, for a change.

The navy, for all its many benefits, didn't give a man

many choices, and Colin was eager to make up for lost time now that he was his own man.

Eager to begin his career as a student, he jammed one hand into his backpack, digging for a fresh spiral notebook and a pen or a pencil to write with. He was positive they were to be found somewhere in the depths of his bag.

Or at least thought they were there.

He was almost certain.

He bit the corner of his lip and made another pass at it. His hand closed over several items, which he grasped and discarded—a fork, a sock without a mate, a baseball, a stud finder he'd been using earlier in the day on his apartment wall in order to hang pictures.

He cringed, squeezing his eyebrows down close around his eyes as he called himself every kind of idiot. It was his first day of school. Surely he had remembered to throw in something to write on. And to write with.

At length, he found the notebook he wanted, but his blue ballpoint pen, the one he'd purchased especially for this new school year, eluded him, until he remembered suddenly he'd shoved it into the back left pocket of his jeans before he left.

So he wouldn't forget where it was, naturally.

Settling restlessly in his seat, he took a moment to look around, tapping his newly found pen on the top of his notebook as a rich female voice resonated warmly from the front of the room, speaking of classroom procedures, what to expect from the course and what homework assignments would be like.

Colin listened with only half an ear. He knew he should be paying more attention, especially on his first day, but he was more interested in his fellow students than what was going on at the front of the room.

Who were these people, and what were they in for? He didn't expect to fit in with a crowd of kids coming straight from high school, exactly, but...

Oh, man.

Old man was more like it. Was he really ready for this?

He was astounded at the profusion of young men in baggy pants, young ladies with fuchsia and other Easter colors striped in their hair, ill-concealed Game Boys peeking out of pockets, coats, dresses and purses. Bodies of both genders were pierced in places Colin didn't even want to think about.

Oh, man.

Where were the people like him? Where were the people who hadn't figured out they needed to go to school until they were—what was a nice way of phrasing it?—well past their adolescent prime?

Looking around him, he felt worlds older than the youngsters in this class, though that was hardly the truth. He was thirty, which wasn't exactly over the hill.

He was probably only a decade older than most of the students. But in experience, he was an antique compared to the young men and women sitting around him.

Or at least he felt that way.

His gaze wandered down to the floor of the auditorium, where a couple of professors, young ladies, were taking turns speaking. The muted sunlight made it hard to see that far down, but Colin's vision was excellent.

He smiled as his gaze shifted from one of the female professors to the other and riveted upon her.

He was much closer in age to that pretty little parcel

with the gorgeous long legs, sashaying back and forth in the front of the room.

Much closer.

He didn't know why he hadn't noticed the attractive twentysomething woman earlier. He had to be really nervous to have missed that bright beacon of light in an otherwise shadowed room, for it was her warm voice lighting up the darkness.

And to think he hadn't even looked to the front of the room until now! Not to look for potential assignments or anything. He hadn't even glanced at the prominent overhead projector illuminating the middle of the room.

To think he'd almost continued on blissfully unaware of the lovely angel who would most certainly transform this class into something, if not pleasurable, then at least palatable.

He grinned. He couldn't help it if he liked a pretty face. He hadn't seen enough of them in the navy. His ambition to become a chaplain didn't make him blind to a pair of pretty eyes or make him immune to the scent of a beautiful woman.

He might not have a lot of relationship experience of his own to draw from, but he'd been around. He'd been there to watch firsthand when his beloved twin sister fell for the love of her life. He knew how it worked.

And to be honest, he wouldn't mind so very much if *it* worked on him.

In his opinion, God had saved the best for last. Women were the highlight of God's creative efforts, and when He'd finished Eve, He'd had good reason to pronounce His work *very good*.

He tossed his pen down on the desk and leaned forward in his seat, intent on a better view. Now that he'd noticed the pretty prof, he couldn't take his eyes off her.

She had long, thick dark brown hair that gleamed with red highlights as it shifted when she walked. And her eyes were a dark, rich green, and the color of Christmas velvet.

Her sharp gaze was, he noticed with a blast of electric shock, pinned directly on him. He had no doubt whatsoever that she hadn't missed his tardy entrance to his first class on his first day of school, or of his subsequent fidgeting around in his seat as he unsuccessfully attempted to get settled.

He cleared his throat aloud.

That could be a problem.

She was obviously his teacher.

His *professor*, he mentally corrected. This was college, not grade school.

Miss Prof. Or was that *Mrs.*?

He flashed her his most charming grin. Surprise flashed across her gaze and her pretty, full lips hinted softly at a grin; but then the moment was gone. She frowned and lifted one eyebrow in silent question.

What was he up to?

He swore he saw the corners of her sweet lips twitch as she shook her head, looking put out and disappointed in that unique way elementary school teachers had of making their students feel guilty for misbehaving in their classroom.

Colin's back went up in a moment, his spine stiffening in stubbornness. If she was looking to make someone feel *guilty,* she was looking at the wrong student. This wasn't elementary school, and he wasn't a child anymore. He was paying good money to attend the seminary, and to take these university classes on the side.

This was his planet, his continent, his day, hour, minute, and he wasn't even counting seconds.

He was here because he wanted to be, and he'd arrive and leave when he wanted. He wouldn't purposely do anything to disrupt the class or bother any other students, but he wouldn't hand over any of his freshly minted independence, either.

He knew his philosophy sounded a good deal like a bad attitude, but it wasn't. He happily extended his generous outlook to the rest of the world, if they wanted it, which he very much doubted. He'd always thought himself a bit of a maverick.

In truth, he just wanted to find out what it meant to be footloose and fancy-free. He'd never had the chance to do that, even in his youth. And now that he had the time and opportunity, he wasn't going to give it up, even to a pretty professor.

He turned his attention to the first lecture, scribbling illegible notes on the first clean, crisp page of his notebook.

Colin was soon lost in thought and note taking as he attempted to follow the lecture. Ms. Gorgeous Legs—he clearly needed to find out her real name—was talking a mile a minute, and very animatedly, about something called the Hierarchy of Needs that some famous psychologist guy named Maslow had come up with.

Projected onto the screen at the front of the auditorium was a diagram in the shape of a triangle. A person, especially a child, the lovely woman explained, was unable to focus on obtaining or meeting the needs on the higher levels until he or she had fulfilled the lower-level needs, the base needs, if you will. Things such as finding food, warmth and shelter.

Colin frowned at the diagram he'd traced onto his paper. The more ethereal needs were indeed placed exclusively in higher rows.

But what about the search for God? Didn't that transcend even the most basic need barriers? As a future navy chaplain, he experienced the insatiable desire to know more, and quickly scribbled his own ideas in the margins.

Since he assumed he'd missed the part of the lesson on how the class was run, he wasn't certain how to go about getting his questions answered. He had no office hours or phone numbers to call.

"Serves you right, Brockman," he mumbled under his breath.

He started to raise his hand, then pulled it back down, deciding he'd ask his question at the end of the class...if he could remember it for that long. There was a lot of stuff to think about, and this was only his first class of the day.

He'd always considered himself a smart man, but not necessarily good at book learning. If he was going to make it in college, he was going to have to apply himself, especially since he hadn't been to school in years.

"Your first assignment is going to feel like a big one," said the beautiful woman in the front of the room, her thick sable hair swishing hypnotically with each movement. Colin pressed his chin in his hand, scratching at the stubble. "But it's important that you take this project seriously, and have it completed by next Monday."

Colin paused in his note taking and scowled, shaking his head in silent dissent.

"Great," he whispered under his breath. "A term paper on the very first week of school."

He was completely serious in his opposition, but the three-hundred-pound jock next to him bellowed out a deep-throated laugh.

"Something funny, gentlemen?" The sable-haired woman in the front of the room was eyeing him again. He bit his bottom lip against a smile. He really needed to learn her name.

"No, ma'am," he called out, and the boy next to him sniggered. Her lovely green eyes grazed over the younger man and landed squarely on Colin. Her gaze glimmered with amusement, though her posture was tight and her expression grim.

He resisted the urge to straighten his shoulders and couple his hands on the desk as he'd been taught to do in military school. Rather, he slid down in his seat just about as far as his large frame could fit.

Maybe his question could wait. Maybe he could simply disappear altogether.

"Your assignment," announced Holly McCade, deciding her best strategy on this first day of a new year of student teaching was simply to ignore the snickering, juvenile troublemakers in the back, "is simply this. Find somewhere you can observe a situation in which children are struggling to meet their basic needs. There are dozens of examples I could give you on where to find these children, but I leave that part up to your discretion and creativity. Please feel free to come see me for help and/or suggestions if you run into any trouble with this part of the assignment."

She paused, struggling, for a moment, with her phrasing. "You must observe those children for at least two hours, but the more time you spend with them, the better of an understanding you will walk away with."

She held up her own three-ringed notebook. "Taking notes would be a good idea, but you are not required to do so. You will be required to hand in a one-page paper telling me who you selected, where they are located and how much time you spent observing."

"Is that all?" asked a surprised young lady in the first row. The girl was obviously just out of high school. She was wearing too much makeup and wore her boyfriend's high school letter jacket around her shoulders.

Holly laughed. "Yes. That's all."

A surreptitious glance at her watch signaled a frenzy of activity as students packed up their books and got their things together.

And she hadn't even said the word *go*, she thought, smothering another smile.

"Remember, if you have any questions, I'll be here for another ten minutes."

A couple of students responded to that call. One obviously wanted to get in good with the teacher and make sure Holly knew who he was. The other was a typical overachiever obsessing about whether or not Holly would give an A+ on the assignment when the student in question was only allowed to turn in one page.

"Take it easy," said a rich, laughing baritone from somewhere behind Holly's left shoulder. "You make it sound like you *want* her to make us write a term paper or something."

"I...well... I..." stammered the girl, and then picked up her books and darted out of the classroom without another word.

Somehow Holly instinctively knew to whom the

voice belonged even before she turned around. She was certain it must be the man she'd noticed sitting at the top round of the auditorium. The man with sparkling blue eyes and an untidy bit of light blond hair.

It felt strange for her, as a student teacher, to be teaching someone older than she was, although the man could hardly be called her grandfather. She guessed him to be around thirty, only two years or so older. Not much of an age difference.

Older people returned to college all the time in this day and age. She'd taught a retired couple last semester and hadn't seen anything strange about that. So it wasn't such an oddity for this man to be enrolled in her class.

But it certainly felt like an oddity, especially when the character in question had spent the study hour cracking jokes with an eighteen-year-old boisterous jock. She would have thought a guy this man's age would have respect for the classroom, if not the teacher.

"Can I help you?" she asked testily.

His grin slipped. "To tell you the truth, ma'am, I don't know."

Was he toying with her? She searched his face, but saw no hint of his intentions. His expression gave her no clue whether he was serious or not.

But dealing with potential class clowns was part of student teaching, and she sighed inwardly, even as she steeled herself to be graceful under adversity, no matter how handsome the package.

With effort, she smiled. "Do you have a question about the assignment?" she asked, rephrasing the query.

"Question, comment, statement," Colin said. "My name is Colin Brockman, by the way." He thrust out his hand with a wink and a grin.

He already knew her name, at least if he'd been paying attention in class. Since he probably hadn't been, and because she didn't want him to keep calling her *ma'am*, she responded.

"Holly McCade," she answered. She hadn't missed a beat in their conversation, but her heart missed several beats as she shook his hand. He had large palms, smooth fingers and a firm but gentle grip.

"My question has to do with that triangle thing you talked about in your lecture," he said.

"The Hierarchy of Needs," she supplied. "The one suggested by Dr. Maslow."

He nodded vigorously. "Well, the thing is, Miss... Mrs...uh, Holly," he stammered, then stopped for a moment and tried again. "I believe there's a bigger base than the one you've—Dr. Maslow's—given."

Intriguing. He *had* been paying attention. "How do you mean?"

"I mean God, ma'am. I think there should be a new bottom row—one reserved for God alone."

Holly's heart stirred. As a Christian, she shared similar feelings, but of course could not teach those beliefs openly in a public classroom. Besides, Dr. Maslow's theory had been used in the psych classroom for years.

"Do you mean," she asked slowly, "in the place of eating and sleeping?"

He frowned and shook his head. "No."

"Please continue, Colin. Keep in mind that Maslow did make room for metaphysical thinking at higher levels of the triangle, addressed after the basic needs have been provided for."

His eyes narrowed in thought, and he stroked the

stubbly line of his jaw. Shaving hadn't, apparently, been the reason he was late for class.

"The more I think about it, the more I wonder if God should really occupy a level at all," he said, sounding surprisingly contemplative, considering his scruffy appearance.

He continued, sounding more confident with each word. "God isn't a system, something you think about or organize with. He's not Someone you can compartmentalize or graph. I guess what I'm trying to say, and not very eloquently, is that I think He's a relationship. *Without* boundaries, or format. He transcends the triangle."

"Maybe He *is* the triangle," Holly suggested quietly. "By and in and through everything—every need, every want, every desire."

Before Holly could catch a breath, Colin pounded a nearby table with his fists and hooted with glee. "That's it! Hot diggity-dog."

She chuckled nervously, brushing her fingers through her hair as she covertly looked around to see if anyone had noticed his outburst. To her relief, the room was empty except for the two of them.

"Ain't life just grand?" he asked with a smile. "Don't you just love it when you *get it*?"

She'd never thought about it that way, but she supposed she did enjoy the thrill of discovery. His childlike enthusiasm was contagious, and she found herself smiling back at him.

And she found herself modifying her initial opinion of her unusual scholar. Colin might, after all, be precisely the type of student she wanted to teach. "Do you know where you're going to go for your assignment?" she blurted without thinking.

He shook his head, his blond hair fluffing out every which direction. He reminded her of a little boy growing out his summer haircut, or maybe of a wild turkey, she wasn't sure which.

Either way, he looked adorable.

"I have a couple of ideas, if you'd like to join me," she offered tentatively, unsure why she was reaching out to him. She wasn't sure she was supposed to be interacting with students on this level. She wasn't even sure she liked him.

"The Christian Relief Center is open to visitors. We could go there," she suggested.

"These are street people?"

"Yes. CRC caters to women on the street who are there due to divorce or battering. There are always lots of children to observe. CRC tries to sweep these women and children off the street and, well, meet their lower hierarchical needs."

"That's a mouthful," Colin said. "Hierarchical. Try saying that three times fast."

Holly felt the heat rush to her face. "You don't have to go with me if you have somewhere else to go."

His gaze flickered with amusement. He reached out and lightly chucked her under her chin. "I have no place else to go. Lead on, fair Holly, and I will follow."

Chapter Two

Holly McCade switched her position on the university park bench, crossing her left leg over her right and stretching her right arm across the back of the bench. She turned her head, taking in the landscape all the way around her. Colorado was gorgeous in the fall, and Greeley was no exception. Though it was too early for the aspen leaves to turn their traditional shades of yellow, orange and gold, the day was still vivid with color.

Greeley lay on the eastern plains, and Holly could see the green and brown patchwork of farmland and ranchland from where she sat. And though there were one or two taller buildings marring the view, she could even see the front range of the Rocky Mountains in all their majestic splendor, far enough away to require a plan, but close enough for a drive.

Students milled around between classes, talking, studying or playing Frisbee on the lawn. Birds chattered from the trees, and there was even a big brown squirrel helping himself to lunch from a convenient garbage barrel.

It was all very nice, and she might even have enjoyed the morning sunshine and the lovely views, except that she wasn't sitting here to spend half her Saturday watching university students play games and hungry squirrels rummage for food.

She was waiting for Colin Brockman.

With a loud sigh, she glanced at her watch.

Again.

She didn't know why she'd offered to do this—meet with a man she hardly knew and wasn't completely sure she liked. Probably she was under some misguided, philanthropic notion that she could help him broaden his horizons on his way to a better understanding of child psychology.

And to have waited over an hour for him—she must really be losing it. She wasn't the young woman with low self-esteem who'd do anything for a man she might have been in her youth. Anything but!

She should go. She could be busy with something else. Her time was important, and Colin obviously didn't respect that. Or respect her, for that matter.

She should have gone with her first impression, she decided. Colin was nothing more than an overgrown kid with mischief in his heart.

She suddenly recalled all those little things she noticed about him that clinched her first opinion—the cut of his uneven hair, the day's growth of beard on his face. Even his clothes looked like he'd thrown them on from where they'd once lay crumpled, probably on the floor of his bedroom.

He was a rascal, all right.

A *late* rascal.

Anger and frustration welled up inside her heart. Anger at herself. Why had she bothered waiting?

She sighed and reached for her bag. She already knew the answer to that question before she asked it of herself.

First impression of him notwithstanding, when she'd spoken with Colin two days ago in the auditorium and he'd voiced his very clever and fervent thoughts on Maslow's theory, she'd sensed something exceptional about him, something that drove away every thought of his scruffy appearance and reeled her in to his charm. He fascinated her with the inkling that there was something more to him than his outward appearance.

Something extraordinary.

His eyes. His beautiful, sea-blue eyes. When he spoke about anything, they danced with happiness and amusement. When he spoke about God, they blazed with love, fire and excitement.

She couldn't help but want to find out more about the man. She wasn't ready to pursue a relationship with anyone, but she could use all the friends she could get. And she wanted to get to know more about Colin.

It wasn't as if she were attracted to him or anything. Not *that* way. He was hardly her type. *Her* type of man was a stylish, well-dressed, aggressive overachiever who cared more about himself and his career than he did the woman he supposedly loved.

Which was exactly why she was swearing off the whole gender. One hundred percent cold turkey.

Except for Colin. And it appeared *he* was swearing off *her*. She glanced once again at her watch and decided she'd waited long enough.

She gathered her bag, concluding it was pointless to

stay any longer. He was obviously not going to show up, and the longer she waited, the more she was going to hurt herself.

Maybe he never planned to come in the first place. And since she hadn't thought to give him her cell phone number, he wouldn't have been able to contact her if something important *had* come up, and he couldn't make it for legitimate reasons.

"Fair Holly, your carriage awaits."

Even as her heart skipped a beat at his fairy-tale teasing, she whirled around on the bench, her gaze narrowing in on the errant charmer. She was determined to give him a piece of her mind before she lost her nerve to the tune of his sweet words.

With a pointed glance at her watch, she stated the obvious. "Colin, it's 11:15 a.m."

He chuckled. "Thank you, Ms. Big Ben, for the update."

"Oh, and Mr. Late ought to be the one to talk. Should you be in kindergarten instead of college? It's apparent you can't tell the time."

To her surprise, he agreed. "I probably should be in kindergarten, at that." He pulled up the sleeve of his black Mickey Mouse sweatshirt and bared his arm to her perusal.

"Showing me your muscles?" she teased.

"Showing you my watch. See?"

"You aren't wearing a watch."

He broke into a grin, as if she'd made some great discovery or major breakthrough, with his help.

"Exactly," he confirmed.

"Exactly…what?" she asked, suspecting she really didn't want to know.

"I don't wear a watch."

"I think we've established that fact." If his goal was to get her laughing, and she thought it might be, he was succeeding admirably.

But there was still the issue of his standing her up for an hour. "We agreed that we were going to meet at 10:00 a.m. sharp, as I recall. If you weren't going to meet me here when you said you were, why did you bother to mention a specific time at all?"

"I didn't mention a specific time. You did. Besides, I'm here now. Isn't that what's important?"

"Isn't keeping your word important?" she shot back, annoyed, but she regretted her hasty words when his face colored scarlet.

He had the nerve to look angry? Indignation rose tightly within her. She pinched her mouth closed, her heart pounding rapidly in her defense. *She* was the one who'd been injured here.

"Yes, ma'am, keeping my word is very important to me," he replied gravely, his golden brows bridging low over his eyes. "I guess I should have told you up front that I—I don't live by my watch," he stammered.

His gaze met hers, then he looked away. "I expected to arrive much closer to our scheduled meeting time than I did. I do apologize for that."

She was intrigued. There was a story here he wasn't telling her. Why would a man forswear a watch, particularly when he was in college, where time was so very much of the essence?

"So tell me, Colin…how do you make it to all your classes without knowing what time it is? Since you don't wear a watch."

He shrugged, and his face pinched up so it looked almost like a cringe. "Well, I know you saw me sneak in late to your class the other day, so I guess I can't deny it. My system's not perfect."

"Oh, it's not *my* class," she corrected, heat warming her cheeks at his assumption. "I'm only a student teacher at the moment. For my doctorate, you know? There are two of us team-teaching the child psychology class this semester, under a full professor's guidance."

"Oh? I thought you were a full professor." He slid down to sit beside her on the bench. "You certainly talk the game. Imagine my surprise when I arrive at my very first college class only to discover that my university teacher is cuter than I am."

Her face was now utterly flaming. He might not be the best-dressed man she'd ever known, but he had the silver tongue of a devil in disguise. She'd have to watch herself around his blatant flattery, or she might just wind up believing him.

"So what about your system? Do you just guess what time you're supposed to be in class?" she asked in a rush of breath, trying desperately to turn the subject away from herself.

"More or less. I do have an alarm clock. On school days I usually haul myself out of bed in time to make it to my first class."

He grinned and gave a casual shrug. "From there, it's just a matter of moving from building to building. The timing is about right for me to make it to my next class with extra to spare, and my courses at the university are all in a row, so I don't have any downtime."

"Not even for lunch?"

"Nope." He winked. "I brown-bag it. Eat in one of my classes. Not yours," he added hastily.

"For some pathetic reason I believe you," she said, shaking her head. "But that still doesn't explain why it took you so long to get here today."

He flashed her a twisted grin but kept silent.

She wasn't about to let him get away with it, even though he was silently begging her for mercy. "You know you're going to tell me, so you might as well just spit it out and be done with it."

He probed her soul with his gaze, looking as if he were about to refuse to say a word. Then, suddenly, his gaze grew clear, and he relented. "I rescued a litter of kittens."

Holly made a little squeaking sound out of the back of her throat—the best she could do for speech at the moment.

He cleared his throat. "I found them abandoned in the Dumpster at my apartment. What could I do? Just leave them there to fend for themselves?"

She couldn't help it. Her heart went soft, and no amount of coaxing could harden it up again. Colin Brockman was a hero, and what was more, he didn't even like admitting to the fact.

Unless he was just teasing her, testing her resistance to the romantic.

"You're kidding, right?" she asked, secretly hoping he wasn't.

His sea-blue eyes widened as he scrubbed his hand through his tousled blond hair. His mouth puckered in a reluctant half smile, and he shifted his gaze back to the ground. "What do you think?"

She sighed and reached for his arm, sliding her palm up to the breadth of his shoulder. Her fingers didn't miss the depth of muscle hidden beneath his cotton shirt.

Colin was every bit as strong as he looked. "I think I'm a sucker for kindness. How many kittens were there? And what did you do with them?"

"One question at a time, please. There were six little kittens. Newborns. Four black, one white and one little guy, the runt of the litter, with black and white patches all over him."

Holly made a tender, choking sound in her throat and Colin lifted an amused eyebrow.

"They were stuck in a shoebox with a lid on top. Someone had taped the box shut with packing tape and tossed them into the Dumpster. I just thank God I walked by when I did."

"Poor little things," Holly cooed. "How could some terrible person abandon a litter of newborn kittens? Who would be so awful?"

"Too much trouble, I guess. Some people can't own up to their responsibilities."

"I'll say," she agreed, righteous indignation coursing through her. Poor little things. "So what did you do with them?"

"Well, I'd like to say I found nice homes for all of them. Someplace with little girls to tie bows around their necks and give them milk when they purred." He smiled grimly. "But I did the next best thing—took the little nippers to the local Humane Society."

She could tell he was choked up about it, though he struggled not to let it show on his face or in his low voice.

"You did the right thing," she assured him, "although I know it must have been tough to let them go."

He laughed, but it was a dry, echoing sound. "You

could say that." He looked around, rubbed his palms together and stood abruptly.

"So…where are we off to today?" He'd switched from melancholy to cheerful in an instant.

She stood and met his gaze, expecting to see the truth hiding under the surface; but his eyes were a clear, bright smiling blue. She couldn't keep pace with him. His erratic hairpin curves in emotion were more than she could navigate.

She took a moment to collect her thoughts. "Actually, we can walk there from here, so we won't be needing that carriage you mentioned," she said, feeling her tone might be a little too bright.

"I thought we were going to a rescue mission or something."

"That was my original plan, but as I was thinking about it, I wondered if we couldn't go a different direction for your assignment. Do something the other students might not think to do."

He smiled, and it lit up his whole face. "That sounds good to me. I'm not exactly your typical student, as if you hadn't noticed. But you know, that brings up another question."

"Yes?"

"Why are you helping me?"

Holly froze inside. She didn't know the answer to that. "We can go the rescue mission if that's what you want to do."

"You didn't answer my question."

She pulled her book bag into her chest, using it as a shield. "No, I didn't."

His voice softened. "Why not?"

"I…" she began, and then her voice trailed off as

her throat tightened. "I suppose I thought you might need help."

Colin tilted his head, silent for a moment. Then he slapped his hand against his thigh and roared with laughter. "I look that bad, do I?"

No, he didn't look bad. He looked wonderful. He'd also looked like a lost sheep that first day in class. Completely out of his element. And she'd always been drawn to the pariah. Perhaps that's why she'd responded to him the way she had.

It was as much a mystery to her as anyone.

"I didn't mean that in a bad way," she amended rapidly. "Actually, I'm just as interested in the topic as anyone."

"I hope so, considering you're a grad student," he pointed out wryly as he reached for his bag. "Is it okay for you to be helping me, Mrs. Prof?" he asked softly as he slung his bag over his shoulder.

"Ms. Prof, thank you very much. And I should think so," she answered, realizing she'd consciously set aside taking into account the ethical implications of her helping one student over the others. Would it be considered fraternizing for her to be here with Colin?

She hoped not, and for more reasons than one.

"I'm a student, too, Colin," she reaffirmed, as much to herself as to him. "I'm helping out the child psych class because my doctorate thesis is in the area of child psychology, but I'm not a full professor. So I don't see any hindrance from us exploring the first assignment, or any other, together."

"Okay," he said easily. "I'm glad."

His simple, straightforward statement took her aback. He could be frighteningly direct at times.

"What's your doctorate thesis about?" he asked as they walked, sounding, to her surprise, genuinely interested in what she had to say.

She laughed. "You don't really want to know, do you?"

He grinned back. "Why not?"

She playfully jostled his shoulder. "Because it's long and complicated. I'll tell you, if you really want me to, but not right now."

"Okay," he conceded, falling easily into step with her. "Later, then."

"Sure. Later. Right now, we'd better set our minds on *needs hierarchies*."

"The triangle is already forming in my mind," he teased, holding one hand to his temple as if he were conjuring the image as he spoke.

"You have some good ideas about where God fits into human need," she said on a serious vein.

"They're just thoughts," he corrected. "I've been mulling it over, but I'm not satisfied with my conclusions. It's a complex topic."

"You sound like you're trying to make it into a theological principle or doctrine of the faith," she teased. "I'd almost think you were trying to set this thing in stone."

"Maybe I am," he confessed with a ready smile. "I'm no scholar. I'm sure you've figured that out by now. But I do know that everything I learn here I'm learning for a reason. I'm also attending Stanton Seminary at the same time as the university."

Holly shook her head, shock reeling through her. As nice as he was, she just couldn't see Colin as pastor material. "You want to be a pastor?"

He laughed. "Oh, no. Not this man. A navy chaplain."

Seminary? A *navy chaplain*?

He would have done better to have left it at pastor. A navy chaplain, Holly could picture. But regret filled her. She'd been enjoying getting to know Colin. And she already knew she couldn't be a part of *this* man's navy.

Chapter Three

Colin wasn't sure what he'd said, but Holly looked as if she were ready to take a nosedive, or lose her breakfast, or maybe both. Her complexion turned white and clammy, and she was clasping her canvas bag to her chest as if it were a lifeline.

Or a shield.

He made a quick mental backtrack. He was sure he hadn't done anything inappropriate, and all he'd said was that he was training to be a navy chaplain. It was as if she'd frozen at the word *chaplain*, though moments earlier her voice had sounded teasing when she'd asked him if he was going to be a pastor.

She'd already made it clear to him she shared his faith. So what could be the problem?

He swiftly reached a hand to her to steady her, but she brushed him off with a scowl. Both literally and figuratively, he suspected.

"What did I say?" He asked the question gently, but that didn't stop her from cringing.

"Nothing." She snapped out the single word, steadfastly refusing to look at him and stepping away as if he were invading her space.

"Come on. Something I said or did made you angry." He set his backpack on the sidewalk and gestured to her with both his hands free.

She shook her head, almost vehemently. "I'm not angry."

"Then what?" he coaxed gently, adding his most winning smile for effect. Surely his immense manly charm wouldn't be lost on her, he thought sardonically.

It had always worked before.

His grin widened just as her frown narrowed. "Have you charmed your way out of *every* difficult situation you've ever found yourself facing?" she asked curtly, propping her free hand on her hip.

He scrubbed his fingers through his already-tousled hair, debating with himself how much honesty was called for in such situations. Finally he shrugged. "Mostly, yes."

She turned on her heel and faced him off with the spit and polish of a drill sergeant. "Well, it's not going to work with me, Colin Brockman."

He pulled in his smile, but knew it still tugged persistently at the corners of his mouth. Her eyes were sparkling with challenge, and he was determined to see them brimming with mirth.

With that lofty goal in mind, he lifted a hand to her cheek and slowly ran his index finger down the line of her jaw. It was extraordinary, how the rough calluses on his finger felt against the silky smoothness of her skin, as if the two were made for one another.

Callus and cream. Direct opposites, and yet the sensation of his hand on her skin was all the more breath-taking for its very contradiction.

Holly didn't speak, not even to turn him away, so he leaned into her ear and whispered, "Don't be so sure about that. I can be charming when I want to be."

Her reaction was classic, and not totally unexpected. Huffing loudly, she began marching in a direct line away from him. She didn't look back, not even to level him with a glare.

And—another point in his favor—she didn't swing her book bag at him, though he could tell the thought crossed her mind.

Laughing, Colin caught up his own bag and followed, loping to catch up with her long strides. "So where are we going?" he asked easily, as if the unusual moment between them hadn't taken place at all.

It was his way, to go on and not dwell on things. He hoped she'd follow his lead.

He'd make a point to find out later what had gotten her so ruffled. Sometimes it paid to wait until emotions had calmed before addressing matters of that nature, anyway.

Not that he was an expert. He strode to keep up with her quick pace.

They walked in silence for a moment, and then her gaze swung sharply up to him. She looked apprehensive, as if she was concerned he might be joking again, and she didn't like that prospect. He smiled to assure her he was on the up-and-up.

"The university has an extension program that works with children who have special needs," she began, putting on her teacher's voice, which Colin thought was for his benefit.

Or maybe for hers. He bit back a smile.

"It's called Marston House."

"I think I've heard of it. They take care of Down's syndrome kids and stuff, right?"

She shook her head, but her eyes were laughing. "And stuff. Oh, Colin, you're hopeless! What am I going to do with you?"

"I can't wait to find out," he quipped.

"You wish." She nudged him playfully on the arm. He grinned, happy that the easy camaraderie was back between them.

"Anyway," she continued, "I've arranged it so the children you'll be meeting today are all deaf. They take special classes to learn sign language and lip-reading, among other things. Eventually many of them learn to speak by themselves."

"Pretty impressive stuff," Colin said, uttering a low whistle. But just as he spoke, he caught the gist of her words and froze to the spot, reaching for her elbow so she wouldn't walk away without him.

"Did you say meet the kids?"

She whirled on her toes, teasing surprise registering in her eyes. "Of course I mean kids. You're in a child psychology class. And that's the assignment. Or have you managed to squirrel that away *out of sight, out of mind*, as well?" She tapped her temple with her index finger.

He grinned wryly. "Something like that. Actually, I was referring to the *meet* part of the sentence. I'm positive you didn't say anything about meeting or interacting with the children we monitor when you gave out your very specific and succinct instructions. The word I remember is *observe*."

She looked flustered for the briefest moment, and Colin grinned. For some reason, it gave him a kick that he could do that to her.

That she could fluster him just as easily was completely irrelevant.

"Observe means to watch, view, scrutinize, monitor," he said as blandly as a walking dictionary.

"I *know* what *observe* means," she snapped, moving rapidly from flustered to annoyed. And while he enjoyed setting her off-kilter, he wasn't so sure he wanted to cross the line.

An angry woman was a volatile woman, and that he didn't need.

"It's no big deal," he said, fibbing through his teeth.

She crossed her arms and raised a dark eyebrow. "Colin Brockman, I haven't known you that long, but anyone with half an eye to see can tell you're not telling me the truth."

He slouched away from her. "How's that?" he asked defensively.

"Classic symptoms. Won't look me in the eye. Hunches away from me. Fiddles with the zipper on his jacket." She smiled, her eyes gleaming with amusement. "I'm a psychologist, remember?"

In the space it took her to say the words, he'd dropped his hand from his jacket, pulled himself to full rigid military attention, looked her straight in the eye and jammed his fingers through his hair just for good measure.

Holly chuckled, but her eyes were serious. "What's the problem, Colin?" she asked, more gently and softly than he would have expected, or maybe even thought that he deserved.

He knew he wasn't making any sense to her. He didn't make any sense to himself at times. She had every right to be annoyed with him.

Still, he wasn't one of those open, sensitive guys who bared their souls on the first date, and Holly was hitting a nerve. Thanks to God, he'd made many resolutions in his life and in his personal relationships, but he still kept his emotions tucked safely away.

Not even this pretty psychologist was going to pull his true feelings out of him, though, if anyone could do so, Holly might be the one.

"I don't like children." He knew it sounded harsh, but it was better than admitting the real truth, that he was afraid of them.

Holly made a sound from the back of her throat that was close to a snort. That was about as much nonsense as she had ever heard from a man, and she told him so.

"You don't have to meet the kids if you don't want to, but I think you may surprise yourself. From everything I know of you, I believe you'd be good for them. They could really use your attention."

Colin raised his eyebrows, and a shield dropped over his eyes. He smiled with obvious effort. "All right, then. Bring them on."

Holly wanted to laugh at his forced bravado, the gravelly sound in his voice making it sound as if he were walking the plank.

But found she couldn't laugh at him. Colin was obviously hiding something, and though she wanted to share his burden, she decided to say nothing and let this hand play out on its own.

Sometime soon, she would discover what was haunting him. What was the mystery, the hidden crisis he veiled so well behind his casual demeanor?

It might be the psychologist in her that wanted to know the truth, but Holly suspected it was the woman.

Very much the woman.

As they entered the school facility at Marston House, Holly greeted the administrator, who led them to a large playroom filled with equipment. A large, multicolored plastic jungle gym took center stage, surrounded by various-sized rubber balls, a teeter-totter and a number of gymnastics devices, including rings, parallel bars, a balance beam and a gymnast's horse.

To one side, a group of elementary-aged children sat in a circle on the floor, practicing their hand signs in an animated display.

Colin stepped so close behind Holly that she could feel his warm breath prickling on the back of her neck, even before he spoke. As if he'd done it a million times, he placed his hands on her shoulders and rubbed his thumbs gently against her sore muscles.

Her own breath caught so suddenly in her throat that she was afraid to speak, for fear he'd be able to hear the emotion in her voice and comprehend how his nearness was affecting her.

"Do you know any of that stuff?" he queried softly. For once, she heard no hint of merriment lining his voice. Awe, perhaps, and a little fear, but not the laughter that was his captivating trademark.

"Stuff?" she parroted, wishing he would step away from her, but not finding it in herself to make the move on her own.

He wrapped his arms around her and demonstrated with his hands in front of her chin.

"This," he said, touching his index fingers together.

"And this." He touched his right middle finger to his left palm, and then reversed the action.

She was impressed. He'd been paying attention.

"And this." He wiggled his fingers in a nonsensical manner. She felt rather than heard laughter frothing to the surface.

She laughed and turned out of his grasp. "The first, I can tell you, means *to*. The second sign is *Jesus*, which is obvious, when you think about it."

"The nails in His hands."

"Right. And as far as the third sign goes, I'd have to say you need to learn how to finger spell."

"And here I thought I was so close." He wiggled his fingers again in nonsense language.

Holly ran down the finger-spelling alphabet with him, amazed at how quickly and accurately he picked up each letter sign.

"Hey, wait a minute," he broke in, midalphabet. "This is a university-run school."

Holly nodded, but didn't comment, not knowing where he was going with his point.

"Why are the children learning how to sign *Jesus*? Isn't that a breach of separation of church and state or something?"

Holly would have bristled at the question, were his tone not so reverent and sincere.

"These kids have to learn everything they need to survive out in the world. Part of that world is faith and God and church. So the kids learn the signs they'll need to know to follow along with the praise songs and hymns, not to mention the sermon. I don't know about you, but my pastor preaches about Jesus a lot."

Colin chuckled, remembering the cantankerous old hellfire-and-brimstone navy chaplain who'd helped him see the light. What if he hadn't been able to hear the old man's preaching? It was so easy to take God's gifts for granted.

There and then he prayed silently in gratitude for his own blessings, and resolved himself to brighten these courageous young children's hearts in some way this day.

His heart felt heavy with their burden and light with God's peace at the same time. It was a funny, choked-up kind of feeling, and Colin wasn't sure what he should make of it.

"Do they have special deaf churches?" he asked in an attempt to cover his own discomfort.

"No." Holly took Colin by the elbow and nudged him toward the group of children. He offered a token resistance, but it was no more than that.

He knew it was a ploy, and he suspected she knew it, as well.

His cover was blown. He did care.

"Most of these kids go to one of the larger churches around town, one of those that offers an interpreter for the deaf. Greeley's a good town to grow up in if you're deaf. The college draws in students wanting to learn to work with the hearing impaired, so there is no shortage of eager interpreters."

"That's good to know," Colin said, but his focus had already shifted to the children.

It was obvious the moment they got the go-ahead to break out of the group and play. Children scattered like a flock of chickens with a fox in the coop. Smiles and laughter abounded all over the place.

"It looks and sounds just like a regular playground," Colin murmured in awe and wonder. "This is absolutely incredible."

"What did you expect?" she asked softly.

He looked down at her warm, velvet-green eyes and shook his head. "I've learned not to have expectations." His voice lowered and he frowned. "Somebody always gets hurt."

She slid her palm over his forearm, intensely aware of how his muscles tightened under her touch. "'Somebody,' meaning you?" she queried gently, keenly aware of the risk she took in asking.

He shoved his hands into the front pockets of his jeans, effectually brushing her hand away from him. "Sometimes."

It was little more than a whisper. Colin obviously didn't want to talk about it, but Holly didn't realize how much until he abruptly turned and strode away from her, taking refuge with the children he'd earlier professed to dislike.

He singled out a young boy who was tossing a rubber Four Square ball against the wall in an empty rhythm. He was all alone in his corner of the room, and he appeared not to notice when Colin approached him.

Holly cringed inwardly. Of all the children to pick, Colin had to go and choose the one least likely to respond to him. He was in trouble again, and he didn't even know it yet.

She started to follow, but her determination to save Colin from himself came to a screeching halt, as did her feet, when Colin appeared to strike up a conversation with the young boy.

It was impossible.

Well, perhaps *impossible* was too strong a word. But highly unlikely, from a large, untrained, blustering hulk of a man like Colin Brockman.

The boy was nine-year-old Jared Matthews, a mildly autistic boy counselors had as yet been unable to reach with any effectiveness. He wasn't deaf, but he often fled reality for a world of his own, somewhere deep inside his head where he could make sense of a life that flew by too fast, too strong and too loud for him.

Like many autistic children, Jared was very smart and clever, amazing others with what he could do. Music was his forte. Without any instruction whatsoever, he could play any instrument given to him. He had a natural ear for music, and played beautiful songs he made up in his mind.

But that was only when he could pull himself from his autism, and it was becoming increasingly difficult for him to do so. More and more, he retreated into a world of his own making, rather than living in the real world.

The fact that he had been shifted from foster home to foster home during his young life didn't help. He'd been all but abandoned by parents who didn't want the trouble of an autistic son, and Holly was certain it wouldn't be long before the parents made it official.

She hoped—prayed—she was wrong.

Parents didn't abandon their children, even those with disabilities. She'd been raised to believe that family took care of their own.

Her heart welled up, as it always did, for the boy and his terrible, tragic situation, especially knowing there was nothing she could do about it.

That was the worst part, knowing she could only help so many, when there were so many more in need.

Colin crouched down to the boy's level, his movements painstakingly and laboriously slow. With even more care, he gently reached toward the boy, and when Jared didn't protest, he tousled the boy's inky black curls.

To Holly's great surprise, not only did Jared not pull away from Colin's touch but, within moments, he'd focused his gaze on the man, and was playing against Colin in a game of Two Square.

Impossible!

Chapter Four

Holly was dumbfounded. Colin was playing Two Square with an autistic boy as though it were no big deal. As if he were an expert in the field. As if he didn't have a care in the world.

This from a man who professed a blatant dislike—or more accurately, as Holly suspected, a *fear*—of children. She didn't know what Colin had done to put Jared at ease, but in her mind, it was nothing short of a miracle, quite literally a work of God.

Surely Colin would have to realize what a special gift he'd been given. And if he didn't know, she fully intended to be the one to tell him. She suspected he'd only deny the truth, but she was compelled to confront him with the obvious.

Someone had to tell him he had a gift, or he might wander aimlessly for the rest of his life. He was a strong man with much to give the world, and if she didn't miss her guess, especially to give needy children.

All that was left was for him to figure that out for himself.

She started across the floor, her pace quick and determined. Her movement alerted Colin, whose gaze switched away from Jared to her. Their gazes met for only a moment, but it was enough for him to realize her intentions, or at least to guess at them.

It was as if she'd pushed his panic button. Alarm sparked from his sea-blue eyes, and in a moment, he was off and running.

Literally.

It was a clear attempt to avoid her, but for some reason, she didn't take it personally. She'd always had a penchant for the tousled stray—this one just happened to be a man. She'd catch up with him sooner or later.

Holly chuckled when Colin began walking hunched over like a big gorilla, touching his toes and making hooting noises. And she wasn't as surprised as she might have been when Jared followed, placing his hands on his toes and echoing the high-pitched monkey sounds.

He mimicked Colin yet again when Colin threw his arms in the air and waved them wildly, whooping like a man gone wild.

The comical little parade didn't stop when Colin braved the balance beam, pretending to waver in the middle and making all kinds of funny faces.

And it was not only Jared aping his antics. One by one, each of the deaf children joined the line, smiling as they pretending to waver in the middle of the balance beam, just as Colin had done, making the same faces he had made.

In and out of tunnels, up and down the slides they went, one by one. Over the vaulting horse and somersaulting across the mats they flew.

Colin led and the children followed. And the merriment didn't end until the regular teacher signaled the close of the session by flickering the lights, so the children would know it was time to return to class from their play.

Colin, his face flushed, and dabbing at his sweaty temples with the edge of his shirtsleeve, looked absolutely elated.

"Did you see that?" he asked, sounding amazed and grateful, and not the least bit superficial.

"I told you, you're a natural," she teased, unable to stop herself from rubbing it in just a little bit. "Do you want to come back again sometime and play with the *children* again?"

His eyes widened, full of emotion she was certain he didn't want her to see.

"Yes." He nodded.

"No." He shook his head.

He halted abruptly, his mouth hanging open, before he swallowed hard and jammed his fingers through his hair, sending it spiking every which direction. "I don't know, Holly. I don't really know what just happened."

His voice sounded strained, as if he were under a tremendous amount of pressure. And maybe he was.

Holly linked her hand through the crook of his arm and accompanied him out of the school. "You'll figure it out," she said gently. "You connected today."

"Do you think?" He sounded genuinely amazed, and more than a little choked up.

"Jared, the young boy you were playing with, seldom responds to contact. What you did today was a major breakthrough for him. The counselors at Marston will be thrilled."

She slid her hand down his forearm and linked her

fingers with his. "I think God has given you a special gift, Colin."

He squeezed her hand and cleared his throat. "I'm humbled."

Holly hadn't expected such a reaction, and her throat closed around the unnamed emotions pounding through her chest. Colin was so strong, his navy background giving him squared shoulders and a powerful bearing; yet for the moment, she sensed a quietness in his soul, a new and tender sensitivity that only served to enhance his masculine image in her mind.

"I don't want you to take this the wrong way," she said slowly, her grip on him subtly tightening, "but I'm proud of you."

A slight flush tainted his tanned cheek, and one corner of his mouth tipped up in a grin. "Do you think?" he asked, his eyes gleaming.

"I think," Holly agreed, her voice scratchy with unspoken thoughts and unnamed emotions. She laughed as she pictured Colin being innocently followed by all those children. "You know what?"

"What?"

"I also think you are a veritable Pied Piper."

Colin stepped into the door of his small studio apartment. Dirty socks hung over the backs of the chairs and clothes were strewn haphazardly around, as if a tornado had blown through. Unwashed dishes were piled high in the sink, and books and papers littered the floor.

He took one look at the utter chaos he'd left in his living quarters and sighed deeply.

It was good to be home.

The last few weeks had proved incredibly busy, as

professors and students alike shifted into high-learning mode. He hadn't been ready for the chaos on the high seas of academia.

Go to class.

Take good notes.

Read the textbooks.

Study for exams.

Colin barely knew what to make of it. He hadn't been in school for years, and had certainly never taken such a heavy academic load. He felt as if he were scrambling to keep up. At his best, he'd never been a model student and he didn't feel remotely close to his best at the moment.

It was the first time in his life he'd really wanted to succeed in school, but he felt as if he was not achieving the levels of accomplishment for which he was aiming.

A weekend of PT and reserve training was a welcome relief. The physical training was a terrific opportunity to stretch his idle muscles stiff from hours of cramped study, and the navy structure a good break from his self-imposed anarchy.

He'd also hoped his reserve work would give him some distance, some perspective on his thoughts, for no matter how hard he tried, or how much he studied, he couldn't seem to get Holly McCade out of his mind.

He'd seen her now and again over the weeks, passing in the halls, before and after class, always greeting one another and promising to get together for coffee, but never quite making the connection.

And he wasn't positive it was all coincidental. On a subconscious level, he thought he might be avoiding her.

Which was ridiculous. He ached to be with Holly. He thought about her every waking moment.

Yet he was obviously avoiding every opportunity to be alone with her. And it was possible she was doing the same with him.

No. He couldn't blame it on her.

He was at fault, and it was about time he acknowledged it, though he guessed that by now Holly might be blaming herself for the fact that they hadn't connected. His limited knowledge of women, mostly from his twin sister, Callie, made him believe they were prone to shoulder the blame in most circumstances, and this was probably no exception.

He only hoped he hadn't inadvertently hurt her. And he kicked himself for only now realizing that as a possibility.

He wasn't even quite sure why he was running away, except that his life was a tangled mess right now and he felt he needed to sort out the pieces before he spent any more one-on-one time with Holly.

Being with her was a roller-coaster ride in itself, without all these other things going on in his life. He was too confused to add his unquestionable attraction to Holly into the equation.

Callie was bugging him to come up to Oregon to be with her and her husband, Rhett, for Thanksgiving, but he wasn't sure he was up for the trip. Being with Callie would simply reopen old wounds about his family.

Bathed in the love of her new husband, Rhett Wheeler, Callie had succeeded in putting the past behind her, where it belonged. Colin knew what he'd find at Callie's—a traditional Thanksgiving dinner with all the fixings, followed by a jaunt to the church for a Thanksgiving praise service. God at the center, family most important and children all around.

Rhett and Callie had two children—a teenage son, Brandon, who was Rhett's from a previous marriage, but whom Callie loved as her own; and a capricious baby girl who was the apple of Rhett's eye.

Between the two of them, there was enough noise to drown out Puget Sound. And more happiness and giggles in one place than Colin thought his heart could bear right now.

He was happy for his sister, but he was envious of her, too. And he wasn't sure that now was a good time to rub his own nose in his shortcomings.

He didn't blame Callie for trying to get everyone together for the holidays. In fact, he appreciated that she always thought to include him, knowing he had no one else and nowhere to go; and no doubt realizing how much she now had, how much God had blessed her in her husband and children.

Colin unbuttoned his dirty blue shirt and twisted out of it, not caring where it dropped. He pulled on his T-shirt to stretch it out, but he didn't remove it. It might be sweat stained, but it was comfortable.

He shifted, grimacing. Neither he nor Callie had many family traditions to pass down to their children.

Oh, his mother, when she was alive, had always prepared turkey with all the trimmings. She'd forced the festivities and brought out the best china. But his father always managed to ruin everything. Sometimes he complained about the food, but more often he complained about Colin. Colin cringed at the mere memory of his father's harsh, grating voice.

You're a complete failure, son. You disappoint me every time I turn around.

Callie should have been born the boy. At least she got good grades and stayed out of trouble.

You're nothing but trouble.

Nothing but trouble.

Colin squeezed his eyes shut and pushed the memories away, burying them in the black recesses of his mind, where they belonged. He shouldn't have gone there, even for a moment.

It did no good to dwell on the past. But it did help him make his decision.

He'd stay home for Thanksgiving and order a pizza. Callie would understand.

He scrubbed a hand over his eyes and tried to concentrate on his future. One thing he *did* know for certain—God was working through all the things that had happened in the past few weeks, including bringing Holly McCade into his life. Colin sensed that He was changing the whole course of his future, not to mention his ministry.

His Child Psych class had started out as nothing more than a requirement on his transcript, and not one he was particularly keen on completing. Now, it had suddenly become the focus of his life, in more ways than one.

Little autistic Jared Matthews was often on his mind, and always in his heart, as he figured out new and original ways he could help the boy. Though he didn't call attention to the fact, he'd visited Jared almost daily since that first time.

Sometimes, he thought he might be making a difference in the boy's life. Often, he felt there was little he could do for the lad.

Except be there. He could do that.

Because of his work with Jared, Colin had also started considering the children of military parents, those he'd be working with as a navy chaplain, those like the ones he'd grown up with.

He desperately wanted to find something he could do for them when he reenlisted. If he could reach the children…

Finally, he felt as if he had some real direction, a place to focus his energy, as he studied and struggled to become a navy chaplain. His work at the seminary and university took on new meaning, and he found it wasn't quite so difficult to pay attention to his studies as it had been before.

He was slowly unraveling one of the most complex strands of his life, and it was exhilarating.

Motivating.

And most of all *confusing*.

The most pressing question of all still loomed in his mind. It was the main reason he'd worked his body so hard this weekend, trying to sort these things out in his mind.

Where did Holly McCade fit in?

On one hand, Colin pictured her as an angel from heaven, and not just because of her beauty. She'd taken the time to help him, to rescue a poor, helpless student when he'd been floundering, even though she didn't have to do a thing.

And somehow, she'd known just what he needed.

She'd discovered his heart, and pegged him right into his future before he himself had a clue. How had she *done* that?

With an almost deliberate intent, she'd forced him into a situation beyond his experience and control. She had lined him up with a real live child, face-to-face, where he was compelled to look into the boy's eyes and confront his own fears.

And discover his destiny.

She was incredible.

She brought out the best in him, and he thought he might be a good influence on her, as well. Was it his imagination, or did she shine a little brighter when she was in his company?

Unfortunately, that was the problem.

Holly McCade was a monumental distraction. Right now and always. He didn't trust his head when he was around her. Or his heart.

Who knew if she might steal it clean away?

He unlaced his spit-polished black boots, groaning as he took them off his feet. If his hard weekend work-out wasn't enough to clear his mind, he was in a whole heap of trouble.

He couldn't stop thinking about her.

It occurred to him on more than one occasion that he might want more from his relationship with Holly than mere friendship. But that was a concept so new, he hardly dared explore it.

With the singular background of a navy career out of high school and his own poor upbringing as a child, he'd never before in his life given thought to having a real, romantic relationship.

He'd dated his fair share of women, but only on a so-cial, casual basis. He'd not taken the same woman out more than a handful of times, and even then, he never remembered feeling remotely as he did now with Holly.

Now he was toying with the concept of making a commitment to a woman. Holly deserved no less, and he wanted above all to give her everything she deserved, the world on a platter.

A real, accountable relationship. Something permanent. Grown-up, even.

It had only taken him until he was thirty years old to meet a woman extraordinary enough to prod him into acting like an adult. Go figure.

He was treading on new territory, and he hardly knew where to begin. He struggled to compose his thoughts.

Women, in his experience, were friends. Occasionally, they'd become innocent diversions. He'd stolen more than one kiss over the years, but nothing memorable.

Shaking his head, he grunted in frustration. A kiss was one thing, but a committed relationship was something entirely different. When he looked at Holly, he heard wedding bells ringing in his ears.

Colin slammed his hand down on the table, slicing through the silence like a knife. He hadn't so much as kissed her yet, and here he was mentally standing at the altar in a tuxedo, holding matching wedding rings in his palm.

He took a deep breath and let it out, relaxed his posture and chuckled aloud.

First things first.

He had to steal a kiss.

Chapter Five

"Holly. Holly McCade. Earth to Holly. Come in, Holly."

"I'm sorry. What?" Holly asked, reluctantly pulling herself from her thoughts.

Sarah Rembrant, her friend and co–student teacher, shook her head and belted out a laugh, loud enough to cause Holly to take a fleeting look around the room to see if anyone had noticed the outburst.

Fortunately, students were only now beginning to arrive for class, milling around with the cluck and gaggle of a coop full of chickens.

"Where were you?" Sarah asked.

"What do you mean?" Holly asked, confused. "Where was I when?"

"Just now. You were a million miles away. If I didn't know better, I'd say you were somewhere in the vicinity of cloud nine. Tell me the truth now. Have you been holding out on me? Are you in love?"

"Don't be ridiculous," Holly snapped back, agonizingly aware of the color rushing to her cheeks even as she said the words.

Sarah's jaw dropped in astonishment. "You *are* in love."

Holly scowled at her friend and waved her off. "It's about time to start class."

Sarah nodded, but the look in her eyes assured Holly this subject wasn't closed.

It should be, Holly thought, crossing her arms about her like a shield. She wasn't in love. No one fell in love at first sight, except in the movies.

This was real life. Savvy women dated awhile before they made a commitment, and even then there was generally a long engagement.

It made sense to take her time to get to know a man, to discover his true character and whether or not she would be compatible with him. Know all his quirks and his faults, not just the charm that made a woman forget her own head.

Then, perhaps, armed with all that knowledge, it would be safe to fall in love.

She wouldn't know. She'd never been remotely close to falling in love. She was no expert in matters of love, by any means. Sarah's teasing notwithstanding.

Reluctantly shifting her mind into teaching mode, Holly let Sarah carry most of the class, and tried not to let her gaze wander too often to the blue-eyed, ruffled-haired, heart-stealing troublemaker seated in his usual seat in the back row.

Class went quickly, to Holly's surprise, and it wasn't long before the bell rang signaling the end of class. And she hadn't looked at Colin more than a handful of times.

She'd just started gathering her notes when she heard a familiar deep, teasing voice speaking to her just over her right shoulder.

"Got a minute?"

How had he managed to sneak behind her when she wasn't looking?

Holly flashed a silent distress call to Sarah, whose eyes widened noticeably at the sight of the good-looking man who cupped his hands on Holly's shoulders and turned her gently but firmly around.

"She's got all day," Sarah said, nudging Holly toward Colin, closing what little distance lay between them.

So much for friendship.

"Thanks a lot," muttered Holly under her breath, but Sarah didn't seem to notice—she was too busy smiling and crooning at Colin, acting like—well, like a woman behaved around an attractive man.

A surge of jealousy coursed through Holly, for which she was totally unprepared, quickly followed by a rush of mortification, flooding through with the force of a deep river current.

Which was ridiculous. She wasn't the jealous type. Not to mention the fact that she had nothing to be jealous about.

She had no claim on Colin. She couldn't keep him from flashing that charismatic grin to all the pretty women he met, nor would she want to. Certainly his charismatic smile would work as well on other women as it did on her, and she was hardly going to be the one to stop it. The Dodgers baseball cap he wore low on his brow did nothing to hide the inherent happiness in his smile or the joy in his eyes.

But there it was, even if she didn't want to admit it, even to herself. Holly didn't like the way Colin and Sarah connected through their gazes, as if they were sharing a private joke meant only for two.

Then the moment was over, and Colin was once again smiling at her. It was funny how he could look at her and her surroundings just melted away. He had a way about him that always made her feel as if she were the only one in the world.

Or at least the only one in the world for him.

"Well?" he queried lightly.

"Well, what?"

"You haven't answered my question yet."

Sarah cleared her throat. Loudly. "I think I better go pick up my notes off the overhead projector," she announced in an obvious attempt to leave Holly alone with Colin. Her wink in Holly's direction was an unnecessary addition to the melodrama.

But it helped nonetheless. Relief washed through Holly along with the realization that Sarah posed no threat, to whatever it was inside her that was feeling threatened.

She steadfastly refused to even *inwardly* acknowledge why it should bother her at all, never mind try to put words to her feelings. It was a free country, and Colin was too handsome a man not to be noticed by the women around him.

She took a breath, but it caught in her throat. Her relief was short-lived and was quickly replaced by panic as she looked up at Colin's sparkling, mirthful gaze and lazy half smile.

"Your friend is nice," he commented, gesturing a nod to the retreating Sarah.

"Yes, she is," Holly agreed mildly, watching Colin's face for a reaction and relieved when there was none.

He turned his warm gaze on her and smiled his enigmatic grin, and her heart did a back flip despite her reservations. Any thoughts of threat or panic dissipated like a bad dream in the daylight. Colin's smile alone was enough to make a woman forget her own name.

"Busy Saturday?" he asked, casually pushing a stray lock of her hair away from her face.

Instinctively, a lie sprang to her lips, a defense against the truth. She immediately set about the task of conjuring up something interesting to say she was doing. Something other than spending the weekend alone.

But before anything plausible came to mind, Colin broke in. "I hope you'll say you're free for the day. I have something I want to show you at my apartment. Something I think you'll like. A lot."

Anything she'd been about to say was immediately lost in her interminable curiosity about all things Colin. If she were the proverbial cat, she most certainly would have expired by now.

"I'm free," she reluctantly admitted. She didn't have time to regret the words, for his eyes lit up like sparklers on the Fourth of July, glittering with delight and amusement.

"I promise you won't be disappointed."

Somehow, she didn't think she would be.

"Why don't you come over in the morning and stay for lunch? I'm a lousy cook, but I'm a whiz when it comes to speed-dialing Chinese food."

"This surprise of yours will take that long?"

His half smile appeared again, along with a healthy shade of red across the top angle against the soft scruff on his cheeks. "Aw, shucks, ma'am." he said bashfully. "You caught me red-handed."

She laughed despite herself. "How's that?"

"Well, I hoped I could persuade you to stay long enough to help me brainstorm a few ideas for my big research project in your class. You gave me a great start on your course with our first excursion, and I thought maybe you could help me out again."

She caught his gaze and held it, questioning him with her eyes. What was really behind this half serious, half flirtatious question?

What did he really want of her?

Somehow, she knew there was more behind his outwardly simple request than met the eye.

"Oh, come on," he pleaded, grabbing her right hand and placing it over his heart. "You wouldn't want your favorite elderly student to fail your class now, would you?"

She chuckled. Aged he was not. "What do you want me to bring?" she said on a sigh. "I make a grand tuna salad, if you're interested."

His blue eyes sparkled like a mountain stream in the sunshine. "Just bring your beautiful self. We'll let the lunch plans take care of themselves."

"Colin," she objected, "you are completely incorrigible."

"I was going to say *adorable*," Sarah inserted as she sashayed by with a load of textbooks in her arms.

"Thanks for the compliments, ladies," Colin said, tipping off his baseball cap and swinging it around in a grand gesture. "I'm going to have such a big head my cap won't fit."

"You consider *incorrigible* a compliment?"

"You don't?" he asked, sounding genuinely surprised.

She nearly choked on her laughter. "Not in the general scheme of things."

"Oh, now, come on! Who wants everything to be the same all the time?" He punctuated the statement with a wide, confident grin that made Holly wave her hands and roll her eyes at him.

"You never know what to expect when you're with me, right?"

That, at least, was the truth.

"It's always an adventure when you're with Colin Brockman," he asserted smugly. "Always fun and games. Something new around every corner."

"You make that sound like a good thing," she muttered under her breath.

He froze in his tracks for a moment, watching her keenly and looking as if he couldn't quite figure out what he was seeing.

She wasn't surprised. She and Colin were as different as day and night in every way.

And yet there was that *adorable* thing.

Colin was that, surely, and Holly hadn't missed the fact. She had to admit she was attracted to him, but she was terrified of him, too. Jumping off cliffs without knowing if there was an ocean beneath her just wasn't her style.

Not anymore.

She gritted her teeth and closed her eyes against the dark memories threatening to surface. Now was not the time to drudge up past mistakes.

She needed to stay with the program. Stay in control of her life and her feelings.

But with Colin, she just couldn't say no.

When he smiled, his whole face smiled. His whole

body smiled. And when he opened his arms to her, she didn't resist. He was tall, and strong, built like a fortress, and navy tough. And he smelled wonderful—a clean, soapy scent that tickled her nostrils and made her want to inhale deeply.

She could feel the rumble of his chest on her cheek as he spoke.

"We'll stick with *incorrigible*, then," he said softly, next to her ear. "The good kind."

"If you say so," she mumbled into his shirt.

"I do," he agreed with a nod. "So hold on tight, sweet Holly, and get ready for the adventure of a lifetime."

Chapter Six

As Saturday arrived, the bright Colorado sun shone high in the sky, promising another fine fall day in the shadow of the Rocky Mountains' majesty. Colin whistled under his breath as he searched for his key to his apartment door, happy, for the moment, just to be alive and breathing.

That is, at least until his gaze rested upon Holly, leaning impatiently against his front door and looking as if she had a few choice words for him. He didn't know exactly what time it was, but he guessed by the exasperated look on her face that she'd been waiting for him a good long while.

He *had* said to meet him here in the morning, he realized with a prickly brush of hindsight that left him feeling genuinely chagrined. Jumping into motion to cover his mistake, he jammed the key into the lock, stumbling over himself as he tried to express how apologetic he felt at having left her waiting.

In the end, he could only state the obvious without blathering on like a complete idiot. "I'm sorry. I know I'm late."

Holly lifted her forearm and gazed pointedly at her watch. "*Very* late."

Colin shrugged and motioned at his wrist. "I don't have a…"

"Watch," she completed for him. "Yes, I know. We've been over this before. Otherwise I would have left a long time ago. As it is…"

"I didn't mean to make you wait," he said, rubbing his palm across her shoulder, brushing back the soft, sable curl of her hair.

She chuckled. "I know you didn't. I came prepared this time." She pulled a paperback book out of her purse and waved it under his nose.

"Something for your doctorate?" he queried, lifting an amused eyebrow.

She flipped the cover to reveal the title. He recognized it to be one in a mystery series, one with a cat as the main character.

"I suppose I should be studying my psych books," she admitted with a grin. "But I thought I'd take a break today, it being Saturday and all."

"Works for me." Colin unlocked the door and gestured her in. "I'm all for taking a break whenever you can squeeze them in." He looked back at her and grinned. "Saturday. Monday. Wednesday…"

He stopped short when he surveyed his apartment, and Holly plowed right into his back, mumbling something under her breath about "brick walls."

He had more pressing matters weighing on his mind. What would she think of him when she saw his living quarters?

If anything, his front room looked *worse* than it usually did.

Was that possible?

He'd been meaning to give his present barracks a thorough scrubbing down this morning, but then an opportunity had come up that he just couldn't pass up on, and he'd gone off without giving another thought to the state of his dwelling.

And now, he was going to live to regret that easy dismissal.

Holly was practically openmouthed as she stared at his living room, arms akimbo as she confronted the slapdash, careless environment that was the true indication of his chaotic lifestyle.

Hopefully she wouldn't judge him too harshly. The mess didn't make the man, did it?

He cringed inwardly and struggled not to demonstrate his discomfort on the outside. He wanted to wiggle and squirm like the worm he was, living in a hole filled with dirt, or at least dirty laundry.

Holly turned to him, her face a mixture of emotions. "The socks strewn across the top of the furniture give the place a certain kind of ambience, don't you think?"

It was the last thing he could have expected her to say, and it threw him off for a moment. "I…uh… That is…"

"I know, I know. Your maid hasn't been here yet today." She moved to the orange patterned couch that looked—and probably was—from the seventies. With a gentle smile, she casually brushed the clutter aside, seating herself straight-backed and elegant, as if she didn't have a care in the world, and wasn't bothered at all by the disorder around her.

He recognized what that action cost her. He'd known her long enough to know she was the queen of order.

If her meticulous appearance wasn't a dead giveaway, her scrupulous school notes and flawless handwriting would be enough to suggest her tendency toward, if not perfectionism, then at least chronic neatness. She was stretching herself for him, and he appreciated it more than he could express.

With a grin, he sprawled on a green armchair across from her, kicking one leg over the arm of the chair and propping one elbow on his thigh. He might not be able to voice his gratitude, but surely she'd be able to see it written on his face.

"So where were you today?" she asked, pulling her legs beneath her and leaning back against the cushion. "Or is it a state secret?"

He chuckled. "No secret. I was over visiting Jared Matthews at Marston House. I try to get by and see him every day, if I can."

Her eyebrows hit the ceiling. "Michelle Walker, the principal at Marston House, mentioned in passing that you'd been visiting Jared occasionally, but I had no idea you were growing so close to the boy."

He looked away and shrugged. How could he explain the feelings he had toward Jared?

In some way, that brave youngster represented the struggle Colin had gone through himself as a boy; and, in turn, every wretched mother's son trying to make the most of a tough situation.

He found he wanted—*needed*—to do something to make Jared's life better, to help him find a little happiness in the world. The kind of happiness Colin himself had missed as a boy.

He couldn't change his own circumstances or his

past, but he would do what he could for Jared. It was the least he could do. And the most.

"Do you think you are getting through to him?" she asked softly. "Is he making any progress?"

Again, Colin shrugged. "Sometimes. Other times it's like he's completely locked away in his own mind, and all I can do is sit quietly beside him and wonder what he's thinking inside."

He crooked his elbow on his knees and gazed out the glass double doors that led to a small wooden balcony overlooking the apartment parking lot. Jared Matthews grabbed at something in his heart. How could he express what he felt, when he wasn't even sure he could put it into words himself?

"Whenever I get through to him," he continued, "I feel like I make a genuine connection. Like the two of us have something special."

He paused and scrubbed his fingers through his hair. "Other times, I just sit and visit with him, talking about all kinds of stuff even though he doesn't respond to me. I'm not completely sure he knows I'm there."

"He knows." Holly's sweet, gentle voice soothed the ache in Colin's heart.

"Yeah," he agreed quietly, closing his eyes to hold on to the comfort. "I guess he does."

"It's too bad Jared's in such a bad situation," she remarked regretfully.

The hair on the back of Colin's neck brushed to attention. He had the distinct impression she wasn't talking about Jared's autism when she mentioned his *situation*.

He cleared his throat. "How's that?"

"You don't know?"

He shook his head.

"I would have thought Michelle or Janice at Marston House would have told you, since you're seeing Jared so regularly."

"Told me what?"

She pinched her lips together before answering, her velvet-green eyes awash with compassion. Colin suspected that emotion might extend to him, as well as the little boy in question, and he didn't know what to make of it. He swallowed hard.

"Jared was just removed from his ninth foster home. He's having a great deal of trouble staying in a foster home setting, and foster parents just don't seem to know what to do with him."

He blew out a low whistle. "Oh, wow."

"Yeah. It's bad. He can't seem to find a good match with a family, and I think he's just miserable. The worst part is that his real parents hardly ever come see him."

"You're kidding." Colin emitted a low growl. He knew what it was like to have a father who paid no concern to him.

"I wish I was." Holly shook her head. "They've practically abandoned him to the state, though they haven't made any formal petition. I have heard they've indicated to the staff at Marston House that they can't handle a little boy with autism. Isn't that sad?"

Colin didn't answer. He was lost in his own thoughts, his mind going back to the moment in his own life when his dad ordered him to leave the house, to attend military school in another state.

Because his father couldn't handle being around *him* anymore.

"What kind of parents abandon their kids, even when

they have problems? Can you even imagine?" she continued.

He could imagine.

He looked up at her, biting the inside of his lip until it bled in to control the emotions roiling through his belly. He was plunging into deep water here.

He hadn't told Holly the truth, or at least not the whole truth. The only ones who currently knew anything about his past relationship with his father were his twin sister, Callie, and her husband, Rhett.

And they never talked about it.

Neither did he.

But he was going to talk now. He didn't know why, but he sensed, somehow, that it was important for Holly to understand where he was coming from, why he believed the way he did about children. About families.

And that meant breaking his self-imposed code of silence.

He cleared his throat. "When I was sixteen, I got into trouble with the law."

He heard her sudden upsweep of breath and grinned mildly. At least he could be sure he had gotten her attention.

"I was arrested for shoplifting at a grocery store. It was on a foolish teenage dare with my twin sister, Callie, and it was only a candy bar."

He waited for her response, but she remained silent, staring at him with wide eyes brimming with disbelief.

He laughed. "I promise I've never done anything as remotely stupid before or since," he assured her.

Her facial color had heightened to a healthy rose, and he wondered if she regretted being here with him now. Was she going to spend the rest of her life staring at him as though he were a common criminal?

He cringed at the thought that he might have impeded on their friendship by sharing such information. Had he said the wrong thing again?

"What happened?" she whispered coarsely, clearly aware that the black moment in his story was yet to come. She sounded a little like a small child eager to hear the ending to a good story.

But at least she didn't sound judgmental. He found the courage to continue in that.

Colin ran a hand down his jaw, reluctantly remembering the moment. "My father hit the roof, and was as close as he'd ever been to hitting *me*."

Holly made a strangled noise in her throat, and he moved over to sit by her, draping his arm over the back of the couch. She leaned in to him, laying her sweet cheek on his chest as if trying to find his heartbeat.

If she *was* trying to find his heartbeat, she'd find it racing. He focused his mind on continuing his story and found his thoughts difficult to collect.

"My dad was so angry, he threatened to send me away to a military boarding school. I thought he was kidding. Or maybe I hoped he was just threatening me in anger, and didn't really mean what he said. But the next day, he was on the telephone, calling around to find me a boarding school. He was looking for something as far away as possible. Out of state, at least. Something in the next galaxy, I think."

He blew out a breath. He thought he'd dealt with all his anger, but it was still difficult to look back to the trauma he'd experienced in his youth without some stirring of emotion. And he sure wasn't finding it easy to talk about, either.

"I can't believe a father would not want to be with his son," Holly said, anger tinting every word.

"Believe it," Colin snapped. "My father just wanted me to go away. In fact, I think he wished I had never been born."

Holly made a strangled sound.

Colin grit his teeth. "When I left home, the only thing he said was that he hoped that the military could beat some sense into me."

"Well, they clearly failed," she teased softly, and Colin's gaze flew to hers. Her eyes were full of sadness and sympathy, but she was clearly trying to lighten the mood, and Colin could have kissed her for the effort.

"So true." He chuckled wryly. "I never could seem to bend myself to appreciate the military lifestyle."

She shook her head and laughed a little too brightly. "That from a career navy man. I don't think I'll ever figure you out."

"Sounds pretty bizarre, doesn't it?"

"If I didn't know you, I'd say *yes*. But I think I understand the paradox in this case. I do want to know what happened, though," she said, once again changing the tenor of the conversation, gently nudging back toward the subject of Jared Matthews. "Having a father turn you away from home is a lot for a young man to swallow. But you turned out terrific, so you'll have to tell me how it's done."

"The word is *abandoned*. No matter how you couch it in other terms, the fact is that he abandoned me. Intentionally."

"Yes," she agreed mildly. "That's exactly what I'd call it. And I'm sorry, Colin."

Her gaze met his, warm and reassuring, and for a moment he let down his defenses, let himself feel once again the pain of rejection.

But this time, he had someone here with him. Someone to commiserate. Someone to care, to comfort him.

He squeezed his eyes closed, gratefulness washing through him as she gripped his hand, linking her fingers through his.

"I can't help being curious...." she said softly, pulling him back to the present.

He opened his eyes, gazing down at her and enjoying the novelty of the soft feelings swirling through his chest. "What?"

"How did you handle yourself when you found yourself in military school?" she asked with a smile that let him know her question wasn't entirely innocent. "Did you make yourself hard to live with? Refuse to concede? You simply don't strike me as the kind of man to give in without a good fight."

"Oh, I fought, all right," he agreed, torn between a smile and a frown. A dull ache started at the back of his neck and throbbed mercilessly into his head.

"What did you do? Act up in class and get kicked out of school? Beat up on other kids and take your anger out on them? Run away from the dorm and get chased through the woods by a pack of baying hounds?"

He blew out a breath. "In a way, I guess, I did all of those things. I certainly got in my share of fights. I tried to get kicked out, and ended up on K.P. or running the obstacle course at midnight in the pouring rain. I learned pretty quickly to keep my mouth shut and my opinions to myself."

"Keep going," Holly urged. "This story isn't over yet."

Colin snorted. "Hardly. I did my time. But my father didn't even bother to come to my graduation ceremony. My graduation." He drew his left hand into a fist, but stopped short of punching it into his right palm. "I decided right then and there I never wanted to see him again, not as long as I lived. I decided to disappear and never be seen again. Someplace my dad would never find me. Somewhere he'd never think to look."

"So you...?"

He unclenched his fingers and ran a hand across his stubbly jaw, concentrating on the prickly feeling against his skin. "I joined the navy."

She laughed and shook her head. "I knew you were going to say that. But it still seems odd to me that a man who disliked military school so fervently would join the navy."

He reached out and pushed a stray lock of soft, sable hair from her cheek. Touching her grounded him, reminded him that he was his own man, thirty years old and not a boy. And he was sitting beside a beautiful, sensitive woman who at times appeared to understand him better than he understood himself.

He had a future to embrace.

But he knew that no matter how personally agonizing it might be, he was obligated to finish his story. Only then could Holly really understand where he was coming from, and what made him the man he had become.

"My joining the navy seems like the action of a crazy man. I know. I've thought about it a million times since that day in the recruiting office, wondering how I could ever have made that decision."

He snorted and shook his head. "All I can say is that it made sense at the time. It might not have been rational, but I did have my reasons. The military lifestyle was familiar to me, however disagreeable it was. And I knew I could disappear quickly into the navy. My dad would never think to look for me in the military."

He paused thoughtfully. "Not that he would think to look for me at all."

"What about your twin? Callie, right? Did you tell her where you were?"

"No. I never told her anything. I didn't make contact with her at all." He chuckled dryly. "She was pretty angry with me when I finally got around to looking her up."

Holly grinned wryly. "I can imagine."

"You probably can," he agreed. "Fortunately for me, she's a kind, forgiving woman, and Rhett's a good, supportive husband. Thanks to him, I didn't have to live in the doghouse too terribly long before she welcomed me back home."

"I'll bet that's a great relief to you."

"It is. I really love my sister. I'm glad we could reestablish our relationship. I've always had a special bond with Callie, her being my twin and all. When we were younger we used to say we could read each other's thoughts. And I think it was pretty near true."

Holly smiled again. "I'm glad for you."

"And in consolation, the navy's been good to me. I've been stationed on both coasts and in the Far East. I've met a lot of good people, some of whom mentored me

and introduced me to the love of Christ. And I have a lot
to look forward to once I've reenlisted as a chaplain."

"It worked out for you, didn't it?"

"God had it all in His capable hands," Colin stated
emphatically, realizing after he said it, that what he
said had was true.

"He does, doesn't He?" Holly parroted softly.

"Which is what we've got to remember as we pray
for poor Jared," he said, stealthily refocusing the spotlight. "I'm sure that his parents feeling the way they do
about him couldn't have helped his autism."

"I think you're right about that. He sometimes re-
treats completely into himself, as you've no doubt seen
when you work with him. He generally doesn't want to
interact with anyone. Especially men."

She smiled gently and nodded in his direction. "And
yet here you are, Colin. You have had the most success
of anybody here in getting through to Jared, and in so
little time, too."

He supposed he should feel proud, but he was humbled by the statement.

"I…" He cleared his throat and ran a hand over his
mouth. "I…really care for the boy."

"Oh, Colin!" Holly launched herself at him, wrapping her arms so tightly around his neck he could barely
breathe. "I knew it."

"Knew what?" he queried, his voice muffled by the
arm of her sweater.

"I knew you'd realize your own potential. Your calling."

"My calling," he parroted, breaking her embrace
as he stood and moved toward his bedroom door. He

couldn't continue all this serious talk. He'd had enough talking and *feeling* for one day.

If he could *do* something, he'd do it. But he didn't want to talk about it.

He opened his bedroom door, and a scruffy little black-and-white ball of fur pounced into the living room, then rolled around and around, reaching for his tail.

Holly squealed in delight. "You didn't tell me you had a kitten."

"I didn't have a kitten, at least up until a few weeks ago. Remember our first date?"

Holly's heart jumped when Colin referred to their first meeting as a date, but she quickly reminded herself how unpredictable Colin was. He no doubt meant the word *date* in a generic sense.

"I remember you were late," she said.

He grinned and nodded. "Right. But do you remember *why* I was late?"

Holly's heart swelled as she recalled the circumstances surrounding his tardiness. She'd been so angry with him at the time, and yet he'd managed to win her over with his pathetic excuse.

And his boyish charm. "You were rescuing a litter of kittens, as I remember. You found them in a Dumpster or something."

"That's right."

"I'm sure I remember you saying you'd taken them to the Humane Society, so they would be adopted out to good homes."

He picked up the wiggling kitten and pulled it in next to his chest, slowly stroking over the small feline's back until he settled down and began purring contently in the big man's arms.

"I did. All except Scamp here. I just couldn't find it in my heart to give him away," he admitted in a low, husky voice.

Scamp. The name fit the rascally black-and-white-patched kitten. And maybe the moniker fit the man the cat had obviously adopted, as well.

"I think you two need each other," she remarked thoughtfully, studying the man and feline together. Scamp was still purring and had curled into a ball, looking as if he was preparing to take a nap right there on Colin's palm.

"Don't let Scamp hear you say that. He thinks he is king of the world."

She laughed as Scamp pawed at Colin's scruffy chin. "He sure acts like he's king. And I'll bet you spoil him rotten, too, don't you?"

Colin chuckled, and his cheeks colored.

"I thought so."

"I'm not admitting to anything on the grounds it might be incriminating."

Holly reached forward, stroking the kitten on his ears. "Your very first kiddo, huh, Colin?"

"Hah!" Colin threw up his free hand, waving her off almost frantically. "That may be. But Scamp is the first and *only* kid I'm going to have in *this* family."

Chapter Seven

"What is that supposed to mean?" Holly snapped, more severely than she would have liked. She knew she sounded desperate, but he'd surprised her.

In a quick, defensive move, she swept Scamp away from Colin and cuddled him under her chin. He purred and rubbed his nose against her.

"Are you saying you don't ever want to have a cat again?"

She hoped.

He winked and shrugged. If he noticed her discomfort, he wasn't showing it. "Kittens are okay. I just don't want to have kids."

"You're joking!"

"After what I just told you about my own youth, you think I'd subject that kind of heart-wrenching agony on a child of my own?"

She wanted to point out the obvious, that it wouldn't *be* that way with a child of his own, but it was patently evident he was already finished listening to her.

Ignoring her attempt at conversation, he had dropped

to his knees and was hissing at Scamp, who obliged by hissing back.

Colin's revelation amazed and stunned her. From what she'd seen and heard, he would make an excellent father. He was kind and compassionate, and full of the type of boyish charm that had Holly picturing him wrestling on the floor with a handful of small children.

Granted, right now it was more like a mangy, half-starved black-and-white kitten.

As bad as his childhood had been, Holly knew he was making the mistake of a lifetime to rule out becoming a father someday.

Why it should matter so much to *her* was beside the point.

Somehow, she decided with a strength of resolve that she didn't want to question, it had become her responsibility to make stubborn, thickheaded Colin Brockman see the error of his ways.

Children were a gift from God, not something to be feared and avoided. They were the very image of one man's love for his wife, and in that love, the image of God Himself.

Holly struggled to see Colin's viewpoint, to understand how he could feel as he did. Children were her livelihood, of course, so she was biased on the subject.

But more than that, she realized, children were her greatest dream.

Marrying Prince Charming and raising a house full of her own laughing children had been her heart's desire since she was old enough to understand what harboring such romantic notions was all about.

And those feelings hadn't faded over time. If anything, the older she got, the more she clung to her fancy.

At her age, it was probably no more than wishful thinking to believe she would—or even could—bear a houseful of children. Men weren't exactly clamoring to play the role of hero and father.

Or more accurately, not the right kind of man.

She peered down at Colin, who was lying on his back with the cat perched on his chest. They were both meowing at the tops of their lungs, and Holly couldn't quite decide who was outhowling whom.

Colin could be her Prince Charming, she realized with a start. If he combed his hair, tied his shoes and stopped slouching, it was possible she could picture him galloping into her heart on a white steed, with a shiny coat of armor dazzling brightly in the sunlight.

She caught her breath and held it, nibbling softly on her bottom lip. Maybe *that* was why she cared so much what he thought.

It was an unsettling notion.

"Do you want to work on your term paper?" she asked briskly, standing. Her head was reeling, and she scrambled to anchor herself back in reality. "That is why you asked me over here, isn't it? To brainstorm topics for your paper?"

He rolled over onto his knees. "I already have a topic."

"But I thought…"

He rose to his feet and grinned. "Okay, you caught me red-handed. I'll admit it—I invited you over here on false pretenses."

"To meet the cat?"

He slid a surprised look at Scamp. "What? Oh. Well, partially, I guess. Mostly I just wanted to spend some time with you."

Her heart picked up pace, sending little, tickling flutters down her neck. "I'm honored. I think. I enjoy spending time with you, too."

She narrowed her gaze on him, giving him her best severe-teacher look. "Are you really that far along on your term paper?"

He chuckled and ran a hand across his scalp, making random points of his thick white-blond hair stand at attention. "I didn't say that. I said I had a topic. It's not the same thing."

She wasn't the least surprised. "Well, I'm glad to hear you've done that much on your paper, anyway. I'm sure it's better than some students have done, though as your teacher, I would highly suggest you motivate yourself in the near future."

He chuckled.

"Care to share?"

He sat up and crooked his arm around one knee. His sea-blue eyes sparkled with excitement. "I thought you'd never ask, Teach."

She sat down cross-legged before him. "Please, Colin. Professor lectures are all over for the day. I promise. I'm here as your friend."

He smiled slyly and ran the back of his index finger down her cheek and across her chin. "Are you?"

She had no idea what he meant by that comment, but her throat went dry and she found she couldn't swallow. "I… Just call me a casual observer, then. I know you've put a lot of effort into this class, and I suspect you've come up with an interesting theme for your class project. I can't wait to hear it."

"A casual observer, huh?" He chuckled. "I'll just bet you are."

She frowned. "What's that supposed to mean?"

"Oh nothing." His smile told her just how far from *nothing* he meant.

"Colin, you have five seconds to…" she threatened with a smile.

"Okay. Okay." He pulled some papers from under the scratched and chipped oak coffee table that looked as if it might have come from a secondhand store, or maybe a garage sale. "My notes are right here. Somewhere."

"So there's a method to your madness," she teased with a giggle. "And here I thought you were living in complete, unsystematic chaos."

"I can find what I'm looking for. Most of the time." He shuffled the papers and cleared his throat. "See? Here it is."

"Please proceed." She slipped softly into an armchair and leaned forward, wrapping her arms around her knees. "I'm all ears."

"My goal in completing this class is to create a program I can implement when I return to the navy as a chaplain. As you know, I've been drawn to the plight of children recently."

He paused and grinned at her. "Anyway, I began to think about the military kids I've run across while in the navy. I'm not a military kid myself, but I think there's a lot of need within the system as it stands today. These children move around a lot as their parents are reassigned to various duty stations. And if Mom or Dad is called in for active duty, the child may not see them at all for a long period of time."

"Wow. I'm impressed."

He grinned and winked at her. "And all this brilliant deep thinking is a direct result of your fabulous teaching."

Holly smiled, aware he was teasing her, but flattering her nonetheless. "I'm glad to hear my lessons are reaching someone's ears. Sometimes when I'm teaching I think I'm speaking into empty space. That enormous vault of an auditorium echoes back at me like I'm in the Grand Canyon. *Alone.*"

"I've been listening," he said softly, rolling to his stomach and tucking his chin into his hands. "Before I started listening to you, I hadn't ever really thought about the needs of children. I certainly didn't consider the kids much when I was working as an RPS in the navy. Of course, Religious Program Specialists get more of the paperwork and less of the interaction than a regular navy chaplain does."

"You do realize that there are outside, auxiliary operations targeting Christians in the military that have programs available for military kids and teens," Holly interjected, thinking of her own experience as a marine drill sergeant's daughter.

She knew the programs well. She was a product of them. Or was that a by-product?

Not that the programs themselves were bad. They just hadn't reached and helped a teenaged Holly when she'd been calling for help.

"So I don't need to create something—is that what you're telling me? King Solomon's *nothing new under the sun* and all that business?" His voice was rough. He sounded frustrated.

"No, no," she protested immediately, causing him to grin at her in relief. "As much as these programs do, they don't reach the kids one-on-one, on a personal level where it really makes a difference. That's what you're talking about, isn't it?"

His blue eyes sparkled. "Exactly. I knew you'd understand where I was going with this."

"In that case, you'll be pleased to know the ball field is wide-open to your unique ideas: And to your enthusiasm."

He gave a low whistle. "It seems like a pretty wide ball field. I don't have a clue where to begin."

"Have you done any research on programs used in the past? Made a study contrasting their goals and effectiveness?"

"No, but I suspect there aren't many programs that would match the organization I've concocted. I can call one of the chaplains I worked with in the navy and ask him for help."

"Excellent start. You don't want to assume anything without doing your research, or you'll inadvertently duplicate something that's already been done."

His brows creased low over his eyes. "Good point, well-taken."

She smiled, glad to be able to use her years of training to help a friend. "You'll want to cross-examine the information you get from the navy with data you get from the other branches of service."

He glazed her with a sugary sweet look that melted her insides and contrarily put her on the defensive in a single glance.

"What?" She leaned forward and narrowed her eyes on him.

"What, what?" he asked, his voice and features dripping with feigned innocence.

"You know *what*. That look you just flashed me. What do you want?"

He looked away and pretended to brush a speck of lint from the shoulder of his white T-shirt. "It's nothing, really."

"If it's nothing, why aren't you telling me what you want?"

"I wouldn't ask, except that it will save me a bundle of time, and you know how you've been getting on me to make better use of my time."

She chuckled. "I just want you to be *aware* of time, Colin. I don't care how you use it."

"Yes, but if you talked to your father about the marines for me—"

"Hold it right there, buster." She stood with alacrity as she cut him off. "I'm out of here."

Her heart was pounding so glaringly in her head she could hardly hear or see, and there was a funny ringing sound in her ears.

All in all, she felt like she might pass out.

Or be sick. Either way, she wanted to be out of Colin's apartment when it happened.

"You'll excuse me, please. I've got to go." Dizziness engulfed her, and she reached for the back of the couch and struggled for a breath.

Colin was on his feet in an instant, his hands on her shoulders in a strong but gentle grip Holly doubted she could break.

"Hold on a second," he said, his voice as soft and low as the purr of his cat. "What did I say?"

"Nothing. I just have to go."

"Holly, I know you better than that. I know I've said

something to upset you, and I want you to tell me what it is."

Holly unclenched her teeth long enough to answer him. "I have not, nor will I ever, go to my father for help or advice. Not ever. If you want to talk to him, feel free to accompany me home for Thanksgiving and ask him yourself."

Colin didn't know which portion of her comments to address first. "Is that an invitation?" he asked, surprised.

Her eyes widened. How had she gone from beelining her way out of Colin's apartment to inviting him home for Thanksgiving dinner?

"Yes, I suppose it is," she agreed reluctantly. In for a penny... "I know my mom would love to have you come up to the lodge with me. Just give me a heads-up so I can tell her to set an extra place."

"Heads-up," he answered immediately, and then paused, dropping his hands from her shoulders as he took a step back. He had to wonder, now that he'd already committed himself, just what he was getting himself into.

He'd accepted this invitation from Holly without a second's thought between his mind and his mouth. And yet his original, carefully thought-out plans included a day of prayerful solitude on Thanksgiving, knowing that right now he had nothing to give anyone, not even his family.

Nothing emotional, anyway.

He'd even turned down the opportunity to share the holiday with his beloved sister, Callie, not to mention the prospect of spending time with his nephew, Brandon, and his new niece, Abigail.

Why did Holly's request feel so very different to his mind and heart?

Holly.

It was definitely Holly.

Holly was watching the interplay of emotions on his face and narrowed her eyes on him when his gaze connected with hers. *For once*, her expression told him, *I caught you off guard.*

If only she knew.

His unruffled, nonplussed, ride-the-wind-and-see-where-it-will-take-you attitude couldn't hold a candle to spending a day in the presence of sweet, spectacular, solidly dependable Holly McCade.

"I'll let my mom know you'll be coming," she said. "But there are conditions, Colin."

"Be on time and wear a tie?" he quipped, trying to coax a chuckle from her.

She looked all too serious as she stared back at him. "You can start with that. My father's a stickler for those kinds of details. But it's actually my father to whom I was referring."

Colin pictured his own very intimidating version of Holly's Marine Corps drill sergeant father in his head and wondered if going to her parents for Thanksgiving was such a good idea after all.

"Should I salute?"

"Colin!"

"Sorry." He did his best to look ashamed, which earned him a reluctant chuckle. He followed with a feigned salute that Holly slapped away.

"Believe me, you'll feel like saluting when you meet my father. *I* feel like saluting him, and I've never been in the military."

He took a loud, sweeping breath and reached for Holly. She stood stiff for a moment, then allowed him to fold her into his arms.

She was very serious about her relationship with her father, and she didn't have to speak it aloud for him to see the tension she was feeling. He was obviously not the only one who had issues with a father. He stroked her hair and murmured soothingly.

He closed his eyes against the sudden longing in his head and heart to protect Holly from whatever it was her father had done to cause her such anxiety.

He'd long since given up the killer instinct that used to rise in him at the mention of the word *father*, but he was still inclined to distrust the title. He'd learned, living through the school of hard knocks, that not every father deliberately set out to hurt his child, but most managed to do a bang-up job in the end, intentionally or not.

Hence the reason he was so disinclined to have children of his own. He didn't want to hurt his own offspring, his own precious gifts of God, intentionally or otherwise.

He had enough to do just comforting damsels in distress over their own father's conduct.

With a shaky laugh, Holly sniffed and stepped back out of his arms. "I'm getting you all wet."

He hadn't known she'd been crying. She was still visibly shaken. Her fingers held a tremor as they wiped a few tears from those velvet-green eyes.

"That's okay. I'm a navy man, remember? We're used to water."

She chuckled again, this time sounding a little stronger and more sure of herself.

"You'd better hit me with those conditions while I'm still agreeable to a coat and tie," he teased in an attempt to distract her from her tears.

"It's nothing, really." She paused and took a deep breath. "Just this. Whatever you have in mind to do, or to ask my father, feel free to do it. I'm sure he'll be very helpful."

She looked over his shoulder and her velvet eyes misted once again. "Just do me a favor and leave me out of it."

Chapter Eight

Holly looked so miserable, so withdrawn, that Colin did the only thing he could think of.

He kissed her.

On hindsight, he realized it was probably not going to be the best idea he'd ever come up with, but at the moment, all he could think of was the softness of her lips, her cheeks, her hair.

Holly stiffened for a moment when his lips first brushed across hers, but she quickly melted into his embrace. With a contented sigh, she wrapped her arms tightly around his neck and pulled his face down to deepen the kiss.

Colin chuckled over her mouth. Perhaps she felt something for him after all. It was enough to make him want to shout for joy, except that he was too busy kissing her to shout.

The sensation of cradling Holly within the circle of his arms was wonderful. Everything *about* Holly was wonderful. But when he tried to express those feelings in his kiss, she backed away.

"What?" he groaned, trying to pull her back into

his embrace. She resisted, turning out of his reach and wrapping her arms about herself in a manner that brooked no argument.

"Colin, what is this all about?"

She was back to her old self, serious, rigid spine and stiff shoulders. He wanted to reach out to her, to make things all right again.

He wanted to kiss her again and have her return that sentiment; but he knew from the look on her face it was a lost cause.

"I don't know what you mean," he denied, his voice low and husky. He tried to make eye contact, but she shifted her gaze away.

"We've been friends for a while, Colin, but there was no cause to kiss me."

He shook his head, disagreeing fervently. "I had a million reasons for kissing you, Holly."

"Oh, I wish you didn't." She slumped down on the couch. "This never should have happened."

Colin's mind was reeling. "I'm confused. I like you. And I think you like me. We kissed each other as a token of affection for each other. Where is the problem in that? What? You don't like me?"

She scrubbed a hand down her face, as if to wipe off the assortment of emotions she displayed there. "I don't want to get into it. I don't even know where to begin addressing the issues that kissing you raises."

She shook her head and waved him off, as if that was that. "I'm not comfortable. Can we just leave it at that?"

But he didn't want to leave it at that. She made kissing sound like some kind of legal issue, or at least a topic for a self-help book.

He merely wanted to know what was wrong. He wanted to fix the problem.

Now.

With effort, he reined in his tender curiosity and crouched before her. Infinitely careful with his touch, he reached forward, suspending his motion until she consented with her gaze. Then slowly, his breath suspended in the moment, he lightly skimmed the palm of his hand down her upper arm.

"Understand one thing about me," he said, his voice low and earnest. "I like you. I consider you my friend. A very, very *good* friend. And I would never, ever hurt a friend."

She attempted a shaky smile, but he could feel her quivering.

"I'm sorry I'm acting like a goose," she said with a wobbly laugh. "Maybe someday I'll be able to explain why I'm acting this way." She looked away, and her eyes became glazed. "But not today."

"Not today," he repeated, half to himself, and half to her.

It didn't make sense. But then, she was a woman. Men and women weren't supposed to be from the same planets, were they? He held her close. "Please don't apologize to me." He crooked a finger and tipped her chin up until her reluctant gaze met his. "You have the right to your feelings."

She pinched her lips. "I don't know about that. But I appreciate your understanding."

Understanding might be overstating it, but there must be some label for the feelings he was experiencing right now. He grinned and tapped her on the nose. "You've got it."

He might not comprehend, but he could be supportive, even if he couldn't shake the feeling that Holly thought they'd—*he'd*—done something wrong.

He summed up his feelings. "We kissed, and it was fun. End of subject."

He stood and pulled Holly to her feet. His mind was still spinning, and his muscles needed something physical to do to lighten the mood and make Holly feel better.

"Now, why don't we go down to the park and see if we can have even more fun?" he suggested with a wink. "It'll take my mind off the pressure of finishing my project for your class."

He took her hand and guided her to the door. "And if you're *really* nice, I might even be persuaded to push you on the swing."

The phone was ringing as Holly entered her apartment. Holly threw her keys down on the table by the door and raced for the telephone.

"Why didn't you tell me?" Sarah demanded as soon as Holly picked up the receiver. "It's not fair for you to keep such a hunk a secret."

Holly's heart raced, and she labored to take in a breath. "I don't know what you mean."

Sarah barked out a laugh. "Oh, right. I'm sure you don't have a clue. As if plucking the best-looking student from the classroom and claiming him for yourself is your usual style."

"I did no such thing!" answered Holly indignantly. "And you know it."

Again, Sarah laughed. "Of course, silly. *I* don't care if you date a student."

"I'm not dating him. And there's nothing in the

student teacher's handbook that prohibits my seeing someone in the class."

"Exactly," Sarah agreed easily. "So tell me all about him. I already know where you met. What else is there to tell? What? Where? And when?"

Holly cringed, knowing Sarah couldn't see her. "I'd rather not."

"What's wrong? You sound shaken up."

"I am. Something happened today with Colin that I—well, I just think I'd be better off to find out a way to avoid him from now on."

"Did he hurt you?" Sarah, her voice defensive, sounded all ready to lay in to Colin, and Holly chuckled despite herself.

"No, of course not. Colin wouldn't hurt me. At least, not on purpose," she clarified quickly.

"Meaning?"

"I just want to back off. Things between the two of us are getting a little too complicated for me." She paused, easily conjuring up the handsome blond sailor. If she expelled her breath on a sigh, it wasn't on purpose.

At least that's what she told herself.

"So he's not a nutcase or anything."

"Oh, no." It was amazing, how quickly she rose to his defense. "Colin is a gentleman in every sense of the word. He's smart. And funny. And I don't have to tell you how handsome he is. I just can't be around him right now. And I can't explain it."

She swept in a breath and darted a furtive glance around the room, searching for something comforting on which to settle her gaze.

But her pristine apartment offered little in the way of consolation. She snatched a pillow from the couch and pulled it close to her chest. "That sounds crazy, doesn't it?"

"You said it, not me. Is he pushing for a commitment and you're not ready for it?"

Holly laughed shakily. "Oh, no. Nothing like that. But I do think he's pushing our relationship toward the next level, something more serious than a casual friendship."

"And?"

Holly clutched the telephone. "Sarah, you are one of the few people who really know me. You *know* why I can't be with Colin."

"I know why you're *afraid* to be with him," Sarah inserted. "Because of your past. But if Colin is half the man you say he is, he'll understand, Holly. You have to be honest with him. Talk to the man. You aren't the only one in the world who has ever done anything in their past they've been ashamed of, you know."

Holly felt her cheeks flushing with warmth. "I don't *want* him to understand, Sarah. I'll die of humiliation if he ever finds out the truth about me. I don't think I could handle that. I want to go back to the way things were before he entered my life."

"You can't do that."

"I know that. But I made a mistake in pursuing a friendship with him. He's just not the kind of man a woman can be friends with."

"Honey, I could have told you that with one look at the man." Sarah laughed. "But I don't mean to downplay how you're feeling. He wants more, and so do you. And it scares you to death."

"That's precisely the point, Sarah. And that's why

you've got to promise me you'll help me steer clear of Colin Brockman, and all the trouble he brings."

"Holly, I don't think—"

Holly cut her off. "Promise. You have to. With your help, I'll be able to put that blond-haired scalawag out of my mind once and for all."

"I promise…" Sarah said. Then she finished her sentence under her breath. "Not to tell you *I told you so* when this all falls apart."

The more Colin thought about his encounter with Holly, the more perplexed he became.

Sure, he'd kissed her without warning her first, but he was positive she'd been receptive to his affection, at least at the moment their lips had first touched.

So what had happened to turn her away from him?

He'd asked himself that question a million times, and each time he'd come up blank. He'd prayed over and over for discernment, for a tiny glimpse into heaven, or at the very least into the complex and bewildering mind of a woman.

No sign, wonder or great revelation came on any front, not that he really expected it. Bright lights were his style, not God's. And Colin was too restless to be motionless enough to hear the still, small voice that might really do him some good.

Worst of all, Holly was obviously avoiding him at all costs. It had been two whole weeks, and he hadn't seen her once.

No. That wasn't completely accurate.

He'd *seen* her, all right. But he couldn't get close to her, no matter how hard he tried. Every day in class, he watched her speaking, teaching a subject that lit her internal fire. He enjoyed the sight of her thick, sable hair swishing in waves across her back, and pictured those velvet-green eyes he'd come to know so well gleaming with brilliance, though he couldn't see them clearly from the shadows of the room where he always sat.

With every breath, he longed to speak to Holly, and his arms ached to hold her, to assure her nothing was wrong between them.

Nothing was wrong.

He remembered back to the first time he'd seen her. Ms. Gorgeous Legs, he'd called her.

She was that, all right. The memory brought a smile to his lips.

But there was so much more to Holly McCade than her pretty face and fine figure, that he couldn't begin to name them all. And there was so much more Colin wanted to learn about her.

It was an insatiable yearning, to know everything about her a man could learn. He knew this much—he connected with her on a level that had made her his closest friend, while paradoxically becoming the greatest mystery of his life.

Holly was kind and sensitive, with a sense of humor that matched his own—except for those few times he couldn't figure out. She was strong in a feminine sort of way. She knew where she belonged, and where she was going.

But she was hiding something. Some kind of secret that was keeping them apart. That was the only reasonable explanation he could fathom.

He'd glimpsed her in a hallway once and had started to approach her, but as soon as she'd seen him—and she *had* seen him—she'd turned and fled in the other direction like she had fire at her heels.

He had no doubt she was running away from him, that *he* was the proverbial fire nipping at her heels. The only question was: Why?

What exactly had he done to strike the match?

Colin wasn't the type of man to sit back when there was a challenge to be met, and he wasn't about to let Holly run out of his life without a fight. She was the closest friend he'd ever had, except for his sister, and since Callie was related by blood, he could hardly count her.

He was going to get Holly back into his life. No argument about it.

Like the military man he was, Colin planned his strategy carefully. He would begin with Holly's friend Sarah, who had been so bubbly and flirtatious before, and had practically shoved Holly in his direction with her encouragement. Sarah now stood as staid and stoic as the walls of Jericho around Holly, acting like a fortress between her bewildered friend and Colin.

When he approached Sarah about Holly's noticeable absences in class, and the way she tactfully avoided him whenever she *was* there, Sarah cheerfully chatted around the issue. When he pressed her, she stoned up.

The walls of Jericho.

Clearly, Sarah didn't know how *that* particular story ended.

If he couldn't go to the source, he would find out through other means what was happening with Holly. Colin waited for the right moment, after class when Sarah was busy cleaning up. Sarah wouldn't run as far and as fast as her friend and colleague Holly. He could feel it in his gut.

When he advanced, it was a full-scale attack. He even sent a couple of figurative spies, in the form of jocks that sat near him in psych class whom he'd made acquaintances with, to spy out the land. They kept Sarah occupied while the classroom exited, luring her off to the side where she would be more vulnerable.

He waited in the shadows until the trumpet was sounded.

Then he charged.

Sarah saw him coming, rapidly interpreting the determined expression on his face, if her flare of panic was any indication. She scurried for her notes and books, but put them down again when she realized there was no immediate means of escape.

Where was there to run? Colin would only follow, and probably cause a scene.

Colin squared his shoulders. He was taking no prisoners. No matter what he had to do.

"I don't even know what I said," he declared boldly, taking a calculated risk that Sarah knew the whole story and would not mistake his meaning.

There was an awkward moment where the air crackled with electric silence. She narrowed her gaze sharply upon him.

Then, all at once, the walls of Jericho cracked, and started to crumble.

With a vengeance.

"Said? What you *said*? It's what you *did*, you dumb overgrown sailor."

Her insults didn't bother him, but her accusation cut to the quick.

He'd never knowingly hurt Holly. And Sarah of all people should know that. Was it only two weeks earlier that she'd been pushing the two of them together? *Women.*

"What I did," he repeated, trying to keep the frustration he was feeling out of his voice. "And that would be *what*, exactly?"

"If you don't know, I'm not going to tell you. You'll have to take that up with Holly."

"In a second," Colin barked back, seething with annoyance. Was it just with him, or did women always talk and not say what they meant? "Except, as you well know, Holly isn't speaking to me."

Sarah shrugged, and Colin thought he saw just a hint of concession in her eyes. "I did tell her she ought to talk to you."

The walls continued to crumble. He grinned. This was one battle he was determined to win.

"I'd never hurt Holly. Sarah, if you listen to one thing from me today, this is it. You've got to believe that."

She pinned him with a fierce, protective glare that spoke louder than words. He already *had* hurt Holly.

"Maybe not intentionally."

He scrubbed a hand through his hair. "Look, I'm trying to fix the problem, whatever it is. Whatever I have to do, I'll do it. If she'd just tell me what's wrong, I'd have a lot better shot at making it better."

He shook his head fervently, his determination to make things right with Holly renewing with every breath he took. He *would* make this work. "At least I'm *trying* to work things out with her, which is more than you can say Holly is doing right now."

Sarah nodded. "I'll admit, that's commendable." It sounded like half truth, half cynicism. She continued to eye him closely, taking his measure.

She was a good friend to Holly, Colin realized, but while he appreciated her loyalty, he also wished he could cut a break with her here. Anything would be better than what he was feeling right now.

It was now or never to blow the ram's horn and shatter any remaining bricks. He cleared his throat and flashed her his best pleading gaze. "Sarah. Please. Give me a break. Help me out."

She narrowed her eyes on him. "I'd like to do that, Colin, but I'm not sure I can. I have a division of interests here."

"No you don't," he replied immediately. "Sarah, we're all on the same side here. You, me and Holly. We're striving toward the same goal. You've got to see that we are."

He pinched his lips together in a straight, determined line. He wasn't going to stoop to yelling at Sarah, but he figured he wasn't beyond a little begging. "Where is Holly now?"

She wavered for a moment before answering, her eyes flickering with uncertainty. "She's back in the psychology office. Doing research, if I'm not mistaken."

"Good."

"I'm sure she doesn't wish to be disturbed."

He waved her off with a shake of his head. "Take me there." It was more of a command than a request.

Sarah flipped her long hair to one side and perched her hands upon her hips. "And then what?"

Colin shrugged. "I guess we'll figure that out when we get there."

* * *

"Got a minute?" Colin peered suddenly around the side of the office door and flashed Holly a toothy Cheshire cat grin.

Holly put a hand to her chest to still her pounding heart. He'd startled her, popping in unannounced as he had; but if she were honest, that wasn't the only reason her heart was beating so rapidly.

It was the man himself. And she had no desire whatsoever to speak with him.

He knew it, and she knew it. He was purposefully backing her into a corner, and she mentally scrambled for the best way to react to his unwelcome presence.

"For you, anytime," she said, then wondering how her lips could so easily form such a falsehood. She tried to smile, and knew it looked more like a grimace, but Colin didn't appear to notice. Or if he did, he was resolutely ignoring her discomfort.

He swirled into the office like a whirlwind, pulled up a wooden, straight-backed chair, turned it backward and straddled it, leaning forward on his arms.

"So what are you up to?"

Obviously not what was really on his mind. Not even a particularly good opening line, from friends who hadn't seen each other in a while.

Holly steepled her fingers and leaned back in her seat, a big black leather office chair that creaked when it moved. "What do you really want?"

Colin raised both his eyebrows. "You know me so well."

"Ha-ha."

"That wasn't a joke."

Holly groaned. "Everything's a joke with you, Colin. This much I know."

"You've got it all wrong," he protested.

"Do I? There is no ulterior motive for your visit today? Nothing you hoped to accomplish?"

He colored. "Well, there is that matter of Thanksgiving dinner."

"See? I told you so," she crowed, delighted at the opportunity to see Colin squirm a little bit.

"Did anyone ever tell you," he replied mildly, leaning his chin on his arms, "that it's not polite to gloat when someone's begging?"

Holly's breath caught in her throat. "You're begging?"

His clear, sea-blue gaze caught hers and held. "Do I need to be?"

She looked away. "No," she said around the catch in her throat. "I guess not."

He smiled so gently, and so completely without gall, that she instantly forgave him everything. Even stealing a kiss.

"Are you sure?" he continued, standing to his feet and yanking his chair out of the way so that the legs scratched against the tile floor. "Because I can get down on my knees right now."

Holly held both of her hands in the air, mortified. "Please don't."

He didn't. Instead, he held his hands out to her, pulling her out of her chair until she was standing face-to-face with him, a little closer than she would have liked, but not so close as to make her back off.

"Am I re-invited for Thanksgiving dinner?" he asked in a teasing tone.

"To my knowledge, you were never uninvited," she reminded him.

"Not technically, maybe."

"Not at all."

"We're going to have to talk, you know." His words were soft, but their meaning was unmistakable. He wanted to know why a kiss could send her off the deep end.

"Do we have to talk now?"

He chuckled. "No. Just sometime."

"Sometime, then." She'd put *that* moment off for as long as possible. Now that she was in Colin's presence again, she remembered how much she liked being around him, and she wasn't quite ready to give that up.

Which she'd have to do when he found out the truth about her. He wouldn't want to be around the kind of woman she was.

"Sometime it is."

"You really want to come?" she queried softly, squeezing his fingers.

"I really do." His gaze told her how much. "I need to speak with your father, remember?"

She did remember. And she thought she should feel insulted, for him to remind her of that. Maybe with another man, she would be.

But with Colin, she somehow knew that while he did need to speak with her father about the marines, he was really coming along to spend the weekend with her. And for now, that was all she needed to know.

Chapter Nine

One look into Colin's sea-blue eyes and Holly's common sense must have floated away. That was the only possible explanation.

And now, on Thanksgiving Day, she had to pay for her moment of weakness.

Holly straightened her jacket and slid a glance sideways at the handsome man standing beside her on her parents' front porch.

He looked straight ahead, his bearing tall and strong. He didn't appear to be looking in her direction, but just the same, as she turned her glance away from him, he reached out and grabbed for her hand, giving it a reassuring squeeze.

She smiled softly. She didn't know whether the reassurance in his grip was more for her benefit, or for his.

It was the first time she'd ever seen Colin look nervous. She thought, given the circumstances, that she might be basking in the pleasure of watching him sweat, but she was more taken in by the moment's witness of sheer humanity.

He wasn't always one hundred percent in control, after all. The knowledge made her like him even more.

Holly was a bit amused by his looks. His jeans and sweater looked as if they might have been ironed. It looked as if he'd bought a new pair of running shoes for the occasion, for the supple white leather wasn't marred by a single scuff.

He'd even combed his hair into a semblance of military precision. Not a single strand of his white-blond hair was out of place, no doubt thanks to a good slathering of gel.

She looked up at him and smiled. She wasn't at all sure she wanted him here with her today, but there was no sense in making him suffer any more than was absolutely necessary. Not that there was any doubt on that point.

He *would* suffer.

Her father would see to that, however shrewdly he crafted ways to turn the screws on Colin. It was going to be an agonizing weekend for everyone concerned, and for her most of all.

Holly made up her mind at once not to be the cause of any of Colin's difficulties. At least not today.

She closed her eyes and sent a silent and uncomfortably overdue prayer of forgiveness heavenward. It wasn't Colin's fault she had a sordid past she was struggling to keep hidden, especially when she was the one who hadn't been up-front with him in the first place. Maybe if she had been…

Stealing a kiss was not a crime.

She might even have enjoyed it, were circumstances different.

But they weren't.

She shifted uneasily. Her parents were taking an inordinate amount of time answering the door. On purpose. To keep them squirming.

Holly knew she'd eventually have to talk to Colin, and tell him the truth. Even if they never took their relationship beyond the friendship they had now, he deserved to know.

But knowing would change everything. And she would put that moment off for as long as she could. She had already waited too long to bare her soul to him, at least with any hope of his understanding. He would want to know why she hadn't been up-front with him.

And to be honest, she didn't know the answer to that question anymore. She wished she *had*.

She wasn't going to kid herself with anything but the truth. He was going to turn around and walk right out of her life when he found out how she'd spent her teenage years, what kind of person she'd been back then.

A shiver ran through her. There wouldn't be any more stolen kisses between them to worry about.

Which was all the more reason to enjoy whatever time she had left with him. She squared her shoulders. She had a lot of memories to make, something she could treasure later.

After.

She glanced sideways to see if Colin was feeling half as impatient with the wait as she was. He wasn't his usual talkative self, if that was any indication.

But when he met her gaze, all her doubts disappeared. The smile Colin gave her was anything but apprehensive, edgy or even impatient, for that matter. It was his usual careless, confident grin, and it immediately made her feel better inside.

Funny how he could reassure her even when he wasn't trying.

Her father swung the door open, and she knew in an instant he'd been making them wait on purpose.

Anger flared in her chest, but Colin squeezed her hand again, as if he knew what she was feeling, and her resolve to make the best of things strengthened. She wasn't going to let her father get the best of her. Not now that Colin was here with her.

"Dad, this is Colin Brockman, the man I told you about."

Holly's father, Ian, his hair cut in a characteristic military crew, and his T-shirt a marine green, pinched one eye closed in that grizzled way he had, then pursed one side of his lip and spoke out of the other. "Navy man, my girl says."

Colin squared his shoulders and looked the man directly in the eye. "Yes, sir. I'm out of the service now in order to attend college and get my master's degree, but I plan to reenlist upon my ordination to the ministry."

"Good man," the sergeant barked, clapping Colin on the back. "Rather you were a marine, but military's always welcome under this roof."

Colin grinned as casual as ever. "Thank you, sir. I'm glad to be here."

"Mrs. McCade will be sorry she missed the chance to be here to greet you, but she had some last-minute shopping to do." Sergeant McCade grunted. "Put a roast in the oven and took off like a whirlwind. Don't know what got in her craw."

Holly giggled and shared an amused look with Colin. She had told him a little bit about her sweet, quixotic mother, and it was just like her to run off at the last minute for some frivolous reason or another when she had guests coming.

She probably wanted to impress Colin, Holly thought, smothering another laugh. Impress him with a new red-checked tablecloth, or turkey-shaped salt shakers or Mother only knew what else.

More likely, when her mother did finally see him, Colin would be the one impressing *her*. It wasn't every day Holly brought a devastatingly handsome and charming man home to supper. Mom was in for a shocker.

With the tender consideration of a true gentleman, Colin placed a hand at the small of her back and accompanied her inside. Without hovering, he remained close to her side, his broad shoulders serving as a protective and very effective barrier between Holly and her father until she was ready to face him.

"Hello to you, too, Daddy," Holly said, giving Ian a perfunctory hug and a kiss on the cheek. He looked older than she remembered, and tired.

Or maybe *she* was the one feeling old and tired. At this point it was hard to tell.

"Sweet Pea."

She blushed at the use of her father's pet name for her. If he was trying to embarrass her, he was doing a wonderful job of it.

"Holly, why don't you go on down to your room, and I'll bring your things along to you shortly. Colin, grab your gear and follow me. I'm putting you up in the spare room."

He paused and looked back severely. "The one on the *opposite* end of the house from Holly, if you take my meaning."

Colin chuckled, but his smile, for once, did not reach

his face. His blue eyes were like ice cubes. "That will be fine, sir."

Holly held back in astonishment that Colin didn't bark back at her father for such insensitivity. He'd had no right, and Colin was his own man.

Sure, he was easygoing, but no man enjoyed being pushed around, and she thought Colin, most of all, would get his back up at being ordered about.

She half expected—*hoped*, she recognized suddenly— that Colin would stand up to her father in the way she'd always wanted to but never had the nerve.

Instead, he was rigidly polite, and clearly military. To his credit, he didn't say a word when provoked, except a brisk, military sanction.

Still, it could happen. Her drill sergeant father was a master at provocation, and Holly was pretty sure he wouldn't let up on Colin, if for no other reason than that she had brought him home.

Hit the right button, and every man would go off.

Even cool, cavalier Colin Brockman.

Colin was obviously a master at maintaining his composure, or else he had an arctic demeanor that was a part of him she hadn't seen before. Evidently, he had some way of shielding his true thoughts and feelings from the world, more than just the carelessness or even world-weariness she'd observed in him earlier.

Had the military given him this rigid self-possession? Or had his youth—his father—cast these scars?

"Young man, there's another thing we'd best get straight about your stay here," Ian continued, as if Colin's icy eyes weren't boring into him. "Something very important. Pay attention."

Holly tensed, anticipating the explosion. Either it would be her father's words, or Colin's temper.

"If I find you so much as in the same hallway as the one where my little girl sleeps, I'm going to tan your hide from here to Texas."

Colin flashed a suddenly warm, amused glance in her direction before he grinned at the sergeant. This time, the smile was real, even a little bit cheeky. Holly knew it, and she knew her father knew it. "Yes, sir, Sergeant McCade, sir. I understand completely, sir."

"What?" snapped the sergeant when Colin looked as if he wanted to say more.

"Well, sir, I was just thinking…"

"Get on with it."

"You've warned me about visiting your daughter's hallway, sir."

"What's your point?"

Colin's gaze met Holly's, his eyes sparkling. "I think it's only fair that you warn her off mine. Or you'll tan *her* hide all the way from here to Texas?"

"Colin Brockman, you are treading on very thin water," Holly warned, holding out one hand and swinging her purse like a weapon.

"Are you being impertinent, son?" Ian McCade asked at the same time.

"I dare you," Colin said to Holly, his eyes brimming over with laughter.

When his gaze shifted to her father, Holly took the opening and nailed him in the rib cage with her purse. Colin was on it in a moment, hooting with triumph as he wrapped the strap around his wrist. He used the momentum of the swing to yank Holly off balance and pull her under his arm, where he tucked her snugly.

"Yes, sir," he said, nodding at her father. "Completely impertinent."

The sergeant roared with laughter. "Glad to hear it. Welcome to the McCades, son. Home away from home."

Colin unpacked his bag and settled in to the small but comfortable room he'd been given. It was sparsely but tastefully decorated in masculine colors of red and blue. The twin bed looked a good deal more comfortable than the naval bunk to which he was accustomed, so he couldn't complain.

Keeping the room neat would be a trial, but not an impossibility. He'd managed in the navy, and he would manage now.

Using the small bathroom to wash up and run a comb through his already-tousled hair, he quickly adjourned to the den, where a roaring fire was blazing in the hearth. It was quiet, dark and cozy, and Colin found himself able to take his first real, deep breath in over an hour.

He covertly scanned the room. He could hear bustling sounds of pots and pans coming from the kitchen from whom he assumed was Mrs. McCade, and there was a black Labrador retriever dozing by the fire, but to his relief, Holly was nowhere around.

Colin had a mission to fulfill, and the sooner he got it over with, the better.

He'd realized as soon as he saw the stern, commanding drill sergeant that the older man had a noticeable soft spot in his heart for his little girl. But he highly doubted Holly had ever recognized that kind of affection from her father. Ian wasn't the effusive type, unless you called barking orders effusive.

For his part, Colin wasn't going to let himself be intimidated by the gruff old man—he'd seen enough hype in the military to know just what Sergeant Mc-Cade was trying to pull.

Colin grinned. A little bellowing wasn't going to keep him from asking Holly's gruff father a very important question.

Sergeant McCade was relaxing on a leather easy chair with his sock-covered feet propped up on a stool. He puffed with satisfaction on a black pipe, his black reading glasses propped on his nose as he perused the daily newspaper.

"Good afternoon, sir." He stood before the armchair as he greeted Holly's father, trying to be convincingly amicable and categorically unmilitary, knowing he succeeded at neither.

Ian grunted and waved toward the sofa, then buried his nose back in the newspaper.

Colin crouched on the edge of the cushion, elbows across his knees, his hands gripped tightly together. "I was wondering, sir, if I could talk with you. If you have a moment. If it's convenient."

He clamped his mouth shut before he said anything else stupid. Before he rambled anymore.

Sergeant McCade pinched the rim of his glasses between two fingers and pulled them halfway down his nose. For a moment, he merely eyed Colin over the rim, then grunted again and returned his glasses to the bridge of his nose, shaking his paper noisily.

Colin took that as a yes.

"Well, it's like this, sir," Colin began, tightly lacing his fingers in front of him. He was careful not to clench his fists. "Lately, I've been spending a lot of time with your daughter, and I want you to know I think the world of her."

Ian grunted harshly. "That so?"

"The truth is, I really like her. But I can't seem to get close to her. She's not the easiest person to reach. Maybe you know what I mean."

He cleared his throat, but found he couldn't look away from Sergeant McCade's stare. He was frozen to the spot, unable even to breathe.

Holly's marine drill sergeant father narrowed his gaze on Colin the way a panther pinned down his prey. His eyes gleamed gray in the firelight. "Close."

"Close, sir, meaning getting to know her better, becoming good friends with her," Colin clarified, finding his breath, and his voice, with alacrity. "I want you to know up front that I'm a good Christian man, sir, and I'm committed to staying—" Colin felt himself stammering "—that is…being—"

Ian actually chuckled. Colin felt the tension ease from the room, and smiled back at the older man. Although he wasn't quite sure what Sergeant McCade found so funny in the situation. While Colin was sweating bullets, Ian was as cool as the proverbial cucumber.

"I get your point," the sergeant replied acerbically. "And while I don't know *why* I believe you, I do believe you."

"You do?" Colin asked in surprise, his face flushed with elation.

"Yes," Ian answered briskly. "I do." He steepled his fingers and tipped them to his chin. "So, then your problems concerning my daughter are merely in the… *spiritual* realm then? Is that correct?" he asked with an amused twist to his lip.

The flush in Colin's face increased until he was sure his skin was flaming red. He cleared his throat against the pressure choking him. "Uh, not exactly, sir."

"Meaning?"

"Yes…w-well." Colin stopped, realizing he was stammering again. That would never do, not with a marine drill sergeant. He'd best just say it like it was and get it over with, since he'd come this far. "The fact is, sir, I kissed her."

Ian didn't budge. Colin expected him to frown, or chuckle or shoot him dead right there on the spot. Ian was a rock, showing not an ounce of emotion.

He did have a few words, however.

"What about your commitment to—" Ian cleared his throat, a little overdramatically, if you asked Colin, but then, drill sergeants were given to the overdramatic.

"Frankly, sir," Colin said, deciding to be blunt, "it seemed like the right thing to do at the time. As a general rule, I don't see anything wrong with stealing a kiss now and again."

"And is that what you did?" Ian's words were straight and wry. Still no bona fide reaction, though, not even in his expression. His gray eyes were as cold as ever. "*Steal* a kiss?"

Colin thought back to the moment he'd kissed Holly, how she'd melted into his arms, how right it felt to hold her and feel her heart beat with his.

"Yes, sir," he said at last. She *had* reacted, but he hadn't given her any hint of his intentions. He'd shoulder the responsibility.

"There's your problem," Ian said with the solemn authority of a father. He steepled his fingers again and looked wise—and unapproachable.

"What's that?" Colin asked, confused. "My problem is that I kissed your daughter? That sounds like just the sort of advice a woman's father would give."

Suddenly the rock broke. Amusement spilled like a water from a broken dam from Ian's gray eyes. "No, young man. Pay attention to what I'm saying. Your problem is that you *stole* a kiss. Like a thief."

Colin's eyebrows met the crook of his nose. "I don't understand."

Ian chuckled. "No, you certainly don't, my boy." He ran a grizzled hand over his wrinkled, clean-shaven cheek. "I think maybe you don't know my Holly well enough to be kissing her."

Colin bristled. "I know her well enough. And if she'd let me—"

Ian silenced him, laying a fatherly hand on Colin's sweatered shoulder and giving it a squeeze. "Take it from her father, my boy," he said in a surprisingly gentle tone. "Holly doesn't want to be trifled with by any young man, most especially a man in uniform."

"Trifled with? Oh, but, sir—"

"I know, son. But trust me. She doesn't see things the way you and I do." He pinched his lips together tightly, obviously pausing in order to choose his words wisely and thoughtfully.

After a moment, he continued. "She's had some… bad experiences in her life."

Colin frowned.

"I'm sure she'll tell you about them when she's ready for you to know. But do yourself a favor in the meantime. Don't steal any more kisses."

"Sir, I would never trifle with Holly." His voice was an octave lower than normal. He was surprised by the fervency burning in his heart, how much he meant what he was saying.

Where had this strength of emotion come from?

He would never have guessed he had it in him, to feel like this. It was a invigorating revelation, but a sober one.

He'd never expected this conversation to take such a serious tone. Nor for his heart to have taken such a serious turn.

He squared his shoulders and looked Ian straight in the eye. "I wouldn't hurt Holly. Not ever. You have my word on that."

"Good." Ian nodded firmly. "But don't tell *me*. Tell Holly."

He swept in an audible breath and turned his gaze away, looking distant for a moment before returning to the present.

He gave Colin a grimace that was an old man's close rendition of a smile. "Holly is good at keeping things deep inside that pretty head of hers, but I can guarantee you she's worrying about it."

"I'll get right on it, sir." Colin stood and nodded at the grizzled soldier, feeling almost as if he should salute.

"Don't push her."

"No, sir."

Ian leaned back in his chair and returned his pipe to his mouth. As he fluffed his paper back to where it had been, he spoke one more time.

"You're the kind of man Holly needs in her life, sailor. A man who faces up to his challenges."

Colin nodded to the older man, but since the sergeant was clearly already engrossed in the newspaper, he decided to go back to his room. As he walked, he mulled over what Ian McCade had said about facing up to challenges.

Colin had been faced with many challenges in his lifetime. Now, with God's help and a great deal of his own determination, he had faced up to every challenge he'd encountered, even the lingering pain of his father's mental abuse, which he knew would never quite leave him alone.

But this—this was new to him.

Being with Holly was a challenge unlike any other he had faced. He paused in the hallway and closed his eyes for a moment, restoring his equilibrium and evening his breath.

He smiled, knowing what lay before him would be worth whatever effort he had to expend; for winning the love of a woman, Colin thought, his chest swelling with newly hatched emotion, must truly be the biggest challenge a man would ever face.

And the biggest triumph he would ever know.

Chapter Ten

Holly didn't remember a Thanksgiving dinner quite as unusual and uncomfortable as this one was turning out to be. She shifted in her seat, vitally aware of the energy crackling in the air. The tension was so thick she thought she might be able to reach up with her hand and touch it, and be physically shocked by the sheer electricity of the moment.

Her father had asked—though it had sounded more of a gruff command than a question, coming from her father's lips—for Colin to say the grace.

The request was met with a smile, as Holly knew it would be. Everyone knew he was a future navy chaplain. This was probably the first of many such requests.

Colin's prayer was simple and elegant, but the words he spoke had Holly wondering what planet she was on. Were these people really her parents? Was the grinning man sitting across from her really the man she had brought home for the holidays?

Thanking the Lord for food, family and friends had been what Holly considered in the normal realm of things, typical Thanksgiving fare. But then Colin started going off on the oddest tangent—something about thanking God for people who chose to forgive, to give old friends a second chance at friendship, and how precious they were in the eyes of God.

She could have sworn she heard her father smothering a laugh.

Her stern, taskmaster father laughing during prayer? *Impossible!*

She looked from one stiff-spined military man to the other, but could find no clues in their expressions. She picked at her meal, no longer feeling hungry.

She didn't like the notion she was missing out on some kind of inside joke between everyone else. What was going on in this house?

Colin didn't appear to have any misgivings about his own meal. He greedily gulped down enormous bites of food, between equally large quantities of conversation. He appeared completely at ease with her parents, much more so than she herself felt at the moment.

Or ever, for that matter.

And her father was watching her. She could feel his eyes upon her whenever Colin was speaking. But if he thought to intimidate her or make her feel funny for bringing Colin home, he'd have to think again.

She reminded herself that she was no longer the small girl trying to win her daddy's approval. She had nothing to prove here today. She was simply eating a holiday meal with the family.

And she'd brought a friend home with her this year. Her mother, at least, was pleased by Colin's obvious enthusiasm for everything around him, the food and gracious company most especially.

Holly put her fork to her plate and decided the best

course of action was to concentrate on her food and let the other details worry about themselves. It was hard to swallow at times, especially whenever Colin looked her way.

All through the meal, it seemed to Holly that Colin was sending her silent messages with his smile, but she had no idea what he had on his mind. She wasn't about to ask him out loud.

Not at the dinner table. And not with her father present. He'd tell her in his own good time, whatever it was that was pressing on him.

She didn't have long to wait. When her mother rose from the table and began stacking the plates, Colin charged into action, charmingly and literally disarming her mother of the dishes, insisting he would do them on his own, since he was the guest.

Holly rose, intending to follow his lead, but he shook his head. "No, no. No dishes for you."

But when she turned away, he was equally as adamant. "No, no. Don't leave. Follow me," he said as he led her into the kitchen. "I just want you to sit and keep me company," he explained as he dropped the dishes onto the counter with a clatter, scraped out a stool from the breakfast bar and gestured her into it.

"What's this about?" she asked as he filled the sink with hot, sudsy water.

He shrugged and set a stack of dirty plates in the water. "I just thought I should do a little bit to help out, since your mom spent the whole day in the kitchen creating that fantastic culinary masterpiece we just consumed."

"That's not what I was talking about, and you know it."

Colin didn't answer.

She changed the subject. "I expect my father is happily ensconced on his favorite chair in the family room by now, puffing on that silly old pipe of his. I've tried to get him to quit, but he's a stubborn son of a gun."

Colin didn't answer, busy as he was scrubbing at the dishes. It was amazing how masculine he looked, his sleeves pushed up, and hunkered over a sink of dirty dishes, a towel slapped over his shoulder.

She shook her head and laughed softly, resuming her soliloquy. "And if I know my mom, she will be sitting at his side, cross-stitching or reading a novel. They've had the same after-dinner routine for as many years as I can remember. It was one of those odd family habits that made life feel the same, even when we moved around the world as a military family. They always made me do the dishes, which I highly resented, of course. Just Dad, Mom and me. Funny, how I remember it so clearly just now."

"I've been smoking this pipe longer than you've been alive, missy," Colin mimicked in a surprisingly accurate rendition of her father, from his low, scratchy voice, all the way down to how he pinched one eye and half of his mouth closed as he talked.

Holly laughed, truly delighted. Her throat was still tight with emotion, but Colin's antics had helped. At least now she could swallow.

Colin chuckled with her, then nodded as he wiped a plate clean. "I've seen him puffing at that old pipe. He's a man with a mission. I don't think I'd want to mess with that kind of dedication."

"When did you see my father with his pipe?" she asked, surprise jolting through her at the odd sensation that something was not quite right.

She hadn't seen Colin and her father together a handful of times since they'd arrived at the lodge; and then never in the den, which was the only place her mother allowed her father to smoke his pipe.

"I saw him with his pipe at the same time he told me why you're so afraid of me," Colin said, his voice soft and even.

Holly blanched. "What?"

Her father had told Colin about her teen years? When she'd rebelled against God and everyone? When she'd run with a loose crowd, both figuratively and literally?

He wouldn't do that to her. Would he?

"I don't believe you."

"It was a good conversation, Holly. We both felt it was very productive."

She stood and turned away from Colin, grasping the back of a chair for support. How could her father betray her trust in so cruel a manner?

And why to *Colin*?

Why not just blare it out over the military megaphone to the whole world and have it over with?

All she'd struggled to build through the years was crumbling down around her in a big messy heap. This was her worst nightmare come true.

Colin knew the truth. He had *sought out* the truth. But she couldn't blame him.

She was the one living a lie.

"He told you all about me, then," she acknowledged, her voice sounding flat to her own ears. But better flat than panicked.

"I already knew everything I need to know about you before I ever talked to your father, Holly McCade," he whispered softly, just next to her ear.

Somehow he'd moved behind her without her knowing. His steady, warm breath both soothed and ruffled her at the same time.

Holly closed her eyes tightly. She couldn't bear to think of Colin picturing her at the height of her immaturity, and she certainly didn't want to see the look on his face right now.

But she'd always known she couldn't hide the truth forever. Purity was something she'd embraced in her early twenties, too late to take back that precious gift God gave only once between a man and a woman.

She'd desperately wanted to believe the lie, as a teenager, that love and sex were the same thing. By the time she'd realized the truth, it was too late to turn back the clock.

If she ever were to marry, it would have to be to a man with a big heart.

Like Colin.

Her own thoughts burned through her. She hadn't realized…hadn't recognized…

"He didn't tell me any state secrets," Colin assured her, running his palms across her shoulders before turning her firmly around to face him. "He was helping me with *my* problem."

"And what would that be?" Holly blurted, eager to turn the spotlight away from herself, even if it were only for a moment. The rush of relief she felt was on an equal par with her curiosity to know what he considered his own quandaries.

"Well…*you*," he admitted wryly as he grinned down on her.

"Me. Since when did I become a problem?"

"Holly, what do you want out of life?" he asked, answering a question with a question.

"More than I can probably get." She looked away, ashamed of the cynical streak that ran through her, but unable to take back the words.

"Meaning?"

She let out an audible sigh. "What most women want, I suppose. A husband. A dozen kids. A home of my own to keep them in."

"With a lock on the bathroom so you can find some privacy," Colin inserted, the gleam in his eyes both teasing and caring.

"That, too." She chuckled.

"What else?"

"What else? Oh, I don't know. The usual. A career. I want to help people, you know?"

He tucked her under his chin and held her there against his chest, where she could hear the strong, even beating of his heart. "Yeah, I know."

"Isn't that what you want?" she asked quietly, her voice muffled against the softness of his sweater. "A home? A family? Eventually, I mean."

She felt his muscles stiffen, though he didn't move away. She slid her arms around his waist and gave him a strong hug.

"I somehow don't think that's what God's got planned for me," he said, and she could hear the tension in his voice.

"Why is that?"

He pushed her away from him enough that he could gaze down into her eyes. "You know better than anyone how bad the military lifestyle is on children. I wouldn't be so brutal as to subject my own kids to that kind of torture, never mind my wife."

"It doesn't have to be that way." She was amazed by the words coming from her own mouth; yet in the same moment, she knew what she said was true.

Her own experiences as a child of military parents didn't preclude the possibility of someone else making it work. And she and Colin had turned out all right despite the problems.

She could make it work.

She could raise military children. She already knew all the pitfalls. She could avoid them herself, and help her own children over the humps.

Of course she would never admit such a thought, most especially not to Colin.

He had returned to the sink and was noisily stacking dishes. His back to her, she covertly admired his broad shoulders and muscular physique.

"Do you think I trifle with you?" Colin didn't give any indication he'd spoken. His words were so low and velvety soft that it was almost as if he hadn't spoken at all.

But that didn't stop the bolt of electricity that sparked through her at his words, nor the heat rising to stain her cheeks in protest.

"Trifle? What do mean, *trifle*? Who uses a word like *trifle* these days?"

The answer hit her just as Colin turned, looking at once amused and sheepish. She blushed to the roots of her hair.

"Colin Brockman, *what* has my father been telling you?"

Chapter Eleven

A week later, Colin still wasn't sure how he'd gotten out of Holly's query about her father without losing his humor or his head, though Holly had threatened both and more.

But now that he was tightly ensconced in his own comfortable—if messy—apartment, he could relax, even if he couldn't quite forget about the close call. He was sprawled on the floor in front of the coffee table, a large, daunting stack of papers and books spread around him.

He had no idea where he should start. The ominous pile gave him a gut feeling that was at least as over-whelming as the one he'd experienced in his first week in boot camp. Only, this time, there was no one yelling in his face to get the job done.

He was so far behind on his studies that he thought he might never be able to catch up. It was amazing what a pretty face could do to a man's mind. Last weekend, at Holly's parents' lodge, his mind had been on Holly alone. He hadn't even thought to crack a book.

Now, when he knew he had to either get with the

program or face the consequences, he was *still* having trouble concentrating, keeping his mind off a certain sable-haired beauty with velvet-green eyes that made a man's insides turn to mush.

He flipped open the book on the top of the pile and tried to read, but he couldn't help reminiscing, even so.

It had been an amazing weekend. Sitting with Holly's mom and dad and having a real old-fashioned holiday meal had been the highlight. That, and his talk with Ian, who had shed some light on Colin's relationship with Holly.

He was especially grateful to Gwen, Holly's mom, who had come into the kitchen to see how the dishes were progressing. If she hadn't stepped in at just the right moment, Colin may have been forced to reveal his hand.

And he hadn't studied his cards yet.

He grinned and chuckled. How providential could a man get?

He'd slipped away without having to say a word. Without answering Holly's query on the word *trifle*. Without admitting how far her father's conversation had gone, how much he now had to think about.

For in truth, he was beginning to think seriously about Holly, wondering if God might have meant for her to be his life's partner. The Man Who Would Be Single was now contemplating matrimony—if not seriously, then at least with some degree of significance.

Marriage.

It wasn't as frightening a concept now that Holly was in his life. If it wasn't for his own fear—that of becoming a man like his father—he'd probably have whisked her off to the altar already.

Any sane man would have.

He chuckled under his breath and tossed aside the book he'd been reading. He picked up the next book nearest his reach. Sliding down to one elbow on the carpet, he yawned widely and forced himself to open the book, wishing not for the first time that he was a better student.

Though he'd never gotten much above Cs and Bs in high school, he knew he could be a good student if he put his mind to it. If he'd learned one thing during his years in the military, it was that he could improve himself, but he had to work harder.

He creased his brow, determined to buckle down.

He'd found his spot in the history book he held, and had read maybe three-quarters of a page when there was a knock on his door.

He groaned. Was he doomed to fail the semester? He was never going to be able to follow his dream of becoming a chaplain this way.

"Just a second," he hollered as he rolled to his feet. He half staggered to the door on legs that had fallen asleep on him, muttering under his breath about not being as young as he used to be.

Still grumbling, he yanked at the knob, determined to send whoever was on the other side of the door running for cover, so he could get back to the mind-numbing tediousness of his own work.

But when he opened the door, all thoughts of books and study were swept from his mind by the sight of Holly, her eyes sparkling with excitement. She shifted, almost bounced, from foot to foot, clearly in anticipation of the words that looked like they were about to bubble right out of her mouth.

Colin grinned and gestured her in. He'd never seen Ms. Straight-Arrow like this, and to say his interest was piqued would have been an understatement.

She made it two steps inside the door before she ruptured.

"Oh, Colin, I'm so excited," she burst out, whirling to pull him in the doorway and close the door. She gave him an impromptu hug that sent them both careening, until he uprighted them with a good show of strength.

He laughed loudly and swung her around. "I can see that. What gives?"

"You won't believe it."

"Why don't you sit down and tell me about it? Do you want a soda or something?"

Holly took off her coat tossed a load of books from an armchair to the floor. "A cola would be great, thanks. With ice, if you have it."

"Coming right up. Make yourself comfortable."

"There's plenty of padding," she teased, "what with all these socks and jackets lying around."

"What?" he squawked in protest. "But I cleaned this week."

Her high, tinkling laughter filled the air, and his throat closed tightly. She sounded like a spring fairy, flittering from flower to flower and laughing joyfully all the while.

Of course, if he told Holly what he was thinking, she'd probably want to crack him alongside the head with a two-by-four. Flittering and fairy weren't probably how she would want to be described.

She was a modicum of decorum, or at least a sleek, contemporary career woman.

Not the flittering type.

Colin grabbed a soda for Holly and one for himself, then kicked the refrigerator door shut with his bare foot and went back and settled himself on the couch, his legs propped on an empty corner of the coffee table.

"So what's up?" he asked with a grin.

Holly took a deep breath, and then let it out audibly. "I've found it!"

"It?" Colin parroted, popping the top on Holly's soda and pouring the bubbling liquid in a tall, ice-filled glass.

Holly looked at him as if he were dense. "Your theme paper. It's practically written itself, thanks very much to me."

"I'm interested." He slid a glance toward the gaping pile of yet-to-be-read books on his floor. Boy, was he interested.

Holly reached out and stroked his arm. "I thought you would be."

"Go on."

"Well, it's like this," she began, as if starting an epic tale.

"Once upon a time…" he teased.

"You'll think it's a fairy tale by the time I'm finished," she promised. "Anyway, to get back to the story, I went to church on Sunday."

"How very pious of you."

"Colin!"

He frowned, trying to look penitent and humble. Kind of. He cleared his throat on a chuckle. "Sorry."

"I'm sure. Now let me get on with the story. When I attended church last Sunday, they had a special program during the service. St. Andrew's does that sometimes, in order to motivate our parishioners to be out *doing* things for God in the world instead of just sitting in the pew thinking about good works. Pastor Freeman is a firm believer in acting out one's faith."

"Good man," Colin agreed. "Not enough people walking the talk."

Holly laughed. "You almost sound like a preacher, Colin Brockman."

"I do?" he said, genuinely and pleasantly surprised. Maybe there was hope for him, yet.

"I haven't even gotten to the good part yet. The program Pastor Freeman introduced last week is called Kids Hope," she continued, smiling. "And it's the answer to your prayers. You can thank me now or later," she teased, laughter glimmering in her green eyes.

"Kids Hope," Colin repeated, smiling just because she did. "Sounds interesting. Tell me more."

He hated to be a pessimist, but deep down, he really didn't really think she had the answer. He was becoming more and more convinced there was no answer. He'd certainly been scoping around for one, and had even tried to come up with a few unique ideas of his own, all to no avail.

Still, he didn't want to spoil her fun, so he smiled his encouragement for her to continue.

"The program joins one organization, in this case my church, St. Andrew's Church, to one public school in their area, again, in this case, Stonington Elementary, which is just down the street from the church.

"At that point, the local executive director pairs adult mentors one-on-one with a child the teachers and parents believe would benefit from this service. The adult and the child meet for an hour every week. And every adult mentor is methodically supported by a prayer partner from the church."

Colin felt pinpricks of excitement brush over his skin as energy pulsed through his veins. Could Holly be on to something? "One-on-one, you said?"

"Exactly. That's the difference. The key. Do you see what I see?"

He did. His head was swimming with the possibilities. "How do you think something like this would work out on a military base?"

"Uh, Colin, that would be for you to figure out. Do you want me to write and type your term paper for you, too, or what?"

He ignored her teasing sarcasm and hooted in delight. "What a breakthrough! I need to start by getting the lowdown on the basic training maneuvers, and move on from there. Do you suppose I could get an appointment with your pastor anytime soon?"

Holly patted both her knees with her palms. "Done. Thursday at 4:00 p.m. I hope that time will work for you. I wasn't sure of your schedule."

Colin squared his shoulders and widened his grin. "I'll *make* it okay. I can't believe you've done this for me. You're an angel."

He stood and extended his arms to help her to her feet. She stood slowly, almost hesitantly. He didn't let go of her hands, choosing instead to run his thumbs across the soft skin behind her fingers.

Their eyes met, and her gaze softened, but she took a single step backward, shifting ever so slightly, putting the subtlest line of distance between them.

"You're a dream," he said huskily.

"Bad or good?" she quipped as she shifted from one foot to another. She didn't quite look at him—meeting his gaze and then looking away.

He wondered what he had done to make her nervous in his presence. But even he could feel the underlying electricity in the air.

Maybe that was it. His heart was buzzing with the exhilaration of the moment, and he could imagine her heart in sync with his.

He raised her hands to his lips and brushed light kisses across the softness of her knuckles. "You're the best kind of dream," he assured her, smiling into her warm, velvet eyes. "A fantasy."

Mere inches separated them. He lowered his head to keep their gazes locked. "Is it okay that I dream about you, Holly?"

A chuckle escaped her lips, but her fingers quivered when he asked the question.

"If I can dream about you," she whispered after a long pause.

The air was suddenly thick with tension, and Colin struggled to pull in a breath. "I wouldn't have it any other way."

He found himself drawn toward her, his gaze wandering to her gloss-shined lips. He wondered if she was dwelling on the word *trifle*.

He hoped not. Because he could no more stop from kissing her than he could make the sun move backward in the sky.

As it happened, though, he didn't have to stop, or even make the first move. Holly, in a sudden impetuous move, put her arms around his neck, grabbed him by the collar and pulled his face down to hers, leaning toward him until their breath mixed.

"Kiss me." Barely a whisper, it was half a request, half a demand.

Colin willingly complied with both. With the utmost awareness, he leaned down and brushed his lips over hers, closing his eyes as he savored the sweet, gentle contact. His senses heightened at the same moment his world focused, until there was only the taste, sight, sound, smell and feel of Holly in his arms.

He closed his eyes, wanting the moment to last forever.

Instead, the atmosphere was instantly and completely shattered by the sound of the telephone ringing. Its shrill clang jolted through Colin's brain like a spoon on a frying pan, effectively dousing his romantic mood.

Even so, he didn't move or pull away, determined despite the disturbance not to lose the moment. He knew it might be a long time before they would reach such a point again.

Holly, however, immediately attempted to push back and break their embrace, turning aside toward the sound of the telephone.

"No," Colin protested, pulling her back into his arms. "Just ignore it."

Holly looked at the telephone, and then him. It was only a moment before she made her decision, melting back into his arms with a contented sigh, just as the answering machine picked up.

"This is a message for Colin Brockman," the woman on the line began. "This is Michelle Walker, the principal at Marston House. I need to speak to you as soon as possible regarding Jared Matthews."

Colin launched toward the telephone, but was too late to intercept the call. With his heart beating in his ears, he flashed an apologetic look toward Holly, tucked the receiver under his chin and rapidly punched out the numbers Michelle had recited.

Please, God, don't let him miss her.

Holly moved to his side and placed a hand on his shoulder, offering instant and silent support. He glanced down at her, flashing her a grateful smile.

She smiled softly in return.

"This is Colin Brockman," he said when Michelle answered, clearing his throat when he realized how low his voice sounded.

"Colin! I'm glad you called back so quickly," she blurted immediately. "I'll cut to the chase. There is a problem with Jared Matthews, and I thought, under the circumstances, that you should know."

"What kind of problem with Jared?" Colin clenched his fist around the phone cord as his throat constricted around his breath, with emotion for the boy he'd come to love.

"I'd prefer to discuss it with you in person, if you don't mind." Her voice was firm, but clearly anxious, and Colin paced back and forth as far as the telephone cord would reach.

"I'll be right over."

He hung up the telephone and reached for his coat. "I'm sorry, Holly. I really want to discuss this whole Kids Hope thing with you, but it will have to wait until later. I'm afraid I have to leave right now. I'll walk you out."

Holly didn't say a word as he helped her into her coat, pulling it tight against her chin, since it was snowing outside, and wrapping her scarf firmly around her delicate neck, against the drafts.

"What's wrong with Jared?" she asked at last, halting him from his erratic movements with a level hand on his elbow.

"I don't know," he answered hoarsely. "Not something good, I'm afraid. I'm sure going to find out as soon as I can."

"I'm going with you," said Holly resolutely as he, equally resolutely, pressed her out the door ahead of him, pausing only to lock the door.

He was about to assure her Jared wasn't her problem, at least not on this day. She should go home where it was warm, not follow him about in the cold chill of the winter afternoon. But something in the look she gave him stopped him from saying a word.

She was *making* it her problem. Because of *him*. Because of what they shared between them.

Again, his throat clouded with emotion. He had already been through a lot today, and he had the feeling the day wasn't over, not by a long shot.

Had it only been a few months ago that he hadn't been attached to a single person in the whole world? He'd been so proud of the fact that he was his own man, all alone with no one to care for, or to care for him.

How had he ever lived that way?

First there was his sister and her new family. And then there was Holly. And Jared. What was a man to do with himself?

He slid a glance toward the beautiful, loving woman at his side. He might not be sure what to do with himself, but he knew *exactly* what to do with her. He kept an arm around her waist as they left.

Together.

Chapter Twelve

Holly was surprised and pleased at how quickly Colin gave in to her request to accompany him.

Before he'd had the opportunity to send her away, she'd already mentally lined her arguments up in a row.

She'd been the one to introduce him to Marston House in the first place. She knew Jared and his case. And, the clincher, she hoped: she was a child psychologist, after all. A professional in her field. Perhaps she could be of some help.

And she'd needed none of it. Colin wanted her to be there. With him. For his own reasons.

He didn't speak the whole way to the school, but she didn't begrudge him the silence. She could tell his mind was on the meeting ahead. So she kept her hands folded on her lap and tried not to think about all the bad things Michelle Walker's telephone call could mean.

His small blue truck was a lot newer, and a good deal fancier, than her Jeep. It held in heat much better, and had a much nicer ride.

It was funny how she'd driven a Jeep all her life, just

because her father's gift to her when she'd earned her driver's license had been a Jeep.

It was one of her best memories. Learning to drive had meant something to her father. He had been so proud of her that day.

She shook herself quickly to the present. Despite the smooth ride, Colin looked like he was bouncing all over—internally, at any rate. His square jaw was locked so tight she could see a tendon straining against his cheek. And he was scowling, something so foreign to Colin, it made Holly want to cringe.

She couldn't stand seeing him look so miserable. His boyish good looks set in a frown broke her heart. It was just *wrong*.

Slowly, so as not to startle him from his thoughts, she leaned toward him, stroking his brow, gently soothing the anxiety marked there.

"Thanks," he said gruffly.

"For what?"

"For being here. With me."

She choked up. "Where else would I be?"

He tossed a grin her direction, but it wasn't more than a decent attempt, and came off more like the grimace he must be feeling inside.

She took his hand and squeezed.

They arrived at Marston House a moment later, and Colin parked, got out of the vehicle and quickly moved around the truck to get Holly's door. He lifted a hand to help her down from the truck, then linked her fingers with his as they entered the school, sending her the silent message that he needed her, that they were in this together.

She squeezed his hand, offering what little support

she could. She was only beginning to realize how important Jared was to Colin, and her respect for the man grew with every moment, causing her throat to tighten as emotion swelled.

There weren't too many men who would put themselves forward for the sake of a helpless little boy, especially a boy like Jared who had special needs.

There weren't too many men like Colin Brockman.

Colin wasn't in Marston House a moment before he'd obviously spotted Jared. With a quick glance down at Holly, he lit off for the playroom where he'd first met Jared. Holly followed.

The boy had climbed up a pile of boxes and was sitting high in one corner of the room, curled up in a ball and looking as if the world didn't exist for him as he rocked back and forth, back and forth, staring into space and mumbling something unintelligible—and repeatedly.

Michelle put an arm around both adults as she entered the room. Frowning, Colin shook her hand off and started for the boy, clearly intent on finding out firsthand what was going on.

The principal stopped him. "Wait, Colin. I know you want to go to Jared, but there are some things you need to know first."

"What things?" Holly asked. It was heartrending, watching the child's visible agony.

"Jared got some bad news this morning. He's been like this all day," Michelle explained gravely. "Our staff hasn't been able to get through to him at all. I thought of you immediately, Colin. I know you've spent a good amount of time with Jared. I'm hoping maybe he'll respond to you."

Colin's troubled gaze met Holly's for a moment, and then he bowed his head. "I'm no expert. I don't know if I can help. But I'll do my best, ma'am."

Holly realized as she watched Colin approach Jared that he hadn't even waited to find out what had happened to send Jared into a downward spiral, though that was clearly a major concern. What could have happened to make Jared revert as he had?

They would find out in due time, she supposed. In the meantime, she'd take her cue from Colin. His first and only consideration was to be with the boy.

Tears pooled in the corner of Holly's eye, and she absently wiped them away. How many men would have made such an emotional commitment to a complete stranger?

Michelle approached Jared first, but when she laid her hand on his shoulder, he brushed her away with a near-violent jerk of his shoulder. She backed away from the boy with her hands held open, giving Colin a chance to crawl up the boxes and move in.

At first Colin merely crouched near Jared, speaking softly all the while, so the boy would know he was there, but not touching him or encroaching on his personal space.

He talked continually and watched unremittingly for a long while, but he didn't shift a muscle, though the minutes wore on.

Colin sat without moving for so long Holly began to wonder if Jared would respond to him, but Colin looked confident, if concerned. He somehow appeared to know instinctively that he needed to wait the boy out, to prove his trust and friendship by his presence and not by his touch.

Any concern he might be feeling in his heart didn't show in his voice. His low, steady baritone assured even Holly, as she listened to the quiet, soothing monotone whispering nonsensically.

Lost in her own thoughts, Holly missed the moment when contact was made, but suddenly the boy was in Colin's arms, rocking back and forth and making heart-breaking little rhythmic sounds that were a lot like sobs.

Colin's gaze met hers, and together they shared a moment of grief. Jared's cry was enough to break any-one's heart; and right now, Holly distinctively heard *two* hearts fracturing.

Colin resisted the urge to move. He wanted to tighten his grip on the little boy, but he knew instinctively it would be the wrong thing to do. Jared needed the kind of tenderness Colin thought that, with his own big, bum-bling body and huge hands, he might not be able to give the small boy.

Yet, it was clear Jared was responding to him, and that, at least warmed his heart.

Jared had come to *him*.

He felt a great deal of responsibility toward the boy, but for some reason that burden didn't frighten him the way he thought it should have, or even would have as short as six months ago.

Had turning thirty somehow made him grow up, mature in some way he'd missed in the past?

Or maybe it was a combination of things—joining the navy, coming to know Christ, deciding to become a chaplain, meeting Holly and then getting to know Jared. Maybe it was a combination of life's events that caused a youth to become a man.

Whatever it was, he was just glad he had what it took

to make the adult decisions and adult commitments it was clear he was going to have to make. At least he was beginning to believe he had what it took.

For Jared's sake, he hoped so.

"What happened to him, to set him back?" he asked Michelle quietly.

"You know he's been in foster care for several years," Michelle said gravely.

"Yes. You mentioned that you couldn't find a good fit for him, that he'd been in several homes over that period of time. Is that what's happening now?"

"Worse than that, I'm afraid," Michelle confirmed, her voice low.

Colin's gaze slid to Holly. She put her palms together and linked her fingers in front of her as their eyes met. Her message was clear.

We're in this together.

He took a deep breath and nodded. Somehow he felt better, just knowing Holly was there.

"His mother and father have abandoned him to the state," Michelle stated without preamble. "He's now officially an orphan."

"How could they?" Holly whispered harshly, her outrage showing clearly on her flushed face. "I've never heard of parents intentionally abandoning their children to the state. Can they do that? What kind of people would do that, anyway?"

Michelle sighed. "Welcome to the world of child psychology. Mothers and fathers don't always act the way you would expect them to, especially when their children have some kind of disability."

"But to abandon them to the state? How can a mother give up her child?"

"Sometimes they believe they are doing what is best for the child, giving him to caregivers who know more about how to deal with him and treat his special needs than they do. Sometimes they just don't want the responsibility of a child who is 'different.'"

"But isn't there another way?" Holly asked, disagreeing with her scowl as well as her words. "I just can't see it."

"Maybe they are poor, Holly," Colin broke in, though he realized he was treading in deep water. He was speaking about something he knew less than nothing about, and was probably better off keeping his mouth shut.

Holly looked up at him, her big green eyes luminescent with unshed tears. "Be that as it may, I don't think I'll ever understand. Or forgive. To me, there isn't a good enough reason in the world."

Holly was quiet the whole ride back to Colin's apartment, and left for her own apartment as soon as they'd reached Colin's place.

Frankly, she didn't know what to say to Colin. He had been magnificent, and she couldn't even find words to tell him how she felt when she saw him holding little Jared in his arms.

But right now she had other things on her mind. Like how she was going to be a total failure in her chosen field. She'd not realized until the moment she'd seen Jared all curled up, helpless and alone in the world, just what being a child psychologist really meant.

What *helping children* really meant.

It meant she'd have to face the tough cases, ones that

didn't work out according to the rules of the book, or even the rules of decent life.

She supposed she'd always known that, in theory, but seeing Jared so helpless today had been all too much reality for her. She'd handled some questionable cases for the state in her college internship, but Jared stepped beyond the realm of books and into the personal.

She *knew* this boy.

And it made a difference.

She held strong feelings for Jared. He wasn't just any little boy, he was someone she knew and cared about, and would wonder what happened to when tomorrow came around.

Was there any way she could look at Jared's mother and father and not want to scream at them, force them to do the right thing, to love and serve this little boy who was such a precious gift in the eyes of God?

She closed her eyes, half in prayer, half in pain. She knew there were many ways to view such a situation, and that the way the state, or any other agency she worked for might not see things her way.

Could she handle being told to do something she didn't believe in?

She searched her soul, and found she wasn't sure of the answer to that question. Her faith was beating strongly in her heart.

She could not and would not turn her back on God. The quintessential question *What Would Jesus Do?* entered her mind.

Except she didn't know the answer to the question this time around. The issue wasn't exactly cut out in black and white.

Did she keep on with her plans for the future, doing

good wherever she could and making the most of every bad situation? Or did she look for another way to serve God and the world?

Was there a way she could use her skills and be true to her faith at the same time? But was that what Jesus meant when He said to go into all the world?

She's never been more confused.

There were other avenues for a trained child psychologist than working for the state. Some were overtly religious, though she'd never before considered such a vocation. Somehow, she didn't see herself as a missionary to the children in South Africa, but odder things had happened.

She wondered what Colin was thinking. Knowing Colin, he was probably out playing basketball or something, his problems already happily forgotten in the fluky, whimsical life he led.

She wished she could throw her own problems to the wind, but she knew that was beyond her capability. She was the proverbial stick in the mud. Her troubles were bound to follow her no matter where she went.

For her, the trick was to turn around and face them head-on.

Colin was not playing basketball. He wasn't playing anything. And he definitely had not been able to put aside his problems.

He slumped back in his chair, brought his hands to his head and brushed his fingers through his already tousled hair.

As soon as he'd dropped Holly off at her car, he'd turned his truck around and returned to Marston House. An idea had popped into his mind during the silent ride home with Holly, and he couldn't shake it no matter how he tried.

He'd spent a few minutes in silent, frantic prayer with God, almost begging to be talked out of the crazy idea. But when he'd felt that gentle nudging of God on his heart, he decided to follow up right away, before he lost his nerve. And that involved speaking to Michelle.

The principal of Marston House had been surprisingly receptive to his plan, but had soon excused herself to get some papers, and was taking forever to come back to her small, sparsely furnished office located at the far east end of the school.

Colin sighed and crossed his arms over his chest, his palms resting tightly over his upper torso.

This had been the longest, hardest day of his life. Even his first few days of basic navy training couldn't compare to the strain he was feeling now.

At boot camp, they battered his body; but today, holding Jared while he grieved, sheltering the precious little boy in his arms, was far worse agony than anything the navy could dole out.

Being with Jared battered his emotions, and more than that, struck at his very soul.

He'd heard Holly's anger when she lashed out at Jared's parents' actions, and he shared in that sentiment. But his mind had been so taken over with Jared's immediate needs, he hadn't wanted to waste any energy on emotion.

What he needed were solutions.

Another foster home wasn't going to be the answer for the boy. Even if he was sent to another home, he'd more than likely be permanently sent back to the state before long.

Maybe someone could reason with Jared's parents, but Colin doubted it. The boy's parents had obviously not come to their decision overnight, and it was doubtful more counseling would change their minds about what they felt they had to do, for whatever reasons they had for making the decisions they did.

Colin couldn't help but feel that Jared, with whatever understanding he had about what was going on around him and to him, was losing hope—in the system, in humankind, maybe even in God.

Colin gritted his teeth and slammed his fist down on the tabletop. He couldn't let that happen to another young boy.

Not while he was there to stop it.

Chapter Thirteen

Holly wasn't sure why her father had called her up to his lodge over the weekend, but whatever it was, it couldn't be good. He'd used his drill sergeant voice when he'd spoken with her, so there was no room to brook an argument.

And her father had emphasized the need to hurry, too, so she hadn't said goodbye to Colin, or even let him know where she was going.

She was sorry she couldn't make contact, but when she'd called his apartment there'd been no answer; and of course, in typical Colin fashion, he hadn't remembered to turn on his answering machine.

Since they spent nearly every day together these days, she knew he would probably, and rightfully, assume they'd be spending the weekend together.

Which they would be, were it not for her father's request.

Even so, she knew Colin wouldn't be angry with her when he found out she was gone, even if he didn't know why or where she'd gone. He might worry a little bit, but it wasn't in his nature to stress over things the way she did, so she didn't worry—too much—that she'd caused him undue anxiety.

She had the oddest feeling, though, that it was a bad time to leave, a time when Colin really needed a friend by his side. She knew he was broken up over what had happened to Jared, even if he hadn't expressed his feelings to her.

For one thing, he'd reverted to his rigid, military posture and stiff upper lip, both literally and figuratively. That was enough to let Holly know something was seriously amiss in Colin's world.

And all the while he was wrestling with the situation with Jared, he was trying to pull things together with his Kids Hope project for her class, which in itself was a huge undertaking. He'd been making phone calls and reading dozens of books, which she knew was not his favorite pastime.

He told her in confidence he was working on a PowerPoint presentation he could use after he graduated, even though she'd assured him he needn't go to *quite* that much effort for her class. He wanted something he could use on naval bases, and was proving himself a lot more focused than Holly would have thought.

She couldn't stop thinking about Colin the whole hour's drive to the lodge, which was a surprise. She was still broken up about her own dilemma, to which she'd come to no decent conclusions.

More than that, she knew she ought to be pondering all the possible reasons why her parents might want to see her. At the very least she should be giving it a guess.

It could be that all they wanted to do was to lecture her about why she wasn't getting married and starting a family. Certainly, bringing Colin home for Thanksgiving might have sparked that old flame.

It was a tune she'd heard many a time before, especially from her mother, although why that should require an extra trip on Holly's part was beyond anything she could contrive.

The truth was, she couldn't think of a single reason why her parents would want to speak to her in person. A telephone call would do for most things she could conceive as a problem, and they could wait until her next visit on anything else they had to say.

Unless someone was sick. But that would mean *really* sick—fatally ill, even.

Her stomach lurched as she rolled the thought over in her head. She pulled the Jeep's steering wheel sharply to the left and slammed her foot on the brake as she executed a sharp hairpin curve on the washboard dirt road, and swallowed hard to gulp down her dismay.

Was her mother incurably sick? Had her dad, her dear, gruff Marine Corps father, contracted some sort of serious illness?

No.

It couldn't be, and she wouldn't let herself consider it for another moment. If her foot came down a little bit harder on the gas pedal, it was purely coincidental.

And it was, fortunately, on a straight segment of road.

Despite promising herself she would do no such thing, Holly had thoroughly worked herself up by the time she'd reached the lodge, simply by *not* thinking about it. She dashed from the car, let herself into the front door and launched into her unsuspecting father's arms, her tears wetting his weather-hardened cheek and dripping onto the plain forest green of a marine-issue T-shirt.

He promptly pushed her aside, squaring his shoulders and frowning over her, though he still supported her with one arm.

"What's this, now?" he barked in his best drill sergeant voice. "Buck up, young lady. We'll have no crying here."

From habit learned in childhood, she straightened herself to military rigidity and wiped her eyes.

And it helped. She was oddly comforted by his gruff actions.

The familiarity of old habit soothed her, however rough it might seem to the outside world. This was a marine daddy with his little girl, and this was the way things ran in her world.

She knew better than to shed tears in her father's presence. In truth, she thought a woman's tears might be the one thing her tough old military father couldn't handle.

"Sorry," she scratched out, her throat dry.

"Done," her father replied with a snappy nod. He'd never been much of one for extended apologies. "But don't let your mother see you this way. You know how your tears upset her."

"Yes, sir." It warmed her heart at the way her father still protected her mother, as if the woman was made of fine china, and was not the strong, sweet woman who had devoted her life to him and was in truth, in many ways, stronger than he ever was.

"How is Mom?" she queried, hoping for information to confirm, or hopefully allow her to discard, her disturbing theories.

Her father's eyebrows creased, but his eyes sparkled with mirth. "Meddling as ever."

Her heart swam with relief, and her breath relaxed as her anxiety melted within her. "She's still trying to get you to quit smoking that pipe, huh?"

He grunted. "The never-ending battle. Maybe someday I'll just quit that old pipe cold turkey and send her into an apoplexy." He laughed good-naturedly. "But then we wouldn't have anything to fight about, and our marriage would be over."

Holly laughed with him. "It would be over? Why is that?"

He gazed at her solemnly, then ruined the impression with a sly wink. "Why, then, we'd have nothing left to talk about!"

Holly laughed with him. "Then neither one of you is ill."

"'Course not. I can't imagine where you'd get an idea like that."

She *could* imagine. And for once in her life, she was quite relieved to be wrong.

"Are you wondering why we called you down to the lodge?" he asked bluntly. "Because if that's what's bothering you, you don't have to get all in a snither about it." He picked up her suitcases and gestured her down the hallway.

She snorted her protest. "I'm not in a *snither*, Dad. But you have to admit you were rather vague about why you asked me to come up here this weekend. Is it some kind of surprise?"

He gave her a half grin and nodded. "You could say that."

For a man who spent his life being inordinately up-front with people, he sure was beating around the bush with her now.

"Is it for me? It's not my birthday," she reminded him. "Nor a holiday."

Her father looked about ready to speak when the doorbell rang. Since they'd stopped in the middle of the hallway in the intensity of their conversation, they hadn't quite made it all the way to Holly's bedroom to drop off her luggage.

In his typical, immediate military fashion, her father dropped the suitcases neatly in a row by the wall, and strode back toward the door with quick, even steps.

Curious, Holly followed, though she lagged behind her father's brisk pace. It really wasn't her business who was at the door—probably the milkman, or perhaps a neighbor calling.

"Colin," she exclaimed when her father opened the door and she caught a glimpse of the thatch-haired navy man standing in the doorway, his back ramrod straight, his broad shoulders even, the very picture of military stature.

Her heart immediately began pounding riotously at the sight of him, especially as much of a shock as it was to see him here.

The only thing to ruin the keen navy image he was obviously trying for, was the slow, lazy smile that appeared on his face. The very same grin that had driven Holly crazy a million times. The smile that said he had everything under control, and maybe, just maybe, he was keeping a secret or two from the world.

As the shock of seeing Colin at her parents' lodge subsided, suspicion bubbled up inside her.

She whirled on her father. "What is this all about?"

she queried, halfway between annoyance and confusion. "I can't believe you summoned Colin out here, too! For what? Are you and Mom trying to embarrass me? Are you trying to play matchmaker? Not like *that's* going to work."

"Missy, I have no idea what you're talking about," her father denied gruffly. "And that's no way to greet a guest in our home."

Holly's jaw dropped and her stomach curled into a knot of astonishment. "Are you telling me you didn't invite him here?"

Her father's eyes narrowed as she took his measure and he returned the favor. After a moment, he firmly shook his head. "No, ma'am."

Her gaze slid reluctantly to Colin, who confirmed it with a shrug and a grin. "No, ma'am."

With a gesture indicating she was close to pulling her hair out, she emitted a long, exasperated groan and reached for Colin's free hand, pulling him inside with her and swinging the door closed behind them.

"Welcome to my parents' home," she said smartly, flashing her gaze to her father, who pinched his lips tightly as if annoyed, though his dark, gray-eyed gaze sparkled with amusement.

She turned to Colin, who just smiled at her. She didn't feel like playing games, and Colin wasn't giving her a clue. Her emotions had been jerked around too much today already, thank you very much.

"What are you doing here?" She eyed the worn backpack he had slung over one shoulder. Clearly he hadn't planned on staying. Long.

But how had he known where to look for her? She gave him another close scrutiny.

His throat was working, but no sound was coming out of his mouth. She decided to help him.

"You were following me?" she suggested, planting her hands on her hips.

Colin didn't know what to make of Holly's audacity. She was clearly upset at someone over something. But he sure didn't know who, or what. This wasn't the way he'd planned his entrance at all.

His gaze slipped unintentionally toward Ian McCade. The man met his gaze head-on, his expression a mixture of welcome and warning.

He wasn't surprised by those sentiments. It hadn't taken long in Holly's father's company to know Ian McCade was going to protect his precious little girl at all costs, and it was a daunting thought.

He swallowed hard. Carrying out this crazy plan to fruition wasn't going to be easy.

He stopped short, wondering for a moment whether he had, once again, dived into the water headfirst without first checking for the depth of the pool. He looked from father to daughter, and thought perhaps there was no water to swim in at all.

He quickly covered the ground he'd tread in his mind, reminding himself of the reason he was here.

Jared Matthews.

When he was searching and praying for an answer to Jared's problem, the solution had come with such ease it had amazed and astonished him.

Jared needed a family. *He* would be Jared's family.

No. *They* would be Jared's family. He and Holly. Together.

In one gigantic flash of insight that was akin, Colin thought, to being hit over the head with a metal beam, clang and all, he had realized the depth of his love for Holly. It was the kind of love a man built the foundation of a family upon.

Not that the idea of loving Holly was such a giant leap for him to make. But the idea of marrying her had popped him *clear* out of the ballpark.

And yet, in that one second he knew marrying Holly was the *right* answer. The *only* answer.

He'd never felt more joy in his life than the moment he'd settled his heart on a life with Holly. And Jared.

He immediately started making plans, starting with a trip up to Holly's parents' lodge to have a man-to-man talk with her father.

It wasn't going to be easy. But he'd known that before he came here.

He just hadn't expected *Holly* to be here. Her visiting here wasn't exactly a typical occasion, from what he knew about this family, and from what Holly had said. She wasn't comfortable here. She didn't exactly come around on a regular basis.

Which meant there was a special occasion of some kind. Or else something was wrong.

He looked from father to daughter, but neither looked grieved, or bereaved, and definitely not overly joyous—only perplexed, and maybe a little annoyed. And curious. Definitely curious.

They wanted to know why he was here. They wanted to know *now*.

And it was a *logical* question, after all.

The only problem was, he didn't have a reasonable answer. At least not one he could share with Holly and her father—yet.

He cleared his throat and prayed God wouldn't look

too harshly upon him for this one little fib. "Yes," he said at last, deciding the best course of action was to follow her lead, especially as he was completely unable to come up with a feasible alternative on such short notice. "I…followed you."

Chapter Fourteen

What else could Colin do, except follow Holly's lead and hope he didn't end up in a ditch? He couldn't tell them the real reason he was here, at least not until he'd spoken to her father alone. And he couldn't think of any other sensible reason he'd be at the lodge.

"I…wasn't able to catch you at your apartment, but I was fortunate enough to see you leaving in your Jeep. So I followed you. Uh…here," he added just for good measure.

"Why?" Her hands were still perched on her hips, and her gaze eagle sharp.

He squirmed inwardly, but was careful not to let his thoughts show on his face. What he wanted to do was to blurt everything aloud and get it over with, but he knew better than to let his mouth start flapping right now. He'd insert both his big feet for sure.

If he had any hope at all of winning Holly's heart, never mind her hand in marriage, he had to do it the right way.

Move in slowly. Plan his tactics carefully. Be romantic.

And he should definitely not embarrass her in front of the father she held in such high esteem.

Besides, Ian McCade was the first step in sealing this deal. Ian wouldn't be any happier than Holly would be if Colin asked her to marry him on the spot, without at least giving them a hint of his good intentions beforehand, and leaving a good impression on them both.

Holly audibly cleared her throat. She was still waiting for an answer.

"I'm trying to finish my term paper and I need some help," he said, grimacing at how lame of an excuse he'd concocted.

At first he didn't think Holly bought it, either, but after a moment's hesitation she shrugged and waved him along.

"Come in and sit down. I'll make tuna-salad sandwiches for everyone. I can't think about school on an empty stomach." She patted her flat stomach and brushed her palm along the curve of her hip.

Colin's eyes followed her movement and his breath caught and held. She was a beautiful woman in every respect. The man who won her regard was a blessed man, indeed.

He only prayed he would be that man.

He knew he wasn't good enough for her. Holly deserved much better, a more stable man, a man who would wear a watch, who she could count on to be on time for their wedding.

But he was in love with her, and he was enough of an optimist to believe love could conquer all. One thing he knew for certain—he'd gratefully spend his whole life trying to make her happy.

And he would wear a watch for their wedding. The thought brought a grin to his lips.

Glad the invisible hand had finally let go of his

chest and allowed him to breathe, he followed Holly into the kitchen. Though the winter morning held a Colorado chill, she was wearing a flowery spring dress that shifted and twirled around her long, sleek legs. He wondered if she'd brought a sweater along, but didn't voice his question aloud, knowing how much Holly valued her independence.

Besides, he hadn't thought to pack any extra clothing at all.

She chatted on about the weather, her Christmas plans and a whole host of other topics, one following closely on top of the other, sometimes with unusual overlaps in thought or subject that made Colin chuckle.

"Are you nervous about something?" he queried, observing that he, himself, was about ready to jump out of his shoes with restlessness.

"No," she denied a bit too quickly. Then she glanced at him and their gazes met and held. Her eyes told him the truth before her lips did. "Yes, I am."

He stroked her arm with the back of his fingers. "What's up?"

She leaned forward until their foreheads nearly touched. "It's my mom and dad," she said in a conspiratorial stage whisper. "I think something's up with them."

Colin lowered his brow. "Why do you say that?" he asked in the same tone of voice she was using.

Holly took his elbow and pulled him into a corner of the kitchen, where she resumed her normal tone of voice. "Well, for one thing, they called me here, but wouldn't tell me why. I asked, but they were vague."

"That does seem a little odd," he agreed. Her parents

appeared pretty straightforward to him; not the type to play games, especially with their only daughter.

"As you can probably well imagine, I was terrified at first, because as you can guess, I rarely receive a summons from my parents. For anything."

At least that explained why she was here. "A summons? You sound like you're talking about the Supreme Court. What did they do, send a courier with a missive?"

"Just about. I was sure someone was dying. Why else would they call when it wasn't a holiday?"

"Your dad seems fine."

"His usual gruff self, you mean. Yes, he is. And he assured me my mother is doing well, too. So well, in fact, that she's out shopping right now." She chuckled.

"So if it's not illness, then what?" Colin found his own curiosity growing on the matter.

"When I find out, you'll be the first to know. I must admit it's nice to see a familiar face up here. What's your trouble with your term paper, anyway?" she asked, clearly finished with the subject of her parents, and ready to swim on to bluer water.

Colin's mind froze for a moment, but his slick tongue quickly recovered. "I'm having trouble wrapping my project up for the class. It's such a big idea. I thought you could take a quick look at it for me and see if I'm going in the right direction."

It suddenly occurred to him that he might be asking too much of a woman who was still technically his teacher, at least until the Christmas holiday. He was always bugging her about this thing or that. Her other students weren't haunting her that way.

"Am I putting too much pressure on you?" he asked

suddenly. "I mean, you being the professor, me being the student, and all?"

She smothered a laugh with her palm. "And you're asking me now?"

He smacked his hand against his forehead. "I've been taking advantage of the professor all semester long! I'm an idiot."

She shifted so she stood behind him, wrapping her arms around his waist and laying her head against the back of his shoulders. She stood silently for a moment, just holding him.

Colin shuddered with emotion and swallowed hard. He wasn't used to feeling this depth of love, or even of labeling the feelings he was just now recognizing as *love*.

It would take some time getting used to. A lifetime, maybe.

"Do you know that you have been the only stable thing in my life this year?" she asked quietly.

He rumbled with laughter. "Me, stable? That's a scary thought."

She was about to say something in reply when her father entered the kitchen. Holly stiffened as if to move away, but she slowly relaxed her arms and locked her fingers, sealing her arms around his waist. Colin knew it was a big step for her, and he rested his hand lightly on hers for support.

Sergeant McCade narrowed his eyes upon that spot at Colin's waist, and his lips pressed and turned at the corner, one eye half-pinched closed.

Colin held his breath, feeling like a teenager on his first date, not a grown man sharing a close moment with the woman he loved. He could sense that Holly had also stopped breathing.

"Did you want a sandwich, sir?" he offered, holding up the tuna salad sandwich he'd just finished slathering with mayonnaise.

"Sounds good," said Holly's father gruffly. "I was just on my way to the den."

"I'll bring it to you there," Colin said quickly, seizing upon the opportunity he suddenly realized had been presented to him.

Sergeant McCade exited just as quickly as he'd entered, pulling his pipe from his shirt pocket without another word to either of them.

"You're sure you want to do this?" Holly asked as soon as her father was gone, her voice muffled against the denim of Colin's shirt. "I guarantee you're going to get raked over the coals on my account the moment you walk into that room."

"Why would you think that?" He turned in her embrace and put his arms around her. "Just because I happen to have tender feelings toward his daughter?"

She broke the embrace and moved to make another sandwich. "When you put it like that, it doesn't sound so awful."

He wondered why she didn't sound happy about what he'd said. He'd been tentative in his statement, probing her feelings in his own backward way.

Could it be that her emotions did not match his? That she was not in love with him?

No. There was a connection between them. He knew it in his gut.

And if an emotionally impeded student could figure

it out, surely a brilliant, stunning professor would have to be in tune with the special bond they shared.

With a forced grin, Holly handed two plates to Colin and gestured toward the den. "It's your skin. Be my guest."

He flashed his most charming grin and gave her a grand wink before heading for the den and the potentially fire-breathing dragon within.

"Sergeant McCade," Colin acknowledged as he entered. "Your sandwich, sir."

The elder man waved him to a seat, and Colin sat uneasily in the blue-patterned Victorian armchair across from the sergeant's easy chair. He sat straight-backed, holding the sandwich awkwardly on his lap.

Ian was already eating, so Colin took a big bite out of the corner of his sandwich. He chewed, but couldn't taste a thing. And the bread must have been too dry, because he was finding it hard to swallow.

He wished desperately he'd thought to bring a bottle of water with him when he'd come in. What good military man made an advance without a good supply of drinking water?

He set his plate aside. He couldn't eat, not when he was literally facing one of the monumental and significant moments he'd ever faced in his life.

Holly's father had no such qualms, and was quietly devouring his sandwich and basically ignoring Colin, which was just as well, as it gave him time to pull himself together, to pull all his military training together to work for him on this one task.

He only prayed it would sustain him.

"Sir," he said, surprised at how full and even his

voice sounded. Maybe the military had been good for something after all.

"Brockman."

"May I ask you a question?"

Holly's father gazed at him for a moment, not looking the least bit taken aback that Colin wanted to speak to him, but with a marked curiosity in his eyes.

Colin held his breath, afraid to so much as swallow or move a knuckle.

After a moment, the sergeant grunted and nodded his consent.

Colin had rehearsed the speech a hundred times in his mind, but now it came out slow and scratchy from his tight throat and dry mouth. He strained to form straight, even words, feeling ridiculously awkward.

"I—um—well, I suppose this doesn't come as a complete shock to you, but I'm in love with your daughter. I guess I have been for a while now, and I'm pretty sure that, as her father, you've probably picked up on those… uh…vibes. Since you know her so well, I mean."

Sergeant McCade didn't blink an eye.

That being the case, Colin forged on. "Sir, I would like to ask for your blessing on our marriage."

The sergeant didn't look surprised, or angry, or happy about what Colin had just said.

In fact, it was almost as if Colin hadn't said anything at all.

Slowly, with agonizing patience, Sergeant McCade reached for the pipe sitting on the table beside him. He licked his bottom lip, stoked the pipe carefully and scratched the tip of a wooden match against the bottom of his slipper in order to light the pipe.

He took a puff, then two, closing his eyes to savor

the aroma. Finally, after what seemed to Colin like a lifetime, he opened his eyes, tipped his pipe out of the corner of his mouth and cradled it lightly between his thumb and forefinger.

"What does Holly say about all this?"

Colin was so surprised by the question he hardly knew what to say. He'd given this so much thought. He'd thought his battle plan to be foolproof.

He would impress the sergeant by approaching him first, in the traditional, old-fashioned way of doing things.

And then he would have the added ammunition of her father's blessing to take back with him when he went to ask Holly to be his wife.

In the back of his mind, he guessed he had half expected the rugged, commanding sergeant to want to make a decision for Holly on her behalf without her consultation whatsoever.

Not that Colin would have accepted any such thing, of course, but the thought had been there, that it might happen that way.

Of all the scenarios he'd run in his mind, though, this had definitely *not* been one of them. "Well, sir, to be honest, I haven't asked her yet."

He pinched one side of his mouth together over his pipe and said gruffly, "Don't you think that'd be a good idea?"

Chapter Fifteen

Holly stepped into her parents' stable and inhaled deeply. The combined smell of horse and hay soothed her. It was one of her favorite smells in the whole world.

She'd inherited her mother's love for horses, and she loved to ride, but didn't get much opportunity to be around horses in the city, or even a small university town such as Greeley.

It was only when she was here, at her parents' lodge, that she could shed reality and indulge her childhood fantasies of roping and racing.

This morning, she'd come down to the stable to see her mother's newest asset, a beautiful, shiny black Morgan-cross mare named Belle; but in truth, she'd also escaped the confines of the house to find some-place quiet to think about what her father and mother had revealed to her the previous evening.

Her parents were set on giving her an early inheritance.

They'd told her over dinner. With Colin in the room, like he was family or something.

For some crazy reason, her father had gotten it into

his head that he wanted to be around to see her enjoy what money they'd saved up over the years.

It wasn't a fortune, they assured her, but it was enough for her to be able to dream a little bit, and it would be a much needed supplement to her measly salary as a student teacher.

Her father had made a big production of the announcement, telling her over the main course so that she choked on her broccoli and nearly made a scene, dropping her fork with a loud clank onto her plate and standing so suddenly, her chair tipped backward with an additional clatter.

She'd glared at her father, but he'd just pinched the side of his lip and looked satisfied with the way he'd goaded her into a reaction.

Of course, Colin had been there to see the whole debacle. Why her parents had decided Colin ought to be present for such a grand announcement just because he was *there* was beyond her.

And it had been his reaction Holly had dreaded most of all.

He'd merely wiped his mouth with his cloth napkin—Holly thought he did that to hide his amusement, which wasn't very effective, since mirth was shining like a beacon from his eyes—and leaned his elbow on the table, as if he were leaning forward in order to hear better.

Apparently, no one had ever thought to teach Colin it was polite to keep his elbows *off* the table. And though, in her present mood, she'd been inclined to tell him, she was too busy rectifying her own breach in manners.

She didn't know what Colin thought of what her parents had just revealed.

She didn't know what to think.

On one hand, she wanted her parents to spend their money on *themselves* in their retirement. She didn't want any of their hard-earned savings.

Yet her mother had stressed, in her sweet, understated way, what a true desire it would be to give their money to their daughter while they were still living. They wanted to see what a difference they could make in her life.

Being reminded of her mother brought her thoughts back to the present, and Holly moved from stall to stall, looking for the special Morgan mare. As soon as she saw it, she realized what a special find the black was, and Holly immediately fell in love with her.

Picking up a brush and curry comb, she entered Belle's stall. She kept up a steady stream of soft, nonsense talk, and the friendly horse nickered softly in return.

"You're a real beauty," she told Belle. "What beautiful little foals you'll have someday."

Belle shied away from the brush, and Holly laughed. "Oh, don't worry. We don't have any stallions in this stable."

Brushing lightly at her glossy black mane, Holly ran a hand down Belle's sleek neck to calm her, and felt the horse's powerful muscles quiver beneath her touch. "Men can be a handful, can't they, girl?"

Holly sighed inwardly. *Colin* certainly could be labeled a handful.

She still didn't know why he was really here, but she'd bet a year's salary that he wasn't here to work on his term paper. She wouldn't even be surprised if his backpack didn't even contain his books and notes. If she were to hazard a guess, she thought the pack might be toting a spare change of clothes.

Besides, he hadn't even mentioned the need to work on his paper the day before, and he'd had plenty of time to broach the subject with her if that was what was really on his mind.

Which meant he was at her parents' lodge for another reason. And that she could not guess.

Holly had just slipped under Belle's neck to brush her other side when she stopped suddenly to the sound of the stable door opening. The door had squeaked for years, but her father, who did not share his wife's love of horses, had never bothered to oil the hinges.

At first Holly thought to call out to whomever had interrupted her solitude in the stable, but something inside her compelled her to remain silent at the sound of the soft but steady footsteps in the hay.

The unidentified person moved from stall to stall, but did not pause to interact with the horses as Holly would have expected her mother to do. And there was no coarse grumbling that would signify her father's role in the life of the stable—the keeper of the chores.

As the footsteps got nearer, she recognized Colin's low baritone, nickering to the horses and laughing when they responded in kind. He walked to the stall next to Belle's and stopped for a moment.

Holly held her breath.

"Good boy," Holly heard him tell an old paint mare as he reached out to touch her muzzle.

"He's a she," Holly corrected softly, extending her head and arms over the top of the stall door and making Colin take a quick step back, surprise written all over his handsome face.

She laughed with him, both at his rookie mistake, and at the way she'd caught him off guard. "Good *girl* would definitely be a more appropriate moniker. Her name is *Contessa*."

The paint pushed against Colin's hand, searching in vain for a carrot or a sugar cube, and he patted her neck awkwardly. Evidently they didn't teach equine aptitude in the navy.

"Why don't you try this?" suggested Holly, coming out of Belle's stall and handing Colin a carrot. When he hesitated, she put her hand under his, slowly stroked his own hand open flat, showing him by example the way to feed the mare.

It was an intimate posture, and Holly was intensely aware of the way her arm brushed against his, and the way the rough skin of his knuckles felt under her palm. It was suddenly as if the world had opened up and her senses cascaded to life.

The smell of the freshly thrown hay was transformed into a brisk, delightful aroma. The sound of the horses was like a symphony.

And the sight of the tall, well-built man standing close beside her was like an artist's canvas. His thatch of blond hair blew lightly in the breeze that crept through the cracks in the wood. His face, flushed rosy from the cold, contained a heart-stopping grin. In typical Colin fashion, he hadn't bothered to shave that morning, but to Holly, his adorable, tousled mane and scruff only added to the colossal masculinity he exuded.

She struggled to pull in a breath, and nearly suffocated on the bite of the wintry air. "Keep your hand out straight and she won't mistake your fingers for that carrot," she said with effort.

He looked apprehensive for a moment, but he soon followed her directions, grinning when the old, biddable mare nibbled gently at the carrot, her lips working noisily against the flat of his palm.

"It tickles," he said with a boyish chuckle.

"She's a great little mare," Holly said, stroking the paint's floppy and multicolored forelock. "Contessa was my first horse. She's a smooth ride and a gentle spirit. I think she'll always be my favorite."

Colin was silent, as if absorbing her words. She handed him another carrot and he tentatively moved on to the next stall and Belle, who nickered gladly for the attention.

Holly didn't know what to say, and felt a little like her babbling was breaking up the moment, so she just stood back to enjoy the sight of the charming man become acquainted with her horses.

"So…what brings you out to the stable?" Colin queried lightly, asking the question as if *he* belonged here and *she* was the trespasser.

She gave him a long look before she answered. His gaze gave nothing away. He showed a mild curiosity, nothing more.

"My mother just got a new mare. I came out to see her. Actually, you're feeding her now. This is Belle. She's a Morgan cross."

"I see," said Colin, as if he did. His voice was a good deal lower than usual, and just the tiniest bit gravelly.

"What are *you* doing in the stable?" she blurted, unable to wait one more minute to find out what she'd been wondering all along. "And don't tell me you came out to see the horses, because I won't believe you."

He grinned. "Of course not, Holly. I came out here to see *you*."

Her heart leapt and started dancing pirouettes in her chest when his warm gaze met hers. Something about the way he was looking at her was *different*. Her heart knew it, as did her lungs, which had suddenly refused to work.

"I'm sorry. Did you need something?" she asked through a clogged throat.

He chuckled. "You could say that."

She leaned her back against the stall door and looked him in the eye. This probably had something to do with his school project, once again.

Bracing herself, she calmed her heart down to below roaring and prepared herself to don the role of teacher, something that was getting more difficult to do where Colin was concerned. "I'm all yours."

Again, he chuckled. "I hope so." This time he sounded nervous.

Colin, nervous?

She *must* be imagining things. Colin was many things, but nervous wasn't one of them. She'd never seen him this wound up before.

He placed his hand on the door above her shoulder and leaned into her, making it more and more difficult for her lungs to discover air to breathe. She inhaled the sweet pungency of soap and man that was the distinctive scent of Colin and thought she might be a little short on oxygen. She was definitely feeling light-headed.

"Were you raised around horses?" he asked, but given the vivid gleam in his eyes, she highly doubted that was the question he wanted to ask.

And she was having trouble forming an answer. The

words were in her mind, but there seemed to be an electric short in the link between her brain and her tongue.

"No," she croaked out at last. "Not as a child, anyway. Horses have always been my mother's dream, but because of the military lifestyle, we moved around too much to own horses."

He leaned closer. "I'm glad she finally had the opportunity to fulfill her dreams. When *did* she get her first horse?"

Again, Holly had the distinct feeling he was postponing the moment when he'd blurt out what he really wanted to say.

"When she was forty-seven years old, although if you tell her I even remotely alluded to her age, she won't talk to me for a week."

"My lips are sealed," he promised in a whisper, marking a silent X across his mouth with the tip of his finger.

Holly smiled gently, both at Colin and at the memory of her mother. "She often tells me her life started when she got her first horse. Except for having me, of course. Though she always adds that part as an afterthought," she said with an edgy chuckle.

She wished she was able to retreat from the feel of his breath on her cheek, and his arms so close about her but not quite touching her. But the stable door didn't give way under the force of her prayer, however fervently made. And it held strong behind her back.

"What are you really doing out here, Colin?" she asked abruptly, deciding to force his hand while she grappled for the stable door handle.

"I want to marry you."

His words, though softly uttered, hit her with the force of a navy torpedo.

What could he be saying to her? She hadn't the slightest idea why he wanted to see her when she'd asked him about his motive in visiting the stable, but a marriage proposal had been about as far from her mind as the earth from the moon.

Marriage. They hadn't even talked around the word, much less seriously worked through the many aspects of their relationship. She wasn't even sure they *had* a relationship.

She pulled in a breath and held it, waiting for time and reality to smooth out her world. She looked back at Colin, focused on his smiling, expectant face, and the plain leveled.

It was *Colin* asking that ridiculous and completely unexpected question. Slowly her heart resumed beating again.

With effort, she laughed and nodded in understanding. It was his idea of a joke, but he'd caught her off guard. "Right. Now tell me what you really want."

To her surprise, *he* looked surprised. Genuinely astonished.

"No, Holly. I really mean what I'm saying. I want to marry you."

"Colin," she warned, trying to keep her voice from shaking.

He was being mean, playing a spiteful joke, whether he realized it or not. It wasn't like him to be insensitive, especially on purpose.

"Holly, how can I convince you I'm in earnest here?" he asked, his voice low and fervent. Determination glimmered from his eyes. "No, wait. I know what will do the trick."

He rummaged through his fleece-lined jean jacket

pocket with his free hand. "Will this convince you I mean what I say?"

Holly swept in a breath. Colin flipped open the top of a small, black velvet box to reveal an engagement ring. A lovely solitaire sparkled brightly even in the dim light of the stable.

"I...don't understand," she whispered hoarsely, clenching her hands together in front of her.

His smile wavered for a moment, but soon his confident grin reemerged. He lifted the diamond toward her, as if somehow she hadn't seen it.

She wasn't blind. Only struck dumb by the irony of the eternal bachelor asking *her* to be his wife.

"It would be great if we could be married as soon as possible," he said, grasping her left hand in his right and rubbing her ring finger with his thumb.

Holly's heart was roaring in her head. All her feelings for Colin rose up to greet her, and she was astonished at the intensity of the love she felt.

How had she not realized this before?

She was in love with Colin Brockman.

Deciding the answer to his question—even if he hadn't quite *asked* the actual question—was one of the easiest things she'd done in all of her life.

Of course she'd marry him.

Or at least she thought she would. Until the next words out of his mouth changed *everything*.

"I've got to adopt Jared Matthews soon, or he'll be sent off to foster care again and I'll lose my window of opportunity."

"What?"

"It will be much easier to convince a judge I'm worthy as a married man. And of course I was happy to hear about your early inheritance," he continued as if she had not frozen in his arms, her jaw dropped in astonishment. "The extra money is going to be like a windfall to mention at the hearing."

The affirmation poised on her lips died a sudden, painful death. The reality of the truth washed through her in wave after nauseating wave.

Colin didn't *love* her.

He didn't really want to be married in the first place. He was doing this for the sake of a *kid*.

She squeezed her eyes closed, as the stain of her own sinfulness crept up to mock her, sneaking into her thoughts again though she thought she'd put the past long behind her.

She reminded herself quickly that God had washed her white as snow. She'd started afresh.

Besides, the rejection she was feeling now had nothing to do with what she'd done in the past, because Colin didn't even know the way she'd lived as a teenager.

But knowing that didn't stop her from embracing the feeling she wasn't good enough for a man like Colin. She couldn't help it. Years of poor self-esteem had set her up for this moment.

The pain of rejection raged through her despite all her inward protests. It seemed ridiculous to feel unwanted when she was being proposed to, but no matter how she tried to look at it, she couldn't break free of the sting of her conclusions.

It was obvious he was essentially settling on second best, asking her to marry him because she was his friend, and the most obvious choice given his present set of circumstances.

He'd do anything he had to do to take care of Jared Matthews, up to and including marrying a decent, convenient woman.

And she was that convenient woman. Money and everything.

She didn't know how she could bear the heart-wrenching pain in her chest; nor did she quite know how she would retain her dignity in the moment. She only knew she must, and she would—somehow.

Perhaps the answer lay with the word *decent*. Colin needed a virtuous and godly woman to raise his adopted son. He was looking to her because he didn't know better.

Well, he was going to know better now. He was going to know the truth. And then he would do what any good, upstanding man looking for a mother for his child would do—get out of Dodge.

"Colin, there is a lot you don't know about me," Holly began, raising her chin and meeting his gaze head-on.

"Of course, sweetheart. I know I'm rushing things, but you know I've got a good reason. And we'll have plenty of time to learn all the ins and outs once we're married, don't you think?"

Holly wanted to groan. He was so naive, it was almost scary. She wouldn't believe he was for real, if she hadn't been around him long enough to know he was the genuine article.

"I think you need to know about me now."

Colin leaned forward, so his breath was brushing her cheek. "Okay. So tell me."

She couldn't think when he acted that way. She shoved him backward with both palms. "You can't marry me, Colin. After what I'm about to tell you, you won't even want to marry me."

"There's nothing you can tell me that will make me change my mind," he vowed.

She laughed without mirth. "Believe me, I've heard that before. No man wants what I have to offer. At least no Christian man."

"And what's that, Holly? What's so bad that I'm going to run screaming from the stable?" He sounded as if he was getting angry now. That was just as well, Holly thought. Better anger than hate or, worse, revulsion.

"Let's just say I wasn't a saint in high school," she said, not knowing how to say what needed to be said, and desperate to have it out and over with. "I didn't become a Christian until college. I drank beer. I smoked cigarettes. I partied with a wild crowd."

"And?"

He was going to make her say it.

She looked away. "I'm not a virgin, Colin. Not even close."

With a muffled sob, she ducked under his arm and ran away, as fast and as far as her legs would carry her. Away from Colin, and any future they might have had.

Chapter Sixteen

Colin didn't know what kind of reaction he ought to expect from Holly after his sudden marriage proposal, but dropping what she must have thought was a bomb on him and then running frantically from the quiet stable wasn't even on the list.

Neither was having her Marine Corps drill sergeant father come raging down on him like a dog on a T-bone steak.

Teeth bared and everything.

That man definitely did *not* like to see his only daughter upset. It was a wonder Colin escaped with his skin, never mind his sanity.

Well, that wasn't quite true. While his skin was still intact, his sanity was questionable.

He hadn't been the same since he'd returned to the unaltered silence of his apartment, the sparkling new diamond ring meant for Holly buried deep in the pocket of his fleece-lined jean jacket.

He'd come home weighing a great deal less than when he'd left. There was an immense, gaping empty space where his heart had once resided.

He slumped onto the couch, groaning half in welcome, half in misery. Rascally Scamp pattered onto his lap and pawed at his stubbly chin for attention.

His kitten was right. Colin knew he looked like a wreck, his green plaid shirt half-untucked from his jeans, and his hair looking as if he'd been raking his fingers through it all day.

He *had* been messing with his hair. Not so much because it was troublesome so much as the fact that he was busting out of his bones, going out of his mind over the way things had worked out. He felt every bit as miserable as he looked.

"Whaddaya think, Scamp, ol' fellow? Did I blow it big time, or what?"

Scamp only purred in response, arranging the untucked side of Colin's shirt into a nice little kitty bed with his paw, and comfortably settling himself upon it with a contented *mew*.

"I wish I was a cat," Colin said grumpily.

Scamp licked his paw clean and swiped it over his fluffy black-and-white ear, the self-proclaimed king of the castle. Colin, on the other hand, felt like a pawn in a game a good deal larger than he was.

Where had he gone wrong?

With what he hoped was a critical eye, he reviewed the series of events that had led up to Holly's stark rejection of his proposal.

He frowned, finding it hard to concentrate. He'd been feeling unusually emotional lately. Ever since he'd met Holly, in fact.

But definitely more so this weekend. He wasn't sure he could trust himself to be rational.

Especially now.

Proposing to Holly had seemed like such a good idea at the time. He, who'd sworn off children as if he were allergic to them, had become father material the moment he'd heard of Jared's dilemma and realized he could provide a stable home where others could or would not.

The next logical progression in his chain of thought was to consider getting married, to improve his chances to adopt the boy and to provide Jared with a stable home with a father *and* a mother.

So he was a little slow on the take. It was only then that he'd realized he *wanted* to get married—to Holly— and not because of Jared, though adopting the little boy made the deal even sweeter in his mind.

Holly McCade was the right woman for him, the woman he wanted to spend the rest of his life with. It had only taken a catastrophe to goad his brain into figuring out what his heart already knew.

Holly as his wife, and Jared as his son. Holly Brockman. Jared Brockman.

Until then he hadn't put a word to his feelings for Holly.

Love.

He wanted to hoot and holler and scream and cry, all at once. His feelings were at once so incredibly simple, and so largely complicated, that it went beyond description.

He was in love with her.

And she, he decided, thoughtfully and carefully, was in love with him. She'd been the sensitive, expressive one in their relationship, and he'd been the big dolt who hadn't known enough to grab on to a good woman when he had the chance. She'd hinted again and again of her feelings in a look, a touch. Even the special meaning she placed upon their kisses should have clued him in.

But he was hopelessly dull in the romance department, and he'd never let on how he felt about her. How could he, when he hadn't known himself?

He'd decided to fix that omission as soon as possible. His heart was in the right place. All that had been left for him to do was to buy a pretty diamond ring and ask Holly to become his wife.

Unfortunately, the actual event hadn't been nearly as uncomplicated as his daydream.

At first, it appeared she hadn't understood the question. Which was highly preferable to what happened when she *did* figure out what he was saying.

She'd been so distressed. Her cheeks had turned an alarming shade of pink, her breath had come in tight gasps and her voice was shrill. She hadn't returned the sentiment he had offered.

Instead, she'd thrown her past in his face. Reminded him of how difficult and different her life had been like before she had found a Savior.

It broke his heart to think of what she must have been through. She'd suffered much. But why bring it up now? Did she think he hadn't been through enough in his own miserable life to be able to commiserate?

There must have been something—something he'd said or done to make her run away from him the way she did. Somehow, he had the gut feeling he was responsible for how their relationship now lay in ruins.

The question was, how was he going to straighten out this big mess?

He didn't have time to ponder the answer to that question because the telephone rang.

Holly!

He rummaged frantically through the basket of unfolded clean clothes he'd left on the floor by the fireplace, sure the ring was coming from somewhere in that vicinity.

It took him three rings to find the receiver and juggle it to his ear, but he answered with a full-toothed grin.

"Holly?"

"Mr. Brockman, this is Michelle Walker at Marston House."

Colin's hopes fell into his gut like a lead cannonball. He recovered slowly. "Hi, Michelle. How's Jared?"

"Holding his own," Michelle answered promptly. "Greatly due to your assistance."

"I can't take credit for that," Colin denied with a grimace. "God's the one taking care of that terrific little boy."

"Yes, well, let us hope so. Jared is the reason I'm calling."

Colin's gut clenched, and he grit his teeth. "Go ahead."

"I've spoken to social services on your behalf. They are willing to hold a hearing on your proposition, first for Jared's placement, and then for his permanent adoption into your household."

Colin squeezed his eyes closed, as close as he'd ever been to shedding tears. This would have been good news, if only…

"I hear a *but* coming," he said wryly, his throat closed and his voice scratchy with emotion.

Michelle gave a nervous chuckle. "Smart man. Here's the thing. Before you can get that hearing, you have to meet with a team of psychologists appointed by the state. It's a five-member panel of men and women from this area who'll be, basically, judging your suitability as a father for Jared."

His suitability as a father.

Colin felt as if he'd had his legs cut out from under him. Five minutes ago, he'd thought himself about as low as he could possibly go.

Now he knew it could be worse.

He had no illusions about his chances to have Jared as his son. As a single man, it would take a miracle for a judge to even consider giving him custody of the young, troubled boy.

And that was when he had only two hearings to contend with.

But now he was looking at standing a minimum of three times up before a judge or panel, and he found he didn't quite believe in miracles anymore.

He silently reached for heavenly support, but his faith was wavering under the strain, and God's comfort seemed far away.

"Don't worry too much about it, Colin," Michelle added when he didn't answer her right away. "These are all going to be friends and colleagues of Holly. I'm sure you'll do fine."

Fine? He clenched his fists and set his jaw against the anger and torrid feelings of helplessness raging through him.

Hadn't he been questioning himself these past couple of weeks? He'd run headlong into the idea of adopting Jared because he knew in his gut in was the right thing for him to do. And because he wanted to do it.

But when the pragmatic side of him sat down and looked at it, there was a great deal more to the story than that. As long as he'd held out hope that Holly would be in the picture, at least he had her loving kindness to fall back on.

Now he only had himself. And he wasn't sure if he could do it. There were moments when he wasn't sure he wanted to do it, wasn't sure what adopting the boy would mean for his career, and now—without Holly— for the rest of his life. Alone.

Jared had special needs. Could he handle it? Could he father the boy and still attend college and seminary full-time? What about the navy after that? What about the moving around?

Could he offer Jared the stability he needed, without Holly there to help?

Colin squared his jaw and his shoulders. Of course he could. He would make it work, just as he'd worked out all the other challenges he'd faced in his life. He would do what was right, and deal with the consequences as they occurred.

Hadn't Jesus Himself said to take it one day at a time?

Slowly, his mental, physical and spiritual strength returned, and with it, his resolve to do what was in his heart. He had to try, for Jared's sake. But could it possibly get any worse?

He cringed. Somehow, he thought if it were possible, it would probably get worse. He'd never been a pessimist. But he'd never felt more alone in the world than he did at that moment.

It had been two weeks, and Holly still hadn't recovered enough to resume her normal activities, including teaching her classes at the university. She'd told Sarah she was sick—and she was.

Sick at heart.

Her parents had been surprisingly gracious, allowing her to stay at the lodge and mope around as long as she wanted. Her mother brought her dinner in her room when she didn't show up for a meal; and to her surprise, her gruff old father didn't say a single word about Colin's misspoken and untimely proposal, not even to say *I told you so*, though she was certain the sergeant knew all about what had happened.

That no one spoke of the matter hadn't kept her from thinking about it, of course. In fact, Colin was about all she thought about, locked in her room with the curtains drawn and the television humming. Every look, every smile, every shared kiss replayed in her mind, a brand of self-torture she hadn't realized she was capable of.

When she returned home to her apartment, it was with a new mind. She let herself grieve for the broken relationship, and though she hadn't been able to sweep Colin completely from her mind, she knew it was time to move on with her life.

And the beginning of any new life, she knew, was a clean house. She started by opening the blue gingham curtains wide to reveal the sunlight. She swept and mopped and vacuumed until every room in her studio apartment was spotless and sparkling.

She prayed, soul searched and found something she didn't realize she had.

Self-respect. And strength. For the first time she had to confront her past within her present reality, and though she thought it might be counted a loss, she decided to count it a win.

She was still standing.

She was ready to make a go of it. She was anxious to get back to teaching. And she was ready to start her career in social services, as well. If she'd learned one lesson from all this, it was that there was very little black and white in the world.

She wanted to fight on the side of the good, make whatever little dent in the world she could make.

And still there was Colin.

Because she wanted to understand, to move on, she returned to the iniquitous moment in her mind, the replay painful but necessary. She knew the words by heart, remembered every movement, every expression.

He'd never even really asked her to marry him, technically, and she wondered if he even knew. And yet, for all that, it *was* a marriage proposal, one with strings attached.

How could Colin, her sweet, sensitive Colin, have treated her with such arrogance, such mockery? After all the time and experiences they'd shared together, she'd thought Colin was her friend—in truth, her best friend, the best friend she'd ever had.

And more, she knew she loved him, though she'd never told a living soul of her feelings. She hadn't been certain of her own heart herself until Colin had mentioned marriage.

Had it only been her imagination, thinking he might reciprocate those feelings?

One would think it to have been a possibility, considering he'd proposed to her. His part of the bargain would have been to have and to hold, as well.

But maybe he wasn't taking into account his own feelings. He'd certainly acted as if her acceptance of his marriage proposal was a given, a done deal before it even started, with no regard to *her* feelings whatsoever.

As if there were no question that she would immediately fall into his arms, or at least agree to wear his ring. As if the courtesy of asking didn't matter. As if her strength and dignity could withstand his callous behavior.

How little he really knew her.

Did he *really* think she would enter into a loveless marriage with him, even for the sake of a sweet little boy like Jared Matthews?

Did he really think love didn't matter?

What kind of a wife could she be to Colin without love? What kind of mother would she be to poor Jared Matthews?

The question echoed through her head, stunning her heart back to life. What kind of mother, indeed?

Tossing the mop aside, she cranked up the stereo with some classic rock music, took a long-armed lamb's wool duster and began dusting the ceiling fans and the tops of the doorways.

Her thoughts turned to the little autistic boy who'd won Colin's affection, as well as hers, over the last few months, and she felt a flash of guilt.

What would happen to the little boy if she and Colin weren't there for him?

She didn't know when Jared had stopped being just one of many kids, and had become a personal issue, but that's how she thought of him now. As her own personal problem. The way Colin obviously thought of Jared, too.

When she'd run away from Colin that day in the barn, she'd been thinking of herself—first, and only.

She'd been feeling so sorry for herself she hadn't given a thought to the plight of that little boy.

Perhaps it was to Colin's credit that he was so set on making this small, but critical, difference in the world. Perhaps she was looking at this whole set of circumstances through the wrong set of lenses. Maybe Colin had never meant to hurt her at all.

He *had* hurt her with his assumptions, but she now acknowledged that it was possible he'd had other things on his mind that day. Noble things.

Like Jared.

Of course, when it came to marriage and a lifetime together, *she* wanted to be the first one on his mind and in his heart, after God. But a precious little boy in distress wasn't a bad runner-up.

It was saying something that Colin was willing to give up his freedom in order to save Jared. She knew how much he valued liberty. Freedom to go and do as he liked was paramount to the man. Hadn't he rebelled against anything remotely stifling and autocratic—even a wristwatch?

He'd always shied away from the idea of marriage, never mind children. He was afraid he was going to turn out like his father.

And suddenly he wanted to take on both a wife and a son?

Michelle Walker had let her know that Colin was going up before a jury of her peers, in order to determine whether a preliminary custody hearing was in order. And while she knew Colin would pass the tests of charm and integrity with flying colors, without her help, he could not produce a wife.

He could not provide the secure, white-picket-fence

kind of household Holly knew the board would be look-ing for. He couldn't show the stability he'd never known and was desperately grasping for.

The truth was there before her, and she knew it. Colin no doubt knew it, too. And it was no doubt break-ing his heart.

No single man, no matter how persuasive and sin-cere, would hazard a chance of adopting a special-needs child like Jared Matthews. Her heart fell for the future of the little boy. And, to her surprise, her heart fell for Colin's future, too.

As suddenly as those emotions overwhelmed her, she knew there was another way.

She could help. She wanted to make a difference in the world.

She could. She could make *all* the difference in the life of one little boy, and Lord willing, in the life of the man she loved.

Even if he didn't return those sentiments.

It was a crazy idea. Yet once the thought had crossed her mind, she couldn't get rid of it. It nagged at her, buzzing around her mind like a gnat.

What if she agreed to marry Colin?

Was it possible God could work through the situation on Jared's behalf? Was it possible Colin might come to love her over time?

In taking care of Jared, she could use all the skills she'd spent a lifetime building. She'd always wanted to do something really special, really meaningful with her life's work. Working with Jared would fit right in with her career in social work.

And old-fashioned as it was, it appealed to her to make a home for Colin and Jared. She thought she might find great joy and fulfillment taking care of her husband and children, at least if her childhood daydreams were anything to go by.

She could build a place where love and laughter spread as much warmth as a fire in the hearth. She could make a place that Colin would look forward to coming home to, and that would give Jared the sense of safety and routine he needed to thrive. And they already had a kitten.

The dream broke through like a waterfall.

Did love conquer all?

Her past rose up to greet her, taunting her, reminding her just how far from *love* she had once drifted. Ironic, how a teenage girl gave up her virtue and her morals looking to be loved.

Really loved.

It wasn't until she'd found God's love that human love, especially between men and women, began to make any sense. Clothed in the mantle of God's love, she was finally able to recognize her own capacity to give love, and hopefully, eventually, to receive love.

A Scripture she'd learned in childhood rose up to greet her like the morning sun. She remembered it word for word, the verse chiming out in her old Sunday school teacher's bell-tone voice, clearly enunciated and ringing with clarity.

Closing her eyes, she smiled at God's wisdom.

There is faith, hope and love. But the greatest of these is love.

It could work. It could really work!

Chapter Seventeen

Colin was sweating. He was *really* sweating, not just politely perspiring. And he knew the droplets forming against his temple and dripping onto his eyebrows weren't helping him look his very best before the five-member psychological panel.

Sweating, whether from stress, or maybe from downright fear, was not the impression he wanted to leave with the state board that held his life—and little Jared's—in his hands.

Trying not to make a big show of it, he pulled a carefully ironed handkerchief from the back pocket of his pants and swiped it surreptitiously across his damp brow and across his freshly shaved upper lip.

He quickly shoved the cloth back into his pocket when the dour-faced, gray-haired woman sitting at the end of the five-person panel—a woman Colin stopped just short of classifying as an old broad, out of kindness, not of truth—caught his attention and sent bolts of alarm through him.

Staring at him coldly, she tapped her pencil against the table in an erratic beat that hammered in a merci-

less, burning rhythm in Colin's brain that made him
want to grab his head and run.

This from a man who didn't *get* headaches. But this
was a special occasion, and the throbbing in his head
matched the painful throbbing in his heart.

Ms. Dour Face stared at him without saying a word.
He met her gaze straight on, letting her know in his own
quiet way that he had nothing to hide.

She, on the other hand, was giving nothing away. If
only someone on the panel would smile at him, give him
some hope or encouragement that they were really considering his request, and not just paying lip service to it.

That he wasn't here on a lost cause.

His worst fear was that they'd made their judgment
before he'd even had a chance to speak his case. They'd
asked a few preliminary questions, but hadn't let him
launch into the soliloquy he'd prepared on Jared's behalf, the one where he listed all the reasons he would
make a good father.

With what he had going against him, it wasn't beyond
the possibility that they'd sealed his fate without listening to a word he might have to say on his own behalf,
or on behalf of little Jared.

He reminded himself that these were Holly's friends
and colleagues, but somehow, that only made him feel
more alone. What he wouldn't give for Holly by his side
right now. He, the king of independence, finally admitting it would be nice to have a woman's hand to hold.

No one had ever accused him of being good on his
timing.

The board stirred, looking at their watches and then
at each other, whispering guardedly behind file folders held up to block their faces from his view. Colin

swallowed hard and resisted the urge to once again swipe at his beaded forehead.

"Mr. Brockman, can you tell the board how you originally came into contact with Jared Matthews?" A pretty young blonde on the panel asked that question.

Happy to have the opportunity to speak, Colin launched into the story of meeting Jared as part of the school project. The board clearly recognized and acknowledged Holly's name and role in this. Colin hoped she wouldn't mind that he'd mentioned her part.

At the board's insistence, he continued with how he'd returned to Marston House and befriended the boy, and then was there for him during various crises the boy had experienced.

"We have testimonials from Marston House on your behalf," the man in charge assured him.

Colin cleared his throat. "You do?"

"Yes, sir. It seems you have worked some miracles with Jared."

He grinned. "Yes, sir. Well, God's in the miracle-working business, but I'm always glad to help."

"Tell us truly," said the dour-faced woman, "why you would want to adopt a boy with autism."

He looked her straight in the face. He looked them all straight in the face. "Because I love him."

It was so quiet in the room, there wasn't a single paper rattling. "That's a good answer," said the pretty blond woman.

The board stopped and conferred with one another behind their files.

They were close to a decision.

Colin's heart was in his throat. When the leader of the board, Trey Adams, stood and nodded to him, he stood, as well—shoulders squared, feet planted and his head held high.

"Mr. Brockman," Trey began, then cleared his throat and looked for support to the four ladies that completed his panel.

Colin didn't like that pause or the way Trey Adams pursed his lips.

"Let me start out by saying I've never met a man with your personal concern for a child not his own, particularly a young man with special needs.

"In my experience, most men don't take an active interest in social work, and certainly not to the point to which you've extended yourself by being here today. We are all very impressed, and you are to be highly commended."

Colin pinched his lips into a semblance of a grin and nodded his head. He could feel a *but* coming, and he knew before the words were spoken that it was going to be one big *nevertheless*.

"You must know that you more than qualify in most of the areas we were looking at today," Trey went on, a little less tentative than a moment before. He steepled his fingers and stroked the bottom of his thick black goatee. "We are concerned, however, that you lack one crucial quality, a characteristic that makes us more than a little hesitant to recommend you."

Colin stood rigidly, military stiff, and braced himself for the unwelcome news.

Trey paused a moment, cleared his throat and continued. "While your integrity and love for Jared are evident and highly commendable, and while you've shown yourself to be a good physical provider with a fine future ahead of you, it concerns us nevertheless that you are an unmarried man."

There it was, out on the table.

Colin fingered the collar of his dress whites. He'd wanted to create a presence with his uniform, but instead it felt confining, wrapping around him like a straitjacket and strangling him like a noose.

Finally, the matter had been voiced. It was out in the open for everyone to see. Now, if they'd only let him openly address the issue, he might be able to persuade them what a good parent he would be.

He had barely lifted his head to begin his first argument when he was stopped in his tracks by a voice from the back of the room, a rich, warm voice he knew as well as his own.

"Oh, but, Trey, you're mistaken," Holly announced, pausing to catch her breath as she entered the room. She'd obviously been running. Her face was prettily flushed and she was obviously struggling to pull in air, one hand propped on her hip, and the other bracing her knee, as if she'd run a marathon.

"What's this about, Holly?" Trey asked, sounding as baffled as Colin felt. "I think I speak for the rest of us here when I say I'm a little confused."

Holly pulled herself upright and marched to Colin's side, her sleek black attaché bouncing on her hip and her high-heeled shoes clicking with every step. She slid an arm through his as if it was the most natural thing in the world, and smiled up at him with a brand of encouragement that left Colin's heart racing and his head reeling.

She'd never looked better.

She turned to the panel with a confident, poised smile. "Trey. Panel members." She nodded to each one, addressing them as if she were the lawyer pleading his case. And indeed, that was what she seemed to be, especially when she spoke her next words.

"Colin and I have decided to step up our wedding plans the tiniest bit so we can take care of little Jared *together* at the earliest opportunity."

The word *together* reverberated through the room, echoing off the walls, bouncing from the window wells and ringing through Colin's ears.

Marriage? What marriage was she talking about? Last information he had, they weren't even on speaking terms, much less conjugal ones.

He slid her a look he hoped she'd read accurately. He wanted to know the truth now, before things got any deeper in the mud!

She refused to look at him straight on, instead choosing to address the panel once more. "Colin and I were going to get married eventually, so moving forward the date makes sense for all of us. Jared will have a real mother and father who love him and are completely committed to him from the first day he comes home to live with us."

She paused, making eye contact with every person in the room except Colin. "Colin and I agree that we want to give Jared a permanent, stable home. As you know, I'm a licensed psychologist, and Colin is currently in seminary to take orders to be a navy chaplain. I assure you that you won't find better parents than Colin and me for that little boy.

"What's more, Jared Matthews isn't just any little boy. We've both spent extra time with him, and we've both grown to love him very much. Each of us has faith in God that Jared can and should be a member of the home we are building."

She pulled tightly but surreptitiously on Colin's arm, nudging him closer to her. He noticed that she was gritting her teeth even as she was smiling, but he put on a good face for the panel, taking a kind of backward joy in the opportunity to wrap his arm around the woman he loved and planting a healthy, smacking kiss on her lips.

"My fiancée," he announced, smugly eyeing the panel of Holly's peers. "She'll make an excellent mother for Jared, don't you think?"

Trey made a surprised sound in the back of his throat and sat down. Again, papers and files surreptitiously covered faces as the panel whispered and deliberated amongst themselves.

Colin stared down at Holly, unable to find his voice through the emotion clouding his throat, but desperately wanting to know what was going on inside that pretty head of hers.

She still wouldn't look at him. Her fingers, gripping tightly around his waist, tapped an erratic rhythm, and Colin could only guess at her nervousness at being here.

His own gut was still tight with anxiety over the situation.

But now, for the first time, there was the real likelihood—the real *hope*—he might have a go at raising Jared.

Thanks to Holly.

Trey smiled as the panel grew quiet. "We want to offer our congratulations," he said, his gaze moving from Colin to Holly, and back again.

"Thanks, Trey," Holly said smoothly, covertly yanking on the back of Colin's uniform jacket to bring him up to speed. Colin couldn't think of what to do besides smile and nod, and let Holly do the talking. She was obviously good at it.

"We think you make a fantastic couple," Trey continued. "And we think you'll make equally fantastic parents to Jared Matthews."

Colin felt a rush of triumph at the words, but not for himself. For his future wife and son! He beamed down at Holly, his angel of mercy.

He offered a silent prayer thanking God for the privilege of being able to love a woman like Holly, and the opportunity to raise Jared Matthews. He knew he'd never be able to make it up to Holly for the sacrifice she'd made today, but one thing he knew for certain— he'd spend his whole life trying.

Colin was only glad Holly had finally come to recognize that she loved him, and that she was showing her commitment to him in a tangible way with her dedication to Jared. No one had to tell him that there weren't very many women in the world willing to make those kinds of sacrifices in the name of love.

Holly, though her face was bright with their mutual success, refused to look him straight in the eye.

After a moment, she placed her knuckles against the table and grinned up at Trey and the board. "We do appreciate your confidence."

"We'll recommend your case be heard as soon as you sign the marriage license," Trey assured them both with a wide smile as he presented them with a variety of legal documents to sign. "Of course, this is only the first step, but we have confidence that you two are going to go the distance. Just let us know what your plans are, and we'll act accordingly."

He'd know, all right, Colin thought. The whole *world* would know when he made Holly his wife. They'd be able to hear him shouting a million miles away.

Nearly shaking with happiness and wondering how he'd ever lived without the emotions he was now experiencing, he took Holly by the elbow and escorted her briskly from the room. He wasn't about to give the panel any time to reconsider their assessment.

"Jared thanks you, and I thank you," he said, planting a juicy kiss on her cheek the moment they were outside.

He'd rushed her out the door, eager to take her in his arms, share the depth of his joy with her and properly kiss the woman who would soon become his wife.

But something in her eyes stopped him. Something was not quite right.

While she looked as radiant as he'd ever seen her, with her cheeks becomingly flushed and her sable hair glistening with red highlights in the winter sunshine, her eyes did not glow with the same intensity he expected of her.

With the same intensity he felt.

Her smile faltered and wavered, and then disappeared altogether. "There are some conditions," she said, her voice cool and collected. Too calm.

"I beg your pardon?" he asked coarsely, wondering how, in his happy delirium, he'd missed the part about the *conditions* of pursuing custody of Jared. Had it been part of the written paperwork they'd signed?

Was it something to do with their marriage? Did he need to purchase a home or jump through some hoop before they could really be a family?

Whatever it was, it would happen. He was determined to see to that.

"I agree to become a military wife," she began, finally looking him in the eye. She looked determined, but not particularly happy.

It wasn't what he expected at all, and definitely not what he wanted. He hadn't expected her to show up today. But when she had—well, he'd at least thought she'd be happy about it.

"I agree," she repeated. "But you, in turn, must let me take care of the children."

Colin felt like he'd been hit in the head with a sledgehammer. This wasn't about the panel, or even about adopting Jared.

He opened his mouth to ask what was really going on, but she held up a hand and cut him short.

"That's right, I said *children*. If we're going to be married, and apparently we are, it is going to be a real marriage, in every regard. A two-way street, with respect on both sides of the fence."

She paused, but he could tell she wasn't finished, so he didn't try to speak.

"I also want a real wedding. I refuse to run away and elope with you."

"Holly, I never said I wanted—"

"My parents won't settle for any less than the works. Dress. Flowers. Cake."

Visions of wedding works danced in Colin's head, and he swallowed hard. While he'd never actually considered eloping with her, he did have to admit the many details of planning an actual *wedding* had escaped him.

She swept in a breath and delivered her ultimatum with a grand gesture of her arm. "And I want children of our own someday."

Colin frowned, perplexed. Of course she wanted

children of her own. She was going to make the world's best mother. There was no argument there. "Holly, I think you—"

Again, she cut him off. "I'm perfectly content with my decision, Colin," she assured him. But somehow that declaration only made him feel more ill at ease with the situation.

"You just caught me off guard, the first time. That's all."

Colin pressed his lips together and took a good look at the woman he was preparing to marry. Perhaps that was what was wrong—that he'd somehow botched the marriage proposal, dashing out to ask her to be his wife without first preparing her for the surprise.

But somehow, he thought it was more.

He *knew* it was more.

Maybe it had something to do with what she was trying to tell him that day in the stable. All that stuff about her past, her life before she became a Christian.

Whatever it was, he had to know.

He took her by the shoulders and locked his gaze with hers, not allowing her to turn away this time. He was a man determined to get answers. "Holly, I want you to take a deep breath."

She complied with an audible sigh.

"Okay, then. Now I want you to tell me what in the world you are talking about!"

Chapter Eighteen

Colin stopped fidgeting the moment he donned his white, navy dress uniform, but his heart was still wiggling around in his chest like a two-year-old on a hard church pew. With effort, he steeled his nerves and faced the mirror, attempting to make final adjustments to his tight collar.

"How do I look, buddy?" he asked Jared Matthews, who was sitting at a table in the corner of a room, assembling a puzzle.

Jared, adorable in a black tuxedo, looked up at Colin and strained to focus his gaze. "Colin…is…good," he pronounced slowly.

Colin laughed. "Wow, pal, I hope Holly thinks so, too. I can't believe how nervous I am."

"H-o-lll-eeeee," Jared agreed happily, before returning his attention to the puzzle.

Suddenly it sounded as if someone was trying to bulldoze the door down, and Colin whirled hastily, his clammy palm slipping against the door handle as he tried to turn the knob.

Ian McCade marched in, looking smart and intimidating in his Marine Corps dress uniform, his shoes spit-polished and his seams straight and even.

The sergeant didn't mince words. He strode to Colin and faced him down—or up, as the case happened to be, since Colin was four inches taller than his future father-in-law.

Colin was almost annoyed by the habitual way his own military training took over. Without a bit of conscious thought, he squared his shoulders, stood an inch taller and tipped his chin up, staring straight forward instead of directly into Sergeant McCade's eyes, which would have been a sign of disrespect.

"Are you ready to get married?" Ian barked into his face.

"What?" What else would he be here for, all decked out in his dress whites and getting ready within moments to proceed into the McCades' great room and stand at the end of an aisle, where wedding bells were ringing?

What was the man trying to insinuate?

In moments, he would gladly join his hand and his heart with Holly forever, giving her his name and his home in addition to his life.

"You hard of hearing, boy?" McCade shouted, stepping an inch closer than before, toe-to-toe and nose-to-nose with Colin. "Are you ready to get married? It's a simple question, young man."

"And I," Colin said through gritted teeth, frantically pulling for answers as to why he was getting such a grazing at this late hour, "have a simple answer. I *am* ready to marry your daughter, sir."

McCade seemed vaguely appeased and took a step

backward. "Good answer. Now, I want you to tell me one more thing."

"What is the point of all this?" Colin demanded, slacking away from his military posture and putting some distance between himself and the crazy sergeant. If it weren't for his love for Holly, he would be thinking twice before marrying into a military family.

He jammed his fingers into his hair, and then realized what he'd done. With a frown, he picked up a brush from a nearby table and brushed his tousled hair back into place. "Why are you acting like the Inquisition when you know as well as I do that in less than fifteen minutes I'm going to walk out that door and meet Holly at the altar?"

"When was the last time you told my daughter you loved her?" Sergeant McCade asked, his voice soft, but retaining its usual gruff quality.

"I told I loved her when—well, I—I—" Colin stammered to a halt.

When *had* he said the words? His face flaming with guilt as he realized his oversight.

His *major* oversight.

"Oh, boy," he squeaked, jamming his fingers back through the tips of his hair again.

"Uh-huh," his future father-in-law agreed. "I'd say. It's just as I thought."

"Well, why didn't you say something earlier?" Colin snapped, then cleared his throat against the high-pitched sounds that kept coming from his mouth. His voice was taking on the tone of an adolescent boy.

"I've got to *fix* the problem."

But *how* was he going to fix the problem? His heart

pounded against his chest. A cold sweat formed on his forehead.

"Don't think of it as a problem, son," Sergeant Mc-Cade advised, patting him awkwardly on the shoulder. "Instead, try to think of it as the building site of a future solution."

At first Colin stared blankly down at his future father-in-law. What was that line of philosophical prose, delivered with equal doses of drill sergeant gruffness and efficiency, supposed to mean?

Love.

Of course. Love was his problem—or rather, the fact that he hadn't actually mentioned the *word* love was the problem.

But love—the emotional candor he felt in his heart and had obviously not communicated to Holly and the world—was the…how did the sergeant put it?

The building site of a future solution.

"Where's Holly right now?" he asked, sounding every bit as gruff as Ian.

"That's my boy," the sergeant commended. "First hall to your right, two doors down."

"Can you watch Jared for a moment?"

Gramps, as Jared called him, was already sitting down at the puzzle, muttering quietly under his breath about how small they made puzzle pieces these days.

Colin took a moment to straighten his uniform and brush his hair. He'd already blown one proposal. He wasn't going to let a single detail go unnoticed this time around.

Never mind the big ones.

How must Holly be feeling? She was preparing to

marry him with no assurance of his love. He couldn't even fathom why she would do such a thing.

She was a brave woman. Crazy, but brave.

He'd have to remember to tell her so.

Holly took a deep breath and sighed. Colin had taken her ultimatums about children and family surprisingly well for a man who claimed he didn't ever want to be saddled with either; but the happiness she expected to feel at winning that argument had somehow got lost in the translation.

The texture of the tea-length white satin wedding dress brushing against the sides of her calves wasn't quite what she expected. She'd imagined this moment a hundred times as a little girl. Now none of it seemed to be measuring up.

Not even looking in the mirror satisfied her, seeing in her reflection lace, ruffles, a bustle and a great big...*frown*.

Bittersweet longing pooled in her heart. Today she was getting married to the man she loved with all her heart and strength and soul.

This wasn't how it was supposed to be.

Her mother, crouched by her on the floor trying to mend a hem before the big moment, mumbled through the pins she held in her teeth, something about staying in one spot before the dress tore or Holly would end up with satin pinned to her ankle.

With effort and an inward sigh, Holly stopped her restless movement and forced herself to be calm and patient, at least on the outside.

Patience was a trait she'd no doubt have to develop,

she thought wryly. She'd be needing a lot of strength and fortitude before this day was out.

And she was looking at a whole lifetime.

The odd thing was, she'd gotten beyond her doubts. Her mind and her heart were completely at ease. She was convinced she was doing the right thing.

She had no qualms about the time it would take to raise Jared. In many ways she was looking forward to becoming an instant mother.

It was instant *wife* that was bothering her at the moment.

"Holly, if you don't stand still, this hem is going to look like a roller-coaster ride."

"Sorry, Mom." She fidgeted unconsciously, and her mother sighed and rolled her eyes.

"Sorry," she said again. She set her jaw and focused all her energy on standing still.

After a few minutes, she'd finally managed to level out her breathing and stop her feet from shifting. She'd even been able to engage in a bit of casual, insubstantial small talk with her mother, who was busy sewing up the final hem.

"All finished," Gwen announced after what seemed like forever. "Why don't you spin around for me? When you were a little girl, that was always the first thing you used to do when you got a new dress—spin around in it to see if it floated."

Holly glanced down at her mother, sharing the moment of nostalgia. Her throat tightened and tears pricked at her eyes.

She remembered.

"Go ahead," her mother urged when she didn't move. "I'll just bet this dress floats like a cloud."

Holly laughed despite herself. Time had proven she was no fairy or a princess, but she didn't see any harm in reliving one whimsical moment. Her dreams of a knight in shining armor had turned into more of a white knightmare, but that didn't mean she couldn't have a little fun this one last time.

She lifted her arms, determined to give her best spin for her mother's sake.

Instead, she spun herself right into Colin's waiting arms. He hooted his appreciation for her effort.

"Colin Brockman, you get out of here this minute!" her mother admonished with a shriek. "You can't see your bride on her wedding day!"

"I need a minute, Mom," he said, grasping Holly around the waist and sweeping her around. "I promise I won't look."

He grinned down at Holly, his eyes sparkling. It was clear he'd already taken a peek, and his gaze told her he liked what he saw.

Well, she had that, anyway. There was nothing conventional about this wedding, anyway. What was one more break with tradition?

Her mother stood and pressed her hands to her hips, her stance belied by a big smile. "It's very unconventional, young man, but I suppose I can give you a minute."

Colin beamed.

"A *minute*," she warned. "No more."

As soon as her mother exited, Holly pried Colin's hands from her waist and held them in front of her, putting a little space between them. She couldn't think when he stood so near her, especially all decked out in his dress whites.

He was an attractive man in any attire, but he was so strikingly handsome in his navy uniform he took her breath away.

"What do you want?" she asked, hoping her voice didn't sound squeaky or hoarse.

He took a step back and brought her hands to his lips, pressing multiple small kisses onto her knuckles. "You look absolutely stunning."

She chuckled despite herself. "You aren't supposed to be looking, remember. And you haven't answered my question."

"Have I told you lately that I love you?"

Her heart bolted to life, though she hastily coaxed it back into its cave. Colin, she reminded herself, often said things off the cuff, things he didn't think about before he spoke.

He'd never intentionally try to hurt someone with his words, of course. He was too good a man for that.

But sometimes he did hurt someone, just the same. He had hurt someone. Hurt her. He'd scarred her heart with his words—or rather, his lack of words.

"You came in here to quote song lyrics to me?" she asked, hoping she sounded light and casual, and hoping she could find something else to think about on her wedding day other than the fact that her future husband didn't love her. This was going to be harder than she'd thought it would be.

He looked taken aback for a minute, and then he grinned, as if suddenly getting the joke. "I'm a man on a mission."

"I hope so," Holly retorted, "or you're going to have my mother to contend with."

He held up his hands. "Don't scare me."

He paused for a moment, then caught in a breath and pulled her back into his arms before she could step away. His expression was as serious as she'd ever seen it, even more so than on the day of Jared's hearing. It made her nervous when he looked at her like that.

"Do you love me?" he rumbled from the back of his throat.

She nearly choked. "What kind of a question is that? I'm marrying you, aren't I?"

"That's not what I asked," he reminded her gently. "I asked you if you love me."

The dam burst, and all of Holly's pain and insecurity, feelings she'd been repressing and refused to deal with, rose to the surface, spilling over in her tears and in her voice.

"Colin Brockman, how dare you ask me such a thing. I've loved you since the first day I looked up into the top of the school auditorium and saw a thatch-haired thirty-year-old with mischief in his eyes causing trouble in my class."

"Yes. I'm a troublemaker. But do you love me? How do you love me?"

Holly laughed despite herself. "Let me count the ways."

He grinned, but his eyes were no less earnest than before. "Because…?" he prompted.

She shook her head and sighed dramatically. "Oh, all right. I love you for the way you are with Jared, so kind and supportive, always knowing what to say and do. I love that you make him laugh, and the way that you make *me* laugh.

"I love the way you smile at your cat. I love the way

you walk. The way you talk. The way you brush your fingers through your hair so it stands on end."

She wiped her wet cheeks with the palm of her hand and chuckled throatily. "Yes…well. I love you. I think you get the picture. Is that what you were looking for? Or should I go on?"

Colin's smile was like sunshine. "I'll take the short version," he teased.

"But you better be ready for the long one," she threatened boldly, laying a hand on his chest, "because you're about to commit to a good, long lifetime of hearing it from me."

He reached up a hand and stroked her cheek, using first the back, and then the tips of his fingers. "I was hoping you'd say that," he said huskily, caressing her jaw with his palm. "Because I love you, Holly McCade-soon-to-be-Brockman, enough to want to marry you, have a dozen kids with you and watch us grow into a couple of old fogies together."

Holly closed her eyes, savoring the sweet words. She'd waited all her life for this moment. But there was still a lingering question.

"Why didn't you tell me you loved me before? Like when you asked me to marry you?" she asked huskily.

"Because I'm an idiot."

She chuckled. "I won't argue. But I think there's more to it than that."

"More to it, how? Holly, don't read a bunch of psychology into it where there isn't any. I just don't always know how to say what I'm feeling. I'm a guy. Cut me some slack."

That might be all there was to it. But even if he meant

what he said—and he *was* pretty convincing—there was still something standing between them.

"There's still a lot that's left unsaid between us," she reminded him. "A lot we have never finished discussing."

"There's nothing you can say that will make me take back my words," he assured her. "Or my love."

"Nothing? Weren't you listening to me that day you proposed to me out in my parents' stable? I told you all about my past that day, remember? I was desperate for love, and I—"

Colin cut her off with a kiss.

When he raised his head, she tried again. "Colin, I'm serious. You need to know about the things I did back then and how I—"

Again, he cut her off with a kiss.

"I don't need to know any more than you've already told me," he muttered, nibbling on her bottom lip and spreading kisses down her jaw. "What's in the past is between you and God. I'm sure you've made your peace with Him, and that's all that matters."

He deepened the kiss for a moment, then backed off again. "I'm not looking back. Only forward."

"Yes, but I—"

He laughed, his eyes shining as he bent his head in for another kiss. "If you don't stop talking, we're never going to make it down the aisle today."

She joined in his laughter and kissed his cheek, which was smooth and clean shaven.

"I love you," he said again, cupping her cheek with his palm. "And I've obviously not said it enough. Believe me when I say I'm going to spend a lifetime making sure you hear it each and every day."

He kissed her again. "I love you."

All her fears and anxiety melted with those three little words. As shaky about herself and her life as she'd been a moment ago, that was as sure as she was now that Colin meant what he said.

It was funny how she only needed to hear the words aloud to know it was true. He'd been showing her all along, if only she'd bothered to listen to what he was telling her with his actions and his heart.

She turned her face into his hand and kissed his palm. "Until today," she reminded him, "you haven't said *it* at all, you big lug."

He grimaced. "I was afraid of that."

Holly chuckled. "I thought it was a rather large omission, myself."

"That's an understatement. I can't believe you never said anything. Or at least hit me over the head with your attaché. But you're a wonderful woman to let me off the hook so easily."

She arched a brow and smiled. "Who said I'm letting you off the hook, sailor?"

His eyebrows shot up. "Yeah? So what do you say to a big dope who doesn't have the sense to tell the amazing and wonderful woman he loves that she means the world to him?"

Holly slipped her arms around his waist and locked her fingers behind him. The intensity of his gaze matched the sharp intake of his breath. He wrapped his arms around her and held her close to his chest where she could hear the fierce rhythm of his heart.

This, she thought, was exactly where she wanted to be, and this is exactly where she wanted Colin—locked in her arms.

He leaned his face down into her hair and groaned. "What do you say to the idiot who forgot those three crucial little words—*I love you*?" he whispered raggedly.

She smiled, happier in this one moment than she'd ever been. "I do?"

* * * * *

Dear Reader,

Christmas is one of my favorite times of year, as we, God's children, reflect back on the precious birth of our Saviour, and look forward to when He will come again in glory. In heaven, there will be no pain, no anxiety and no tears.

In the meantime, we live in a world where mistakes and misunderstandings happen all the time. As Colin did with Holly, sometimes we, or those we love, say and do the wrong things—or say nothing at all. I don't know how many times I've misread a loved one's signal, or jumped to a false conclusion. How wonderful that our God is a God of forgiveness, and He uses our mistakes and sins for our good and His glory. Hallelujah!

On another note—Kids Hope USA is a real, wonderful program through which individual churches and organizations can make a difference in their community schools by mentoring one child at a time. You can contact Kids Hope USA at 100 S. Pine St., Suite 280, Zeeland, MI 49464 or at http://www.kidshopeusa.org.

Do you have a comment or a prayer request? Contact me through my website, www.debkastnerbooks.com.

Deb Kastner

SEASON OF JOY

Virginia Carmichael

This book would not exist if not for the support of many different people, old and young, near and far. Thank you to my daughters, Isabel and Ana, for being my beta readers. I'm sorry for the smooching. It just had to be in there somewhere. For Jacob, Sam, Edward and Elias, thank you for every time I asked for one more minute to write and you ignored me. Cruz, I want to say Marisol's food terms came from Google. Really. Thank you to my sister, Susan, who never reads this kind of book but was willing to put in serious time proofreading and giving comments. If I could write a good ghost story, I would, but that gene was passed to you alone. Thank you to my brother Dennis for making time to read and comment on all sorts of things, giving tech advice, big business advice and keeping a sense of humor through it all. For my brother Sam, who always keeps a clear view of what's important in life, sort of like Grant. For my parents, Murphy Carmichael and Bonnie Reinke, thank you for raising me in a house with more books than our local library. Bibliophiles unite!

Most of all, thank you to the fine ladies over at seekerville.blogspot.com who started this ball rolling in the first place. Your constant encouragement and advice is invaluable.

I have other sheep that do not belong to this fold.
These also I must lead, and they will hear my voice,
and there will be one flock, and one shepherd.
—*John* 10:16

Chapter One

A dark tidal wave of fear swept through Calista Sheffield as she paused at the door of the Downtown Denver Mission. She took a deep breath and wiped damp palms on the legs of her jeans. Her image was reflected in the glass door as clearly as in a mirror, the bright Rocky Mountain sunshine as backlighting. Giving her casual outfit a quick scan, she tucked a strand of honey-blond hair behind her ear and tugged at the hem of her black cashmere sweater. She prayed no one in the shelter would be able to tell the difference between Donna Karan and a knockoff, because she wasn't here to impress anyone. She was here to volunteer.

Her reflection showed a pair of large green eyes shadowed with anxiety. Calista squinted, hating her own weakness. There was no reason to be afraid when she ran a multimillion-dollar company. She gripped the handle and swung it open, striding inside before the heat escaped.

The exterior of the five-story mission was a bit worse for wear, but the inside seemed clean and welcoming. In the center of the enormous lobby, a tall pine tree bowed under the weight of handmade ornaments and twinkling lights. Calista's gaze darted toward a group of men clustered near the double doors at the far end. Probably the cafeteria. Maybe she was just in time to help serve a turkey dinner with trimmings. A vision of handing a plate piled high with steaming mashed potatoes and gravy to some desperate soul passed through her mind's eye. This was going to be great.

No, this was going to be more than great; the start to a whole new life. Not like the lonely existence she had right now with only her passive-aggressive Siamese cat for company. No more pretending she had somewhere to go on Thanksgiving, then suffering through everyone else's happy chatter after the holiday. It was her own fault for letting work take over her life, but that was all in the past.

This Christmas would be different.

Calista scanned the lobby for a secretary. The long, curving desk spanned the area between the elevator and far wall, but it was empty. An oversize wooden cross took center stage on a staggered section of ceiling that connected the lobby to the upper level. A small smile tugged at her lips, thinking of how that sight would have made her cringe just a few months ago.

A young man with the mission staff uniform and close-cropped dark hair exited the double doors, papers in hand. Calista stepped forward into his path.

"Excuse me, I need to see Grant Monohan," she said, in the tone she reserved for secretaries and assistants. Her eyes flicked from his deep brown eyes to the ID badge pinned to his shirt to the solid pattern of colorful tattoos that covered both of his arms from biceps to wrist.

He paused, frowned a little, glanced back at the empty desk.

"The director," Calista added, hoping she wasn't speaking the wrong language. His dark coppery skin and angular features made her think of paintings she'd seen of the Mayans.

"Just let me drop these papers in the office and I'll tell him you're here," he said, waving the stack of papers at her. He started off again without waiting for a response and punched in a series of numbers at the keypad by the far door.

The brown patterned couches were arranged in groups of three but none of them were occupied, except the very last one, near the large windows that faced the street. An older woman sat hunched in the corner, rocking and murmuring to herself. Her brown shawl slipped off one shoulder and pooled at her feet like a stain. Dark tangles framed a wrinkled, but somehow expressionless, face. Calista swallowed a sudden wave of anxiety.

A door swung open to her right and a wheelchair-bound woman rolled to a stop behind the desk. Her short gray hair was spiked on top and touched with violet. She maneuvered to the middle of the desk just as the phone rang.

"Downtown Denver Mission, this is Lana. How may I help you?" she responded in a cheerful tone.

None of this should have made her feel queasy, but the combination of the rocking elderly woman, the young man's tattoos and the purple-haired handicapped woman had Calista struggling with her resolve. She wandered toward the windows and gazed out at the snowy sidewalk, taking deep breaths. Life isn't pretty, she should know that. But after ten years of clawing her way to the top of the business world, Calista had buried any memories she had of imperfection. Memories of her own rough childhood in a place where there were worse things than purple hair and tattoos.

"Ma'am?" She snapped into the present at the word spoken quietly behind her. The young man was back. "The director is just finishing up but he can see you for a few minutes before his next appointment. Go ahead and have a seat."

Calista nodded and smiled brightly. "Thank you," she chirped, hoping she oozed positivity and enthusiasm. They wouldn't want unhappy people around here. She was sure they had enough of those already.

Grant Monohan checked the balance-sheet numbers for the third time. He knew better than to get upset at the decreasing number in black and the increasing number in red. The shelter scraped by most of the year until they got to the season of giving, or the "season of guilting," as Jose called it. God had provided every day of the past seventy-five years, so he wasn't going to start worrying now.

A light knock at the door and Jose popped his head in. "We got another one."

Grant wanted to roll his eyes but he nodded instead.

"Actress?" Aspen's popularity had been great for them, even all the way out here in Denver. The mega-rich had started to settle in the area a decade ago and it showed right around the holiday season. Every year, right when the store windows changed to sparkly decorations and Santas, the famous faces started appearing. Most were dragged in by agents or managers, but a few came on their own. They would spend a few days, sign some autographs and go away feeling good about themselves. He wasn't one to turn away help, especially when it came with good publicity and a donation, but it got real old, real fast. Last year they had a blonde starlet stumble in with a twenty-person entourage. Most of them were as high as she was. He cringed inside, remembering the scene that erupted as he informed them of the "no alcohol, no drugs" policy.

"Not sure. She's pretty enough but she came alone." Jose shrugged. Grant wished he would come all the way in, or open the door wider, but Jose always seemed to be in constant motion. It was all the kid could do to hold still for a few minutes.

"Why didn't Lana call back here?"

He shrugged again. "The lady just came up to me and said she had to see the director."

Grant frowned, wondering if it was worse to have a volunteer who demanded special treatment, or a volunteer who ignored the disabled secretary. He stood up and stretched the kinks from his back. Maybe he'd look into a better chair after the crazy holiday rush was over. The ratty hand-me-down was obviously not made for a six-footer like himself. Or maybe turning thirty was the start of a long, slow slide into back trouble.

"Tell her I'll be right out." Jose's head disappeared from the doorway. Grant crossed the small office space and absently checked his reflection in the mirror near the door. He was looking more and more like his father every year. Women told him what a heartthrob he was, like a classic movie star. They never knew how close they were to the truth. But what he saw—instead of the dark wavy hair, strong jaw and broad shoulders— was the man who walked away from his mother when he was just a kid. Grant shook his head to clear it. *All things are made new in You, Lord.* He had a heavenly father who would never run away and he needed to remember that.

Grant pushed open the heavy metal door and stepped into the lobby, letting the door close with a thud behind him. It wasn't hard to pick out the new volunteer. It wouldn't have been hard to spot her in a crowd at the Oscars, she was that pretty. She had the California party-girl look with an added healthy glow, but had wisely left the party clothes at home.

At least she was dressed conservatively. If you could call cashmere and designer jeans conservative. He sighed. Rich people could be so clueless. He watched her for a few moments as she stood near the window, arms wrapped around her middle. She sure didn't have the confidence of a professional actress. Unless the whole nervous attitude was an act.

She turned suddenly and looked straight into his eyes as if he had called her name across the lobby. Grant felt heat creep up his neck. He must look like a stalker, standing there silently. He strode forward, forcing a welcoming expression.

"Grant Monohan," he said, extending his hand. She took it, and he was surprised by the steadiness of her grip.

"Calista Sheffield," she answered. "Wonderful to meet you." The name sounded familiar. Her smile was a bit too wide, as if she was worried about making the wrong impression. Or maybe she was turning on the star power. As if that sort of thing worked on him.

"Jose told me you wanted to see me. Would you like to sit down?"

She frowned down at the couch and said, "You don't meet with anyone in your office?"

"Actually, I don't. We have meeting rooms for groups, and we have a reception area. There's another building at the south end of the block that we use for most of our administration needs."

There was a pause as she tilted her head and regarded him steadily. He could see her processing that information. "Is it a shelter policy?"

She was quick, this one. "It is. To protect the residents and myself from accusations or suspicion. We have plans drawn up for a new office that will have glass partitions but that's still a few years away." He motioned toward the long lobby desk. "So, for now we have Lana get pertinent information on visitors first."

She surprised him with a grin, green eyes crinkling at the corners. "That's usually the way it's done, isn't it?"

Grant hesitated, adjusting her age upward. Not for the laugh lines but for the gentle ribbing. He'd been told before he was slightly intimidating but she seemed able to hold her own.

"There was no one at the desk when I came in, so I just asked Jose."

He gave another tally mark, this time for remembering Jose's name. She might not be a total loss after all. He wasn't such a fool to think she'd stay more than a few days, but maybe she could do more than sign photos.

Grant motioned to the clean but worn couch behind her. "Let's sit down and you can tell me why you're here."

She settled on the edge, hands clutched together. Her

anxiety was palpable. "I'd like to volunteer on a weekly basis. Not just for Thanksgiving or Christmas."

He plopped into the corner of the couch angled toward hers, putting a good three feet of space between him and those green eyes. "Why?"

She opened her mouth, but then closed it again. He raised an eyebrow and waited patiently. She looked down at her hands, then up at him again, emotions flitting across her face. Confusion, sadness, yearning.

Grant wanted to wrap his arms around her and tell her it was going to be okay. Shocked at how fast he'd forgotten his professional role, Grant frowned, eyes narrowing. She was good at playing the little lost girl, that was clear.

"Miss..." He struggled to remember anything more than those eyes trained on him.

"Sheffield," she whispered.

"Miss Sheffield, let me tell you a little about the mission. We welcome any and all support. Seventy-five years of serving the community of downtown Denver has made our organization one of the most respected in the country. We provide shelter, addiction counseling, parenting classes, transport for schoolchildren and job training. There are five separate buildings and almost a hundred staff members." He paused, making sure she was following him. "But everything we do here is aimed at one goal, meeting the deep spiritual needs of all people. We want to be the Gospel in action, be His hands and feet in this world."

Usually at this point in his speech, the new recruit's eyes glazed over. They nodded and smiled, waiting for him to finish. She leaned forward, eyes bright.

"So, you mean to say that you provide for the physical needs but the spiritual needs of the person are just as important?"

"Just as or more. If it makes you uncomfortable, there is also the Seventh Street Mission a few miles away. They are a very respected shelter that doesn't adhere to any spiritual principles."

"No, it doesn't bother me at all," she said, her whole face softening. Grant struggled to reclaim his train of thought. Maybe he needed a vacation, had been working too hard. He felt as if he was a knot with a loop missing and that smile was tugging him undone.

"Good," he said, eyes traveling toward the plain cross on the balcony overhang. "That's the only reason we're here. The only reason *I'm* here." He sure wasn't in it for the money. He paused for a moment, trying to get the conversation back on track. "Did you have anything specific in mind?"

"What about the cafeteria?"

A vision passed before him of men, young and old, lined up for limp broccoli served by a stunning blonde, while the regular servers stood abandoned, lasagna pans growing cold. "How about intake or administration? You would be working with Lana to get the paperwork in order and maybe interview new visitors or assign sleeping places."

She blinked and then nodded. "That sounds fine."

"We'll need to get some basic information and do a background check for security reasons. But you can start today, helping out in the cafeteria. We've got a lot of prep work for Thanksgiving."

"Of course."

"Lana can help with the details." He stood, offering his hand once more. "It was a pleasure to meet you and

I'm grateful for your willingness to serve the disadvantaged in our community."

She stood, gripped his hand and whispered, "Thank you."

Grant's heart flipped in his chest as their hands met and he looked into her eyes. Her heart-shaped face shone with hope and her bright green eyes glittered with unshed tears. There was more going on here than a rich person's guilty conscience.

But there was no way he was going to try to find out what. He had enough trouble keeping the mission afloat without adding a woman to the mix. Even a beautiful woman who reminded him that he might need something more than this place. Plus, with the secret he was carrying around, no woman in her right mind would want to get anywhere close.

Calista stood up, gripping the director's hand, his movie-star good looks bearing down on her full force. The man should have a warning sign: Caution: Brain Meltdown Ahead. She could just see him in a promotional brochure, that slightly stern expression tempered by the concern in his eyes. He reminded her of someone, somehow.

But her heart was reacting to more than his wide shoulders or deep baritone. The man had sincere convictions, he had substance and faith. There was nothing more attractive, especially in her job, where image was everything. She wanted to have a purpose in her life beyond making money and losing friends. She wanted to wake up in the morning with more to look forward to than fighting with her board of directors and coming home to a cat who hated her guts.

She met his steady gaze and felt, to her horror, tears welling in her eyes. She tried to smile and thank him for the chance to work at the mission, but the words could barely squeeze past the large lump in her throat. Heat rose in her cheeks as she saw his look of confusion, then concern. He probably thought she was completely unstable, crying over a volunteer gig.

She dropped his hand and immediately wished she could take it back. His hand was warm and comforting, but electrifying at the same time. A short list of things she hadn't felt in a very long time.

"Let's go get those papers from Lana, all right?" His voice had lost its brusque tone somewhat, as if he was afraid of causing her any more distress.

Calista cleared her throat and said, "Lead the way." She blinked furiously and turned toward the desk, hoping he couldn't see her expression. If only he hadn't sounded so sympathetic. If only he was pleasantly distant, the way a CEO is with employees. But he wasn't like that; he wasn't like her.

Grant introduced them quickly. Lana was ready with a stack of papers and handed them to Calista. She could see why the mission had a purple-haired secretary. The woman was efficient and friendly.

"Tell me when you need me and I can adjust my schedule pretty easily." Calista bent over to fill out the papers. One of the perks of being CEO was she could take time off when she wanted some personal time. Not that she ever had before.

Grant's eyebrows went up a bit. "We're short staffed right now and we could really use some help in the mornings. Maybe Wednesdays?"

"Sure, I can be here at seven." As soon as the words

left her mouth, she wondered if that was too early. Maybe the staff didn't get here until nine. But Grant only nodded, the corners of his mouth lifting the smallest amount. She wondered for just a moment what he looked like when he laughed...

Calista's cheeks felt hot as she dropped her gaze to the papers. Grant turned away to speak to a slim young man who was waiting behind them and Lana took the papers, glancing over them. Her eyes stopped at the employment section. "You're head of VitaWow Beverages? I could use someone with a knowledge of grant writing."

"I've written a few grant applications but they weren't for nonprofits. And it's been a while."

"It was worth a shot," Lana said, shrugging and stacking the papers together.

"But I'm sure I could work on whatever you need," Calista said quickly.

Lana looked up, and Calista saw genuine warmth in the woman's eyes. "That's the spirit," she said. "We have a grant-writing team that meets on Thursday evenings. There are only two of them right now because it's the holiday season and everybody's busy. It would be great to get some of these applications turned in before the January deadlines. Is that a good day for you? They might change the meeting time if you can't come then."

"That's fine. Thursday's fine," Calista said. Any evening was fine. Five years ago she'd been busy with the dinner-and-drinks merry-go-round. Once she was promoted to CEO, she cut out almost all the dinners. Of course, after she'd done so, Calista realized her schedule was completely empty. She was friendless and alone.

"Grant is on the team, too. He can fill you in."

"Does the director usually work in the evenings?"

Lana laughed, a lighthearted chuckle. "You don't know the man. It's all about the mission, all the time." The smile slowly faded from her face. "I know he feels at home here, and we could never survive without him, but I wish…"

Calista waited for the end of the sentence, but Lana seemed to have thought better about what she was going to say. She regarded Grant, deep in conversation with the young man, and a line appeared between her brows.

"You're afraid he'll wake up one day and wished he'd put more time into his own life, something apart from the mission?"

"Exactly." She appraised Calista with a steady eye. "You're good at reading people."

"I suppose I know what that feels like. And you're right, it's no fun." Calista dropped her eyes to the desk, wondering what it was about this place that made her feel she could be honest. She wasn't the CEO here; she was just a woman who had lost her place in the world.

She turned back to her paperwork and said, "I can find my way to the cafeteria—"

The end of her sentence was lost in the explosion of noise that accompanied a horde of children entering the lobby. They seemed to all be talking at once, the polished lobby floor magnifying the sounds of their voices to astounding levels. Just when Calista decided there was no one in charge of the swirling group of small people, two young women came through the entryway. One was short and very young, with a thick braid over her shoulder. The other was a powerfully built middle-aged woman with a wide face and large pale eyes. They were both wearing the mission's khaki pants and red polos under their open coats. They were laughing about something, not concerned in the least that their charges were heading straight for the director.

"Mr. Monohan!" A small girl with bright pink sunglasses yelled out the greeting as she raced across the remaining lobby space. She didn't slow down until she made contact with his leg, wrapping her arms around it like she was drowning. He didn't even teeter under the full impact of the flying body, just reached down and laid a large hand on the girl's messy curls.

A huge smile creased his face and Calista's mouth fell open at the transformation. He was a good-looking man, but add in a dash of pure joy and he was breathtaking. She tore her gaze away and met Lana's laughing eyes behind the desk. Of course, the secretary would think it was hilarious how women fell all over themselves in his presence. Calista gathered up the papers with a snap, when she realized she was surrounded. A sea of waist-high kids had engulfed them, with the two women slowly bringing up the rear.

She sidled a glance at Grant, hoping he would tell them to clear out and let her through. But he was busy greeting one child after another. How he could tell them apart enough to learn their names was really beyond her. They just seemed an endless mass of noise and motion, a whirl of coats and bright mittens.

"Miss Sheffield, this is Lissa Handy and Michelle Guzman. They take the preschoolers down the block to the city park for an hour every day." He was still mobbed by coats and children calling his name, but his voice cut through the babble.

Calista raised one hand in greeting, trapped against the desk, but only Michelle waved back. Lissa seemed to be sizing up the new girl.

She stood with her arms folded over her chest, unmoving. But Michelle reached out and touched her on the shoulder. "It's wonderful to have new volunteers," she said, her voice warm and raspy, as if she spent too much time trying to get the kids' attention. She smelled like fresh air and snow, and Calista smiled back. Her clear blue eyes reminded her of Mrs. Allen, her third-grade teacher. That kindhearted woman had given her confidence a boost when she was just like these little people.

"I don't know how you keep them all from escaping. It must be like herding squirrels."

Michelle laughed, a full-throated sound that came from deep inside. "You're right. The key is to give them some incentive. They head to the park okay, and then I tell them we're coming back, but Mr. Monohan will be here. Easy as pie."

Calista glanced back at Grant, his wide shoulders hunched over a little girl who was excitedly describing something that needed lots of hand waving. He was nodding, his face the picture of rapt attention.

"He seems really good with the kids. Does he have any of his own?" She suddenly wished she could snatch the words back out of the air, especially since it was followed by a snort from Lissa.

Michelle ignored her partner's nonverbal comment. "No, he's never been married. I keep telling him he needs to find someone special and settle down. He was one of the youngest directors the mission had ever had when he started here, but this place can take over your life if you let it."

"But that's what he wants, so don't stick your nose in." So, Lissa did have a voice. A young, snarky voice, coming from a sullen face. She flipped her dark braid off her shoulder and stuck her hands in her pockets. Calista wondered how old Lissa was, probably not more than nineteen. Just the age when a girl might fall in love for the first time.

"You'll understand when you're older, Lissa. But there's more to life than work, even if your work is filled with people like ours is here," Michelle said.

Lissa's face turned dark and threatening, like a storm cloud. "You always say stuff like that. I don't think my age has anything to do with my brain."

Spoken like a true teenager. Calista tried to smooth ruffled feathers. "Michelle's right that everyone needs a family or friends separate from work." Lissa's face twisted like she was ready to pour on the attitude. Calista hurried to finish her thought. "But not everybody is happiest being married, with a family. Like me. I don't think it would be fair to have a boyfriend when my work takes up so much of my time."

Lissa's eyebrows came up a little and she shrugged.

"But I could always use more friends." That last part was a gamble, but Lissa seemed to accept it at face value. She relaxed a bit, the smile creeping back into her eyes.

"Don't know why you'd be looking for friends at this place, though."

Michelle gave Lissa a squeeze around the shoulders. "Come on, you found me here, right?" Lissa responded with an eye roll, but Calista could tell the young woman appreciated the hug and being called a friend.

"Fine, but we got enough pretty people in here slumming it for the holidays. We don't need any more."

"I can wear a bag over my face, if that helps."

Lissa let out a surprised laugh. "Yeah, you do that. Maybe you'll start a trend."

"Maybe so." Calista took one more glance back and started to laugh. Grant had a pair of bright pink sunglasses on his face and the kids were howling with laughter. Parents had started to show up to collect their children and they acted as if the scene wasn't unusual at all.

"Those are Savannah's glasses. She never goes anywhere without them. He's sure got a silly side," Michelle said, chuckling. "But you'd never know it at first glance."

No, you wouldn't. Not with that frown and the serious gaze. As if he could feel her looking at him, Grant glanced up and she saw the smile slip from his face. Calista felt her heart sink. Then again, she wasn't here to get a boyfriend or find true love. She was here because her life had become a self-centered whirlpool of ambition, with her swirling around at the bottom like a piece of driftwood.

Grant seemed to come to some kind of decision. He waded through the kids until he was standing next to them. "Miss Sheffield, it's almost lunchtime. Why don't you come in for something to eat and then I can introduce you to the kitchen staff?"

Calista darted a glance at Lissa. The teen probably thought Calista had been angling for an invitation all along. But she couldn't resist jumping at the chance to get to know this man better. She nodded quickly and he turned toward the far side of the lobby.

"Is there a kid version of catnip? If there is, you must be stuffing your pockets with it."

"Nope, I just listen to them. It's funny how many

people forget that kids need someone to hear them," he said, his words serious, but a grin spread over his features.

At that moment, as they stood smiling at each other, the other side of the cafeteria door swung open and nearly knocked Calista off her feet.

"Watch out! You shouldn't stand in front of the door," an old man shouted at her as she stumbled, struggling to regain her balance.

"Duane, please keep your voice down." Calista could tell Grant was angry, maybe by the way his voice had gone very quiet and dropped an octave or two. "Are you all right?" He reached out and rubbed her left shoulder, which had taken the brunt of the impact.

She nodded slowly, distracted less by the pain than by the warmth of his hand. "Fine, not a problem." Meeting the old man's eyes, she was surprised to see such animosity reflected there. "I'm sorry I was standing behind the door." When both sides were at fault, it was always best to be the first to offer an apology.

But if she was hoping for reciprocation, it didn't come. He blinked, one eye milky white while the other was a hazy blue, and sniffed. "You're still standing here and I gotta get through."

Calista moved to the side immediately and let him pass. As they walked through the doors into the full dining hall, she glanced back at Grant. "Off to a good start, don't you think?"

Again that warm chuckle. She could get used to hearing that sound, even if she couldn't get used to the way it ran shivers up her spine.

"I think we're off to a great start," he said, and something in his tone made her look up. His smile made her heart jump into her throat and he stepped near. Although she knew the whole cafeteria was watching behind them, she couldn't tear her gaze from his.

Calista watched those blue eyes come closer, her heart pounding in her chest. Her brain seemed to have shorted out somewhere between the shoulder rub and the chuckle.

Grant leaned forward, his gaze locked on hers, and then he looked directly behind her. "Scan it twice, please. She doesn't have her guest pass yet."

Calista blinked and turned to see him holding out a security badge with a small photo in the middle. A pretty young woman sitting at a small table took the badge without comment and passed it twice through a card reader. Her dark eyes flicked up and down Calista's outfit, then handed Grant the security badge.

"We use visitor passes to keep track of how many meals are served," he explained.

"I see," she said in a bright tone, but clenched her jaw at her own stupidity. Was she so lonely that any good-looking man caused her brain to shut down? Did she think he was leaning over to kiss her, in the doorway of the mission dining hall? She was so angry at herself that she wanted to stomp out the door. Except she had vowed to do something useful. Which did not include mooning over the director.

She stood for a moment and gazed around at the dining hall. It was much bigger than the lobby and had an assortment of elderly, teens, women, men and what seemed like a hundred babies crying in unison. The noise was horrible but the smell wasn't bad, not even close to what she remembered from "mystery casserole" day in grade school. The rich scent of coffee, buttery rolls, eggs, sausages and something sweet she couldn't identify made her mouth water.

"I haven't eaten with this many people since college." She peered around. "Is there a cool kids' table?"

He grinned. "Sure there is, but I don't sit there." He led her forward to the long line of glass-fronted serving areas. "Here are the hot dishes. We try to keep it as low-fat as possible. Over there—" he pointed to a wall that held row after row of cereal dispensers "—are the cold cereals and bowls. The drinks are self-serve, at the end of the row. Milk, juice, coffee, tea, hot chocolate. We don't serve soda anymore."

Calista nodded. "I see that trend a lot."

"In schools? I'm sorry. I didn't catch what you do."

"I'm the CEO of VitaWow." She felt her cheeks heat a little at the words and was surprised. She was proud of her job, of how she'd turned the company into a national brand. But standing here, in this place, it didn't seem as important.

She watched his eyes widen a little. "I've heard good things about your company. Didn't the city honor Vita-Wow with a business award?"

"Best of the best." She liked saying the words and couldn't help the small smile. "I'm proud of our product and our commitment to health. But I also care about our employees. We have excellent benefits and give every employee a free pass to Denver's biggest fitness center."

He smiled, and she was struck once more by the difference it made. He seemed like a friend, the kind she wished she had.

Calista nodded.

"Our main goal is to provide a safe place where people can fill their spiritual needs. But we also want to make sure the people have healthy food that gives them a good start to the day."

He lifted a tray from the stack and handed it to her. "I don't recommend the hash browns but the breakfast burritos aren't too bad."

"I like having a food guide." A quick peek at the hash browns supported his opinion. They were soggy and limp. The metal serving dish was full, proving the rest of the cafeteria avoided them, too.

He moved down the line behind her, sliding his tray along the counter. "If that's a job offer, I have to warn you that I have great benefits here. Unlimited overtime, my own coffee machine, a corner office with a wonderful view of the parking lot."

Calista couldn't help laughing as she spooned a bit of scrambled egg onto her tray. "Sounds like my job, except I have a view of the roof of the building next door. And lots of pigeons to keep me company."

A short, wiry woman smiled at him as he reached for a biscuit. "Mr. Monohan, it's good to see you having breakfast. You have to eat and keep strong." Her softly curling hair was covered by a hairnet and she wore a brightly colored apron that was missing one large pocket in the front.

"Marisol, this is Calista Sheffield. She's a new volunteer."

Calista hoped the emotion that flickered over the lined face was curiosity, and not skepticism. "We can always use more of those, eh, Mr. Monohan?" The thick accent was a bit like Jose's but more lyrical, as if she was more used to singing than speaking.

"We sure can. When are you going to cook me some

of your arroz con pollo? I've been dreaming of it all week."

Marisol beamed with pleasure. "Anytime, Mr. Mono-han, anytime. You tell me and I cook you a big dinner. Maybe you bring a friend, too? How 'bout that nice Jennie girl?"

Calista studied the biscuit on her tray, wishing she couldn't hear this conversation.

"Sadly, Mari, I don't think there's much future for us," Grant said, sounding not at all sad about it.

"Oh, no." She wagged her finger over the glass case at him. "You let her get away. I told you, she's a nice girl and you work too much." She seemed honestly grieved by this new development.

"You wouldn't want me to be with the wrong girl, would you, Marisol? And she wasn't right for me." Calista glanced at him and could tell Grant was trying not to laugh, his lips quirked up on one side.

"But how you know that when you only see her once or twice? You work all the time and the girl decides you don't like her. That's what happened." She was giving him a glare that any kid would recognize from the "mom look."

"No, I made time for her. But it just didn't work out." He smiled, trying to convey his sincerity but Marisol was not budging. Finally, he sighed. "I don't want to gossip, but I'll tell you something she said."

"Go ahead," Marisol dared him, frowning. Calista couldn't imagine how long it was going to take to convince this little Hispanic woman that Grant hadn't done Jennie wrong.

"She said I was too religious."

Calista felt her eyes widen, a perfect mirror to Mari-

sol's own expression. They both stared at Grant, dis-
believing.

"Oh, Mr. Monohan. That's bad. Very bad." Her eyes
were sad as she shrugged. "Because you don't drink?
Did you tell that girl your mama drink herself to death?"

"It wasn't that. And I never told her about my
mother." His words were light, with no hint of anger.
He could have told Marisol to zip it, but he looked more
amused than anything.

"Well, good thing she's gone. You tell me when you
want me to cook. Maybe I bring my niece, that pretty
one? She's in college and wants to be a social worker!"

Calista bit back a laugh at how quickly Marisol had
let go of Jennie as Grant's future wife.

"Thanks, I will." Grant nodded at Calista and she
figured it was safe to move on.

They got glasses of orange juice and he chose a table
near the entrance. As they settled on either side of the
long table, he extended his hand to her, palm up.

She stared for a moment, uncomprehending, then
remembered how her sister, Elaine, always held hands
with her husband as they said grace before meals. It had
made Calista uncomfortable a few years ago but she felt
her heart warm in her chest now. She placed her hand
in his and bowed her head. The steady strength of his
fingers sent a thrill of joy through her. He spoke simple
words of thanks and asked God's blessing on their day.

He let go of her hand and she put it in her lap, feeling strangely lonely without the pressure of his hand.

"Did she really say you were too religious?"

"I wouldn't lie about that," Grant said, grinning. He
paused, as if choosing his words. "And I'm sorry about
Marisol. Too much information on your first day, right?

But she doesn't mean any harm. She thinks everyone will accept people for who they are, not holding the sins of their parents against them."

Calista dropped her gaze to her tray. She'd worked hard to reinvent herself from a poor girl from a tiny Southern town, the one with a mean father and a dead mother, into a polished and beautiful businesswoman. But there was only so far you could run from yourself. Then it was all about facing your fears and being bigger than your past. She was ready to be what God intended her to be, no matter how crazy it seemed to everyone else.

Chapter Two

"You don't seem very upset about losing your girl-friend."

He took a sip of his orange juice and paused, a small line between his brows. "You know that moment, when you're not sure exactly which way to go, when opposite choices are equally attractive?"

"Of course." She hated that moment. The indecision nearly killed her.

"That was how I felt about Jennie. She was smart, caring, made good conversation. Everybody thought we'd be a great couple."

Calista groaned and he raised his eyebrows in question. "Every time a friend tells me that I'd be great with someone, I know it's doomed." Jackie, her assistant, never tired of setting her up. It was always a disaster and Jackie always enjoyed the dramatic story the day after. Which made Calista wonder if she picked the men for her own amusement.

Grant laughed out loud and nodded. "Maybe I should have known, but my best friend, Eric, set us up. Well, he brought her in to volunteer and he knew we'd hit it off."

Calista took a bite of her biscuit and chewed thoughtfully. Eric thought they'd hit it off because they were so alike, or because Grant went for pretty volunteers? The idea that she was sitting in a spot where twenty other girls had been made her heart sink.

"She's an attorney and spends most of her time as a prosecutor for the city's worst abuse cases. She also handles some family law, but mostly fights for the weakest of our residents. He knew I'd appreciate her passion for protecting vulnerable kids."

The buttery biscuit turned to ashes in her mouth. Grant would certainly not appreciate her own passion for building a vitamin-water empire. There was nothing admirable about getting folks to pay a lot of money for something that didn't really make them any healthier.

"And I really did—I mean, I do—think she does a great job. But we just didn't seem to connect." His voice trailed off and he took a bite of scrambled egg. "But I knew that before she told me I was too religious, so it only made it easier to leave it at being friends."

Calista took a sip of her juice and pondered his words. Elaine told her once that if a man wasn't in contact with any of his ex-girlfriends, then he was a bitter and spiteful person. So, maybe staying friends with Jennie was good.

"I'm just wondering…" She shook her head, trying to formulate her thoughts. He watched her, waiting. "Why did she say that? Was it something you did? Or said? I don't want to pry, but it's an odd comment. Don't you think?"

He grinned at her and she felt her brain go fuzzy around the edges. "Not odd at all. Most people consider anything more than a passing gesture to be too much. Sunday service is okay. Giving up a big promotion because God is calling you in another direction is not. Saying a blessing before eating is fine. Praying for your future spouse is not."

Calista paused, her fork halfway to her mouth. "Future spouse? What does that kind of prayer sound like, if I can ask?"

He shrugged a little. "Uh, I don't usually focus on that, since I have bigger fish to fry. But let me think. I usually pray for her health and safety, for her to grow in God's grace."

Her fork was still poised above her tray. She hadn't spent much time praying in the past ten years, but if she had, it wouldn't have been for anyone else. It would have been for herself. Was there a man praying for her right now? One she'd never met, but who cared for her already? She dropped her gaze as the thought brought sudden tears to her eyes. Could she be loved and not even know it yet?

"That sounds weird to you," he said lightly, but she heard the hint of something in his voice, maybe disappointment.

"No, not weird." She looked up at him. "It's beautiful. I'd never thought of it before, praying for your future spouse."

"Really?" He sounded surprised.

"Really. I'm pretty new to this." She waved a hand between their trays, meaning the blessing. He frowned, trying to understand. "Blessing your food, asking for direction in your life."

He nodded. "How new? Like, today new?"

She laughed. "Not that new!"

He grinned back at her, his broad shoulders relaxing

a little. She wished she could tell him that there were years of prayer behind her, that she was a seasoned Christian. But she was practically a newborn, trying to understand what God's will was in her life.

"New enough." She sighed. "It's a long story but I grew up in a place that was less about the truth and more about what made a good show."

His eyes were sad as he searched her face. "That could be anywhere. I think once pride gets center stage, God's truth is hard to hear over the noise."

She nodded, thinking it through. "You're right. It's probably a pretty common thing. But I let it get between me and God for a long time."

"But not anymore." Grant's eyes were soft, his biscuit forgotten in his hand.

"No," she said, unable to keep her smile from spreading as she gazed back. "Not anymore."

Calista slipped out the mission's door into the mid-November chill. She had been so nervous about volunteering that she had forgotten her coat and gloves in the car, but now she felt the wind whip through her expensive sweater. Tucking her hands in her pockets with a shiver, Calista glanced up at the snow-covered Rocky Mountains. It was hard enough to be homeless in the winter, but it was downright deadly in Denver.

She walked to the secure parking behind the mission, hardly noticing the people passing her on the sidewalk. Her mind was full to bursting and she struggled to squelch the feelings Grant brought to the surface. She'd told Lissa the truth: she was way too busy to date and it never worked out anyway. No guy wanted to be known as "Calista Sheffield's boyfriend" instead of by his own name. There were very few men her age who earned more than her or had more power. The ones who were eager to take on the role were only interested in the boost it gave their own business reputations.

Her mind flashed back to Grant's face, his appraising glance. He hadn't seemed interested in her job so he probably didn't care. That would be a good thing. Her life had become so consumed by her success that she had let her soul wither away. She felt as if she was just a husk, dried up and empty inside. Where there should be something vibrant, something connected to God, there was a pitifully weak, underfed shadow.

But she was ready to change, to let God call the shots for a while. She wanted to feel joy, like the look on Grant's face when the little girl had practically tackled him with her hug. She pressed the button on her key ring and her Mercedes beeped in response. Sliding into the leather seat and reaching for the buckle, Calista felt her whole self yearn for purpose in her life. Her God was a God of second chances so she didn't have to wallow around in her sad and lonely life.

Now, if she could just get everybody else to give her a second chance at being a decent human being, then she'd be all set.

Her cell phone trilled in her pocket. And she answered it automatically.

"I'm sending you the report on the new building sites and you have four urgent messages." The voice on the phone belonged to Jackie, her personal assistant, who sounded calm and collected as usual. She rattled off the messages in rapid-fire.

Calista tucked the cell phone into her shoulder and turned onto the freeway. "Tell Jim Bishop that Branchout

Corporation's new commercial is encroaching on the VitaWow brand and we need to send them a cease and desist letter. Also, get Alicia down to tech support and make them promise not to wipe the hard drive on my laptop ever again. They said they were cleaning it, but all my temporary files disappeared into thin air." She could hear Jackie typing at a frantic pace.

"How was the appointment?"

"What appointment?" Calista asked, before remembering that she'd told Jackie she had a toothache and was going to the dentist. "Right. The dentist was great. All fixed."

The sound of Jackie's laughter made Calista glare at the freeway in front of her.

"This is why I have complete faith in VitaWow's CEO. You can't tell a lie to save your life."

"Why do you think I'm lying?"

"You never forget details, but more importantly, nobody ever says their dental appointment was *great*."

Calista let out a sigh. "Fine. I wasn't at the dentist. But I'll tell you about it later. This traffic is just crazy in the afternoon." Cars were slowing to a crawl in front of her. "Good thing I'm always at the office until late. I completely miss rush hour."

"Are you using your headset?" Jackie asked suddenly.

Calista already had one ticket for cell use while driving. "I was, but I dropped it when I got out of the car and it shattered."

"New headset," Jackie mumbled into Calista's ear as she typed another note. "Okay, I'm hanging up now because it would be extra bad for the company image if you racked up another ticket."

"All right," Calista said. "See you on Monday."

Jackie snorted. "And talk to you tomorrow, you mean. You don't take weekends off. Which means I don't, either."

She frowned, easing into another lane of slow-moving traffic. "Well, that might have been true before. But I'm determined to make it a priority to enjoy some free time. I don't want to wake up at eighty and realize I worked my life away."

"I never thought I'd hear you say that. How surprising."

"Realizing your only friends are people who get paid to talk to you will do that to a girl."

Jackie laughed and her infectious giggle made Calista grin long-distance. "I thought it was your biological clock ticking away."

"I'm not that old! I just need to expand my horizons," she said huffily. But the thought had crossed her mind, right about the time her sister, Elaine, had given birth and Calista had seen the pictures of all her friends gathered to meet the new baby. Calista wanted a family, but she wanted the whole picture. She wanted the faith that brought fullness to life, and the friends to experience it all with her.

"And I mean it about the weekends. I might pop into the office on Saturdays but no more Sunday work. I want to get a real life."

"Hey, as a card-carrying member of your current life, I don't appreciate you getting a new one unless I'm in it. But this is sounding stranger and stranger." Jackie's voice was still light, but Calista knew her words concealed real worry. And she had cause to be worried because Calista had made no secret of how her hypo-critical father had ruined her life.

"It's a long story."

"Then Monday it is, and be careful driving in that traffic," Jackie said, sounding uncharacteristically ma-ternal before she hung up.

Calista focused on the road in front of her and tried not to think of the horror stories she had told Jackie. None of them had been exaggerated.

Her father had been the most respected man in their dusty, Southern town, but he ruled their little house like a dictator. He acted loving and gentle in front of their church family, but told his own family when to eat, sleep and pray.

The blaze that burned her house to the ground and took her mama's life told her for certain that God couldn't be trusted. So, she would have to make her own way in the world, without His help. Her choices were either go to college or settle down with Ray Col-lier, the football coach's son. Ray was a good guy, but he would never have been happy with her. She had too many opinions and didn't like football. Her sophomore year in college she heard he'd married Tina Bowdy, a pretty girl whose father owned the gas station. She hoped they were a lot happier than she had been the past fifteen years. But her unhappiness was her own fault. There was ambition, and then there was insanity.

As Calista turned the car into the private parking ga-rage under her condo, she felt hope rising in her chest. The mission was going to be a good place to spread her wings. She could be wealthy and successful, and have a few friends, too. As Grant's face crossed her mind, she willed it away. She wasn't volunteering so she could meet a nice guy. Even if she never saw him again, she knew this was the beginning of something…something real, something she'd been missing so far. It was time to stop hiding who she was. She had been born for a purpose, and she was ready to find out what it was, even if it meant admitting to the world that she wasn't the perfect woman they all knew as the VitaWow CEO.

Chapter Three

"You haven't cashed my check." The low growl on the other end of the phone set Grant's teeth on edge.

"I tore it up. Don't send another because I don't want your money." He worked to keep his voice steady and even, but his heart was pounding in his chest.

"You're a fool. Or a liar. I've heard the mission is in big trouble. I know you need the cash." A thick, mucusy cough followed the last word, and Grant flinched as the sound echoed in his ear.

"I do what's best for the mission and that would never be accepting your money. You'd always be there, try-. ing to worm your way into every decision I make." His voice had risen higher as anger threatened to choke him. They'd had this conversation ten, twenty times. He was sick of it.

"You're right. I'll always be here, whether you take the money or not. But thanks for letting me know I need to have my accountant send another. This time, to the board." Then there was silence.

Grant stared into space, then slowly replaced the receiver. The board consisted of nine very respected and dedicated professionals, from bankers to business owners to pastors. All good people who would wonder why Grant wouldn't take money the mission desperately needed for repairs and upgrades. Especially from the state's richest man. But he couldn't. It was tainted, stained. It was money made off the backs of the poorest of the poor. Taking money from a man who wouldn't even provide his workers with decent health insurance was like making a deal with the devil.

He dropped his head in his hands and groaned. *Lord, I'm not asking for You to stop the sun from rising. I just want him to go away. He had his chance and blew it. Isn't it enough that I forgive him?*

The sudden sound of a throat being cleared, loudly, brought Grant's head up with a snap. Jose was standing in the doorway, shifting his weight from foot to foot, his thick arms folded over his chest. "What's up?"

"Nothing," Grant answered tersely. Jose had the habit of appearing and disappearing without a sound. He should put a cowbell on that kid.

"Alrighty then," he said lightly, but his face was creased with concern. "Just wondering what you thought about the new chick."

Grant struggled to regain his composure, feeling like a gorilla at the zoo who just had his cage rattled. He stood up and stretched. "She's not a chick. And she seems all right. Should be good for office help, at least. She wanted to work in the cafeteria."

Jose chuckled. "Yeah, that would have been a disaster. She's so pretty the line would have taken forever. She's like, more than the usual pretty."

Grant didn't want to discuss the "new chick" but he nodded. "Yup, certainly got blessed in that department.

But she seemed sort of…" His mind thought back to the tapping foot, the arms wrapped around her middle.

"Nervous?"

"Right. Or sad. I don't know." He shrugged and checked his watch. "But then again, it was probably because her car might get broken into out in the parking lot."

Jose's eyebrows went up. "She has a sweet ride, for sure. But, boss…"

"Sorry." Grant couldn't shake off the irritation that wrapped itself around his neck like a scarf. He rubbed a hand against the base of his skull. "I'm just on edge. True, everyone carries a burden. We'll probably never know the whole story because after Christmas, she'll be gone."

"She said that?"

"No, but you know how it goes. Guilt sets in, they come sign up for a few meals, then January hits and they feel better about themselves so they never come back. Until next November."

Jose nodded. "Well, probably a good thing anyway."

"Why? You know something I don't?" No matter how careful or protective he was of the people here, there would always be those who came to prey on the weaker ones. He had set up several lines of defense with background checks, personal references and lots of observant employees. But there were cracks in every fortress.

"Nope. Just thinking she's definitely your type." Jose grinned and waggled his thick eyebrows.

"That's unprofessional," he said, frowning. Unprofessional and unsettling. She wasn't anything like his type. He felt comfortable with women who were reserved, even a little distant. The woman who came here today was a bundle of emotions; they flickered across her face like pictures on a screen.

"Yeah, it is, but it's still true. Plus, how would this place survive if you actually got a life?"

"I do have a life. It's just very quiet."

"You mean, boring." And with that Jose popped back out.

Grant sighed and pushed back his chair, stretching his long legs out under the old wooden desk. He was busy. He didn't have time for a girlfriend. At least, that's what he told himself.

He rubbed a hand over his face. Sometimes, when it was just a little too quiet, he thought about his mother. A beautiful woman ruined by her addictions, heartbroken when she trusted the wrong person. She never stopped reminiscing over how rich his father was, how success-ful. It almost seemed as if she didn't remember that he'd left her with nothing but a baby to raise. The memory of the fast cars, wads of cash and fancy parties blurred her focus, polluted her heart. The love of money was the root of all evil, right? Grant straightened his shoul-ders. He was never going to be sucked into that fantasy world. He was happy, right where he was.

His mind flicked toward the image of Calista's face, her large green eyes sparkling with hope. He wished her well. He really did. But people like that didn't stick around places like a homeless shelter. The pull of money was too strong. And money was one thing the mission didn't have.

If God didn't nudge somebody to donate really soon, and in a big way, they might not even have to worry about Christmas preparations. The mission would have to close. But he would do everything in his power to make sure that didn't happen.

Calista slid her car into the open space at the parking garage behind the mission and tried to calm her pounding heart. She allowed a small smile to touch her lips as she thought of the irony of the situation. Just that morning she had brokered a huge deal with a company in Northern California. It had been months in the making and if it succeeded, their production and distribution would be on the fast track to making VitaWow a nationwide phenomenon. Before ten this morning, she was CEO to a company that was a regional star. After ten, she was CEO to a company that could be as widely recognized as Coca-Cola in just a few years.

The irony of her anxiety now was that she hadn't felt a bit uncomfortable going into a meeting that could decide the fate of her company. She knew business and marketing, she understood the language and the terms. More than all of that, she had a gift for business. Calista took another deep breath and shook her head.

But this mission gig had her stomach in knots. Definitely out of the comfort zone, right where God wanted her.

The short walk to the front doors of the lobby seemed to take forever but finally Calista stepped into the warmth. She headed for Lana's desk, unbuttoning her bright red wool peacoat on the way.

The secretary glanced up and raised a hand. "Glad to see you. You're early. I just love early people."

Calista felt her heart lift. Lana sounded like she really was glad to see her. "I was raised in a family of chronically late people so I rebel by arriving just a bit early," Calista said, trying not to look toward Grant's office. She wondered if he was at the mission, or if he was in a meeting somewhere, and then was irritated at herself for wondering.

"Just a bit early is perfect. Then there are those people who come twenty minutes early for everything." Lana rubbed the spiky ends of her hair, and Calista recognized the gesture from her last visit.

"What do you need me to do today?"

"Thanksgiving is a really busy time for us. Not just for meals. There's lots of paperwork. It would be a relief to have someone do a little filing. We have a skeleton crew for the office right now, since two of our part-timers left for other positions."

"You're at the front desk a lot of the time?"

"Right, so when I'm out here, I can't be in there," she said, waving a hand toward the locked door on the right.

Calista's mouth went dry and she cleared her throat. "So, I'll be working with you at the desk, or back in the offices?" She added hastily, "I can answer phones, too. If you show me your system." She actually hadn't worked a switchboard since college but the thought of working in close quarters with Grant sent a thrill of alarm through her.

"Because of privacy issues, you should probably work in the office area. We can have you organize files into specific cabinets, without having to look at the papers, since they're all color coded."

Calista nodded, resigned to the fact she was going to bump into the man. She would just have to get a grip. "I'm ready," she chirped, hoping she was convincing enough.

Lana must have thought so, because she pushed a button on her phone and said, "Grant, Calista's here."

"Be right out." The answering voice was familiar, in a tinny way.

Lana let go of the button. "Thanks again for the help. You're saving me a headache."

She smiled automatically but her mind was whirling. "Jose's not here? I would think Grant's way too busy to show me the filing system."

"He's here, but the director asked to be the one to show you around the offices." Lana's words were followed by the appearance of the man himself.

Calista heard the door and turned her head in time to see him open the door with speed. He looked a little harried, his red tie crooked and crisp white shirtsleeves rolled halfway up his forearms.

He was happy to see her. At least, his expression changed from something like worry to pleasure. His lips quirked up and his eyes radiated warmth. She couldn't stop herself from responding. It had been so long since anyone had looked happy to see her. She let her eyes drift over him for the briefest moment and then clamped down hard on any desire to give a closer examination.

"Glad you're back. Come on in," he said, motioning her through the door.

It was just a common phrase, but her smile only got bigger. It was like she'd swallowed a happy pill.

"I'll show you the offices first, then the general meeting rooms and the break room." He strode down a carpeted hallway and stopped at the first door, knocking lightly.

The affirmative answer from the inside sounded muffled, and she saw why when Grant pushed open the door. Jose was crouched near the desk, piles of power cords in his hands.

"This power strip is dead. I'll have to get another from the supply closet. Maybe they only last a few—" His sentence trailed off as he finally caught a glimpse of his audience. "Hey, Calista. Glad to see you back."

"Hi there," she responded, grinning. Three people had welcomed her in less than ten minutes. She felt all warm and fuzzy inside. It had been a very long time since anybody had said "hey" to her. People didn't say "hey" to the CEO.

"Jose's office. He oversees the group that works with the food boxes distributed to needy families. He also organizes social activities for the residents."

"Yup. And I say we spring for a real Santa this year. The kids are starting to suspect the truth when Santa has a Tex-Mex accent." He grabbed his stomach and tried a few "ho ho ho" sounds.

Grant laughed and waved a hand. "You know you love it. All right, on to the next stop."

The next door was an empty office that had a high window with a pulled shade. "One of our three empty offices. Soon to be filled, God willing. The person here handles class scheduling and addiction support. The main counselors and teachers are doing well right now, but it helps to have a manager type to handle any conflicts."

Another short walk to the next door and Grant pushed it open without knocking. "My office. Lana started calling it my 'man cave' after Jose brought in a small fridge."

"Got it stocked with beer for those slow afternoons?" She chuckled to herself the split second before she realized her mistake. "Oh, Grant. Sorry. That was stupid." His mother was an alcoholic, Grant didn't drink, and she'd just made a beer joke. She wanted to fall through the floor.

To her relief he seemed to shrug off the insensitive comment. "No big deal. And no beer."

Calista gazed around the space and wondered why Grant didn't have a nicer office. As the director, he needed to give the impression that he was the head of a thriving organization. People donated to the cause they thought would succeed—it was human nature. Maybe it was because the donors always met in the conference rooms. Or maybe with nonprofits, it might not work as well to flash too much wealth. In her world, understated luxury was the only way to go.

His office was more than understated; it was shabby. An older-than-Methuselah desk, a battered chair, a few framed photos, his diplomas and the small fridge.

"How long have you been here?"

"Five years as director, about eight altogether."

"And you don't even have a plant?" She turned to him with a curious look.

To her surprise, he flushed. "I should make it a little homier, considering all the time I spend in here."

Calista nodded. "I don't know much about charities, but if you're bringing donors through this hallway to get to the boardroom, you had better keep this door closed."

He let out a sound that was more of a startled cough. "I don't think it's all that bad, personally."

"It's not bad. But it doesn't look good. And donors will judge the entire mission on you and your space." She surveyed the room once more. "Maybe a nice framed photo of the staff, right here, that you could see when you passed down the hallway."

Grant frowned. Putting money into furnishings when there were people who didn't even have shoes was unthinkable. And a photo? He hated anything done for show. It smacked of insincerity to have a photo taken of his staff, even though they were his friends, just to show it off to donors. But he tried to take a mental step back and look at her advice with a cool head. He knew better than anybody that donors saw him and the mission as inseparable. He was the human face they could put on the problems of hunger and homelessness in their community.

"I suppose I can see your point. I'll look for something that might go in that spot. I appreciate the advice."

People didn't usually thank her for the advice she handed out. Probably because she made it a habit to break the cardinal rule of giving advice: wait for someone to ask. She turned, surprised and ready with a quick retort if she saw the faintest suggestion of sarcasm.

Their eyes met. Time seemed to slow as he stood very still. His gaze wandered down to her mouth. It had been so long since any man had looked at her like that and she read in his blue eyes exactly what was going through his mind.

He moved a half inch forward. Calista felt a thrill course through her and couldn't stop her breath from catching in her throat. The tiny noise she made seemed to remind him where they were and what they were doing. He blinked, and his gaze flashed back to the empty spot on the wall.

He cleared his throat and stepped back into the hallway. "I'll show you the filing room so you can see the mess we have in there." His voice was rough.

Calista nodded, following his lead without comment. She really needed to get a grip. All of this talk about purpose and change, but here she was ogling the director. Of course, there were some major sparks flying, but the poor man had enough on his plate without adding a woman like herself to it. She trudged behind him down the hallway, barely listening while making appropriately interested sounds. Everything about Grant Monohan made her want to be a better person, and that meant learning not to indulge every wish and whim. Not something she was really used to, but she was determined to make herself useful at the mission…and stay out of his way.

Grant struggled to put words together as he led Calista down the hallway toward the file room. His mind churned as he pointed out stacks of loose files, gave her a quick tutorial and then made as quick an exit as was humanly possible.

He reentered his office and shut the door, leaning heavily against it. What on earth had just happened there? One minute she was giving him sound business advice, and then next he was about to make a move on the pretty new volunteer. He felt a shiver of fear run through him. Maybe all the stress of making their low funds stretch through the holidays was messing with his head. Maybe he needed to get some counseling to make sure he was staying on track.

And being seconds from kissing a woman in his office was about as offtrack as he could get.

He didn't even really know much about her, except

she was smart, bossy and emotionally vulnerable in a way that made him want to protect her from the world. But she didn't need him to do that. Rich people just hired someone to protect them. Grant rubbed his temples and tried to corral his thoughts.

In a job like this, you had to understand the danger of becoming too emotionally close to the people who needed your help. It was okay to make friends, to give support and encouragement; it wasn't okay to let attraction lead to actions. To be fair, it was definitely a mutual attraction. The way her eyes looked at him told him that.

And she wasn't a resident or someone in need of counseling. But she had already said she was working her way back from some kind of traumatic past. Her faith was new, untested. He had no right to get in the way of what God was working in her heart. It was too much, too soon. The "new chick" was going to have to find her way without any of his attention. Plus, he had bigger problems on his plate, starting with a leaky roof and a Thanksgiving dinner for five hundred. After that, he had to take another look at the financials. If anything else went wrong, anything at all, their reserves would be tapped out.

Chapter Four

Calista's usual morning routine began with two pieces of seven-grain toast, some orange juice and a long run on her treadmill. This Wednesday was no different, except that she pounded out a solid five miles with an overwhelming feeling of happiness. The awesome view of the Rocky Mountains never got old. She couldn't wait for the next snowfall, a few days from now, if the forecast was right. Last year she'd been too busy to enjoy any of it, practically living at the office. But this year would be different.

It would be the perfect winter moment: watching big flakes drifting past her tenth-floor windows as she read in her favorite chair, wrapped in a cozy blanket and sipping hot chocolate. In her mind's eye, there was someone new in the picture. Someone tall, handsome, caring. Calista shook her head and turned off the treadmill. Grant was never going to end up in her condo, sipping hot chocolate or not. To him, the luxury high-rise would be a disgusting waste of money.

Mimi wandered into the kitchen and surveyed her domain from the end of her squashed and furry nose.

Cruella De Vil could have learned a thing or two from Mimi. The cat was bad to the core. Deceptively sweet on the outside, Mimi would wait for Calista to leave before she took her revenge, usually by chewing on her nicest pumps.

Calista put out a tentative hand, hoping for the hundredth time that they could be friends. The Siamese cat waited for her to get closer, then darted forward with lightning speed to nip Calista's fingers with her tiny, sharp teeth. She yelped and snatched her hand back. Mimi made a slow-motion about-face and presented her fluffy behind before she sidled out of the kitchen.

Calista sighed and headed for the master bathroom.

After her shower, she decided on a simple tailored white shirt and khaki pants. She let her blond hair dry naturally so it curled a bit and swiped on a light pink lipstick.

Calista took a long look in the mirror. She tilted her head and squinted, watching little crow's-feet appear at the corners of her large green eyes. She had always taken care of her skin and watched her weight, but no more than most women. Calista knew she had a lot of spiritual work to do but at least she wasn't obsessed with her appearance.

It was a strange feeling, looking at her own personality under the microscope. She'd spent so many years gliding by on power and position that she wasn't even sure what her weaknesses were.

She closed her eyes for a moment, praying that God would reveal her faults to her. *Just not all at once, please*, she thought hastily. Maybe she could tackle one issue a month. And this month would be…being a better friend.

She opened her eyes and grinned at her reflection. This would be the ultimate makeover, from the heart on out.

"Glad to see you this morning," Grant said.

Calista knew it was just words, but she couldn't help grinning every time he said it. "Thanks, I can't seem to stay away."

He reached out a hand and she responded, feeling the warmth and strength that she had missed ever since the first time they'd met. She struggled to sort her feelings, to narrow down the whirl of conflicting emotions. But all she could feel was the touch of his hand, and hear the steady beat of her heart against her ribs. As he let go, she noticed dark shadows under his eyes and there was a persistent frown line between his brows.

"Everything all right? You look tired."

His shoulders straightened a bit and he glanced out the lobby window behind her, watching the residents filing in from the halls. "Fine. Just the busy season."

"Does your family live around here?" As she asked the question, she wished she could snag back the words. He probably thought she wanted to know more about his alcoholic mother. Her cheeks went hot.

His gaze traveled back to her and he frowned, thinking. "My family…is here. At the mission."

Well, that was clear enough. He could have waved a sign that said, "None of your business. Stop prying." Calista nodded, biting her bottom lip.

"Mr. Monohan?" A young man with a long, lean face approached them. He was wearing one of the red polo shirts that identified him as a mission worker and it hung from his thin frame.

"Hi, Jorge." Grant turned his attention to the mission worker. "What's up?"

Deep brown eyes flitted to Calista and then away. He cleared his throat, his Adam's apple bobbing. "Your girlfriend is on the phone."

Calista's stomach suddenly fell to her feet. There was no reason on God's green earth that she should feel anything at those words. She looked around desperately for Lana and pretended she couldn't hear the conversation only a foot away.

"My *what*?"

"Jennie Close, that lawyer? She said to tell you that your girlfriend was on the phone." His eyes flickered nervously between Calista and Grant again.

Grant opened his mouth, then seemed to think better of what he was going to say. "Tell her I'll be right there."

Jorge nodded and slipped back through the door to the offices.

"Lana should be here in just a bit. She has some projects she wanted to show you."

Calista forced a bright smile. "Great. I'll wait right here."

As Grant walked away, Calista felt her face grow hot. No wonder she was at her best in the boardroom. She was a total failure at normal conversation.

"Hey, Calista, did you want to grab some coffee with me in the cafeteria? Then I can show you the filing system." Calista turned her head in surprise, then readjusted her gaze downward.

"Lana, that sounds great, actually."

Lana wheeled past her, leading the way to the cafeteria. She handed Calista her badge on the way. "Here's your ID. Go ahead and slip it on. You should have it visible at all times, especially since you don't have a uniform."

Calista took the square badge and slipped the lanyard over her neck. She was thankful she didn't have to wear that awful uniform. Then she squashed the feeling down, irritated with her own shallowness. At least the shirts weren't yellow. She looked awful in yellow.

They swiped the badges at the front and went to the coffee bar. Lana balanced her cup on a tray settled on her knees. Calista hovered, undecided, then said nothing. Lana had lots of practice carrying her own cup. She should probably just back up and let her do it.

Lana stopped at a table, scooted a chair to the side, then wheeled into place. "You're a godsend for the mission, you know."

Calista choked, the bitter liquid burning its way up her throat. She took a few seconds to clear her airway, her mind spinning. Of all the things she had expected Lana to say, this was close to last on a very long list. "Why do you say that?"

"Your business background. We're in big trouble here and I think someone with your experience could get us back on track."

Calista stared into her cup, watching the overhead lights shimmer on the black surface. "I hadn't heard that. I don't know anything about nonprofits. I wish I did, truly, but—"

"How different can it be? We need money, you know how to make money." Lana leaned forward, her usually pleasant expression now serious. "Grant doesn't want to alarm anyone, but this is the worst situation we've been in for years. Our funds have been low, but this is scraping the barrel."

"What's the problem? Did you have a big donor back out?"

Lana sighed. "The day care area needed to be updated to keep in line with federal standards. Then we had to widen all the doorways and bathrooms for handicapped access." She glanced up. "Don't get me wrong. I'm all for being able to get to the bathroom. But the board thought we should widen everything, not just have one designated exit or bathroom on each floor. That was early this year. Right after that, the classrooms had to have all the electrical redone to be up to code. Then the state recommended every public space have an emergency contact system put in, so we had to put in a PA system."

Calista nodded. Sometimes things snowballed and there wasn't anything you could do about it. "So, how bad is it? The financial situation, I mean."

"Bad. The roof is leaking, so it has to be fixed, and soon. We've got another four months of snow. We'll have to close that building if we can't fix the roof. Thanksgiving is a huge expense, and then winter comes right on top, so we'll be full to the brim. If it was June, we could probably make it through. But as it is right now..." Lana's light blue eyes dropped to her cup, her lips thinned out in a line. "Even with Christmas donations on the way, we won't make it into December at this rate."

A woman appeared behind Lana, her round face pocked with acne scars but her dark eyes were bright. "Lana? Jose needs you at the desk. There's some question about the switchboard. They can't transfer a call."

Lana nodded. "I'm coming." She motioned to her

cup. "Finish your coffee. Come on back when you're done."

"Thanks," Calista said and watched Lana push herself with powerful arms toward the doorway. She couldn't shake the sense of alarm that threaded through her at Lana's news. The mission had serious money issues and they thought she could help? How? A for-profit company sold stock or got investors and promised some kind of return. What kind of return was there in giving cash to a homeless shelter? No wealthy person she knew would be willing to donate the kind of money they needed. There was nothing in it for them.

Calista's shoulders straightened. She would just have to figure something out. But first she needed to get a specific idea of what kind of numbers they were talking about. She glanced around, feeling like the new kid in junior high who had to eat lunch alone. The cafeteria had emptied considerably in the few minutes they'd been talking and the kitchen staff had come out to wipe down the tables and collect trays.

Marisol directed several groups in aprons as they cleared the food trays out of the warming areas. The small Hispanic woman was a blur of movement as she bustled between workers. She spotted Calista sitting alone at the table and paused, frowning. Seconds later she was standing before her, hands on hips, lined face creasing with displeasure.

"Did they go and leave you alone?"

Calista considered her options. She could rat out Grant and feel a little satisfaction after being dumped for Jennie-the-lawyer-but-not-girlfriend. Or she could be honest.

"Lana was here, but they needed her back at the desk." She tried a placating tone, hoping for an undercurrent of nonchalance.

"That's no excuse. Where Mr. Monohan?" If anything, Calista's explanation made the frown even deeper.

"He got a phone call. It was Jennie, the girl you were asking about." She had no idea if that would be helpful, but she felt as if she'd been called to the principal's office.

The noise that came out of Marisol's mouth made her think of an angry goose. An angry mama goose. "So! He leave you to go talk to the girl who says he love Jesus too much!"

Calista felt her face start to flush. The cafeteria crowd was sparse, but there were still a few curious looks being cast in her direction. "It's fine, really. I don't mind."

Her dark head was cocked slightly, eyes appraising Calista. "Oh? You think he is too religious, like that crazy girl?"

Calista's gaze swept the cafeteria for any sign of rescue in the form of Jose. "No, he's perfect the way he is. And I don't mind eating by myself." Or she didn't until the cafeteria matron came to give her a hard time.

As if someone had flipped a switch, Marisol dropped her fists from her hips and slid into the seat across from her. "I'm sorry if I make you feel upset. I want him to have a family, a wife who love him, but he is so busy."

At least she knew when to back down. Her cheeks still felt hot but Calista said, "That's all right. I can tell you care about him."

"Oh, yes. Mr. Monohan save my life." She said this as if she was simply giving the time of day.

* * *

Grant laid the phone in its cradle and dropped his head in his hands. What an awkward conversation. He never wanted to repeat anything like it, ever. Jennie wanted to give it—them—another shot and well, he didn't.

Jose peeked in the door and gave him a sympathetic glance. "Looks like that went about as well as I thought it would."

"Yeah, you called it." Grant stared at the desktop, shoulders slumped. "I'll have to call Eric and tell him he's banned from setting me up with anyone, ever again."

"It's not his fault. You have to admit, she's pretty good-looking."

Grant frowned. "So, how did you know that she…?"

"Wasn't your type?" Jose sidled a glance at him and then chuckled at his boss's irritated expression.

"Right. Did you give her a personality test when I wasn't watching?"

"She wasn't interested in the mission. Just you. And that was never going to work."

"Not interested? Why else would she be here? I'm pretty good at spotting the fakers and the takers." He'd spent close to ten years at the mission, on and off, and after a while he could smell a user at fifty yards. Not a drug user, but a people user. Although he'd gotten pretty good at spotting the addicts, as well.

"Simple." Jose's black eyes were restless, like a bird's, as he glanced around the lobby. "She never tried to talk to anybody else but you. Not the kids, not the staff, not Lana or Michelle or Lissa, or the residents."

"I can't believe that she never talked to anybody. There are hundreds of people here every day."

"I didn't say she didn't talk to them. I said she didn't try."

Grant frowned, trying to remember. "Well, make sure you use your superpowers the next time, okay? You can save me some time."

He turned to see a huge grin spread over Jose's face. "Now what?"

"You sure you want me to put on my cape and tell you who to ask out?"

Grant rolled his eyes. "Sure, why not? Just don't make the list too long. I'm not made of money, you know."

"How about the new volunteer?"

"Oh, right." Grant paused, struggling to come up with a reason that Calista was not his type. He decided not to argue with the type just yet. "Well, I don't think it's a great idea to be using the new volunteers as my personal dating pool. Eric introduced Jennie and me, so it was all right for us to go out socially."

Jose continued to grin. He stuck his hands in the pockets of his slacks and rocked back on his heels, looking like a man who knew more than was good for him.

"And then there's the matter of faith." Grant wouldn't normally share that kind of conversation, but Jose was killing him with that smug expression. "She just said that she's new to all of this. That's how she said it. *All of this.*" Grant waved a hand, indicating the cross on the wall, the lobby, everything.

"That's a bad thing? I'd rather have a fiery convert than a lukewarm cradle Christian."

Grant had to admit he agreed with him there. He

tried a new tack. "I really don't think someone who wears Ralph Lauren to a homeless mission is my type."

The smile slipped from Jose's face. He crossed his arms over his chest and said, "Lana and I were talking about that. What? We weren't gossiping." Grant had opened his mouth to remind Jose that the mission was a "no gossip" zone. There was too much real drama without creating any of their own. "She was wondering if she should mention it to her, just ask her if she could dress down a bit since some of the residents might feel uncomfortable."

Grant nodded. That was one of the reasons they wore the red-polos-and-khaki-pants outfit. Of course, they were easy to identify, but it also took some of the pressure off the staff. It was hard to wear nice office clothes when you worked with people who only had one pair of pants to their name. He should know, because he'd been on both sides of that fence.

"She makes me think of myself, when I first came to Denver." Jose's jaw tensed as he spoke those last words and Grant remembered clearly how troubled the young man had been. "All I knew was how to be tough and I dressed the part. Almost everybody I knew back in El Paso dressed like that, even my family. I knew it made people think twice about messing with me, but I didn't know it made them think twice about giving me a job or being friendly."

Grant had thought more than twice about being friendly. Jose had been positively lethal looking. He had been fighting his way out of alcohol dependency and he'd radiated anger.

"What I wore didn't mean the same thing to me as

it did to everyone who knew me here. But I gradually learned to let the gang clothes go."

"So, you think she doesn't realize that wearing a hundred-dollar shirt is a bit offensive in a homeless shelter?" Grant couldn't hide the skepticism in his voice.

Jose uncrossed his arms and gave him a steady look. "I'm not sure what's going through her head. Maybe she doesn't think anyone will recognize the brand. Maybe she's so rich that these *are* her casual clothes. But I know she'll figure it out and she'll care when she does. And I'm telling you, she's your type."

Grant threw up his hands at the last words and started to laugh. "Okay, I give up. No more talk about dating because I'm probably going to end up a bachelor forever at the rate I'm going. What's so wrong with being single, anyway?"

"Nothing, if you want to be, if you're supposed to be. There's room for everybody, right? But see, Cassandra showed me how happy I can be. I just don't want you to miss out on something good."

There was no way to argue with that. Jose had never been so happy, or so determined to stay sober, as he was now. Cassandra was a small woman with a huge laugh. She'd grown up in the roughest part of LA and was part of the day care staff. Their wedding a few months ago was one of the highlights of the year, in Grant's mind. Two incredibly happy people, making a lifetime commitment before God, inspired them all to be a little gentler to each other.

"Cassandra is a direct message from God to you."

Jose grinned and nodded. "You got it. Anyway, where's the new recruit?"

"I think Lana's showing her what to do."

"Why not you? There's nothing on the schedule this morning, and Lana's busy enough as it is. She asked me to do it but I've got a meeting in ten minutes."

Grant shoved his hands in his slacks' pockets and stared at the floor. He knew he was being ridiculous, but he was afraid if he spent too much time with Calista then his life was going to get a whole lot more complicated. And he liked it simple. Or as simple as it could get at this point.

"Take a chance, boss. You never know what good things are planned for you today." Jose's voice was teasing but Grant got his meaning loud and clear.

"All right, but I'm not saying anything to her about her clothes." Grant stood up with a frown and brushed past Jose, who was struggling to suppress a very broad smile.

He pushed open the dining-room door, feeling a wave of warm air against his face. The smell of casseroles mixed with overcooked vegetables was as familiar as his mother's perfume. Calista probably thought sitting in this place was the worst possible way to spend a Wednesday but it felt like home to him.

He turned toward the table where Calista sat and halted midstep. Her back was to him but she might not have seen him even if she was facing him. Her bright blond head was bent toward a familiar dark one. Marisol had one hand on Calista's arm and the two women looked like they had known each other forever.

"Oh, yes. Mr. Monohan save my life. Is a very long story." The woman waved a hand like she was swatting flies.

"I know you're busy, but I'd like to hear it." Calista

glanced back at the groups wiping tables and clearing dishes.

"Well, I tell you a little." She paused, staring at her hands that were clasped together, dark fingers intertwined. "I came to Denver for my son. He come over to work. His papa died many years ago, it was just us. He sent me an address and money but when I get here, he was gone." Her eyes settled on the wall behind Calista, as if she was seeing something very far away. "I was so scared. I run out of money, not knowing where I can go, what I can do to get home. Then I see the mission sign."

It sounded like Calista's worst nightmare, being stranded, penniless. A horrible dilemma. To stay and search for her son while trying to keep off the streets, or go home and always wonder what happened. She shivered, rubbing her arms through the expensive cotton shirt. Calista tried to swallow past the lump in her throat. "So what did you do?"

"I spend my day looking, hoping. But I need a job and Mr. Monohan asks me if I can cook." She grinned, bright teeth shining again in her dark face. "And that is the end of the story."

Except for Marisol's son. Calista was afraid to ask, but couldn't help herself. "Did you—did you ever find out…?"

Tears welled in her brown eyes but her voice was strong. "I think my Gabriel is gone from this life and he is with *Nuestro Señor*, Jesus. He would have found me by now."

Calista nodded, blinking back her own tears. What would it be like to be loved so deeply? To have someone sleep on the street, to live in a shelter, to refuse to leave a foreign land, just to find you again? "That's a mother's love," she said, almost to herself.

Marisol regarded her for a moment. "*Sí.* Your mother is close to you?"

"My mother died when I was young."

"Ah, *mija.*" The older woman sighed out the words and reached over to pat Calista's arm. "There is nothing sadder than a girl without a mother. Nothing."

She didn't know if that was true, even as her heart was aching in her chest. "Even sadder than a mother without a son?"

To her surprise, Marisol nodded. "*Sí.* I miss my son, it's true. I am sad that he did not have a wife or *niños.* I will never be called *abuela.*" She wiped her eyes with the edge of her apron. "But I have everything I learned from my mother. Her cooking and her stories, how to rock a baby and how to feed a man."

Calista squeezed her eyes shut for a moment, feeling the loss of her mother acutely. "But Mr. Monohan has no mother and he looks like he's doing perfectly fine." She didn't know why she wanted to argue about it.

"Oh, *Dios,*" the woman exclaimed, clapping her hands together in grief. "Poor man, he is an orphan. Worse than an orphan! But he is strong, he works hard and his faith will keep him on the right path. He is busy making the world better."

And that was the difference between them.

Grant had put all of his heart into helping others and he was surrounded by people who respected him, loved him. *I'm sure when he walks into the mission Christmas party, the room doesn't fall completely silent.* No, he was swarmed by kids, beloved by bossy old ladies, protected by friends. Calista felt self-pity well up in her and wondered if it was too late for her to get a real life, one like Grant's.

"Don't look so sad, *mija*." There was that word again, whatever it meant. And the comforting pat on the arm. "There is room in his life for a woman. He works a lot, but I know he is lonely, too. I think if you show him what you feel, there is a chance for you and Mr. Monohan."

Calista shook her head, trying not to laugh as she tried to make sense of such an odd comment. Then there was the ominous sound of someone clearing his throat a little too loudly. She turned her head, knowing before she saw his face that Grant Monohan had heard the last few sentences and was coming to a very awkward conclusion.

Chapter Five

Grant cleared his throat and waited to be noticed. His mind was reeling from the words that had just come from Marisol's mouth. He was busy but was he lonely? And the new volunteer had feelings for him?

Calista turned toward him, her face the color of fresh beets.

His thoughts stuttered as he tried to make sense of what he'd heard. Did she care for him? But they hardly knew each other. He took a deep breath and gave them both a steady gaze. Whatever was going on, he needed to be as professional as possible.

"Mari, thanks for keeping Calista company."

"My pleasure, but you should be ashamed of yourself. You leave this beautiful girl to talk to the crazy woman? No wonder you still not married." This all came out in a rapid-fire, heavily accented stream. The words were a little unkind, but Marisol softened the blow by standing up and placing a loud kiss on Grant's cheek. "And you need a haircut. Is getting too long. Soon, no one will know whether you are a resident or the director. You come over next week and I trim it for you."

Grant felt heat creep up his neck but he nodded. He'd never get used to being treated like a kid, because he'd always taken care of himself. If his hair started to curl over his collar, then he was the only one who ever noticed, until he met Marisol. There was no halfway with her. Once he'd been adopted by the fierce little woman, she got full rights to his grooming, love life and nutrition, in no particular order.

"I got to go make sure they don't break all my dishes." Marisol swept up the tray from the table and turned to Calista. "You come back next weekend and I'll give you some tamales to take home. It's a tradition. Tamales at Christmas." With that last bit of bossiness, she turned and disappeared into the kitchen.

There was a moment's pause while Grant wondered what to say and how to say it.

Calista stood up, grabbing her coat off the back of the chair, and brushed back a wavy curl from her face. Grant wondered what she looked like when she laughed, then felt irritation at wondering.

"I need to go find out what Lana needs me to do," she said, her smile a perfect balance of friendliness and distance.

He knew she was being helpful, being flexible about all the upheaval around the mission, but somehow he felt disappointed. Part of him wished she would seek him out, make an effort to be around him. He realized that even though they'd only known each other a few days, he felt absurdly relaxed around her. Except for when he stood a little too close or looked too deeply into her eyes, and then he felt the very opposite. "I let Lana know I was coming in here. I'd like to show you the rest of the complex, if that's all right."

Her eyes crinkled with pleasure. "Lead the way." Her whole figure seemed to exude high energy.

As they walked through the almost-empty cafeteria toward the double doors at the far end, he glanced at her. "Are you a runner?"

She almost stopped in surprise. "How did you know that?"

"Because of the way you move." The words were out of his mouth before he really thought through them. He hurried to elaborate. "Runners have a confident stride. My friend Eric ran in a marathon last month and he walks like you do."

"I'm no marathoner," she said, laughing. "Those people are nuts. I've done a 10K and a half marathon, but the real deal is way beyond me. I started running when I was in college to relieve stress."

"I hear you. I swim every morning at the Y. When I don't get in my laps in the pool, I feel out of sorts."

She turned to him as he opened the door and motioned for her to pass through. "Earth and water. Those two elements don't mix, do they?"

For a moment, their eyes locked and he felt his brain shift from small talk to something deeper. Her smile faltered as she waited for him to say something, anything. His gaze slipped down to her lips. He struggled to find the thread of the conversation. "Um, I think that's fire and water."

"Right. I don't know why I said that."

Again, that long, loping stride. He grinned, thinking of how many times he'd had to slow down because his long legs left friends behind. Their strides were well matched, in tune.

"We'll start with the recreation areas so you can

get an idea of the different buildings." He pushed the long handle of an exit door and they came out into the mid-November sunshine. The snow-filled courtyard was empty except for two men talking at the far end. Buildings rose on every side, warm-colored bricks offset against the cool blue of the sky. The snow sparkled in the bright sun and the air smelled like it had blown straight down from Mt. Evans.

"We have five separate but connected buildings. The largest is the residence hall, which can house up to two hundred men, and has one hundred cots for emergency overflow. The women and children are housed here—" he pointed across the grass "—and we have family housing on Ninth Street, in an apartment block. The lobby, offices and cafeteria are behind us, of course, in the main entrance areas. In the cafeteria they serve almost three hundred people, three meals every day.

"To your right we have the old classrooms, which we use for addiction counseling and parenting classes and anger-management classes. Then over here we have the recreation areas and the day care rooms. We have a small library that's stocked with children's books, thanks to a community reading program."

"A library? Now that's a good thing. I think books were my best friends when I was little. Maybe they still are." She glanced around, sizing up the buildings. "Which one has the roof that needs replacing?"

He glanced at her in surprise. He opened his mouth to ask, but she was already talking, eyes fixed on the building ahead.

"Lana mentioned it. She also says the mission is running on fumes, financially." She sidled a look at him. "Running a business isn't easy, to say the least."

Grant didn't know whether to be irritated or relieved. Part of him wanted to impress her with how well the mission was doing, but it was true they were in serious trouble.

"What's the fund-raising like here? Do you have a special board? Is there a general fund or are there building funds and program funds? Is the money accessible or is it in trust?" Calista was frowning slightly, a hand over her eyes as she surveyed the building, one hand tucked in her jacket pocket.

"The board handles most of the financial decisions. The money is in a general fund unless a donor asks for it to be earmarked for a certain area, like the children's playground. We have a charity drive twice a year, once in December and once in July." He had to admire her questions; they were thorough and intelligent.

"Have you ever had a fund-raising for a specific cause?"

Grant shook his head. "You mean, like when they have the big thermometer with the red line pointing out how much more needs to be donated?"

Calista's broad grin flashed in the sunlight. "Exactly. And everybody fights to be the one to move the arrow every time the money gets recounted."

The thought of Lana and Jose wrestling over the red arrow made him chuckle. She glanced back at the building, her smile turning serious. Grant dropped his gaze, wishing that he could say something to make her laugh again. The two men who had been talking near the far end of the courtyard disappeared through the doors to the recreation building.

"Grant, it really shouldn't be hard to raise that kind of cash."

He opened his mouth to argue, to tell her how hard they worked for the donations, then thought better of it. He had a business degree, but most of his concerns were wrapped up in the health and safety of his residents. "You have any ideas?"

She nodded, still surveying the area. "Absolutely. You need to involve some bigger sponsors than the neighborhood grocer or carpet-cleaning service." She turned, green eyes serious. "You know what I mean? Big sponsors. Like Denver Bank or the big chain stores or even my company, VitaWow."

"That's not going to be a conflict of interest?"

Grant wanted to smooth the tiny wrinkle that appeared between her brows.

"Why would it be? We partner with charities, especially during the holidays. If I make up a list, you'll need to start reaching out to them right away. Like, tomorrow. Before all their holiday charity funds are snapped up by the bigger places."

"I suppose I can manage that," he said. He laughed and realized with a shock that he didn't mind some wealthy volunteer giving him orders. How did she do that? How did she boss him around and tell him what to do, and make it feel good? The only other person who could tell him what to do was Marisol.

Which brought back the words he'd heard when he'd entered the cafeteria. *He works a lot, but I know he is lonely, too. I think if you show him what you feel, there is a chance for you and Mr. Monohan.*

He cleared his throat and thrust his hands in his pockets, shifting his feet in the snow. He really didn't want to bring it up, but living with an alcoholic had made him allergic to secrets and lies. He didn't have time to wonder what she was thinking, or what Marisol was trying to tell her.

"Calista, do you mind if I ask you a personal question?"

He watched a look of wariness settle in her eyes. She lifted her chin and straightened her shoulders, as if she was waiting for him to say something awful. For the first time, he wondered what, exactly, she was hiding. How anyone could top the burden of shame he carried around, day and night, he couldn't imagine. But something about the fear and courage that battled in her eyes told him Calista Sheffield just might have bigger secrets than he did.

Chapter Six

Calista's heart pounded in her chest. The look on his face was so grave, it sent her warning sirens blaring. Had he heard something about the horrible CEO of Vita-Wow, the one who made the secretaries cry? That was all in the past. She was a kinder, gentler person. The kind who would let everyone decorate their cubicles and chew gum and cook nasty frozen entrees in the micro-waves. Of course, she'd have to put all the microwaves back in the break rooms, but that was a small step.

"What exactly did Marisol tell you today? When I came back from the lobby, I heard something and I—"

Relieved laughter bubbled up and she cut him off midsentence. "Oh, Grant! That woman is priceless! Promise me you never, ever let her leave." She clutched her middle and struggled to catch her breath. "She's just the greatest. And the way she was fussing over your hair." Another wave of laughter rocked her. She was so thankful his question was about Marisol's silly advice that she wanted to turn a cartwheel.

He was grinning right along with her, although his blue eyes remained shadowed with curiosity. "She's a keeper. And I suppose I shouldn't have wondered, but what I heard was so strange…" He shrugged sheepishly.

Calista felt a tiny bit of irritation at the word "strange," but shoved it down inside. Of course she didn't have a chance with Grant. "I know, right? We were just talking about, I don't know, everything." She struggled to remember the entire conversation. "She told me how she got to Denver, about Gabriel, about how you and the former director tried to help her."

"She told you all of that?" His tone was a little sharp. For the first time Calista noticed a dimple in his chin that must only show up when he was frowning.

"I'm sorry, I didn't mean to bring up bad feelings for her. But she said that you'd saved her life and I asked her to tell me her story. If I shouldn't have done that, I apologize." She felt as if the sun had cooled a little and she rubbed her arms through her jacket.

"No, not at all. It's just that she doesn't usually share her story. It's very painful for her, even after all these years."

Calista nodded, remembering Marisol's tear-filled eyes. "She seems resigned to never seeing her son again. And then we were talking about whether it was better to be an orphan or to lose a child."

Grant made a sound of surprise, somewhere between a cough and an exclamation.

She felt heat creep up her neck and squinted out toward the snowy square. "I didn't ask her that. It just sort of came up." She darted a glance at him and was surprised to see his lips quirked up in a half smile.

"It's nice to hear. That she was talking, I mean. Marisol is a good supervisor, friend and grandmother type. But she doesn't open up to a lot of people."

Calista mulled that over. She decided to take it as a compliment. "I'm glad she felt safe with me. Anyway, we were talking about losing parents and—"

"Are your parents living?"

The question startled her, although it was a natural one. "My mother died when I was in high school, and my father and I don't really get along. Too much bitter history." She watched his eyebrows rise but didn't care. Better to have the truth out as soon as possible.

"I'm sorry for your loss. And does he have anything to do with the faith you mentioned, the one that puts the show before the truth?"

She was surprised he remembered her exact words. "Right. So, Marisol was saying you were like an orphan but your faith would see you through and I was feeling a little sad that I had spent so much time building a life that didn't have anything worthwhile in it, and she completely misunderstood my expression and thought I was upset that you were too busy for a girlfriend. And then you came in."

Calista hauled in a breath. She desperately wanted the conversation to veer back into something safe, like planning for the new roofing fund. But his blue eyes were locked on hers. The emotions that flickered over his face were unreadable.

The sudden sound of the door slamming open behind them interrupted whatever thought he had been forming.

A young couple with a small child waved as soon as they caught sight of Grant. They changed their trajectory across the snowy courtyard to meet Calista and the director. The girl had shoulder-length hair with a strip of bright pink on one side and her dark brown eyes were heavily rimmed with liner. She had dark circles under her eyes but walked quickly, holding the baby on one slim hip like a bag of flour. The little girl's curly brown hair bounced with every step her mother took. The young man's shoulders were hunched under his thick, oversize sweatshirt and the hood was pulled over his head. As they got closer, Calista noticed a large tattoo covered the area from his collarbone to his jaw.

"Hey, Aliya, Josh." Grant put out a hand to Josh but was pulled into a bear hug. Aliya grinned and stepped forward to give Grant a squeeze. The little girl reached out for Grant and he took her in his arms. Calista felt a tug around her heart at the ease of his gesture. She couldn't remember the last time she had held a child, let alone had a child reach for her like that.

"Miss McKenzie, you look happy today." The little girl beamed in response and said something that might or might not have been English. Grant looked to Aliya for help and the young mom shrugged, laughing.

"She talks like that all the time. We have no idea what she means, either."

"Calista, this is Aliya and Josh, and their daughter McKenzie." Grant made the introductions and Calista felt the couple's curious gazes. She smiled and held out a hand, which they both shook without comment.

"You guys come for breakfast? Or are you heading for the recreation rooms?"

"Naw. We're gonna go to a class. McKenzie will be in the day care for a few hours." Josh looked dangerous, but his voice was quiet, almost childlike.

"Which class? We've got a great list this month."

"The job-prep class. I think Miss Borne is teaching it. I like the way she gives lots of examples and we read articles from *Newsweek*." Aliya brushed back the pink shock of hair and said, "I don't want to work in fast food forever."

"Glad to hear you like her teaching style. Some people think she's mean." Just yesterday there was a middle-aged woman who had come directly to him to complain about the homework load. But if they were going to give credits for the classes, they had to keep track of the homework, he'd told her.

"Well, if you're dumb enough to give a presentation without doing your work, yeah, she can be pretty mean." Josh ducked his head, as if he knew exactly how that felt.

McKenzie let out a stream of syllables and poked her finger into Grant's ear. He winced, laughing. "All right, missy. Back to your mom before you stick that finger in my eye." He passed the chattering toddler back to Aliya and waved as the couple headed across the courtyard and to the door that led to the classrooms.

Calista watched them walk away, her mind turning on the young couple. "That's really encouraging."

"That they're taking classes?"

"I mean, they could just get on welfare, right?"

Grant was silent for a moment. He seemed to be considering his words carefully. "After a while, if you stick around, you'll realize that many of these people are very proud in their own way. Those two were street kids and are trying to work their way back from some serious mistakes. Josh doesn't look like much, but he's gentle and wants to provide for his kid."

Calista felt shame slice through her. She turned to face him, noting how the bright winter light brought out tiny gold flecks in his blue eyes. "I didn't mean…

I wasn't trying to say…" Her voice trailed off, wanting to defend herself but knowing he was right.

"I know. There are the ones like Duane who will take everything you offer without any gratitude, but he's not the norm." His eyes were troubled, almost sad. "Anyway, let's get started on this tour. I want to make sure you've got a good idea of where everything is in case we need you to volunteer in different sections."

Calista nodded and tried to cover her shame. "I'm ready." As he headed for the dormitories, she sneaked a glance in his direction. The strong shoulders, the slightly wavy black hair, even those startlingly blue eyes were nothing compared to what was inside. His dedication to the mission and his faith in the people shone like a beacon.

As they passed from room to room and into other buildings there were more introductions and more warm greetings for Grant. Calista had an eerie knack for remembering names and faces, and she absorbed the small details of the tour. But half an hour later, her heart was fuller than her mind. Every time she saw him shake a homeless man's hand, touch the shoulder of a teenage boy, kneel down to talk to a little child, the scene dropped into her heart like something warm and substantial. She could feel the weight of it pressing against her ribs, like a hug from the inside.

Calista exited the elevator at full speed and narrowly missed the building's snack cart. Mrs. Benjamin let out a yelp of warning but they were both saved only by Calista's last-second dodge to the left.

"I'm so sorry, Miss Sheffield," the older woman said while picking up the snack-size potato-chip bags that had been jolted off their hooks when the cart stopped on a dime.

A surge of irritation flared in her chest. She didn't have time to be dodging old ladies pushing food carts today. *Love is patient, love is kind.* The verse came out of nowhere and all the words she wanted to say, about not standing in front of the elevator, of moving more quickly, died in her throat.

"It's my fault. I shouldn't have been running out of the door like that." Calista bent down and retrieved one small bag from under the cart's front wheels. "This one looks a little squashed. Let me buy it." She dug in her shoulder bag for a dollar and deposited it on the tray. "Have a good day."

Now the proud owner of a seriously smashed pile of chips in a cellophane bag, Calista continued toward the glossy black desk that designated the waiting area for the top floor of VitaWow. Renee sat motionless, her almond-shaped eyes fixed on Calista. Her shiny, flame-colored bob was lacquered in place and accentuated her sharp cheekbones. Calista had hired Renee for her speed and professionalism, but the woman would have looked at home in the biggest corporations in the country. She was beautiful, educated and had just the right mix of charm and aloofness.

"Morning, Renee." She didn't usually interact much with Renee, since Jackie was her go-to girl, the ultimate personal assistant. But maybe it was time to start reaching out. She stopped in front of the desk and admired an arrangement of exotic flowers. The deep red blooms were striking against the shiny black desk and the scent was strong and sweet. "These are pretty. Did you order them?"

Renee slowly nodded, her eyes still fixed on Calista. "Yes, I order the flowers for the main desk downstairs, the departmental secretaries and your reception area every week."

"Oh." Calista felt her cheeks grow warm. It was not as if that was something she should have known. Deciding who ordered the flowers was not her job. But still she felt a niggle of embarrassment. She'd never even noticed any flowers before. She usually flew right past the desk while yelling instructions. Well, she might slow down just a mite to snag her phone messages out of Renee's outstretched hand. She cleared her throat. "Any messages?"

Renee held several small pink slips of paper and Calista took them, grateful to have something to distract herself. "Thank you," she called on her way into her office.

The reception area of the top floor was empty but the hallways were bustling with employees. Calista stood for a moment, watching the movement of the staff. She felt her brows draw down. Long aisles were bound on each side with half-walled cubicles, but most of the staff seemed to be walking around. Walking wasn't really the word. They seemed almost frantic. In fact, she was sure that one man had just entered and left the same cube twice in one minute.

"What's wrong?" Jackie's voice cut into her thoughts and she turned to see her personal assistant wandering toward her, a stack of collated brochures in her arms. Her hair was brushed back from her face but fell in small ringlets to her shoulders. As she came nearer, Calista saw dark circles under her deep brown eyes. Competent, capable Jackie. Of course, she had her own life, probably filled to the brim with friends and family but Calista couldn't name a single one.

"Nothing." She turned back to the hustling crowd. "It just seems like everyone's on red alert. What's with the running around? See, that guy there with the green striped tie, I swear he just went to check the fax machine for the third time."

A snort of laughter came from behind her and Jackie shook her head, curls bouncing every which way. "Are you serious? Of *course* they're all on red alert. The boss is standing there with a face like thunder and they want to look busy."

Calista whirled to face her. "I'm not some whip-cracking taskmaster. Plus, I come through here all the time."

A single, well-groomed eyebrow lifted in response. "All the time?"

She felt her face grow warm. "At least once a day. Just to hang out."

Now both eyebrows had gone up. "Just…to hang out." Jackie could really pack a lot of meaning into four little words.

Calista frowned furiously and went back to studying the wide-open office space. Could the twenty-five employees who worked on the top floor of VitaWow really have that much dislike for their boss? She tried to think of the other departments. She'd always been warmly welcomed when she visited the lower six levels. Of course, there was usually a reason she was there. A meeting or an announcement. Or to find out who had dropped the ball on some project. Now that she thought of it, those warm welcomes were just a bit tense.

"Okay, not to hang out. To survey my domain.

Happy?" Bitterness crept into her voice. "But that's my job, isn't it? Not to make friends with everybody."

"Right." She could see Jackie nodding out of the corner of her eye. "But it wouldn't hurt to make friends with, say…one or two."

And there it was, out for all to hear. She had no friends. She felt her heart sink in her chest.

"Are you going out for dinner after work?" Jackie sounded contrite and rushed to change the subject. "You sure look nice."

Calista crossed her arms over her light blue linen dress. After the mission she'd made a special effort to choose something that wasn't a slacks-and-jacket set. Now she felt plain silly.

"No, not going to dinner. I just felt like wearing something pretty." She'd had enough of surveying. Time to let the employees relax. She turned back toward her office and Jackie followed beside her.

"So, how was the dentist?" Again that sly note in her voice spoke volumes.

"It wasn't the dentist, as you know. Come in and I'll tell you all about it." Calista led the way into her office and closed the door behind them. She crossed to the small coffeepot in the corner and dumped in some French vanilla. But decaf, since she'd had enough excitement this morning, thank you.

The bright light streamed through the floor-to-ceiling windows and she began to pull the shades on the four windows that flanked her desk. Calista liked her corner office for the stunning 180-degree views of the Colorado Rockies, but directly below the mountain range and too close to ignore there was the mass of air-conditioning units on the building next door. Plus, afternoon sun could really heat up the room and when she used the pull-down shades, the whole room took on a sepia tinge. But all of that would change when they built the new VitaWow headquarters. State-of-the-art glass would adjust to the direct light. The plans had been revised about ten times, but her top-floor corner office was set in stone. Or so the architects had said.

She pulled the last long acrylic shade down over the view, blocking out the sun and the ugly sight of the AC units. By this time next year, her view would be about twenty floors higher up and duct-free. They hadn't picked a location, but the board was fielding offers and counteroffers. Within months, she would be helping break ground on a brand-new building. The thought filled her with satisfaction. She'd grown this company from the very beginning so it was sort of like expecting a baby. A twenty-story, smoked-glass-and-steel baby.

"So, spill it." Jackie perched on the edge of a leather plum-colored armchair and gave her best "I'm listening" look.

Calista plopped into her chair and planted her hands on the top of her mahogany desk. "I'm volunteering at the Downtown Denver Mission. Probably once a week, maybe more if they decide they need me to help them with fund-raising."

There was a beat of silence that became two, then three. Jackie blinked and cleared her throat. "And why would the CEO of this fine company be volunteering at a homeless shelter?"

"Because I woke up one morning and realized I was a terrible human being."

"Just like that?"

Calista sighed. "No, not quite. And it would have been nice if you'd argued just a little with that statement."

Jackie had the heart to look sheepish. "You're not a terrible human being. You're just not very approachable. Or sympathetic. Or caring about anybody's personal life. Or—"

"All right! I got it." Calista stood up and paced back and forth in front of the shaded windows. The watery, muted sunlight made the room look especially monochromatic.

"But I think you could be helpful there."

She turned, hope making her voice rise. "You think so?"

"Definitely. Especially the fund-raising. They can give you the figures and you can whip up some marketing scheme. You probably won't even have to go into the shelter after the first day."

Calista felt her insides tighten with anxiety. Jackie didn't think she could do anything other than make some money. "See, I don't want to just fax over papers or visit with the board. I want to do something real." That sounded ridiculous. They both understood that money was as real as it got.

Jackie looked at her hard for a moment. "You mean, you want to make a difference in someone's life." Her voice had a cautious tone.

"Exactly."

"Don't you think spending time at a homeless shelter is a bit…ambitious? You could always mentor some business majors or even build some relationships here at the company. I'm sure they would appreciate your mentoring a few pegs down on the totem pole."

"You know, that's a great idea." Calista stopped pacing for a moment and put a finger on her lips. "I'll bring that up to Human Resources and see what they say. But I'm still going to volunteer. This morning I took a tour and met most of the staff."

Jackie seemed like she was still struggling to grasp the concept of her boss spending time out of the office, with people who weren't rich or powerful.

"The director is very inspiring, too." Calista left this last comment hanging in the air as she fiddled with the large leaves of the potted banana tree near the window. She tried to make her voice light, but every time she thought of Grant, her stomach did a little jump.

"Inspiring how? The shave-your-head-wear-a-sheet-give-all-your-money kind of inspiring?"

Calista snorted. "Not quite." But she had to admit, it was pretty close. And that was a scary thought. Because if there was one thing Calista Sheffield did not do, it was play "follow the leader." She stared out at the snowy peaks of the Rocky Mountains, letting Jackie's light conversation wind around her. There was nothing else to do except make sure her focus stayed on the mission and not on the director. That gorgeous smile could turn anybody's head but he didn't need another groupie. He needed someone who could raise some cash. And that was what she was going to do.

Chapter Seven

"Hello, *mijo*," Marisol said, loading a giant aluminum pot into one of the three commercial-grade dishwashers. Grant reached over the petite woman and positioned the pot. The steam from the last batch of dishes snaked out of the metal machine in tiny wisps. He slid the door closed and flipped the switch, careful to avoid the hot metal of the utensils in a small green basket she had just removed.

"Looks like you have experience. You want to be the new dishwasher?" Marisol's teasing tone helped the knot ease at the back of Grant's neck.

"Anytime. At least this doesn't include any long meetings."

Marisol laughed, a light, carefree sound that seemed to belong to a much younger person. "No, *gracias a Dios*, no meetings." Tucking one dark brown hand into the pocket of her apron, she waited for him to speak. He rarely came into the kitchen unless he had a purpose there.

He cleared his throat, looking for the right words. He'd heard Calista's version, now he wanted to hear what Marisol had to say.

"Why did you tell Calista I was busy, but she had a chance with me if she showed her feelings?" He didn't know if he was asking out of insanity or sheer curiosity. Part of him wanted her to give a perfectly normal explanation and another part—the part that had him thinking about Calista nonstop since the moment he'd seen her—wanted Marisol to tell him Calista cared for him.

"She said you were perfect. I was just making her feel better because she look so sad." Marisol shrugged, as if that statement hadn't knocked Grant's world for a loop.

He felt his eyes go wide. "She said those words, those exact words?"

Marisol beamed again. "She did. I knew you would like that."

"No, Mari, I'm not perfect. You know I'm not. I'm so far from it that I should come with a warning sign. I get wrapped up in my work, I care way too much, I have a temper." He ticked off his faults in rapid-fire, while holding up one finger at a time.

To his surprise, Marisol laughed, the sound mingling with the clanks and clatter of the busy kitchen. "*I* know that, *you* know that, but *she* doesn't know that."

"And lying to her is okay with you?" He couldn't stop the bitter note of accusation that accompanied his words.

She sighed and reached out a hand to touch his arm. "*Mijo*, I would not lie to the girl. And she is not one to believe a lie. But when the heart first loves, it only sees perfection. With time, the love remains but the heart knows the truth—no one is perfect. Only God. That is what I mean." Her brown eyes were wide with earnestness. "So, when she says you are perfect, and those were her words, it made me happy. That is always how it is in the beginning."

Grant wanted to tell her that she had no right to discuss his personal life, especially with a woman he barely knew. He wanted to be angry that she could laugh about Calista thinking he was perfect, when he was so far from it. But he couldn't. A strange sensation had crept over him while she spoke. It was a mix of yearning and dread, of excitement and fear. He felt as if he were standing on the edge of a cliff.

"Let's not get ahead of ourselves." He worked to get his voice under control. "A lot of people throw that word around."

Marisol nodded in a way that didn't fool him in the least. Her eyes were still bright as she turned to accept another large pot coming from a worker. "You are right. We cannot jump ahead. Let us go one step at a time."

Which made his stomach drop again, as if he really had just jumped off a cliff. Because the next step was going to be seeing more of Calista. Maybe he should ask Lana to assign her some scheduled hours when he was sure to be out of the building. If they never saw each other, then their friendship would never turn into something else. And she would never know he was anything less than perfect, which might be what he really wanted, a small voice reminded him. He heaved a sigh and resigned himself to the fact that he had to trust God. He knew what He was doing. Even if it looked like He was trying to throw Grant off a cliff.

Jackie poked at her iPad, tapping and scrolling through screens. Another crazy Tuesday morning. But Calista didn't mind because she had tomorrow morning at the mission, which was absolutely the best part of her week. "I'm assuming you're not attending this year's Christmas party," Jackie said, not bothering to glance away from her glowing screen.

"Actually, I think I will."

If Jackie had been the excitable type, she would have bolted from her perch on the armchair and let out a screech. But all she did was raise both eyebrows and let her mouth fall open a little in surprise.

"And stay for a while." Calista dropped the words into the space between them as casually as if she had been present for every single VitaWow party for the past five years. Which she hadn't. Well, not really. She would show up for fifteen minutes, shake some hands, watch the party fizzle out to almost nothing, then make her exit. Last year, she swore she could hear sighs of relief on her way out. She was the original wet blanket.

"Is it because it's being held at the Grant-Humphreys Mansion? You said you didn't really care, so I thought it was time to make a change from the Ritz."

"Now you're making me feel unwelcome."

"No, I think it's a great idea." Jackie nibbled a nail, still focusing on her boss. "Are you bringing a date?"

She pasted a noncommittal look on her face and shrugged. "I'm sure someone will pop up."

"Right." And with that, her assistant dropped her gaze to her lap and continued jotting notes.

Calista swiveled in her office chair and gazed at the scenery outside. Little fluffs of white snow were falling lazily from the sky and the peaks in the distance were almost obscured by the low, heavy clouds. Was it possible that she could combine work and play? Just once? If she brought Grant to the party, he could really make some contacts. Enough with the fifty-dollar-a-month donations from old ladies down the block. The man needed to find some serious donors. The guest list had some very influential business owners, and she could certainly pull in a few more. A very small part of her insisted that she wasn't being completely honest. *To thine own self be true.* She sighed and admitted that, just for a moment, it would be nice to go to a party and have a good time. Maybe dress up and dance a little.

The corners of her mouth tugged up. She would ask him today. Her stomach gave a shiver of nerves but she straightened her shoulders. She was done investing time and effort into projects that didn't make her happy. The mission made her feel useful, and she'd made friends there. And Grant… She didn't quite know if the feeling she got around him could be contained in that one word, but happy was definitely part of it.

Grant stared at his desk calendar and counted back the days. Almost Thanksgiving already. It had been three weeks since Calista Sheffield had walked into the mission. She was coming more than once a week now. Even though she spent a lot of time in the filing room at the end of the hall, there was a standing need in the nursery on Friday evenings, when the women's Bible study was held in one of the classrooms. Thursday evening was the grant-writing team meeting and they worked side by side perfecting the applications. And Saturday morning was Marisol's cooking class and Calista had been thrilled to find out there was still a place for one more.

At first, he tried to ignore her. Impossible. He found himself staring into those bottomless green eyes, just seconds after he had decided to ignore her, again. The days when she wore her hair soft and loose, he swore he could smell the delicate scent of her shampoo when she passed his door.

Avoiding her worked a bit better, except that he never saw Marisol when Calista was around because the two had become fast friends. And he could never quite seem to forget she was here, in the building, somewhere close by.

So, finally he decided he would treat the situation like a twelve-step program. *The first step is to admit you are powerless.* He couldn't control his emotions when she was around. It was useless to try. He would just turn it all over to God.

Of course, that didn't mean he was luring her into his office for another near-miss kiss. It just meant he couldn't fight what he was feeling. It was a huge relief. Now all he had to do was battle the insane impulse to follow her around, just to be in her presence.

And he wasn't going to let himself go there, because she was going to leave. Maybe not today, maybe not after Thanksgiving, but for sure when the Christmas tinsel came down and reality set in. If the mission could stay open that long. He might not even have to worry about Calista leaving if he didn't get some big donations real soon.

What if they had met at some sort of business function, not as director and volunteer? Would they have had a chance? There was that edge-of-the-cliff feeling again. He grimaced and tried to calm his breathing. But nothing would be able to get past the fact that she believed in the power of the almighty buck and he didn't.

He didn't think he could be with someone who spent all their time making money.

He rubbed a spot in the middle of his chest, a dull ache. Was it stress or something else? He chuckled at the question and then a knock on the door made him nearly jump out of his skin.

Lana rolled her chair toward his desk, an envelope in one hand.

"This came in the mail today and I wanted you to see it before the board does," she said, her blue eyes narrowing with anxiety.

Grant frowned and took the plain manila envelope. The paper inside was folded in thirds and as he spread it against his desk, the first thing he noticed was the crude handwriting. The next was the message scrawled in black ink.

I know who you are, Grant Monohan.

Under that was a line that made the hair on the back of his neck prickle.

Time to make Daddy's little boy pay.

Lana waited, watching Grant with worry etched in every line of her face.

"I guess it's time, then," he said. "This is the fourth one this month and now there's a threat attached."

She nodded and reached for the paper. "It was bound to come out sooner or later." She folded the paper back into its envelope. "There's nothing for you to be ashamed of, you know."

He rubbed a hand over his face, feeling the stubble

that appeared right around this time of day. "I know, but it doesn't make it any easier. People will come to their own conclusions, no matter how I spin it."

"Then let God handle it, no spin required." Lana was unshakable in her faith and Grant loved that. He felt as if he was holding on to his by a thread most of the time. No, he had plenty of faith, but the doubts were constant reminders of how far he had to go.

"Right. Will you help me craft the statement? I'll give this to the board tonight. We can set up a media announcement for Friday morning. Then we have to turn it over to the police." Standard procedure when there was a threat of any kind. And a big place like this attracted a lot of crazy stuff. Good thing their financial statement was up to speed. Last year's audit was ready if the press started slinging mud.

Lana ran a hand through her short gray-purple hair. He felt himself relax at the sight of the familiar gesture. The secretary had been a good friend these past years, like a steady rock in the storm. "The day after Thanksgiving? Well, that will be a way to avoid Black Friday sales, for sure. I'll get right on it. Short and sweet?"

"Probably better that way, don't you think? It's going to cause enough publicity as it is." His stomach twisted at the thought of making a public statement about his personal life, the past he'd been hiding. No, not hiding but avoiding.

"Grant, you know we all love you." She fixed him with a steady gaze and Grant felt affection for her well up inside, his anxiety replaced with gratitude. His throat closed a bit and he said huskily, "I know, Lana, and I won't forget it."

She smiled a little sadly and swiveled the chair toward the door. She turned back for a moment and said, "You're used to expecting the worst out of the world. You just might be surprised about how this all turns out."

Grant nodded and she wheeled out the door, strong arms propelling the metal chair across the threshold. He stared for a moment at the space she'd left behind. Maybe she was right, but years of seeing the worst in humanity had trained him to prepare for disaster.

When he announced to the world that he was the only child of the wealthiest businessman in the state, his life would never be the same. He gazed around the small, plain office and shuddered at the thought of paparazzi camped out in the lobby, harassing the homeless people. The preschoolers would be frightened and confused by the camera crews. The everyday folks who came here for addiction counseling and spiritual support would feel too intimidated by the cameras to get near the door. He dropped his head in his hands and tried to slow his breathing. Maybe it would be best for everybody if he resigned. Maybe he could continue to work in some other capacity, like board members did.

But the thought of leaving the only place he had ever felt at home made him sick to his stomach. The father who had abandoned him to an alcoholic mother, who'd never sent a penny in support, who'd jetted around the world while his own kid had dug in Dumpsters for food, was not going to run Grant's life.

Grant straightened up and took a deep breath. *Lord, You've been with me every step of the way. Help me to remember You're the only father who matters. Wherever You want me to go, I'll go.* He closed his eyes and waited in silence, feeling as if words had failed him but knowing God read what was unfinished in his heart.

The file room at the Downtown Denver Mission was a little gray box with scratchy carpet and a window too high to let in much light. After twenty minutes that first day, Calista started to sympathize with the VitaWow employees who worked in the basement. She would never again complain about the fact that her office got a blinding dose of afternoon sun. As soon as she'd returned to her office, she'd authorized some very nice coffeemakers and a new set of leather couches to give their break room some extra perks. For the past three weeks, she'd also thrown in movie tickets for every basement-level employee, to sweeten the deal.

But no matter how nice VitaWow's basement was now, this little file room was still a claustrophobia-inducing box. She'd never liked small spaces, especially after the house fire. Her mind flashed on the old wooden porch, blackened and listing to one side. Before she could stop it, images flickered of the living-room floor burned through, the basement where the fire broke out, where her mother had been doing laundry. Finally, where her mother had been trapped when the old wooden steps into the low-ceilinged basement had collapsed.

Calista took a breath and closed her eyes. *Lord, I trust in You.* That was all she could pray when the images began to flash before her, especially in the middle of the night. There was no way she could try to explain why her mama had to die like that. She was a gracious and kind woman, who brought dinner to sick folk and took in stray dogs. How could it ever be made right?

But her faith told her to trust that it would be made clear someday. Right now, all she could do was trust.

Eric knocked and opened Grant's office door at the same time. He stood there looking exceptionally grouchy. His best friend's bright red hair stuck up in tufts like it always did when he'd been clutching his head. It would have been funny except for the frosty glare underneath.

"Hey, what's up?" Grant waved him toward a seat and grabbed two sodas from the mini fridge. Maybe a cold drink would buy him some mercy. He was pretty certain he knew what prompted Eric's visit.

"So, you dumped Jennie and now you won't even talk to her?" He didn't make a move to sit down or take the soda.

Grant winced. "Happy Thanksgiving to you, too. I told you that she wanted—we both wanted—to be friends."

"She just paid me a visit to complain that you weren't answering her phone calls."

"I'm not."

Eric's frown intensified. "Well, must be a story there because you're not usually the type to freeze someone out. Spill it." He plopped his lean runner's body into a chair.

"Well, she said I was too religious, decided we should be friends. Then she called here, saying she was my girlfriend. I think she knows there's something more to be gained by dating a poverty-stricken shelter director after all."

Eric sighed. "Wow. So you think she knows about

your father? She seemed so wounded this morning, she was almost crying."

Grant almost snorted soda up his nose as he thought of how many tears would be shed when he made that announcement. "I have no doubt she was." He straightened his shoulders and rolled his neck, trying to ease some of the stress in his muscles. "I'm holding a press conference tomorrow."

Eric's eyebrows shot up. "Time to get it out in the open?"

"I suppose so. There was another threatening letter today…" His voice trailed off as he remembered the awkward scrawl.

Eric shook his head, staring into his can. "I'm sorry. What a mess. And to think I've always envied you."

Grant looked up in surprise. "Me?" He was speechless for a few seconds as he processed that information. "Because I'm the heir to a fortune made by barely legal activities? Because my father just recently decided that I exist and he wants me to pretend we're best buds? Now, you, you have more talent than anyone I know, a beautiful wife who loves you, a baby on the way and an extended family that makes the mob look disloyal."

He nodded. "Thanks, and she does and they do. But I always thought you had it better because of… Well, everybody loves you on sight. You never have to work to make friends. If you had five minutes alone with him, you could get the Grinch to give this place a donation."

Eric continued. "I had to work for every date. I'm still shocked that Marla even gave me a second glance. But you just smile, and women fall all over themselves."

Grant knew where this was going and got a sinking feeling in his stomach.

"But now, you're way worse off than I ever was. After you tell the world that you're Kurt Daniels's son, it'll be like you've got the relationship version of the Midas touch. Every girl you meet is going to want to date you and you'll never know for sure if they really care. That just stinks."

He couldn't help laughing. It was all so awful, and so painfully true, that it was more than a little funny. "You've nailed it, as usual."

Eric shook his head and took a sip. "I guess I can stop trying to fix you up."

Grant nodded, chuckling. "That would be a welcome change. I don't think it's a good time to be dating any-body right now."

Another knock at the door, and Jose poked his head in. "Michelle wanted to know if the new chick could help her in the day care."

Grant sighed. "Her name is not 'the new chick.'" Maybe it was time for some sensitivity training. The mission was a safe zone, for all people.

"Okay, the new girl. Is she stashed back here some-where?" Jose jerked his head toward the offices.

"Yeah, she's in the filing room, but let me get her." Grant stood up and took a slug from his cold soda. It felt as though he was getting ready to face some un-known danger, the way his heart started pounding. He could feel his body temperature rise about ten degrees.

"I want you to meet our new volunteer. She's been helping with fund-raising. And no smart comments, got it?" He ignored Eric's expression of open curiosity.

His oldest friend flashed him a grin. "Scout's honor."

They headed out the door and Eric paused, his head cocked to one side.

"This is new, this picture here."

Grant nodded. "Calista thought I should make my office more personable."

Eric raised his eyebrows. "I take it that's the new girl. And this was your solution?"

"I think it's perfect." He regarded the crayon drawing of a fluffy cat wearing pink sunglasses. Savannah was an excellent little artist.

"Better than one of those awful head shots with the fake trees in the background. Plus, the kitty is way better looking than you are."

Responding to the gibe with a good-natured punch to Eric's arm, Grant headed out the door. Halfway down the hallway he had misgivings. Introducing Calista to Eric wasn't something he should do. He should keep her separate from his personal friendships. She wouldn't be just a volunteer anymore if she made friends with Eric. And if he wasn't wrong, that was exactly what was going to happen.

Calista wondered if Grant was still at the mission. She hadn't seen him at all today. Not much at all last week, in fact. But he'd been downright friendly on Saturday, helping Marisol with her kitchen class. The man could definitely cook. One more point in his favor, as if he needed any more.

It must be the Thanksgiving spirit. She almost wished he'd go back to staying out of her way. She'd wondered about him all day if she didn't force herself to concentrate on something else. Which was staying on task and having a purpose. And it was going very well, so far. She opened her eyes and decided she'd been sitting for too long in one spot, plunking folders in color-coded file boxes. Reaching high above her head, she laced her fingers together and felt the pleasant strain on her muscles. Her light blue linen jacket had wrinkled at the elbows and the matching pants were looking a little worse for wear. Calista leaned over, arms outstretched, eyes closed and a blissful feeling spreading through her body. Until she smacked into a pile of folders she had just placed on the edge of the desk and several slipped out of sight into the crack against the wall.

Very smooth. She heaved a sigh and glanced around. The metal desk was about five feet long and weighed a ton. Beyond old-school, this thing must have been around when the mission was founded. Calista tried to tug an edge, but realized all her other carefully sorted piles would have to be moved before the desk budged an inch. Nothing to do but crawl underneath. She wasn't a big girl by any means, but it took a bit of maneuvering to get her body wedged into the small space between the built-in drawers.

As Calista pried the stiff manila folder from the crack, there was a light tapping on the half-open door. She froze, hoping against hope it was Marisol. Or Jose. Or even Lissa.

There was no way to see who it was without backing out, so she did an awkward reverse crawl that seemed to have a lot more wiggling involved than it did on the way in. She refused to imagine what she must look like from the door, but all the same, her cheeks were scorching by the time she got turned all the way around.

Of course it was Grant. His face was a mixture of surprise and something that might have been barely concealed laughter. Oh, that gorgeous smile... And he'd brought a friend, who seemed to find the whole thing very interesting.

Calista popped to her feet and brushed off the knees of her pants.

"Sorry. Some files fell behind the desk." She brushed the hair back from her face and wished she had an excuse to turn her back until her face lost what must be a lovely shade of pink.

"Calista Sheffield, this is my friend, Eric Young. He works over at MusiComp as a composer." Grant's voice was steady but his eyes were crinkled as if he were still laughing inside.

Calista forced herself to look away, hoping her face didn't betray anything of the warm glow that flared inside. She dragged her gaze from Grant's and reached out a hand to Eric, surprised at the genuine warmth in his grip. "Nice to meet you. Do you volunteer here, as well?"

Eric snorted. "Are you kidding? I can't stand listening to Grant boss everybody around."

She felt her mouth drop open a little. Grant didn't really boss anybody, ever. He had a quiet kind of authority that most people responded to without argument.

Grant rushed in to fill the awkward pause. "You'll have to excuse him. He's hardly ever serious."

"True," he said, grinning. "My wife takes about a tenth of what I say at face value."

"But how does she know when you're serious?"

Eric laughed outright. "Practice."

Calista shook her head, bemused. She couldn't imagine a relationship with that much teasing and goofing around. It sounded like fun. His laughter sparked an idea in her, an image of Grant, relaxed and grinning.

How would it be to spend time with him, just getting to know what was behind the quick smile and the sad eyes?

"Do you work here in the city? I think Grant said you were helping him with fund-raising."

"I'm the CEO of VitaWow." Calista felt her face warm just a little. It was nothing to be ashamed of, but she was pretty sure it was the first time she had said the words in front of Grant. She sidled a glance at him and his expression was inscrutable.

"The vitamin-water company? That stuff's great." Eric nodded his head. "And it's encouraging to see new volunteers around this place. Will you be here for Thanksgiving? You can meet my wife, Marla."

"Wouldn't miss it for the world." And she meant it. For the first time in years she actually had someplace to go.

Eric seemed to weigh her words, a gentleness in his eyes. "Excellent. It's a total madhouse. We always need the extra hands. Will you be here for Christmas, too?"

The innocent question threw Calista for a moment. Of course she was staying for Christmas. And the next. And the next, if she had her way.

She finally opened her mouth to respond but Grant spoke first, his tone brisk, almost cold. "Let's not plan too far ahead."

Eric blinked, then shrugged.

Right, the mission was way behind on funds. Maybe it was still touch and go. But she had a plan and she was going to put it in motion just as soon as she got the chance. "Well, I better get back to work. Lana wants this last pile cleared up before the new office recruit comes in tomorrow."

See, easy peasy. Calista felt satisfaction with her

businesslike attitude. That was always something she could fall back on, professional distance. And with Grant, any distance was a good thing.

Grant suppressed an urge to slap his forehead as he remembered why they'd come down there in the first place. "Actually, I was wondering if you could go help Michelle in the day care. She's short staffed this morning and they finger paint on Wednesdays."

He glanced at her light blue linen jacket and the cream silk blouse underneath and hoped they had enough aprons. Then he jerked his gaze away as he realized she might not understand his concern. His face went hot.

"I'd be glad to," she said, eyes widening with surprise, sounding genuinely happy about being given finger-painting duty.

"Don't worry about the files. We'll get to them later today. You've really cut down the stacks in the past few weeks."

She flashed him a bright smile and gave another quick dusting to the knees of her pants. "I'll head right over. Nice to meet you, Eric."

They both moved out of the doorway as she slipped by and headed down the hallway. A light fragrance followed her and he resisted the urge to take a deep breath. The view from the back brought the sudden image of her wiggling back out from under that desk. He ran a finger under his collar and frowned. "They must have the heat on high in this room."

Eric let out a laugh. "No, buddy, it's just you. Not that I'm blaming you, you understand."

Grant glared at his oldest friend and refused to take

the bait. "Whatever. And what was that about staying for Christmas?"

Eric threw up his hands, as if to ward off Grant's unhappiness. "A perfectly reasonable question! And don't worry. She's not going anywhere. She's so into you."

He had turned back toward his office but he swiveled to face Eric. "Why do you say that?"

A huge sigh escaped Eric's lips as he shook his head. "Are you saying you just can't tell, or are you saying you're not sure if she's sincere?"

Grant blinked. "Well, if she did feel something for me, then I think she's sincere. She seems that type. Honest, straightforward, doesn't play games."

"I agree. And to answer the first question for you, I say there's a whole lot of something going on there. I don't think she was blushing for me."

Grant continued down the hallway, letting Eric carry the conversation alone. He held open the door to his office and was glad of the momentary pause to collect his thoughts. He wanted to lean his head out the little office window and shout to the world that Calista— sharp, clever, sweet Calista—felt something for *him*. It was almost unbelievable. What did she even see in him? His whole life was wrapped up in the mission, in these people who were struggling just to survive.

But then he thought of the one thing they could never conquer, and slumped against the desk, legs outstretched. *You can't live your life for making money and be able to let it go at the same time.* And working at the mission was all about letting it go.

"Is she Christian?" Eric settled back in his chair and Grant snapped back to the moment. He'd asked the one question that made Grant want to give him a high five.

That was why he was a good friend, a best friend. He knew where the bottom line was in Grant's life.

He leaned against his desk, smiling. "Yes, but she's sort of making her way back from a rough childhood."

"That can be awkward, if one of you is farther along on your faith journey." Eric's tone was cautionary. He had been in love before he met Marla. And the woman just never could make up her mind. In the end, he broke his own heart rather than marry a girl who didn't even believe in God. It was a horrible time and Grant remembered the sadness that shadowed Eric's eyes.

Grant nodded. "I know. But..." He stared at his shoes for a moment, frowning. "There's something about her, the way she makes friends. She listens to the old people and the kids. And Marisol." He rubbed a hand over his face. "I can't explain it. She seems to have this *joy* about her." He shook his head, frustrated with his inability to nail it down, whatever it was.

"Whatever it is, don't worry so much. God's will comes first. Everything and everybody else falls in line. Or not." Eric's expression hardened, probably thinking back on his own wasted attempt to convince God that he knew better. "And if she's on the same page, then there's nothing to worry about. She'll be searching for His will, too."

Grant hesitated, contemplating the strange new idea that there was more to his future than leading this mission. He felt at home here herding kids, counseling parents and raising funds. But God knew his needs, knew his heart inside and out.

He rubbed his jaw and voiced his doubts. "I don't want it to take away from my work here, to be a distraction."

"I know. That's why you're great at what you do. You really care about keeping your commitment to these people. But remember that verse in John, the one that says Jesus came so that we might have life and live it more abundantly? If it's right, you won't be carving out a piece from a pie, diverting your attention away from this place. Your life will be more abundant because of her."

Grant nodded, feeling the tension in his neck ease at the reassurance. Eric was an excellent sounding board. For years, he'd been bouncing doubts off his red-haired friend.

"You're a good man, you know that, right?"

"Yup. But ten years from now, when your house is overrun with little kids, just remember I had nothing to do with it," Eric said, his voice full of laughter.

Chapter Eight

"**D**o you have any experience with children?" Michelle shot Calista a dubious look as they set out the pots of finger paints. Lissa and two helpers were leading the preschoolers in a rousing game of "duck, duck, goose" while the craft tables were readied for the onslaught of small artists. A CD of Christmas music played softly on a stereo. Nobody seemed to mind that they'd started the season just shy of Thanksgiving.

"Um, well…" Calista didn't quite know how to answer the question. She had done a little babysitting in high school. It wasn't exactly rocket science. "A little."

"I guess I'm trying to ask whether you know what you're getting into here." Michelle stood up and put her hands on her hips, eyeing Calista as if she was applying for a position at the FDIC.

She nodded, lining up small tubs of primary colors next to large sheets of glossy white paper. "Kids don't bother me. I know they can be noisy, have snotty noses, cry a lot. But I'm made of tougher stuff than you might think." She looked up at Michelle and flashed a bright smile, but only got silence in return. "How hard can it be to keep a bunch of little kids occupied for a few hours?"

Michelle let out what sounded suspiciously like a laugh disguised at the last minute as a cough. "Exactly. How hard can it be?"

Calista went back to setting out finger-paint pots and paper, trying to squelch the fear that was rising in her chest. She had nerves of steel. She brokered deals with huge corporations, oversaw hundreds of employees. A group of preschoolers wasn't going to be a problem. Was it?

Grant stood in the open classroom door and fought to keep his expression neutral. Michelle was holding her own at a long table of squirming children dripping with paint. Most of the color was getting onto the paper and the rest was dabbed on the oversize smocks the kids were wearing. Michelle's helper looked like a Ping-Pong player, balancing on the balls of her feet as she waited for the next semiemergency and her chance to swoop in for the save.

Lissa's table was about the same, maybe a little noisier with mostly little boys. They bounced in their chairs like jumping beans, constantly in motion. There was one small child who had smeared paint in his hair and all the way up both arms, but Lissa didn't bother to wipe him clean. As soon as the paint was put away they would have to hose him down.

But the next table was a disaster. Calista was lost. As thoroughly lost as if God had plunked her down in the Gobi Desert without any water. And she didn't even seem to know it.

She met his eyes and smiled hugely, blue paint

smeared over one cheek, waving to him with a hand covered in green paint. He raised a hand in greeting, wishing he could take a picture, just for posterity. Her face was pure joy, as if she had waited her whole life to finger paint with a group of four-year-olds. The dark-haired teenage girl at the end of the table was shooting exasperated glances at Calista and the rowdy bunch of children as they splattered paint on each other and the table. She urged them to stay seated, reminding the worst offenders that they were going to have to wash the table if they didn't behave. At any one time, half of the children were out of their seats, borrowing more paint or wiping their hands on their neighbor's smock, or even their neighbor's hair.

Grant stared as Calista carefully removed a little boy's sock and painted his bare foot a bright green. The blond-haired toddler shrieked with laughter as she worked, then he stood up unsteadily, still grinning. Calista slid a piece of paper under his foot and he pressed his foot onto the paper. As he proudly showed off his work, most of Calista's crew started to take off their shoes and socks, ready to follow suit. The assistant waved her arms in the air, eyes wide at this alarming development.

He figured he better lend a hand and strode toward the group. Savannah stood up from Calista's table and waved energetically. "Mr. Monohan! I made another picture for your office and it has a kitty."

He caught Calista's look, her eyes bright with surprise.

"Beautiful, Savannah," he responded enthusiastically. The little girl held up her new masterpiece, the paint glistening wetly. A blue cat with red sunglasses stared back at him. Of course it was a kitty. Savannah swore she was going to have her own someday, when she was in a real home.

"Isn't she talented? Aren't they so creative? Look at this one!" Calista pointed out a little boy's rocket ship. And there were Christmas trees and orange lions and lots of turkeys and all manner of blobs and squiggles. The chatter was deafening but he hardly noticed as he patted shoulders and complimented the artwork. Calista's happiness was infectious. He wanted to sit down and join their table, take off his shoe and paint the bottom of his foot. But that's not what you did when you were trying to keep kids under control. You had to keep a kind but stern demeanor. Calista looked like she followed an "if you can't beat 'em, join 'em" motto.

"Very creative, but let's keep our shoes on, okay?" He laid a hand on the shoulder of a curly-haired little boy who was struggling to untie his laces. The boy frowned but turned back to his paper, his fingers covered in brown paint.

He glanced over at Calista, who was carefully wiping off the boy's foot with a wet paper towel. Her light blue linen suit had more paint on it than a lot of the papers. "I think your suit is a lost cause."

"Oh, for sure." She grinned up at him, brushing the hair away from her clear green eyes with one forearm. She was so happy, she was shining with it.

Something about that gesture, and the light in her expression, caught at his heart. Eric had asked him why Calista was different and he hadn't been able to say. But he knew now, watching her in this room. She wasn't afraid to grab every opportunity and wring something good from it. He flashed back to how she had looked that first day, arms wrapped around her middle, fear hovering behind her eyes. She'd reached out to Marisol and Lana, become friends with Jose and Lissa, worked side by side with recovering addicts and teen parents clearing tables in the cafeteria. He'd heard her laughing this morning when she walked into the janitor's closet by accident. *I come that they may have life and have it more abundantly.* That's what she had, like the verse said, life abundant.

Grant felt his heart contract with the sudden realization that he cared for her in a way he had never cared for anyone before. A surprised smile spread over his face. He wanted to stand up and holler that he finally got it.

"Did you...want to paint?" Calista's hesitant voice brought him back down to earth. Her eyes were watching him steadily. Yeah, he got it, but he sure wasn't going to yell about it here and now. Calista would be off and running the moment the words came out of his mouth. She would think he was crazy.

"No, thanks." He cleared his throat. "I was just thinking how great this is for the kids. They go through a lot of upheaval and a little finger painting goes a long way toward making them feel normal."

"It's true, everyone should try it. When I think of all the years I paid for therapy when I could have just been making footprints..." She shook her head, laughing.

Lissa walked over, arms full of empty paint pots. "We've got about five more minutes and then we'll need to clean up. If any of your kids are finished, try to get them to slip off their smocks by the sink and wash up." She flicked a glance toward the disaster that was Calista's table and rolled her eyes. "Or maybe we can just declare this a national emergency and call in the troops."

"I'm sorry. I don't know how you get them to stay in one place." Calista stood up to start clearing the table, her voice registering the admiration she felt for the day care staff.

"It's a gift. And I can look really serious when I have to," Lissa said, her face relaxing. She seemed relieved that Calista wasn't going to skip out on the hardest part of the activity: the cleanup.

"All right, kiddos, put your hands in the air." Grant demonstrated by putting his palms up high. "Walk with your helper to the sinks. We're going to get cleaned up so we can have snack time."

The response was a burst of excitement, followed by the assistant helping the group line up for the sink. He winked at Calista as they filed past. "The key is to give them a little incentive."

"That's just what Michelle said," she responded, stacking lids and gathering up papers. "I guess I need to write that tip down somewhere."

"Planning on another stint in the day care?"

She frowned up at him, green eyes clouding over with confusion. "I'd like to come back here again. Unless Michelle thinks I wasn't up to spec today."

"I'm sure you were fine." He hesitated, wanting to say so much more, but knowing the time wasn't right. Not just yet. "I'm glad you had fun."

"More fun than I've had all week. Thanks for letting me help out."

"So, if you had to choose, it would be little-kid chaos over filing?"

She laughed again, that sweet sound that drew him toward her like she was pulling on a string. "This beats filing any day."

"I can name a few people off the top of my head who would rather have teeth pulled than spend the morning in here." Like Jose. If he ever wanted the young guy to quit, he could have him transferred to day care. Jose thought little kids were germ factories.

"There's nothing like tidy paperwork. But this—" she waved a green-colored hand at the room "—is beautiful. These kids are a treat after spending the day with businesspeople." She turned serious for a moment, weighing her words. "They're honest. You don't have to wonder what they're thinking. And they don't care what you're wearing or what kind of car you drive or how big your company is."

He wanted to say something, but he couldn't seem to form words. His fingers itched to reach out and brush back that strand of hair that kept falling into her eyes. Her face shone with that fragile sweetness he'd seen the first day she came to the mission.

"And they don't care who your parents are," he added, his voice sounding huskier than he'd intended.

"Exactly." She nodded, her gaze locked on his. "I always thought that verse about being like little children meant we were supposed to be gullible. But that's not what Jesus meant at all." She watched a little girl run toward the door, excitedly waving her art project in the air as her father grinned in greeting. "He meant that we needed to believe first, and doubt later. Not the other way around."

"Sort of the way that little kids love you first and ask questions later?"

Her face lit up at his words. "That's just what I mean."

Love first, and ask questions later. Great for kids,

but it was the very worst advice he'd heard for adults. And still, that was what was happening in his heart. It was almost enough to make him open his mouth and blurt it all out, tell her how thankful he was that God brought her through the mission doors.

Instead, he managed to look away, his heart pounding. "Kids. You gotta love 'em." Probably the dumbest rejoinder in history, but it was either end the conversation or ask her out to dinner. She'd probably appreciate not being covered in paint when he took a step in that direction. "I better help Janice."

"Janice?" Calista's brow furrowed in confusion.

"Your assistant. She's got about ten kids left to scrub down."

"Oh, right. And I'd better clean this area or I won't be invited back." She grabbed another handful of paper towels and started to swab off the tiny chairs.

He stood there for a moment, debating. Lana had set the time for the media announcement. He should probably say something now, before Calista saw it on the news.

"I know you won't be here on Friday morning, but I wanted—"

"Actually, I'm filling in for Lissa for an hour." Calista smiled up at him, hands full of soggy towels.

Grant paused, struggling to find his place again. This shouldn't be that hard. No harder than telling the whole nation. But what did he say? *Hi, you know the guy who owns half of this fine state? Well, he's my dad. But not really, because he abandoned me and my mother when I was born. He really wants to know me now, so I guess I get to be his son whether I like it or not.*

Calista was watching him, a frown appearing between her brows, green eyes turning serious.

A wave of shame flooded him. He couldn't do it. "Great. Michelle needs the help."

Grant ducked his head and crossed the room to where toddlers stood in line for the sink. Janice helped them stand on the stool, soap up and rinse off. Some were spick-and-span in no time. Some would need a thorough dunking. They chattered and giggled, chubby fingers leaving colored prints along the sides of the white porcelain sink. Grant grabbed the dispenser and delivered dollops of soap into waiting palms, all the while replaying their conversation.

He wished he could just blurt it out. But she was going to hear the ugly news the same way everybody else would: on the news. *Love first.* He felt the words echoing around in his brain, in his heart. He was used to being careful, wary, never taking anyone at face value. Was it possible he should trust that Calista was going to stick around? He wanted it so badly that his teeth ached with it.

But before he could build any kind of life with her, he had to bring his ugly little secret out into the light. Tomorrow would be his last Thanksgiving—no, his last *day*—as Grant Monohan, mission director, and not Grant Monohan, Kurt Daniels's illegitimate son.

Calista wiped down the table and gave herself a quick pep talk. It was now or never. She knew she should probably wait until she was looking her best, or even just a little less colorful, but he seemed so friendly, so open.

She kept glancing back at him, watching the line

get shorter and shorter at the sink. Finally, he was almost done. Janice led a little girl toward the door and her waiting mother. Calista took a deep breath. It was just a Christmas party, not a wedding. She marched up behind him and cleared her throat.

He looked back, tilting his head down at her, dark hair just a bit mussed as usual. She picked up a faint woodsy smell, his cologne, and for some reason it was her undoing.

"Grant-Humphreys," she started, then slapped a hand over her mouth.

He blinked. "Excuse me?"

Calista felt heat creep up her neck and wanted to press the rewind and delete buttons. "Sorry. That came out wrong. I was wondering if you wanted to come to the VitaWow Christmas party in a few weeks." There it was. Out, for better or worse.

He turned, helping a little boy with jet-black hair down from the step stool. "Let me guess. It's at the Grant-Humphreys Mansion?"

Calista couldn't help the snort of laughter that answered him. "Sorry. I haven't asked anybody to a dance since my Sadie Hawkins days."

"I'm sure you haven't." He leveled a gaze at her, something in his eyes she couldn't quite define. "And I'd be honored to go."

"You don't even know the date yet," she protested, feeling unreasonably happy, her voice losing its anxious tone.

"Don't need to, but you can tell me anyway. I'll just make sure I'm free." Then there was that smile again, the one that made her brain take a leave of absence.

"It's the fifteenth," she said briskly, working hard

to keep herself from puddling at his feet. *Get a grip. You're not a teenager!*

Grant said nothing, just inclined his head a little, as if that smile was just between the two of them. As if there weren't thirty small children still rocketing around the room. "Yup, definitely free."

She stood there half a second too long, her gaze locked on his. "I thought it would be a great opportunity to meet some really big donors. I've already made sure the guest list has a few considering a sponsorship of the roof project and the classroom remodels."

His eyes went dark as if someone had hit a switch. "Gotcha."

Something about that one word rang a warning bell in her mind. But she couldn't figure out why. The mission needed money, right?

"We can talk specifics later." And he turned back to the sink, running the water and washing the sides of the porcelain with a sponge.

Calista nodded, to herself, since he wasn't even looking, and wandered to the door. She had done something wrong, but she couldn't figure out what.

"Calista, can you be here in ten minutes?" Jackie's rapid-fire speech interrupted Calista's vivid daydream. Something about Grant and kids and lots of laughter. She adjusted her Bluetooth and glanced at her car's dashboard clock.

"I can't. I have to get home and change. Isn't my schedule cleared until one?"

"It was, but then the PR director from Genesis Drinks decided we needed to approve some paperwork

ASAP. I didn't think it would be a problem to tell him to come on over. Can't you leave early?"

"I'm already on the road. But I can't come straight back to the office, so he'll have to wait until I get there."

"You got a hot lunch date?" The curiosity in Jackie's voice should have made Calista smile, but part of her wanted to keep Grant safely away from her other life. Which was how she was starting to think of VitaWow.

"No, but thanks for asking. There was a little mishap and I need to change. I'll be quick."

There was a pause, long enough for Calista to imagine that Jackie had disconnected the call. "A mishap." She repeated the words carefully, as if debating whether she really wanted to hear the details.

Calista peeked in her rearview mirror and changed lanes without dropping her speed. "Nothing too awful. Just paint."

"You were painting? Couldn't they hire some of the homeless people to do that?"

She squashed the niggle of irritation at Jackie's tone. "Not that kind of painting. It was finger-painting day at the day care."

"The day care?"

Calista heaved a sigh. "You know what I've always loved about you? You're so quick on the uptake that I hardly ever have to repeat myself." She pulled onto the exit ramp and tapped her brakes. A long line of cars were queued at the intersection leading to her condominium.

Her sarcasm startled a laugh out of Jackie. "Sorry. You've just always been work first, play later. This new you takes some getting used to."

She pulled through the intersection and took a quick

right. "I'm almost home. Give me about fifteen minutes and I'll be back on my way to work. We can conference call while I drive over, if he really can't wait."

"I'll try and stall until you get back. We've got some cookies around here somewhere."

"Okay. And you can always try the basement break room. They get a shipment of bakery goodies from Les Amis every few days."

"They do? No wonder everybody's trying to get transferred down there. When did you start that?"

"About a month ago. It's a long story," Calista said shortly, sliding her car into the parking spot in front of her condo.

Calista hung up and jumped from the car. If she didn't take too long, she might even get there before the press people. She pushed open her apartment door and kicked off her shoes. Probably better to throw the clothes away than try to dry-clean the fine linen. She paused, fingering the sleeve of her jacket, a smile tugging up one corner of her mouth. Streaks of red paint slashed from her elbow to her wrist. She remembered a little boy tugging her sleeve, wanting her to see his creation. There had been so many little hands and chattering voices, she couldn't even keep up with them all. But Grant was a natural, the way he crouched down to talk to them and let a hand on their small shoulders speak volumes. She ran her hand along the dry paint, smiling at the visible memento of a perfect morning.

Grant's words echoed in her head, about loving like children. She allowed herself to wonder, just for a moment, how Grant loved. Was he someone who fell in love at first sight? Or did he have to warm up to a woman? Any woman he loved would be amazing. She'd certainly have a rock-hard faith, a real purpose in life and a clear calling.

Calista sure had the rock-hard, clear and real part down. But the faith, life and calling was still a work in progress.

She needed to get her priorities straight before she ended up going to the mission just to see Grant. It was so easy to get wrapped up in his purpose, his joy. But she was trying to help other people, not satisfy her own needs.

She'd spent years focusing on herself and now it was time to let God use her for something important, which did not include daydreaming about Grant Monohan.

"*Mija*, take this pan to the front line, please." Marisol passed a large tray to Calista and pointed to the far right, her bright eyes flashing with energy. "The smashed potatoes are almost gone. We cannot have a good Thanksgiving without the smashed potatoes."

Calista bit back a smile and carried the metal serving dish as quickly as she could out into the serving area. The noise of the packed cafeteria was almost deafening, lessened only by the high-ceilinged room. Everywhere she looked there were tables of people, talking and laughing. It might have been a big party, if not for the number of old men in shabby coats and hollow-cheeked women. If you didn't look too closely, it was a happy gathering. If you focused on each person, you started to see the tiredness in their faces, the discouragement in the set of their shoulders.

There was a traffic jam near the end of the serving area. Calista stopped, feeling the muscles in her arms start to protest. Twenty pounds of potatoes must multiply exponentially when you added butter and milk.

"Can I take that?"

Calista felt her cheeks grow hot before she could even register the words. All she knew was the voice, and the man it belonged to. She turned her head and smiled, hoping her face wasn't as sweaty as it felt. Her light cream sweater was uncomfortably warm. "You miss your weight training today? Because a few reps with this pan and you'd be good to go."

Grant chuckled, already lifting the heavy dish from her hands. She could see the darkness where he'd shaved, how his tan skin contrasted against his white shirt collar. His cologne was woodsy, virile. She wanted to lean in and inhale.

"Marisol takes this day very, very seriously," he said, indicating the long rows of serving dishes. "If we run out of something, she thinks she'll be barred from heaven."

"Especially the 'smashed' potatoes," Calista said, lips twitching.

"And the 'corns' and the bread 'balls' and the 'staffing.'"

She couldn't help laughing out loud, and then put a guilty hand to her lips. "Is that rude? She's learned a lot in two years. I don't think I could learn that much Spanish if you gave me ten years."

"She doesn't mind. It's not personal for her. But the food is. We make fun of the cooking and we're all in trouble."

Calista nodded, vividly imagining how the fierce Hispanic woman would shrug off her mispronunciation, but be horrified if the potatoes were lumpy. The woman in front of them moved to the side and a place opened up for Grant to rest the dish against the long countertop. Calista deftly lifted the empty tray from its resting spot, careful not to burn herself with the hot steam underneath.

Grant slid the full tray in place and Calista took the spoon. The line was moving steadily, even though the dinner had been going on for more than an hour already. A young woman with two small children glanced up and smiled tentatively. Calista served a portion on each plate and watched the smallest child's eyes light up. "Some! Some!"

Calista giggled and the mother shushed the little boy, her face going pink. "He loves mashed potatoes," she said, her voice a half whisper.

"Don't we all," Grant agreed, smiling. The little family moved on, the baby still shouting "some" at the top of his lungs.

"Are you going somewhere for dinner after this?"

Calista should have been prepared for the question, but she wasn't. Surprise lanced through her and she focused on the tray in front of her. *No, because I don't have any friends and no one invited me. Thanksgiving stinks when you're all alone.* Probably not the best response.

He waved a hand, the one holding a large serving spoon. "Sorry. I wasn't trying to pry. Just making conversation." His voice was light but his back seemed to stiffen as he spoke.

"I don't care if you ask me personal questions," Calista started to say, pausing to serve another spoonful of potatoes and give a warm smile to the old man holding the plate.

"Really?" He packed so much disbelief into that one word that she had to grin.

"Really. At least, I don't mind the way you think I mind."

"Ah. So, you're saying that you do mind, but I'm mistaken in the exact manner in which you mind my asking."

"Exactly."

His deep laugh kindled something in her chest, and the warmth spread outward, making her fingers tingle. She sidled a glance his way. How she loved that smile. The deep creases around his mouth, the way it transformed his face from almost severe to incredibly warm, the way his eyes crinkled at the edges. She watched his grin slowly fade into something softer, something more like wonder. He cleared his throat and indicated the potatoes. "Someone's waiting."

Calista snapped back to her task, face going hot, plopping the creamy side dish on a plate with a little more force than necessary. Yeah, definitely wonder. *He's wondering why I'm staring at him with my mouth hanging open.* She would have given up her Mercedes to be able to erase the last minute and a half. It was like junior high all over again. And she knew better than to try to be cooler than she really was. It never worked out. You were always caught out in the end.

"I'm not going to another dinner. I haven't been to a Thanksgiving dinner in years."

He paused, scraping corn into a pile in his silver serving tray, waiting for the next customer. "Why? Not your favorite holiday?"

She shrugged, suddenly tired. "Because I haven't been invited."

He didn't respond to that and they worked in silence for a few minutes. Calista chewed the inside of her lip, wishing she could lie and say she was rejecting offers every holiday. Then she was angry at wishing it, then finally sighed under the confusion of it all.

"But you're right here, at my Thanksgiving dinner."

Calista turned to him, ready to roll her eyes, and then hesitated. He looked serious, solemn. "I'm a volunteer."

"And you're my guest." He playfully bumped her with an elbow. "I always make my friends work for their keep. You didn't know what you were signing up for, but you've got years of this ahead of you."

Calista scooped up another spoonful of potatoes for the next plate that slid into view, a goofy smile plastered to her face. She knew he was just being kind to her, making conversation, acting like the concerned shepherd to the lost sheep, but she couldn't help it. Those sweet words made her heart full to bursting. She was a friend, a guest, someone who was welcome. *Years of this ahead of you.* Oh, how she wished it was true.

Chapter Nine

The media descended on the mission before the sun had risen above the snow-covered peaks of the Rocky Mountains. Vans plastered with channel numbers lined the streets and camera crews jostled for position on the sidewalk. The mission doors wouldn't unlock to the public until six o'clock but that didn't keep the reporters from tugging at the handle every few minutes. Last night's press release had caused a frenzy. The man who owned a business empire had fathered a child by a drug-addicted C-list actress and then refused to acknowledge his paternity. Then the actress drank herself to death and the kid had lived on the streets. Definitely newsworthy by itself, but add in the enormous fortune that awaited the only child of Kurt Daniels and the fact that this child was now running the area's biggest homeless shelter, and the story couldn't get any bigger. Everyone was desperate to know everything about Grant Monohan, from his love life right down to what he ate for breakfast.

On the other side of the glass door, across the lobby and down a carpeted hallway, the city's newest celebrity sat with his head in his hands. He slumped in his chair at the long conference table, which was empty except for two other silent individuals. Jose took a gulp of steaming hot coffee and set his mug back on the table, face solemn. Lana sat next to Grant, one hand gently kneading his shoulder. There was nothing she could say that would make this any easier, but she couldn't bear to see him sitting there so alone. Grant raised his head and gave her a tentative smile that he hoped looked stronger than it felt. Lana had been through some rough times herself after her abusive husband sent a bullet through her spine and left her a paraplegic. She'd found her way to the mission the same way he had, wanting to make a difference in a world that could be heartless and cruel.

"Almost time, boss," Jose said, breaking the silence. He looked like he was swallowing glass. His thickly muscled arms strained his polo shirt yet his expression of anxiety made him look like a vulnerable child.

Grant nodded. "Well, let's pray, then go get this done." They bowed their heads as he spoke simple words of praise, because even in this moment Grant was thankful. God had never let him down and never would.

As they stood up, Grant felt as if he was heading to his own execution. His palms were sweaty, his heart was racing. He had never had such an urge to flee in his entire life. The years he'd spent on the street had been rough, but this was worse. He couldn't suppress the twist of his lips at the irony. Announcing that he was the heir to an enormous fortune was worse than sleeping in doorways and begging for handouts.

"Showtime," whispered Grant and they headed for the lobby. Lana asked the residents to clear the space as they prepared for the media to flood into the mission.

Most of the homeless were more than eager to get out of the way. Old Conchita refused to budge from her spot on the last couch, rocking and mumbling, so Jose let her be. A few curious stragglers huddled by the double doors that led to the cafeteria. Breakfast had been served an hour ago and the clang of dishes being loaded into the enormous dishwashers echoed dimly in the silent lobby.

The moment he unlocked the front door would stay with Grant forever. Flashbulbs blinded him as he stood in the entryway, grimly waving in the reporters and cameramen. He hated the way they swarmed into the lobby and invaded this place of refuge.

"As soon as you can arrange yourselves, I will make a prepared statement and answer a few questions." Grant's voice felt uncertain but he cleared his throat and waited for the reporters to stop jockeying for position. He glanced at Lana, who gave him a thumbs-up sign, and Jose, who nodded encouragingly.

Taking a deep breath, he read from a paper he clutched in his hand. "My name is Grant Monohan and I am Kurt Daniels's son." He paused as the cameras flashed like strobe lights. "I have always been aware that he was my biological father. My mother, Annie Monohan, struggled with drugs and alcohol before passing away ten years ago. As a teenager, I spent several years living on the streets of Denver. I came to know the good people who ran the Denver mission and they encouraged me to finish my education. The previous director, Edward Thompson, helped me apply for scholarships, and I earned a degree in business from UC Davis. I returned to the mission to take a position as assistant director, and then was hired as director five years ago." Grant paused, hoping against hope that the frantic scribbling from the horde of reporters would include actual words from his mouth.

"I understand the fascination with celebrities but I am asking you to respect my privacy and the privacy of the mission residents. This is a place of refuge and solace for many people struggling in difficult circumstances. Do not film or record any area of the mission without permission, and do not approach the residents. After I am done answering questions, I will ask you to leave. If you have further questions, I can be reached through the main phone number."

He put the paper away in his pocket and lifted his head, waiting for the onslaught. "Now I will answer a few questions."

The resulting din was deafening as every reporter shouted to be heard above the others.

Grant pointed toward the newscaster for a major Denver news channel. The dignified-looking man lifted his microphone and said in his best dramatic tone, "Is it true you drive a Ferrari while pretending to the homeless population that you aren't wealthy?"

It took several seconds for the question to make sense. Grant's mouth hung open in surprise before he snapped it shut and glared. "No, that is false. Are there any serious questions here?"

Another wave of shouting assaulted his ears and he pointed to a narrow-faced woman in a bright green jacket. She stepped forward. "Can you tell us why you refused to accept any money from your father, when the mission could use the funds for a new roof?"

Again, Grant stood speechless, eyes narrowed. How did she know that he wouldn't cash the check, and that the roof was in need of replacing? He searched around for an answer. "The policy of the mission is to rely on the generosity of the many, rather than depend on large gifts from a few. We also adhere to federal standards for nonprofit organizations, which prohibits some types of donations."

The woman spoke again before he could turn to another reporter. "Surely accepting one gift from Mr. Daniels wouldn't hurt."

The words left Grant's mouth before he thought them through. "My father tends to spoil everything he touches."

The resulting chaos was impossible to calm. Grant waved his hands for quiet but the reporters yelled questions over each other. Finally the mob subsided into restlessness, waiting for him to choose another reporter. But he had had enough.

"That's all I have to say at this time. Please exit the lobby and clear the sidewalk in front of the mission. This is private property and we will call in police assistance if necessary. Thank you for understanding." He pointed to the front doors and his eyes swept over a familiar face at the edge of the surging crowd.

Calista stood to the side, her brow creased with worry, hands up to her mouth and eyes wide in shock. His gut twisted in response as they locked eyes. He wanted to take it all back: the whole morning, the board's approval of the media statement, the threatening letters. He wanted to go back to before she left Thanksgiving night. He felt steel bands tighten around his chest and he struggled to look away from her face. She slowly dropped her hands and gave him a slight smile.

He struggled to look as if nothing much had changed.

But if there was anything that Grant Monohan knew, it was that there was no erasing the past.

Calista watched Grant Monohan face a room of screaming reporters and thought she had never witnessed a braver act in her life. He was tall and straight, head held high as he read from a small piece of paper in his left hand. She knew what it was like to have a painful past. Her throat ached in anguish as he gave the briefest description of his teen years. It sent shock waves through her system to hear him say he was Kurt Daniels's son. He was as recognizable as the president, like Colorado royalty.

Grant's life was never going to be the same after this moment. She watched him plead for privacy for the residents and visitors. And then he had made the fatal mistake of answering a few questions. The first rule of a press conference was control, and in a madhouse like this, control meant no questions.

The first question was the sort of ridiculous gossip she was prepared to hear. Calista could tell that Grant wasn't, because his mouth dropped open a little. She could see the emotions flitting over his face: disbelief, anger, frustration. She wanted to walk in there and grab his microphone. He was going to be chewed up and spit out on national television.

The next question was strange, but Grant's response was even stranger. He didn't deny that his father had offered support or that he had refused help. And then he spoke from his gut, which broke rule number two of press conferences: if you can't keep your emotions in check, don't answer the question. Calista felt her hands go up to her mouth and stifled a groan. It was like watching the proverbial train wreck and knowing it was going to replay in a constant loop for the next week.

Grant looked up at her, right after he'd refused to answer more questions, and she tried to give him an encouraging smile. At least he'd stopped them at two, instead of twenty. She didn't think she could have watched another five minutes of this. The look on his face was difficult to interpret. He turned and strode through the door to the offices.

She knew how it felt to have a past that was beyond your control, and a family that you did not care to own up to. What happened when they came out of the shadows to interfere with your life? Her stomach turned icy at the thought. But Grant's bombshell was delicious for the gossip hounds because he was so *good*. People just loved to see a fall from grace. And pretending to be a normal guy who cared about the homeless while being a millionaire was a pretty big bombshell.

Several large men wearing the mission's signature red polo shirt directed the crowd of reporters to the door. Calista wound her way through the throng, dodging enormous cameras and trying not to trip on long cords strewn over the lobby floor. It sounded as if most of them would be content to park across the street and wait for another opportunity.

Lana rolled into her spot behind the desk, her face pale, dark shadows under her eyes. "Hi, Calista," she said in a friendly tone. Her gaze darted behind Calista, and she said more loudly, "I will not answer any questions."

There were two paparazzi standing a few feet away, apparently hoping for some kind of statement. A tall, thin young man with a baseball cap on backward smirked and said, "You probably will, for the right price."

Calista sucked in a breath and felt anger spread through her limbs. But Lana spoke first, and her voice was controlled. "You can't put a price on friendship. I'm sure you understand."

The man rolled his eyes and turned to his friend, laughing. But the other man shook his head, dark eyes gazing at the ground, and replaced the lens on his camera. His tan face was somber, even sad. Calista wondered if he had seen that friendship almost always had an asking price.

"Very nice. You should have made the statement to the press." Calista hoped Lana would take the compliment the right way, not as a criticism of Grant.

The secretary ran a hand through her short gray hair so that the purple ends stood up straight. "I told him that. But he didn't want to look like he was running away."

"Well, it certainly didn't look like he was running." Calista couldn't keep the admiration from her voice. "How is he? I mean, with all of this?" She didn't know why those words came out of her mouth but she didn't want to take them back, either.

Lana shrugged. "He's tough. He's been through a lot worse than a press conference with some silly reporters."

She nodded. It sounded like Grant was made of steel to survive that kind of abandonment and not be bitter. "He seems so…" Her voice trailed off as she struggled to grasp the word. Hopeful? At peace? "I'm sorry, I guess I'm in awe of his ability to forgive his dad."

Lana's eyes narrowed. "I don't know if he has forgiven him, but I do know he doesn't consider him his *dad.*"

Jose came through the office door, his usually mild expression gone. His brows were drawn down, lips pressed together. A coffee mug gently steamed in his hand. He held the door open behind him and Grant followed. His powerful frame seemed to swallow up the space as he came toward the desk. The dark blue suit coat was gone and his dress shirt was rolled up at the elbows. His red tie was still on, but the knot seemed looser. His face was calm, but Calista saw sadness in his eyes.

"That wasn't enough to scare you away?" Grant stopped a few feet from her and his tone was teasing, but his face said that he thought she should run while she could.

"Nothing scary about it except that it was done all wrong," she replied, sneaking a glance at Grant's face. She was taking a chance, but from what she'd seen, Grant was the type to put his ego on the back burner and take help if it was offered.

"Oh, so you know how to do it right?" Jose leaned against the desk and set his coffee cup on the smooth wooden surface.

Grant said nothing, but his eyes were bright with laughter. Calista sucked in a breath at the sight. She could see his star pedigree in the strong jaw and the high cheekbones. But she was right that his ego wasn't bruised by her honesty.

"Grant probably had a few media classes with that UC Davis business degree. He can tell you what he did wrong." She could feel Lana's gaze on her and Jose made a sound in the back of his throat.

"She's right. It was a total disaster and it didn't have to be," Grant said, nodding. "I shouldn't have taken any questions. As soon as I saw the crowd, I knew this wasn't a normal news conference. Most of them were from the tabloids."

Calista said nothing, hoping her face showed the sympathy she felt. Jose looked from his boss to the new girl and back.

"And then I lost my cool." He shook his head, as if he still couldn't believe he'd let a reporter get the best of him.

"It happens. Have you always handled the press for the mission? Maybe it's time to assign that to another staff member." She looked at Lana, who had taken the paparazzo's gibe and turned it around.

"Are you saying you'd be willing to take that role?" His words were light, but Calista could tell Grant was more than half-serious.

"Not me, I have a quick temper," she said, laughing. "I'd just make it worse. But Lana seems like she'd do a great job."

To her surprise the secretary shook her head. "Now, that should be some rule of working with the press. Don't choose the middle-aged woman with purple hair in a wheelchair."

Calista couldn't keep surprised laughter from bubbling out of her throat. "Whatever you all do, just choose somebody who can keep calm and—"

"Avoid insulting Kurt Daniels?" Grant's voice was cool. The smile had slipped from his face.

"How about not giving them anything to make into a headline," she shot back. She was on his side, whether he believed it or not.

Jose took a sip from his mug. The smell of fresh coffee made Calista's mouth water. She'd had enough espresso, but it was definitely time for a real breakfast. As if in response to her thoughts, her stomach let out a rumble that seemed to echo in the high-ceilinged lobby. Her cheeks went hot.

Grant grinned. "Sounds like it's breakfast time. I didn't eat before the press got here because I was too nervous, but I'm starving now. Want to join me in the cafeteria?"

The idea of spending some one-on-one time with Grant was tempting. "Sure, I'll join you."

"Well, I'll see you two later," Jose called as they headed for the double doors on the far end of the lobby. They both lifted a hand in response.

"He has a mild form of obsessive-compulsive disorder and can't handle the crowd in here," Grant said in a quiet tone.

Calista looked up, surprised. "Would he mind you telling me that?"

"It's better if you know. He's learning coping mechanisms, but he still would feel very uncomfortable if you touched his mug or his food." He reached for the door and looked her in the eye. "You seemed the type of person that's sensitive to others' feelings and would appreciate the heads-up."

She didn't know what to say. She wanted to agree, to say she cared enough to avoid hurting people or offending them. But all that came to mind was Liz Albrecht, the new secretary in Human Resources at VitaWow. She had been sent up to take Jackie's place for a few hours last week. The girl was not the brightest bulb in the firmament and Calista had made it clear that she would not be making another trip to the top floor. Her cheeks flushed a little as she remembered how Liz's eyes had filled with tears as she corrected her again and again. She could have been gentler. Calista dropped her gaze and waited for Grant to open the door.

"And thanks again." His voice was still quiet.

"For what?"

"For being honest. When you're the boss, people have a hard time telling you the truth."

She nodded, knowing exactly how that was. It made her paranoid some days, just thinking of the things she could do without a single employee speaking up. She wanted them to think for themselves, not just their paycheck.

"I have a feeling that's going to be a much bigger issue, now that you've let the cat out of the bag."

Grant laughed out loud, his blue eyes crinkling up. "Great, I feel tons better."

"Lana, I was wondering if I could ask you a personal question." Grant stuffed his hands in his pockets and tried to stop fidgeting. It had been a tough weekend, dodging reporters outside his apartment. But there was a more pressing issue than paparazzi. He'd spent an hour browsing online flower shops, not the greatest way to spend a Monday morning. He'd visited two flower boutiques over the weekend. None of it had felt right. Especially not the little glass doodads he'd seen on the festively decorated shop shelves.

Behind the lobby desk, Lana lifted her head and grinned hugely. "Well, that took long enough."

"What did?"

"I thought you were never going to ask my opinion about whether Calista's a good catch."

Grant choked back his surprise. "I'm not."

Lana's wide blue eyes blinked in confusion. "Oh, sorry. Go ahead."

He shuffled his feet and leaned against the desk. The lobby was bustling with residents on their way to dinner. But if he waited for perfect privacy, that moment would never come. Plus, he needed an answer before Calista showed up for the fund-raising meeting in an hour.

"I was wondering, if you wanted a man to show interest in you, what would you want him to do? Give you flowers? Or maybe a little gift?"

Lana's brows drew down. "I thought you said this wasn't about Calista."

He could feel the warmth spreading up his neck. "I just wanted your opinion. As a woman."

Now Lana's eyes were wide, and a look of alarm crossed her face. "Okay, let's just be clear here. You're not asking me what I would want a man to give me because *you're* the man, right?"

"No! I mean, not because you're not attractive or a nice person—"

"Oh, Grant." Lana started to laugh. "You almost gave me a heart attack. But can we just be honest with each other? We're friends, and friends can tell each other things in confidence. So, talk to me before you do something crazy, like follow Eric's advice." She blinked innocently up at him, a sly grin crossing her face.

"Did he talk to you?" Surprise made his voice rise.

"Nope, Eric is as good as gold that way. Not a peep to me. But I figured you would ask him for advice before me or Jose or Marisol—"

"I get the picture." Grant rubbed a hand over his face and wondered how many people in this mission had noticed his feelings for Calista.

"Look, I saw this coming a long time ago and it's a good thing. She's got a strong faith and a soft heart, but she's as tough as nails when she needs to be. You can't beat that combination."

Grant interrupted her with a groan. "See, I agree with all that. I'm not asking for your opinion on *her* exactly." He paused, trying to speak past the sudden tightness in his chest. "Honestly, I have a lot more reservations about myself than her, if we're talking about relationships."

"I'm not following you." Lana frowned up at him, then let out a low whistle. "Oh. You think because your father's a jerk, you've got some inherited flaw? You think you're going to walk out as soon as the going gets rough?"

He didn't answer, just tried to compose his expression into something other than fear. "I know that loyalty and faithfulness are choices we make. But I don't want to mess up. I don't want to hurt anybody."

"Oh, Grant. You won't. You're not that type of man." Her eyes were soft with sympathy.

"Thanks, Lana." But he couldn't take all the credit for the kind of man he was. God had more to do with it than anyone. "Anyway, what I was going to ask you, before we got sidetracked, is about flowers. Do you think…?"

Lana opened her mouth to answer, but then her eyes flicked behind Grant and widened. "Um, well, let me see. I think most women like flowers. But let's ask Calista what she thinks."

Grant felt as if someone had dumped a cold bucket of water over his head. He steeled himself to turn slowly. Had she heard his doubts and Lana's advice? He was caught between hoping she still thought he was perfect, like Marisol had said, and understanding he came from a man who couldn't stay faithful if his life depended on it.

"The fund-raising meeting isn't for another hour." He frowned toward her, trying to cover his discomfort.

"Two of our board members are stuck out of town, no flights in or out of Denver, so my schedule got cleared for the morning. I decided to come in early." She was brushing snow out of her blond hair, loose to her shoulders, and her nose was pink with the cold. Bright yellow mittens were a new addition to her red peacoat.

Lana grinned at her. "And how I love you early types." She peered over the desk. "Those are pretty mittens."

"Thanks. I made them myself." Calista held up both hands and beamed. "I've been trying to learn how to knit. This one is a little bigger than the other because I got distracted and added too many rows."

"They're supercute. Anyway, we were debating and maybe you could settle the argument."

Calista's eyes were bright with curiosity, her tone light. "I can try. What are you all arguing about?"

Grant's noted the "you all" and filed it away. "Do women really like flowers?"

Calista nodded. "Lots of women do."

"What about you?" Grant hoped his voice was extra casual.

She hesitated.

"And those little cut crystal figurines, like teddy bears or roses?"

Her grimace was all the answer he needed. "You mean, for a Christmas gift?"

"No, more of a romantic thing." Lana's words seemed to startle Calista, who glanced between them before answering.

"I would say I'd rather have a man offer me something that he can't buy. Like time. It's easy to buy something and have it wrapped up nicely. But to let someone into your life, to introduce them to your family and friends, take them to church with you… That's a commitment of yourself. I would find that very romantic."

Lana was nodding as she spoke, but Grant couldn't tear his gaze from Calista's face. *That you might have life and live it more abundantly.* He'd never needed anything more than this place and his friends. His life was full, complete. But now he felt God nudging him toward something more.

"Calista, would you like to come to church with me this Sunday?" The words came out a little quicker than he would have liked, but they felt so right he couldn't help the huge smile that spread over his face.

There was a beat of silence, then another, as Calista looked from Grant to Lana, and back again. She took a breath and said, "I would really like that." Twin spots of pink appeared on her cheeks by the time she finished the sentence.

He wanted to pump his fist in the air but settled for a more sedate response. "Good." He couldn't seem to stop grinning.

Lana sighed and swiped a finger under each eye. "I love the Christmas season. I just love it."

Chapter Ten

Calista slipped on another dress and gave her reflection a critical eye. The pale pink wool shift dress showed off her trim figure. Too girlie? The last one had been too dark. The one before it had been a sweater dress and was too clingy. The one before that was from last year's Christmas party and was really too fancy.

She dropped onto the edge of the bed and stared morosely at the pile of clothing on the floor. It had never been a problem to grab an outfit for church before, especially since she didn't know that many people. She had more trouble finding the hymns than anything else.

A glance at the clock reminded her that she had just a few minutes before Grant showed up. She felt her stomach knot unpleasantly. What would he think when he saw where she lived, how she lived?

Lord, You know my heart. I'm learning to be more like You every day but I know how far I have to go. Calista sighed and went to pick out a pair of shoes. As she swung open the separate closet for her shoes, Mimi darted in, tail held high.

"No, you don't!" She swatted at the Siamese shoe terror and managed to reverse her trajectory.

Just as she picked out a pair of pale pink pumps, the doorbell rang. Calista jumped as if she'd been electrocuted. She slammed the shoe closet closed and ran to open the front door barefoot.

Her heart almost stuttered to a stop as Grant flashed her that perfect smile. Nice suit, check. Fresh shave, check. Delicious smell of soap and aftershave, check and check. She could have stood there and cataloged his attributes all day.

"Hi, come on in." She stepped back and waved him inside.

"Nice place." He took a few steps into the room and gazed around.

Calista couldn't help seeing everything new through his eyes. The wall of glass emphasized the cool steel accent points at the ceiling and the avant-garde table with minimalist modern art above it. It all looked so cold and...expensive.

"I think we share a fondness for a certain artist." Grant's lips twitched as he nodded toward her latest acquisitions. A wall full of Savannah's crayon drawings might be a bit much but she couldn't bear to throw them away. And for every picture she accepted, there was another one a few hours later. They were all kitties with pink sunglasses, most of them by a Christmas tree.

"She told me they were limited edition, but apparently I've been conned."

He reached out to the delicate side table and picked up a silver-framed photo of Elaine's new family. "She looks like you."

"My sister. That's her husband and their new baby."

Calista loved that photo of the three of them, lost in love with their new baby, wrapped up in themselves.

"They live near here?"

"No. I wish they did. But they might be coming to visit in the spring, when the baby's a little bigger."

"You'll certainly have enough room for them." Again his gaze swept the apartment. High ceiling, track lighting, minimal furniture, wide-open space bordered only by the sheer glass wall. The living room alone could hold a family.

"I probably won't be here when they visit, though."

For a moment, she thought he hadn't heard her. Grant was motionless, his head turned toward the awesome view of the mountains. Clouds were moving in over the peaks. He frowned into the distance. "You're leaving Denver?"

"No, no, I mean the condo." She watched him visibly relax, his expression turning to curiosity.

A little sound near the couch made them both turn their heads. Mimi stood, her fluffy head cocked to one side.

"Is that the evil cat?"

"Yup. I better get my shoes on before she takes her chance."

Grant let out a laugh that made even a shoe-destroying cat seem like a wonderful thing.

Calista beamed in his direction as he helped her into her red peacoat and they made their way out the door, but her stomach dropped. How could orchestrating a corporate merger be easier than Sunday services with Grant? She felt like an impostor.

She was barely beyond thinking she was the center of

the universe. She swallowed the lump in her throat and lifted her chin. Well, everybody had to start somewhere.

She sneaked a glance at him as they walked. A lock of dark hair fell over his forehead and Calista realized with a jolt how very much he looked like his famous father, right down to the same perfect mouth. A mouth that was tugged up a bit at one corner.

He reached out and took her hand, the pressure of it short-circuiting her thoughts. Calista felt the tension ease in the pit of her stomach, loving the warmth of his touch.

At that moment, as if they were in an old-time Hollywood movie, fat snowflakes began to drift down around them. Calista's eyes widened and she held out her free hand to catch a falling clump. "Perfect," she whispered.

Grant lifted a hand to her cheek, running his warm thumb across her cheekbone. "Yes, it is." And the look in his eyes made her want to believe it was possible. That a man like him could love a woman like her. Was God that good, that forgiving, to give her such a gift when she hadn't done anything to deserve it? Sudden doubt coursed through her. Grant didn't even really know her yet.

"We don't want to be late," she said softly.

He dropped his hand and grinned. "Definitely not. Especially if you're one of those early people."

She shot him an amused glance and let him lead the way.

Calista had always heard that phrase "church family" but had never really known what it meant. Maybe because her own had been so twisted by her father's need for control and her own fear. Whatever it was, she got it now.

Grant held the hymnbook for them both and she sang along with the familiar stately tune, but inside she was anything but sedate. She had never felt so at home since her mother died. From the moment they stepped through the doors, they'd been greeted and hugged. Grant had already fielded three offers of lunch by the time they'd made it to a pew halfway up the sanctuary.

The little church was filled to the brim and after an hour all the bodies had made it pleasantly warm. She glanced around as the organist paused, then started another verse. Old people, families, singles, teens, everybody was here. A little boy directly in front of them sat sideways on the pew and ran a tiny toy car up and down the wood. His mother, without pausing from her song, reached down a hand and rubbed it through his soft black hair. They all seemed so at ease, so *happy*. She never remembered church this way. Her father had always parked them in the front row and they were bound for a whipping if they even twitched during the service.

As the last notes faded away, Grant turned toward her and said, "I forgot to tell you, we usually go to the parish hall for doughnuts. Is that okay?"

Calista blinked. Doughnuts, too? This was definitely not the church of her youth. "If you knew me better, you wouldn't even have to ask that question."

He let out a soft chuckle and helped her into her coat again. "Someone has a doughnut problem? But I thought you were a runner."

"That's *why* I'm a runner," she said, giving him a quick wink. "On the other hand, maybe we should skip the after-church social because you just might see a side of me that's better off hidden."

"I'll take my chances." He shook hands with an older man whose white mustache bristled as he smiled.

They walked the ten yards to the parish hall and joined the after-church crowd. It seemed as if everyone had stayed for coffee. A giant poster was taped to the front door announcing a spaghetti dinner and silent auction to benefit the Downtown Denver Mission next Sunday. The kids shed their coats and ran through a pair of doors into a modern-looking gym.

"Hi, Eric." Calista didn't know why she was surprised to see Grant's best friend here.

"Hi there, new girl." His wild red hair had been tamed a bit, probably by the dark-haired woman next to him. As she came around her husband to give Grant a hug, Calista saw her rounded tummy. Eric introduced her, with a flourish. "This is my wife, Marla. And our baby."

Marla took Calista's arm, steering her toward one of the tables. "Don't mind him, he's never serious."

Eric was certainly a lighthearted guy.

"Let's park it here while the men get us some sustenance." Marla gestured to the chair across from her and they sat down, leaving Grant and Eric to wait in line.

"When is your baby due?"

"Three weeks. Right in time for Christmas." Marla flipped her long dark hair over one shoulder and rubbed her tummy.

Something in that gesture touched her heart. How would it feel to have such a tiny person to hold for the first time? "I guess you can't wait."

"I feel like I've been waiting for this baby my whole

life." Her smile was tender, then wry. "And at this point, I swear I really have been. It's hard to waddle around with twenty pounds strapped to your front."

Calista laughed. No wonder women felt so off-kilter. She felt a pressure on her shoulder and turned her head to see a very old woman standing next to her. She was tiny, with curling steel-gray hair. Her brown eyes were fixed on Calista, and although her mouth was smiling, nothing was getting past those eyes.

"Are you Grant's new girlfriend?" Her tone was light, conversational.

Calista shook her head, struggling to marshal her thoughts. Out of the corner of her eye she could see Marla laughing into her hand.

"Well, if you've got plans for the boy, I want you to know we're all very fond of him. We want the best for him, especially now after all that trouble with his father."

Calista's face went hot. Did this little old lady think she was a gold digger? She watched the woman's eyes travel over Calista's outfit, stopping at the hem of her dress, right at the knee.

"I understand." That was all she could manage. Her voice seemed to have become stuck somewhere in her throat.

"Mrs. Herne, how are you this fine morning?" Grant's deep voice behind them cut through the chatter in the parish hall. Calista wanted to bolt from the scene but instead she turned and met his laughing gaze. His smile faltered at her subdued expression and he looked from Mrs. Herne to Calista and back again. He laid the small paper plates of doughnuts on the table and cocked his head.

"Now, see here. I won't bring her back if you're going to give her a hard time."

"I wasn't! Not at all." To Calista's surprise, the old woman's lined face turned pink and her eyes widened. "I was just letting her know how fond we are of you."

"Uh-huh." Grant folded his arms over his chest and pretended to fix a beady eye on Mrs. Herne. "I bet you were. I can take care of myself, you know. I'm a big boy."

By this point Marla was wiping tears from under her eyes and her shoulders were shaking with suppressed laughter. Eric dropped into a chair across from them and bit into a doughnut.

The old woman stood her ground. "Yes, Grant, dear, but even big boys get their hearts broken." And with that she gave his arm a little squeeze and walked away.

"I just love her," Eric mumbled through his doughnut. "I could have used her five years ago when I was dating the wrong girl."

Marla wrapped her arm around his shoulders and gave him a tender kiss on the cheek. "But you've never been on the other side. She scared me silly when I first met her. And plus, your broken heart was very attractive to a shy girl like me."

Eric glanced up into his wife's eyes and frowned. "Broken heart? Did I have a broken heart? I can't seem to recall…" He leaned in and pressed his lips to her forehead, dropping a hand to her tummy.

Calista watched them, her throat feeling tight. Her life was so empty of anything that truly mattered. She shot a glance at Grant, and met his eyes. He was studying her face, wondering. It probably wasn't hard to tell what she was feeling. She suddenly felt like the poor cousin at the family reunion, the one everybody felt sorry for.

"Hey, I saw the poster for the spaghetti dinner next Sunday." It wasn't a great transition, but it would have to do. Anything except broken hearts and babies and true love.

Grant nodded, taking a sip of his coffee. "We can pull in three or four hundred dollars in a day."

"But the roof will cost a whole lot more than that."

Eric shrugged. "It probably doesn't sound like much to a CEO like you."

Calista put down her half-eaten maple bar. "I do think it's a lousy way to make money, but not because I'm a CEO. It's basic business. You're on a deadline, you know your target and you're doing a church dinner?"

"And what do you suggest?" Grant's voice was light but there was steel in his eyes. "Ask my father to pay for it all?"

Grant's heart was pounding. Did Calista really think he would take the easy route and ask his father for money? Money that was probably made less than legally?

Her eyes widened, then narrowed. "I can see you're too proud to take that route."

"Proud? Because I won't accept money from Kurt Daniels?" Just saying the name made him angry.

"No." She sat back, choosing her words. "There are other deep pockets in this city. But you're too proud to go where the money is, and ask for it."

Grant almost stood up, he was so surprised. "I'm asking! I spend all day on the phone, calling donors. I send out fliers and do news pieces. I'm practically the poster boy for begging."

She was shaking her head, blond hair falling around her shoulders, green eyes deadly serious. If he wasn't so mad, he would have stopped to enjoy how close she was, how great she smelled.

"You're begging where you feel comfortable." She waved a hand. "Here, your friends. It's a lot easier to ask your favorite brother to loan you ten dollars than to ask a rich stranger for much more."

Grant gripped his head, running his hands through his hair. "Why would I ask a rich stranger for money, when I have close friends and family?" This conversation was so crazy, so unbelievable, that he felt as though all the logic had fallen out of it.

She laid a hand on his arm, leveled her gaze. "Grant, listen to yourself. It's not about *you*, is it?"

Grant stared at her, their gazes locked. Understanding flooded through him, followed by a healthy dose of shame. He'd been proud. Too proud to beg for himself. But it wasn't about him; it was about the people who didn't have a voice.

He nodded slowly. "I see your point." He watched her hand drop from his arm, and immediately wished they were still arguing. She picked up her maple bar and took a satisfied bite.

"Good," she mumbled. "Because that roof was never going to get fixed on spaghetti dinners."

Grant glanced across the table, remembering for the first time in several minutes that Eric and Marla were there. They wore matching expressions. And he knew exactly what they were thinking. He had met more than his match. This beautiful girl with the sharp mind and the bright green eyes, the quick blush and the fighting spirit, she was the one he'd been waiting for.

And she loved doughnuts, to boot.

"How did the visit to Grant's church go?" Lana's bright glance added to the friendly tone of her question.

"Amazing." Calista paused on her way back to the offices, handing over a double-shot caramel mocha and a large plate of homemade cookies. It had felt wonderful to hold the steaming drink on her trek down the snowy sidewalk, dodging foot-high drifts. Another Wednesday morning in her favorite place on earth.

"Ooh, thanks. You sure know how to get on my good side." Lana accepted the hot coffee and took a careful sip. "So, elaborate on amazing," she said and bit the head off a gingerbread man.

"Well, everyone was welcoming, the music was beautiful, the sermon was inspiring and nobody gave me the third degree except one little old lady. I think she has appointed herself Grant's personal protector against women."

Lana snorted, nodding her head. "That would be Mrs. Herne. When my son and I visited Grant's church last year for a special concert, she spent ten minutes asking me about my romantic history."

"Yikes." Calista couldn't help laughing, imagining the tiny elderly woman badgering Lana. "But it's kind of sweet that she's watching out for him."

"Did you pass inspection?"

"Not on your life. I think my dress was too short for her liking."

Lana grinned over her coffee. "I just love that nosy old lady. She'll keep you in line for sure."

"Well, it's not like I'll be seeing a lot of her."

Lana waggled her eyebrows. "We'll see about that. I heard a rumor about a Christmas party at the Grant-Humphreys Mansion."

Calista felt her cheeks flush and was annoyed at her own reactions. "Oh, that. It's nothing—"

Lana burst out laughing. "It's hard to take someone seriously when they're blushing and glaring. I would say it's definitely something."

Before Calista could do more than shrug sheepishly, the office door swung open and Jose wandered over. "Hey, ladies. Who's up for some filing?"

The two women glanced at each other and laughed.

"When you say it like that, it almost sounds exciting." Calista waved to Lana and headed for the office door.

"Like a lamb to slaughter," Lana said, laughing.

Another day, another list of phone calls to make. Grant raked his fingers through his hair and stared down at the page. Most of these people should have sent in their Christmas donation by now. Maybe they thought Kurt Daniels's son didn't need their hard-earned money this year. The idea made his gut twist in anger. He felt as though his father was circling like a vulture, getting closer and closer to cornering him.

He hadn't called since their last conversation, but he was sure Kurt Daniels was going to send the next check straight to the board. And Grant would rather leave the mission than watch it become one more trophy for his father. When he wanted something, he got it. Companies, homes, political influence—it seemed like there was no end to his father's desperate grabs for power.

On the surface, he looked like a man who was active in his community. Underneath, Grant knew that taking money from him was like making a deal with the devil. He had watched political careers soar, then falter when Kurt Daniels decided he wanted the candidate to flip-flop on a campaign promise. Whatever his father touched withered and spoiled. End of discussion.

Grant shook the disturbing thoughts away and refocused on his long list. Calista had given him a list of corporations and by the middle of the week, he'd begged enough corporate sponsorships to get the roof replaced. It wasn't hard at all, once he got his head around the fact that he wasn't as humble as he'd thought.

But they were still behind where they'd been last year. He rubbed his eyes, wishing that he could stop worrying. God provided; He always had. But it was an uphill battle to have faith when he saw numbers like these.

He needed to try on his tuxedo and make sure it still fit. Not that he'd changed since the last time he'd worn it at his cousin's fancy wedding. He was sort of looking forward to the party. It was strange because he hated functions like that, with women so overly glamorous you couldn't recognize them from their everyday selves. He wondered what Calista would wear, couldn't even wager a guess. Black-tie parties were carte blanche to layer on the jewels and the fur. Whatever she did, she would look amazing, that he knew for a fact. A corner of his mouth tugged up as he thought of her with the finger-painting crowd. The girl glowed, whether she had blue paint in her hair or was dressed to the nines.

A tap on the half-open door announced Jose...or

rather Jose's head. "Marisol wants to know if the new chick can work in the kitchen."

Grant opened his mouth to correct Jose and then decided against it. He was going to save his energy for a real battle, and he was tired of reminding him that "new chick" wasn't Calista's name.

"She's in the filing room. I can go get her." It would be a welcome distraction from his morning's work. But then, Calista was a welcome distraction at any time, he thought with a grin.

The small room was almost completely clear of files, with only a few boxes left on a long desk near the door. Calista looked up at his quiet knock, a smile spreading over her face.

"Hey, you." The warmth in her voice was like a physical touch.

"Hey, yourself." Not the most brilliant response, but his brain had gone blank at the sight of her.

"Have you come to observe me in my purgatory?"

"I've come to release you." He couldn't help taking a step closer. She smelled wonderful, like vanilla and cinnamon.

"Excellent! What's the plan, Mr. Director?"

"Marisol needs an extra kitchen helper, if you're willing."

"Really? I've been dying to get in some kitchen time. It's like a private club and no one will share the secret handshake." She tucked a file into its place and grinned up at him.

"Today's your lucky day." His fingers itched to tuck the blond lock of hair behind her ear but he had to remind himself that they were at work, and professionalism was key. He cleared his throat. "I really enjoyed Sunday."

"I did, too." Her cheeks turned pink and she paused, chewing her lip. "And Mrs. Herne was very interested in my past. We had a long conversation. Well, she asked questions and I answered them."

Grant couldn't suppress the laugh that rose up in him. "I should put her on a retainer. She's as good as a private investigator. Between the questions and the fear, I can weed out all the weak candidates."

Calista's happy grin slipped a little. "She's good. You definitely need her."

Grant regarded her for a second, trying to decipher the emotions that flitted over her face. When he figured it out, he stepped forward and lifted her chin with his fingers. Professionalism would have to wait. "There have never been a lot of candidates, and there's only one right now."

A smile played around her lips. "And what did Mrs. Herne decide?"

"She told me we'd make beautiful babies."

Calista's eyes widened in shock, and her face flushed a deep pink. "She did not!"

"I'm telling you the truth. Those old ladies have only one thing on their minds." He shook his head in dismay. "Grandchildren."

She snorted and swatted his arm. "I better get to the kitchen."

"Tell Marisol I'm dying for some tamales."

"Will do." And she flashed him one last lingering smile that deepened as she slipped out the door.

Chapter Eleven

"There you are," called Marisol from the other side of
the kitchen. She waved cheerily and beckoned Calista
to the long metal table that took up most of the far wall.
Calista snagged a burgundy apron from the hooks by
the door, careful to choose one that didn't have a name
embroidered on it. Before she slipped the halter over her
head, she removed her jacket and hung it up. Her short-
sleeved silk shirt underneath was a bright red, for the
Christmas holiday, just days away. The apron wouldn't
save her clothes if she dropped a pot of chili, but if she
was just chopping vegetables it was probably going to
be all right. She washed her hands at the sink near the
door and headed for the rest of the group.

She came to stand beside the short Hispanic woman.
She noted once more the worn apron, the leathery hands
and the familiar smell of chili powder. Her quick glance
was paired with a wide smile. Marisol's quiet joy was
visible in everything she did. Calista's heart rate slowed
to a comfortable rate as she took in the pleasant chatter
around her. The kitchen was hopping today. Not like the
filing room. She was so glad to be out of there she could

have skipped down the hallway. Except that Grant had been watching. She felt her cheeks warm at the thought of his fingers tipping her chin, his assurance that she was the only one he was interested in right now. She struggled to refocus on the task ahead.

"What do you need me to do? I'm ready and willing."

"I'm making vegetable beef stew for dinner and the big chopper broke." She waved a hand toward a large appliance that looked like a mixer, but much more dangerous. Sharp blades showed where a brushed metal hood had been removed. A middle-aged man peered into the innards, a scowl on his face. There was a cart underneath that was half-filled with potato pieces.

"I've never seen anything like that," Calista said, then jumped as the man flipped a red switch and the food processor roared to life. The kitchen workers paused collectively to watch, but then turned back to their tasks as the motor coughed and died.

"It also does french fries and carrot sticks, shreds lettuce, all sorts of things. I sure hope Jim can get it going." Marisol was chopping furiously while she talked.

Calista grabbed a large knife and a potato. "Is it very old? It might still be under warranty."

"No, is too old for the company to come fix. Maybe we can call a mechanic if he can't make it work."

"How much does it cost to replace?" The knife was making quick work of her small stack of potatoes, and Calista made a mental note to sharpen her own kitchen knives.

"That one cost about ten thousand, but that was a while ago."

She gasped, startled, and her knife narrowly missed her own index finger. "Ten thousand *dollars*?"

Marisol nodded, her brown eyes fixed on her work. "Kitchen equipment is very expensive. And costs to run, too. Lots of electricity for the hot water, the stoves, the dishwashers."

Calista stared around the kitchen, suddenly seeing it in a whole new light. The enormous side-by-side refrigerators, the pots that looked as though they could hold a whole turkey, the two large stoves, metal cart after metal cart. Grant needed to have major funds just to keep the kitchen going, let alone the rest of the mission. She started to wonder just what kind of budget a homeless shelter needed.

"I always thought the food was the most expensive part."

Marisol chuckled. "No, we get lots of food donations. Two big bakeries downtown give us all their day-old bread. In the summertime, the local growers bring us fruit. Christmas is a big day, lots of people, but we already have the turkeys ready in the freezer. It is the machinery that is so hard to get." She shook her head, her brow furrowing. "Poor Mr. Monohan. He has too many things to fix."

Calista was silent. A place as famous as the Downtown Denver Mission shouldn't be hurting for support. Times were hard in Denver, just like they were everywhere because of the economy, but people still tended to give at this time of year.

"Christmas is a good time for donations, right?"

Marisol reached for another potato and shrugged. "It can be. But Lana says the donations are down this month. Probably because of Mr. Monohan's father."

Calista felt a wave of pure anger sweep through her. They were holding it against him, and Grant had never asked to be recognized as Kurt Daniels's son. Plus, it was unfair that he had to bow to the pressure and give up his privacy. She couldn't imagine how it felt to be exposed that way.

The pile of whole potatoes was almost finished and Calista felt satisfaction at their quick work. Then Marisol reached under the metal table and tugged a fifty-pound sack into the light. Calista peeked under the table and almost groaned. Four more sacks lay side by side. This was going to be a long morning. But it was still better than the little filing room.

Marisol called a worker to come collect the sack of potatoes for washing.

"Okay, I am going to get the stew meat. Is all chopped and ready." Marisol pointed to a large metal door with a long, flat handle. "You can come with me so you see the inside."

Putting down her knife, Calista dutifully followed Marisol to the door, then gasped as it swung open to reveal a full-size room. The walls were lined with floor-to-ceiling shelves and buckets were tidily lined up on the lowest areas.

"This is a refrigerator?" She should have known that the fridges out in the main area couldn't contain enough food for several hundred people.

"Yes, and we have two walk-in freezers. Always take your coat in when you go."

Calista shivered, partly at the chill and partly at the thought of being stuck in a freezer without coat. As the door eased closed behind them, she resisted the urge to push it back open. The handle on the inside was reassuring, but it was still unnerving to be standing in a steel fridge with only one way out.

Marisol lifted a long packet of stew meat and handed it to Calista. Then she hefted the other into her arms. "Oh, now, see here." She nodded her head in the direction of the shelf.

She was no weakling, but there was at least forty pounds of beef cubes in her arms. Calista leaned over, feeling the strain in her biceps. Light red puddles rested on the floor. Beef blood had dripped from the packages, through the wire shelving and pooled on the concrete.

"We will bring these out and then I have to clean. I tell the workers to always have a drip pan under the meat but sometimes they do not listen."

"Do you want me to clean it? You can keep supervising the stew." Beef blood was on her list of things to avoid, but Calista shrugged off the thought. She wanted to be useful.

"No, *mija*, but thank you." Marisol beamed at her as they reentered the warm kitchen. "I have to wash down the floor with the hose, then spray it with bleach, then scrub. I have a thick coat so I will not be cold." She set the tray near the stove and turned to eye Calista's outfit. "You always look so pretty."

For some reason, Marisol's compliment lightened her heart. Maybe because she was sure it was sincere. At work, compliments flowed freely, but were rarely worth more than the breath they took.

"Thank you. I'll keep working on the potatoes, then?"

Shrugging into a heavy work jacket that was much too big for her short frame, Marisol nodded and headed toward the refrigerator, stopping to grab a hose from where it was neatly coiled on the floor.

Her table was covered with freshly washed potatoes and Calista wondered if this was what it was like to get kitchen duty in the army. The sound of the power hose washing down the cement floor echoed faintly through the crack left in the closed door. She worked in silence, glancing up every now and then to watch the workers in the kitchen. Marisol pushed the door open and recoiled the bright yellow hose, then twisted the faucet closed with sharp movements. She disappeared back into the refrigerator, this time closing the door with a firm thud.

Calista shivered at the sight. It looked like a bank vault from the outside.

At that moment, a large squeal sounded above the stove. She dropped her potato in surprise, then saw the source of the noise. A ceiling fan, several feet square, had decided to stop working. Grant really had to make a list of items that needed to be replaced. She would talk to him about the ideas she'd been working on for fund-raising.

That was the last thing that went through Calista's mind before she saw the flames. Flickering orange, the fire licked along the edges of grating that covered the fan and grew several feet in just seconds.

"Thank you for your generous support of the mission. As a long-time donor—" Grant's attempt to connect with one of the many people who had not given their usual Christmastime donation was interrupted by the piercing wail of the fire alarm.

Just peachy. He gave an internal sigh and hurriedly finished leaving the message.

But this wasn't a drill. Lana always let him know when she was going to have a drill and which building it was in. Grant jumped to his feet, feeling a sudden contraction of fear in his chest.

The hallway was empty but he jogged to the filing room, just in case Calista had come back. His heart was beating so loudly the fire alarm was hardly noticeable. The room was empty. He closed it and hung the All Clear sign that was previously hanging on the inside, then did the same for the other offices. Probably it was nothing. Most likely it was just a false alarm.

Out in the lobby, Lana was giving directions to the residents who were filing by the decorated fir tree, toward the front doors. She caught his eye and called, "Kitchen fire! The meeting rooms on this side are cleared. We're heading out the front."

"Offices are clear," he called back.

Calista. His mind flashed on horrible scenarios of flaming grease or exploding stoves and then he shoved the images away. Marisol would never let her handle anything dangerous without training. And Marisol would make sure everyone was out safely. Every worker was trained in fire exits and procedures. Each supervisor would help clear the building, and herd other workers out. The other buildings would evacuate to the parking lot and the sidewalks. He should be following Lana to the street since he was in the office area but Grant had to look. It was probably just a dish of something going up in flames.

The cafeteria was empty except for the last of the workers trooping out the back exit. Grant ducked into the kitchen, holding his breath against the thick smoke. Bright flames were all too visible as they shot from the ceiling and licked along the edge where the ceiling met the wall. An industrial-size fire extinguisher lay spent on the floor and Grant felt his heart drop into his shoes. This fire was too big to put out. He peered through the black smoke, crouching low to get a better look. He reassured himself the kitchen was truly empty.

Everyone was out. The rest was in God's hands.

He jogged through the cafeteria, letting out a deep breath he'd been holding in the smoky kitchen. The outside door swung open at his touch and he sucked in the fresh air. The mission's fire protocol stated kitchen workers would gather on the far side of the courtyard, which was their rendezvous point. The snow reflected the sun and he squinted toward the workers, searching. They huddled together, some with their arms around the shoulders of friends. He scanned the group for Calista's blond hair, trying to recall her outfit. With the mass of red polos and khaki pants, it only took a second to realize Calista was not there.

Fear gripped him like steel bands tightening around his ribs. He strode over, determined to be calm. His eyes searched the group for Marisol and what had been fear turned to outright dread.

"Mr. Monohan!" A young woman rushed up to him, her red hair escaping from the standard-issue hairnet. Her eyes were streaming tears, but whether from the smoke or the shock of the fire, he wasn't sure.

"That new girl, she was with us but then she went back!"

Grant felt his limbs go numb. He wanted to move, wanted to ask her a question, but for several seconds his mind shut down completely. Went back in? But he hadn't seen anyone, and the offices were clear.

He spun on his heel, staring at the closed cafeteria door. Was it possible she had made it back to the kitchen by the time he had crouched down in the doorway to make sure it was clear? Could she be in there now?

"Did she say anything?" He said the words calmly but his voice broke on the last word. "And where is Marisol?"

The young woman started to sob in earnest. "I don't know. She wasn't in the kitchen with us when the fire started. The new girl got the fire extinguisher and tried to put it out, but it was already burning through the ceiling."

Grant stared at the roof of what was the kitchen. Smoke billowed from the vents and long red flames appeared in the northwest corner. His heart thudded in his throat. He knew the very worst thing was to go back into a fire, for any reason. Everything could be replaced except for human life.

Lord, show me what to do!

In answer to his prayer, the pieces of the puzzle clicked into place. "Were they working together, before the fire?"

She coughed, struggling to suppress her sobs. "I think so. They were chopping potatoes at the long prep table."

Marisol was in there. And Calista knew where. The wail of the fire trucks sounded in the distance and Grant was already moving toward the cafeteria door. He heard several voices calling him back but he ignored them. Within seconds he reached the door, pulled it open and entered the cafeteria. Only it wasn't a cafeteria any longer. It was as black as night with acrid smoke and the heat buffeted against him in waves. He crouched down but could see only marginally better.

"Marisol! Calista!" He called out as loudly as he could, then sucked in a breath. That was a mistake. The coughs that racked his body made it impossible to call out again. He stumbled forward, squinting against the smoke, and ran directly into Marisol's soft, familiar form. He barely recognized her face, blackened with smoke, eyes wide with fear. Calista supported her on one side and her eyes were streaming. He grabbed hold of Marisol's other arm and sped her toward the outside door.

The clear sky above them and the crunch of the snow underfoot were like heaven as they burst out of the cafeteria. Grant supported Marisol and was relieved to notice that she was uninjured, as much as he could ascertain in the few seconds before they reached the kitchen workers huddled in the far corner. She was enveloped by the group and hugged over and over. Calista stood still, panting slightly, streaks of soot on her face. Grant looked over at her, a question on his lips, his fear finally ebbing at the sight of them. He wanted to ask, but before he did he simply held out his arms.

Calista walked into them as naturally as if she had been born to rest there against his chest. He could feel her trembling, her arms locked around his waist. Squeezing his eyes shut, he spoke a prayer of thanks into her hair.

He could have stayed that way for hours, feeling the beat of his heart slowly return to normal.

The sound of water being sprayed at full force onto the roof brought him back to reality. The fire trucks had unrolled the long ladders and were directing water to the hole in the kitchen where flames were still emerging.

"She was in the fridge," Calista choked out. Her green eyes were bloodshot and soot was smeared along one cheek.

Grant stepped back, struggling to make sense of her words. "The walk-in refrigerator?"

Calista nodded, swallowing hard. One arm was still around his waist, under his jacket, and he could feel her shaking. "I panicked when the fan caught on fire. I tried to put it out but then I just ran out with everybody else." Her face collapsed with the weight of her tears and she pressed a fist against her mouth.

"You did what you were supposed to do," he said, pulling her against him again.

"I forgot she was there, trapped in that place," she said and began to sob.

Grant could feel the hysteria rising in her and lifted her face to his. Her tears were hot under his fingers. "Calista, you saved her life. There's a light that flashes in the fridge when the alarm goes off. She should have seen it. You did the right thing, and more."

"When I opened the door, she was on her hands and knees scrubbing the floor. She didn't see it flashing." She shook her head and squeezed her eyes shut, tears leaking out from under her lids. "It felt just like last time."

Grant frowned and moved his hands from her face to her shoulders. "Last time?"

"My mother died when our house caught fire. She was in the basement. Doing laundry." Her eyes were still closed, face tight with fear and pain.

He felt the blood rushing to his head. He couldn't

fathom that she had gone back inside, in the face of all her fears.

"Grant, can I sit down?" She opened her eyes and swayed a little as she spoke.

He cursed himself for letting her talk when she needed to be wrapped in a blanket and checked out for burns. He slipped out of his jacket and wrapped it around her shoulders.

Marisol was still cocooned in several pairs of arms, her heavy coat hardly visible. Grant gently led them away from the group, his arm around Marisol's shoulders, Calista's hand firmly in his, and the three of them made their way down the sidewalk. Marisol mumbled a few words and Grant wondered if she was in shock.

The ambulance crew gave them both a thorough examination, thankful there were only two victims of the smoke. Grant hovered, his heart torn between watching the progress on the fire and making sure they were okay.

Savannah ran toward him from across the parking lot, her pink sunglasses slipping down her nose. Her mother trailed behind, a hand to her mouth in shock.

"Mr. Monohan! There was a fire and everything burnded! Even the pretty Christmas tree!"

He stooped down and caught Savannah's small figure in his arms. There were rules about hugging the residents, especially children. An arm across the shoulders was fine, a handshake was better. But today, he didn't feel like following the recommendations. The little girl was frightened and a hug was really all he had to give. That, and his assurance that everything was going to be okay.

"Savannah, don't worry. It was a kitchen fire and the firemen got it under control."

She tipped back her dark head and searched his face. "Is that a lie, Mr. Monohan?"

He tried to smile at the question, but his sadness got in the way. She was used to adults saying one thing and meaning another. "Nope, not a lie."

"'Cause it looks like everything got burnded up."

"Burned, not burnded. And no, it was just the kitchen. The tree is fine. Everybody is okay." His gaze went straight to Calista, then Marisol.

"Then why is Miss Calista in the ambulance?" Savannah pointed toward Calista, tears threatening to spill over onto her round cheeks.

"They're just making sure she's not hurt. It was scary, but the firemen came and are putting it out."

Savannah rested her head on his shoulder for a moment, her small body relaxing against him. Her mother stood off to the side, transfixed by the smoke that streamed from the kitchen roof.

"Okay, I believe you."

Grant felt his heart constrict with the power of those words. There were so many people who needed reassurance. *Lord, help me show them Your faithfulness.*

"But what are we gonna eat now if the food is all gone?"

"I promise that no one will be hungry."

"Good. I hate being hungry." The little girl shoved her sunglasses back up her nose.

"Why don't you go say hi to Miss Calista?"

Savannah nodded and went over to her mother, slipping her small hand into hers and tugging her toward Calista. Grant watched them with a heavy heart. So many people depended on this mission, on him.

The fire raged on, the hoses poured thousands of gallons of water on the flames, and through it all, Grant had a running conversation with God about Calista, the mission, his future, his father. *Why, Lord? Why now?* And then he would glance back at Marisol resting on the ambulance table and gratitude would sweep over him again. *Thank You for keeping them safe.*

"Are you the director?" A slight man in a fireman-captain's uniform appeared at the side of the emergency vehicle.

"I am." Grant stood up, his body tensing with the news he knew was just seconds away.

"Well, you're really lucky no one was seriously injured because electrical fires spread quickly. We've got it contained now. But the kitchen is a total loss."

Chapter Twelve

Calista sat huddled in a blanket, taking tiny sips of coffee and watching flames shoot through the roof of the Downtown Denver Mission. Marisol was a few feet away, staring blankly into the smoky sky. Calista didn't know if she was praying or in shock. She hadn't said much of anything since Calista had led her out of the refrigerator and through scorching flames.

She was aware of the bitter smell of burned hair and for the first time Calista put up a hand to her head. Sure enough, clumps of hair came away when she ran her fingers through it. She sighed. How many days had she gone to work with her hair down? Two, maybe three? But she had wanted to look nice for Grant and left off her usual French chignon or softly made bun. The irony of it was almost laughable. She would have to call her hairdresser and have some sort of stylishly short 'do for a while.

Calista shook the hair off her fingers and went back to watching the fire. Or watching Grant watching the fire. He stuffed his hands in his pockets and paced for a few minutes. Then he ran his hands through his hair, looked over at Marisol and back at the fire. Then he started with the pocket stuffing and pacing again. She knew what it was like to watch your home burn to the ground. But she had no idea what it was like to watch your home burn, and know hundreds of people depended on you for survival. Their Christmas was ruined.

Lissa and Michelle weren't too far away, surrounded by kids, waiting for parents to come. A few of the little ones were crying but most were jumping up and down in excitement. Two firemen walked over to hand out stickers and show the kids the gear.

Lissa caught Calista's gaze and wandered over, her arms wrapped around her thin waist.

Calista blinked up at the teen, and forced a smile. "How are the kids?" She couldn't imagine herding dozens of small children out of a building with the fire alarms wailing.

Lissa bent down and gave Calista a fierce hug, then stood back. The expression on her face was a mixture Calista couldn't quite decipher.

"And that was for…?"

"For asking about the kids when you're the one who's sitting in the back of the ambulance."

"I'm actually on the bumper, but I see your point." Calista grinned, wondering how Lissa managed to be so defensive and endearing all at the same time. "And thank you for the hug. I needed it."

Lissa nodded, her gaze fixed on the man who paced the sidewalk. She flipped her dark braid back over one shoulder and said, "I wish a hug fixed everything, but it doesn't."

Calista sighed. "Truer words were never spoken."

"I've got to get back to the kids. Michelle says this

is the very first class we've ever run in the parking lot, with firemen as assistants."

She laughed, and raised a hand to Lissa's coworker, who looked ready to hand out kids as party favors. Lissa went back to her group and the kids surrounded her. She was sarcastic and tense, but something in that girl touched Calista and reminded her of her own teen years.

Her gaze was jerked back to the scene in front of her as the fire chief interrupted Grant's twentieth tour of the sidewalk and delivered what must have been the bad news. Calista wasn't near enough to hear the words, but she was near enough to see his shoulders slump. He nodded, his features stiff, and shook the chief's hand before the fireman went back to his crew.

Calista wanted to run to Grant and throw her arms around him, as if that would shield him from what had already happened. She knew there was no use in trying to pretend it was all right, or put a positive spin on the situation. The mission was crippled, maybe permanently.

She raised her eyes and saw him regarding her steadily. She slowly lifted a hand, maybe in greeting or in goodbye since she wasn't sure where he would go from here. Maybe this would be one of the last times they saw each other. He was going to have way more on his mind than getting to know her. She felt as though someone had grabbed her by the throat, the feeling of loss was so sudden. Tears sprang to her eyes and she furiously blinked them away. How ridiculous to cry over Grant, when hundreds of vulnerable people in poverty were in a truly terrible situation. But it was no use yelling at herself; the tears continued to flow down her cheeks. She ducked her head and swiped at her face.

"You need to go home and get some rest," he said, suddenly a few feet away.

Calista frowned, mopping her face one last time with the edge of the blanket. "I'm okay," she said, trying for confident but sounding argumentative.

He sat down next to her and was silent for a moment. They watched the firemen winding their hoses back on to the trucks. Most of the workers had gone home, but Jose hovered near the fire trucks and Lana remained near the corner, giving periodic statements to reporters when needed. Calista felt a surge of gratitude for the middle-aged secretary.

"I can give you a ride home."

Calista glanced up, surprised. Did he think she wasn't able to drive herself? She must look worse than she'd thought.

"I'm really okay. It was pretty darn scary, I admit. But everything worked out…" The words trailed away. It didn't work out for the people who relied on the mission for meals. She jumped back in before Grant could speak. "Is there anything I can do? What's the plan for providing meals? I'm sure you've notified the board and there's probably an emergency backup plan."

He turned to look her full in the face and she struggled not to let another tear slip away from her. His expression was so raw, his despair so clear, that it took her breath away.

"The board has been notified. The residents may stay in the unaffected buildings, so they'll be able to sleep here and have classes. Our paperwork and computers survived, which is a blessing. But the kitchen…" Grant turned back toward the smoking corner of the main building. "The kitchen is the heart and soul of this mission's outreach. A lot of people would never come through these doors if they weren't hungry. Once they have a hot meal, they can face a lot of their other issues."

Calista stared at Grant's profile, finally understanding. "It all started with the kitchen, didn't it? When it was founded?"

He nodded.

"So…" Calista hated to say anything that might bring back that look of despair. But what was the plan? Did they all just go on without a kitchen?

"So," he repeated, sounding a little stronger. "We'll be assessing the damage and probably have some smoke issues with the lobby. I think the offices were spared any smoke damage because the main door was closed."

She felt a burst of relief, hoping that meant she was supposed to come back. He moved to sit down next to her on the ambulance bumper and stared at the smoking kitchen.

"You never did tell me how much of the funding is earmarked for repairs. How long would the board take to authorize construction on a new kitchen?"

He turned to face her, bright blue gaze soft on hers. "You're right. I forgot to outline all of that." He paused. "You know, Calista, I wanted to thank you for being here. Not just what happened with Marisol." He paused, swallowing audibly and glancing away for a moment. Calista waited, scanning his face for the little flickers of emotion that hinted at everything he held inside.

"I wanted to thank you for taking an interest in the mission. A lot of people don't want to be bothered with the paperwork or the dirty details of fund-raising."

Calista let out a breath she didn't know she'd been holding. What did she think he was going to say? That he was glad for her sparkling personality? She swallowed back her disappointment and nodded brightly. "Well, that's what I do best, Grant. Some people lead the sing-alongs or wipe noses. I like the paperwork. And I'm more than willing to help organize the fund-raising for the new kitchen project."

"I've seen you wipe a few noses." He contradicted her, his tone teasing.

"True, but if it's a choice between paperwork and wiping a nose, I choose paperwork any day."

He laughed. "We're two of a kind there, I guess."

She glanced at the smoking ruins and continued in a softer tone. "I know it must be so hard to see all your work ruined, but the faster you start rebuilding, the better it will be for the mission."

"And that's what I'm talking about, right there. Someone else might say that a disaster like this is a huge setback and we should take our time, maybe even close down for a while."

Calista shook her head, struggling to keep her thoughts straight under threat of that smile. "Sure, that would make sense if we weren't talking about *people*. Buildings can wait, stores can open months later than planned, but hungry people can't wait."

He didn't answer, just kept smiling. Then he slowly reached out a hand and ran a thumb along her jaw.

Calista felt as if her whole body had been thrown into a pot of hot water. Her cheeks flushed and she wanted to say something, anything. But her voice was gone, along with any ability to form a complete thought.

"You have soot on your face," he said, very softly.

"Oh."

His eyes crinkled with laughter. "Yes, oh." And then

he was leaning closer, one arm resting lightly behind her back. For a fleeting moment, Calista flashed back to the first time he had been this close. She had thought he was going to kiss her and he was actually giving his security badge to the cafeteria girl. Maybe she should turn and look behind her, just in case he was reaching for something in the back of the ambulance?

The next moment she knew for sure. Grant's lips pressed softly against hers and she couldn't keep her eyes open one second longer. She was lost; his arm against her back and his lips against hers were the only important things in the entire universe.

He sat back a few inches, still close enough for her to see the rough stubble on his jaw and the thick dark lashes that rimmed his bright blue eyes. "Now I know."

"Know what?" Her voice came out all breathless.

"That you won't run away if I try that."

The idea of turning tail at the sight of an impending kiss from Grant startled a laugh out of her. "Why would you ever think I'd run?"

His lips curved up, even as sadness flared behind his eyes. "Plenty of reasons. This isn't a nine-to-five job. And a lot of times I get wrapped up in the problems the residents are having. I should be more distant, but I just can't be."

Calista lifted her hand to his cheek and whispered, "That's what I like about you. Of all the people I've met, you would have the best excuse for being distant. But you're not."

He shook his head, the movement insistent against her palm. "Because I'm not bitter that things haven't always gone the way I've wanted?"

Calista waved her hand at the smoldering ruins of

the kitchen. "This is a little more than not getting what you want. This is watching hard work, effort, hopes and dreams…" Just the words made the reality of the situation so much more real, Calista felt overwhelmed. She struggled to speak past the lump in her throat. "I've been here two months and this fire breaks my heart. It makes me wonder what God is thinking."

Grant sighed and wrapped an arm around her shoulders. "I know. But in Jeremiah it says that God wants to show us great and marvelous things. So, maybe He has to burn down a kitchen or two in the process."

Calista stared out toward the smoking lobby area, the firemen sorting their gear into piles and wrapping up hoses. The snowdrifts were black and dirty, puddles of water mixed with slush. She thought of her mother, and the fire that took her life. What great and marvelous things came from that? Pain rose up in her chest like a wave of icy water. She struggled to take a breath. *I trust in You, Jesus. I trust in You.* Calista rested her head on Grant's shoulder and closed her eyes, fighting back the fear. Fear that she was all alone in the universe, that God was a myth made by fragile, human minds.

"Mija?" Marisol's trembling voice shook Calista out of her thoughts. The older woman walked toward them, still wrapped in a brown emergency blanket.

She stood up and hugged Marisol for all she was worth. "I'm so sorry," she said, her voice catching. "I'm so sorry for leaving you in there."

"But *mija*, you did not leave me! You saved me." Marisol's tone was indignant.

Calista just shook her head and hugged harder. Finally, she stepped back and wiped the fresh tears from her face.

"And we are all safe, that is what matters," Marisol declared, her brown eyes flashing. "And plus, it seems some good has come out of this already." She nodded her head at Grant and gave Calista a huge wink.

She felt the heat rise in her cheeks but couldn't suppress the grin that spread over her face.

"I knew it would take something very big to get Mr. Monohan to show his feelings to you. And for you, too, Calista." She shook a finger at the two of them, each in turn.

Grant made a choking sound and started to protest. "It wasn't the fire, really..."

But Calista never heard the rest because the fire chief came over then.

"We're heading out, Mr. Monohan. Again, I'm sorry about what happened to the mission. If there's anything we can do, let me know. Maybe we can help with fund-raising."

Grant thanked the chief for the team's efforts. "I'll be sure to give you a call when we get a plan."

As they watched him walk away, Marisol said, "Mr. Monohan, I better get home and wash these smoky clothes. Jose said he'd give me a ride home." She gave them both one last hug and walked over to Jose, who gave them a sad-looking wave before heading home.

Calista sighed. "Me, too. And call my hairdresser."

For the first time, Grant seemed to notice Calista's damaged hair. His mouth dropped open in shock and he gently ran his fingers through one side of the sooty mess. Broken and singed strands came away with his hand.

"Oh, Calista," he whispered. "I'm so sorry."

She couldn't help laughing. "You're sorry about my hair? The mission kitchen just burned down and you're worried about my hair?" The more she thought about it, the funnier it was. Soon, she was doubled over, tears leaking from her eyes. Grant watched her, bemused.

"Let me take you home," he said, concern edging his voice even though his expression was light.

Calista took a deep breath, and straightened up, struggling to keep her face straight. "Sorry, maybe it wasn't that funny. I definitely need a hot bath and some calm music." She handed her blanket back to the ambulance crew and turned just in time to see Jackie running toward them.

"Calista! I've been calling you for hours." Her voice was high-pitched with panic, eyes sweeping over the scene and Calista's ruined clothes.

"Jackie, everything's okay, we're fine." She rushed to reassure her friend, reaching out with one sooty hand. "Did you see the fire on the news?"

Jackie stepped back from her touch, careful not to get her pale violet suit smudged. "No, I didn't. But you missed the big board meeting at one and since no one could reach you, the directors were having fits."

Grant watched Calista's eyes change as if a door had slammed shut inside. Where there had been softness and vulnerability, there was only icy silence.

"It's time to get back to your real life, boss, because the office is falling apart." The pretty girl flicked a curl over her shoulder as if she was talking about the weather.

When Calista found her voice, the tone was impersonal. "My phone is in my purse, which is in the file room." She turned to Grant, face expressionless. "Is it all right if I go back inside?"

He nodded, but held up a hand. "You two can talk while I go get it." And he walked away without waiting for an answer.

The door was propped open and he stepped carefully through the flooded patches in the lobby. His heart was pounding, but not in anticipation this time. He was angry, and he needed a few minutes to compose himself or he was going to give that woman a piece of his mind. Calista had been in a fire, saved a friend, confronted her worst fears, and all she could say was that Calista missed a big meeting? He felt the blood rushing in his ears and shook his head.

What was all that about her "real life"? He pushed back a whisper of fear. She had a job, a high-powered position that she didn't make any effort to hide. He was just reacting to the stew of lies his father concocted. It was an offhand comment and nothing more.

The hallway to the offices was a little hazy, but otherwise there was no smoke damage. He stopped to open a few windows at the end of the hall then headed for the file room. Calista's small black purse was sitting on the desk by the door. Grant grabbed it and her coat, and walked back toward the lobby. His head was still whirling with relief and anger and disbelief when he walked through the lobby door, straight into his father.

Kurt Daniels stood at the front of the Downtown Denver Mission as if he owned the place, but that's how he looked wherever he went. With thick, wavy hair that was more silver than black and a stature that made other men feel small, the powerful businessman didn't have to work for respect. It just came to him naturally, whether he had earned it or not. A suit that must cost as much as the average mortgage payment was the final touch.

He was awesome to behold. As long as you didn't know what kind of person was on the inside.

Grant planted himself a few feet away, waiting for his father to speak. Those dark blue eyes were exactly like his own, except for the calculating look.

"I have to talk to you." The gravelly voice was utterly familiar and it set Grant's teeth on edge.

"So you can force me to do everything your way? You're absolutely predictable." He was too tired to argue about this, not now.

"Please." Kurt Daniels held up a long, elegant hand.

Grant waited, eyebrows raised, not trusting for a moment that his father actually had a valid reason to be here, at this moment.

"I made a mistake."

Grant couldn't keep from shaking his head and taking a step toward the parking lot.

"Grant, you need to hear this, no matter what's between us." The intensity of his tone, the set of his jaw, slowed Grant's steps.

After a short debate, he said, "Five seconds. Which is more than you ever gave me until this year."

His father sighed, closed his eyes for a moment and then said, "I hired someone to convince you to see things my way, to make sure you let me get involved in your life. I didn't know what he was doing." He stopped, looking up, pain in his eyes. "No, I made sure not to know. Which is different."

Grant's mind was stuck, spinning like car wheels in the snow. "You…hired someone to write me threatening letters?"

Kurt Daniels glanced at the parking lot, the reporters with camera equipment. "I thought it would hurry things along, if you thought you had to admit to the world we were related."

Grant heaved a sigh. "I don't even know what to say. I'm glad to know who was behind it all. But this is a bad time to be having this conversation. As you can see—" he swept a hand behind him at the smoking shell of the mission "—we've had a fire."

His father stepped forward and grabbed his arm, eyes flashing. "That's why I'm here," he hissed.

Grant jerked his arm away. "What are you talking about?"

"I think the man I hired started that fire."

He felt the words drop one by one, like ice cubes down his spine. "You...did this?" Even after all he knew about his father, he could never have imagined this. It was too horrible, too evil.

"I didn't know, I swear. I thought he was trying to scare you with anonymous threats. When I saw the fire on the news, it occurred to me for the first time that he might do something more."

Grant shook his head, hardly able to form words. He looked over at Calista, standing near the ambulance. How could she ever want to be part of this soap opera? People could have been hurt; Marisol could have died. Fury choked him and Grant struggled to speak calmly.

"If you're here to beg forgiveness, that's not for me to decide. The police will be involved if this was arson, and I'm not going to jail for you." With those words he stalked past him into the parking lot.

Calista stood with her arms folded across her waist, while Jackie paced a few feet away, speaking urgently into her cell phone.

"I'm sorry for the delay." He handed over her purse, hoping he didn't sound as furious as he felt.

Calista accepted her purse without comment, but she shot a dubious look behind him.

"You don't want to know," he said, trying for black humor and ending up somewhere near bitterness.

"Grant, I'm going to go home and get cleaned up, then head back to work so I can handle the crisis that erupted there today. But…" She fixed him with a steady look. "I'm hoping we can talk tomorrow. I don't understand why you can't take his money."

He felt her words like a slap to the face. Of course, everyone wanted him to take the money. That was all that really mattered, unless you knew the truth.

She seemed to read his thoughts because she said, "It just doesn't make sense and I want to understand, if you'll trust me."

Her look gripped his heart and he hauled in a deep breath. He did trust her. As much as he trusted Marisol or Eric, friends he'd known for years. There was a powerful ache to tell her the whole story right here and now, but not because he thought she wasn't going to come back. His heart told him Calista was here to stay. He glanced behind him and wasn't surprised to see Kurt Daniels had already disappeared. He was good at that.

"All right. But it's not a pretty story."

"I wasn't hoping for a fairy tale." Calista's lips twitched for a moment and Grant felt his heart lighten at the sight. This woman could lead him anywhere with one word, one look. It would be sort of scary, if it didn't feel so right.

Jackie snapped her cell phone closed and strode over to them. "We've got to get moving. The board has called a meeting for this evening. I told them what happened and that you needed a few hours to get ready." She nodded at Grant, her eyes taking in his appearance from his head to his shoes, then flickering past him to where his father had been just minutes before.

Calista nodded, her expression all business. "Let's go." She hesitated, and Grant wished he could give her a kiss goodbye. But Jackie was waiting and Calista reached out a hand to touch his sleeve, then turned away and walked toward the far parking lot.

He watched them until they had turned the corner. *Please keep her safe.* Because whatever had gone wrong today at VitaWow, her expression showed that it was a bigger threat to her peace of mind than a raging fire.

Calista flipped the switch inside that took her from normal girl to CEO. It wasn't a hard move, considering she had spent the past decade being fearlessly in control. But this time there was a piece of her, her mind or even her heart, that seemed stuck back in the Downtown Denver Mission parking lot. She could almost feel Grant's thumb moving along her jaw, his warm lips on hers. She struggled to focus on Jackie's fast-paced chatter.

"The board received a last-minute offer on a new location for the headquarters. It's better than the last by a long shot. It's so good I thought it was a joke. As soon as I heard this morning, I tried to call you about twenty times to give you a heads-up before the meeting but you must have had your phone turned off."

Calista frowned, shaking her head. They were standing in front of her car, Jackie's sports car pulled up at an angle to hers. A testament of how panicked she'd been when she'd arrived. Not for her safety, of course, but because of the meeting. Calista swallowed the hurt that swamped her and focused on what seemed like the palest details in a dramatic day.

"I never turn my phone off, but I did go to the kitchen around ten because they needed help in there. I forgot to take it with me." Forgot because she'd been rattled at having a sweet conversation with Grant about babies. Instead of smiling at the memory, she felt her jaw clench. Grant's presence had thrown her into a blushing frenzy, like a teenager. She couldn't even trust herself to keep track of minor things like her phone when he was around.

"Then when the kitchen caught fire, I panicked and got out." Calista left the rest of the story for another time. Or maybe never. She was so tired her teeth ached but she still needed to get cleaned up and head to VitaWow.

For the first time Jackie seemed to consider the implications of finding Calista sitting in the ambulance. "Are you sure you're okay to meet with the board this evening? I could try to get them all rescheduled for to-morrow morning."

Calista almost snorted. Of course she wasn't, but she didn't really have a choice. "It's fine, but see if you can get my hairdresser to meet me at my apartment in thirty minutes. Tell her it's an emergency."

Jackie nodded, eyes wide. "Oh, wow. Your hair is really…going to need some help."

She sighed, hating to admit how shallow Jackie was, if her hair got a bigger reaction than the mission losing a major part of its operation.

Chapter Thirteen

Grant felt a buzz in his pocket for the tenth time that hour. He resisted the urge to throw the cell phone out the open window of his office and answered it like the good director he was. But if today got any longer, he didn't know how much goodness was left in him.

"I saw it on the news. I'm on my way over."

Eric's statement, instead of a greeting, made Grant smile in spite of himself.

"You were just here. There's not much difference except the big black, smokin' hole where the kitchen used to be."

"Be there in ten." And with a click, Grant was reminded why Eric was his best friend. He closed his own phone and laid it on the desk, wanting to lay his head in his arms and close his eyes. The few minutes of quiet in his office was supposed to give him energy to get through the day, but all it seemed to do was remind him how very tired he was. And smoky. And wishing Calista was still here.

Instead she was on her way back to VitaWow, which wasn't fair because she needed to go home and rest.

Jackie's lack of compassion to Calista irked him every time he thought about it. She was supposed to run off to a meeting after what had happened here? Poor woman, no wonder she felt as though she had no real friends if that was as close as she got to friendship. But somehow Calista showed compassion, loyalty, generosity, when she was at the mission…and amazing bravery today. *Give her strength, Lord, for what she needs to do today. Whatever it is.*

His father jumped to mind and he shoved the image away. He just didn't have time to even consider the implications. Was his father really so unhinged he would hire someone to burn the mission down? Just to get attention?

His desk phone rang and he stared at it. What he wouldn't give to pretend he wasn't sitting six inches away. He rubbed a hand over his face and picked it up.

"Mr. Monohan, this is Chief Andrew Neilly of the Denver Police."

That got his attention.

The chief continued. "Just wanted to confirm the fire chief's finding of an accidental fire. Since you've had trouble with the threatening letters, we want to be doubly sure."

"As far as I know, it was a fan that shorted out. A kitchen worker also witnessed the fire start. But I need to tell you something about those letters."

"Go ahead." Grant could hear the chief tearing a sheet of paper off a notepad.

He took a steadying breath and gave the chief as much information as he had, about his father and the man he'd hired.

"Oh, boy."

Grant smiled a little at Chief Neilly's comment. "Oh, boy" didn't really cover it, but what else was there to say? "If the fire is accidental, then I don't want to press charges. I'm going to try and talk to him, see if we can reach some kind of understanding."

There was a pause. "I understand. But Mr. Monohan? Be careful. And if you ever need help, be sure to call."

Careful. He wished he knew if it was wise to even speak to his father again. But something in the old man's face today was different. He seemed to realize, for the first time, that he couldn't always get his way. Grant thanked him and hung up the phone. Another knock at the door announced Lana.

"I know you're taking a break, but I thought you'd want to know about the call I just got from Janet Jeffrey at Seventh Street Mission."

He came around the side of his desk and leaned against it, stuffing his hands in his pockets. "Janet's probably wondering how many people to expect over there."

To his surprise, Lana grinned. "Not exactly. She's been on the phone as soon as they heard about the fire. They've got some meals lined up, dinner for starters."

"Dinner?"

"Yeah. They pulled in some favors and dinner will be coming to the mission at six, right on the dot. A full, balanced meal for two hundred and fifty."

So his residents didn't have to find somewhere else, at least for the immediate future. He felt as if an enormous weight just lifted from his shoulders. "Well, that's some seriously good news. I guess we'll worry about breakfast later."

Lana ran her fingers through her hair and stared

innocently at the ceiling. "Maybe we will, maybe we won't."

"What does that mean?"

She laughed outright, glee written on her features. "Calista sent out a petition and they've already got donors scheduled for the next two weeks. Every meal is covered at least that far, maybe farther if they keep at it."

Grant felt his mouth drop open. He leaned heavily back against the desk, his mind spinning. "How? She's back at work."

"You've got to hand it to the girl. She knows her stuff." Lana shook her head, eyes bright.

"What do you mean by donors?"

"Hospitals, a few sports teams, banks, corporations, you name it!" She was laughing as she ticked off the places on her fingers. "Isn't God amazing, Grant? I could hardly believe it when that assistant of hers called. I asked if she wanted to tell you, but she said she was supposed to keep working and see if they can get the whole month covered."

"Unbelievable. We can set up the classrooms as meal rooms. Maybe use some of the bigger cafeteria tables, if they'll fit. Some of them might have to go in the lobby." He frowned, working the logistics in his head. So many people, so little space.

"Outdoor Rentals called and said they had some all-purpose tents that can be used with a wooden floor for outdoor seating if we need it. It comes with a few heaters. They'll be over later to set it up, just in case we need it for overflow."

It was so much to take in, he had to sit down. Grant went back behind his desk and carefully lowered his long frame into the chair. His legs felt numb. Maybe he was having a delayed reaction from the fire. "Why would they do this? I've never even heard of Outdoor Rentals."

Lana wheeled closer to the desk and reached out for his hand. "Grant, they've heard of *you*. And not because you're famous now. Every phone call I've taken since the fire, and I've taken dozens, has been someone asking to help, wanting to give back to the mission, the same way this place has fed and sheltered people in need."

As if a warm blanket had settled around his shoulders, Grant felt the truth of her words. Calista had told him that there were so many good corporations out there, wanting to help. But every year he had watched downtown businesses call for the city to close the mission and to "clean up" the area. What they really wanted was to hide the problems of homelessness, abuse, addiction and hunger. Every year the city refused to bow to the megacorporations. But he had wondered how many were on the side of the mission. A few? A handful?

He didn't try to hide the moistness in his eyes. "I feel like Jimmy Stewart in *It's a Wonderful Life*. You know, the part where everybody starts throwing money into a big pot?"

Lana chuckled. "Does that make me the goofy angel, Clarence?"

"No, no, you're definitely Uncle Billy," Grant teased, lacing his fingers behind his head.

"And we all know who plays Mary in this version. I saw a little lip-on-lip action this afternoon." She gave him a wink, then started to laugh. "I don't think I've ever really seen you turn that color, boss."

He shrugged, wishing he could force the grin from

his face. But with the immediate needs of the residents taken care of, his mind was free to wander back to Calista…and that kiss. "It was the world's worst timing but it somehow felt right. And she didn't run."

"Always a good sign," Lana agreed. Her eyes were bright with happiness. "Forget about her superhero powers and lining up all these donors. I knew you were meant for each other from the very beginning. Remember the day she told you not to handle the PR for the mission?"

Grant groaned. "How could I forget?"

"A woman who can be that honest is a treasure. I just prayed that everything else would fall into place."

He nodded, feeling the certainty of her words and the faith of her prayers. As soon as he could, he needed to return the favor and be as honest as possible about his past. He didn't want anything to stand in the way of their future, least of all a man like Kurt Daniels.

"That's a great style. Trying something new?" Catherine Banks peeked over her bifocals to get a better glimpse of Calista's hair. The fiftyish woman was not a rabid fan of fashion but the atmosphere in the boardroom was as tense as a war zone and she seemed desperate to lighten the mood.

"I was in a fire. My hairdresser did the best she could with what was left." She ran her fingers through the sleek style that fell to her collarbone and kept her expression affable, enjoying the look of shock on Catherine's face. She understood the woman was elected to the board because she was one of the top shareholders but she sure didn't contribute much. When things got tough, Catherine was the first to change her vote to side with the loudest complainer and Calista didn't respect a woman who couldn't make up her mind.

Brett Caldwell cleared his throat and stacked a pile of papers on the surface of the long mahogany table. "Let's get started. We've got everyone here, finally."

Calista suppressed a retort and pasted an easy smile on her face. As CEO, she had always gotten along well with the twelve board members. They'd hired her, after all. She made VitaWow profitable, and they made sure the profits were dispersed fairly to the stockholders. Not hard to get along, usually. But right now she was sensing wariness from most, and downright hostility from a few. Choosing the site for the new building wasn't in their purview, and they knew it, but somehow it was coming through the board first. Her stomach gave an uncomfortable wriggle of foreboding.

She glanced around the long table at the ten men and two women. Something serious was happening and she was the last to know.

"There's been a new development in the search for a building site. Calista, this is a copy of the formal offer given to us by the board of the Downtown Denver Mission." Brett passed a folder to his right and Calista flipped it open before he'd even finished speaking.

He continued. "They have accepted a generous donation that includes a brand-new facility on private land. The donor wishes to remain anonymous. There are several unusual stipulations to this donation and one is that they offer the current site of the Downtown Denver Mission to VitaWow at a steep discount."

The mission? Why did the mission board want to sell now? Was the money situation worse than she'd thought? Calista scanned the document as swiftly as she could, her mind filing away facts and figures. Something was very wrong with this offer but she couldn't point to a single major problem.

"The anonymous donor wishes the transaction to be agreed on by Christmas Eve. That is why we are here, why some of us have delayed departing on a ski vacation with our family." He straightened his tie with a jerk. At least one member didn't appreciate the donor's need for a speedy resolution.

"The mission site was on our list of possible land options but the board refused to sell at the time we approached them in the spring. We asked only about the north end of the block, which is some sort of a community garden, but this offer includes all the mission property. It seems with the sudden appearance of this very generous mystery donor, they've changed their minds."

Calista sat shaking her head. Page after page of legal documents had already been drafted, waiting for signatures. She didn't see Grant's name anywhere yet. How had this all been prepared so quickly? "When did you first hear from the mission board?"

Brett glanced around, waiting for someone to answer. He shrugged. "I received a call this afternoon at one."

Her mind was spinning but she forced herself to take a slow breath. "So, the fire happened around ten. By one, the mission board had been approached by this donor, who also wants VitaWow to buy the property. Why?" She tapped a pen on the desk.

Alan Johnson groaned and said, "If the mission board agreed, then why should we concern ourselves?"

Several members nodded. "If it works out well for everyone involved, why not?" asked Gerald Manley.

He wiped his balding head with a hankie and tucked it back in his pocket.

Helen Bonnet pursed her bright orange lips and wagged a finger at the group. "Calista is right to ask the question. We can't afford to be involved in a shady deal."

Gerald snorted. "Shady? What makes you think there's anything other than good business going on here?"

Helen leaned forward and glared across the table. "I know good business. I built a company from the bottom up and sold it for millions. Nobody gives that kind of donation and demands the papers be signed in a deadline. Something stinks."

"Now, now, Helen. Let's not be dramatic." Brett adjusted his tie again and Calista saw drops of sweat appear at his temples.

"I have a few questions." Calista kept her tone light, but her heart was pounding. The board could decide whatever they wanted without her approval. And she had a feeling that her usual hard-line tactics were not going to serve her well here.

"Did the donor make a similar offer to the mission before, but was refused? Does the mission board feel that they have no choice to accept because of the fire today?"

Brett sighed. "Does it matter?"

"It might." And now for the biggest question. Calista searched each of their faces, wondering which of them knew who was behind this fiasco. It was someone powerful, well connected and immensely wealthy. Grant's face flashed into her mind and she felt a pulse pounding at her temples. "Why VitaWow? How did this donor know that VitaWow approached the mission back in the spring?"

"Again, I don't think these are serious issues." Brett huffed out the words.

"Maybe not by themselves. But if we add the fact that Grant Monohan has been refusing significant monetary assistance from his father, Kurt Daniels, then things get more complicated." Calista was taking a risk.

"Wait, we don't know for sure that Kurt Daniels is the donor." Gerald waved a hand in the air as if to dispel the entire argument.

There was a silence and Calista almost laughed as the members exchanged glances. Of course it was Kurt Daniels. These men and women may be willing to overlook a questionable deal, but they weren't stupid.

"Fine, let's just assume it is. That's not really a problem, is it?"

Helen leaned forward. "How do you know Grant Monohan refused his money, dear?" Her pale gray eyes sparked with curiosity.

"He said as much at the press conference. And today, after the fire, I saw Kurt Daniels at the mission."

Brett shrugged and said, "He's obviously holding a grudge against his father for having a less-than-perfect childhood."

Calista wanted to slap her hand against the table and shout that *less-than-perfect* did not describe what Grant lived through. But she took a breath and smiled calmly. "I'm not sure what his reservations are, exactly, but I can guarantee they're more serious than being estranged from a wealthy businessman."

Calista closed her eyes for just a moment and breathed a prayer. Now was the moment she needed to convince them that they had to look beyond a generous land transaction. The people needed food and a place to stay today and tomorrow and the next day. They couldn't wait years for a new site to be built.

"This company has thrived because of dedication, focus and drive. But we're also active in the community, support local charities and are working to reduce our carbon footprint. So, maybe we should look at all the angles here. Even the ones that don't directly concern VitaWow."

Helen nodded, listening intently. Brett stared at his papers and didn't respond. Calista continued, hoping her words would make them think, just for a moment, about the people that didn't get a vote in this decision.

"If the mission sells to VitaWow, the demolition would start immediately to keep our own building project on time. That leaves at least two years without any place for the homeless to go. Although the new mission site will be state-of-the-art buildings with extra security and a playground—" she held up the pages, pointing at paragraphs "—it is also situated five miles outside the city. The residents need the central location for school and jobs." But from a business owner's viewpoint, it was a win-win. No more poor people wandering about, disrupting the beautiful views.

"There are other missions. Some of them are just a few blocks away," Catherine interjected.

"Seventh Street Mission is a quarter the size and has no classrooms or day care."

"What is your relationship with the director?" Brett's question came out of nowhere and Calista felt as though the air was driven from her lungs.

"I'm a volunteer."

"Is that all?"

Calista stared, wondering where Brett was headed with his interrogation. Admitting that she was in love with Grant wasn't going to help her argument. "If we're more than friends, won't it look even worse for Vita-Wow to buy the mission property at a huge price cut?"

Silence pulsed in the room and Calista could hear her heart thudding in her chest.

"Like I said, something stinks here." Helen sat back in her chair with a decisive motion. "Why would Kurt Daniels force the sale of the mission and build a new one against his son's wishes?"

There was no good answer. Calista wished she had taken the time to get the whole story from Grant right after the fire.

"I'm not sure. Now, you all know that in business we have to take risks." She paused, looking each one of the board members in the eye. "I don't think this is one of those times. There are too many unanswered questions, too many potential negatives. Whatever ugly war is brewing between Kurt Daniels and his son, it shouldn't involve VitaWow."

Chapter Fourteen

A week. That was all the time the board would give her before they made a decision. Calista dropped her head in her hands and stared at the top of her desk. It was covered with little slips of paper, messages that needed to be answered. Jackie was out calling the donors, getting the month of meals covered.

Lord, I'm so confused. I don't know what You want me to do. She knew that closing the mission for twenty-four months would be devastating for the residents. She knew that VitaWow needed to make smart business decisions. But everything else was a fog, a blur of conflicting advice. She wanted to talk to Grant about it, but he wasn't just her friend. He was the director of the mission and would be absolutely livid when he heard the VitaWow plan. Maybe he already had.

The idea that he was sitting in exactly the same posture, miles away, made her groan. What a mess. It would be awkward enough if she was just a volunteer, but she was more than that. Wasn't she? Calista sat up, trying to shake the confusion from her mind. There didn't seem any way out of it. If she stopped volunteering, the mission wouldn't be a conflict of interest for her. But she didn't want to leave them, or Grant. Not now. If she resigned her position as CEO, the board was much more likely to take the offer. She laid her hands on the table, startled. Was she even considering that? Her whole life was wrapped up in this company. Would she walk away if it meant saving the mission?

There was a knock on the door and Jackie came in, carrying a large clothing bag. "I think your dress is here."

If Calista could have let out a scream of frustration and gotten away with it, she would have. She had completely forgotten about the party, just days away...the party she was attending with Grant.

"Right. Let me take a look. The boutique had to make a few alterations." She tried to be calm and act naturally as her fingers fumbled at the garment-bag zipper.

Jackie let out a low whistle. "Well, now. This isn't your usual little black dress." She cocked her head, surveying the fabric as she lifted it from the bag. "When you got that new red coat, I wondered if you were on a red kick. This proves it."

Calista smiled, hoping it didn't look as brittle as it felt. "Do you like it? I just wanted more color."

"Put it on, I have to see."

It was the last thing she wanted to do at the moment, but Calista shrugged. She might not even get a chance to wear it. No harm in playing dress up now.

A few minutes later, she emerged from the bathroom and had to smile at Jackie's expression. The formfitting bodice gently followed her curves to the hip, where the bright red silk fell in a full skirt, gathered every so often in a draping effect. A large black velvet ribbon was wrapped around her waist, and the ends trailed to the hem. It might have made a woman look like a giant Christmas present, but the creative genius of the designer only made it seem charming. It looked sweet. Young. *Joyful.*

Calista smoothed her hands down the dress and felt her eyes fill with sudden tears. She wanted one evening of magic with Grant. One evening when he was just a man and she was just a woman. She came to a decision, standing there in her party dress, wishing life was different than it really was.

"I think it fits. Now, I better get out of this dress and get cracking. We've got a lot of work to catch up on today."

Jackie grinned, reaching out a hand to touch the black velvet sash. "If you say so. But I'm so into the Christmas spirit now, I'll need some cookies to get me through the day."

"It's a done deal." Ralph Maricort leaned back in his chair. The older man's face was deeply lined but his dark eyes were like a robin's, bright and quick. Only a day after the fire, the smell of smoke was still thick in Grant's office.

"Ralph, I'm stunned. When did this happen? How could the board make this kind of decision without even consulting me?" Grant was struggling to keep his voice even but it seemed like all his breath had been driven from his body with Ralph's news. "If it's about the fire, we've already got the next two weeks' worth of meals planned, and the other buildings weren't even touched." His voice was rising in anger. "There's no legal reason to close the mission. The fire was an accident and everything was up to code. The fire chief said it was an electrical issue, a faulty wire."

"Grant, I knew you were dealing with a lot here, so the board just decided to wait a bit before telling you. And I know this is hard, but it's a temporary closure. The new complex will be built within twenty-four months. We've been deeded the land, seen the plans, and the company is thrilled to get this spot. They approached us back in April about the empty lot by the parking area, but we didn't want to lose any more space, in case we had to expand."

Nothing was making sense. He felt ambushed. Grant shook his head, his mind racing to catch up with the older man's words. "I remembered something about an offer for the community garden area." The board fielded a lot of inquiries about the mission land, since it was a prime downtown spot.

"They've outgrown their building on Plymouth Avenue and have plans for a pretty nice high-rise, complete with a new corner office for the CEO. And she deserves it. Calista Sheffield has worked wonders for that water company." Ralph smirked at his weak play on words.

"Excuse me?" The question seemed to be dragged from somewhere deep in his chest, pulling his heart up into his throat.

"The CEO. She's a real dragon lady. I heard she brokered a deal last month that had the Genesis board quaking in their boots."

If he hadn't been sitting down, Grant would have sunk to the floor. He felt his legs go numb, his mind stutter. Of course. It couldn't be just any company; it had to be VitaWow. What were the odds?

"When did you say this offer came through?"

Ralph wrinkled his brow, thinking. "The day of the fire, and then the VitaWow board met that evening. The CEO asked them to wait a few days, I think, to make sure the papers were in order."

His head pounded as he tried to understand the situation. The mission would close. These people who were struggling with unemployment, hunger, abuse and addiction would be forced to start over. And all because Calista Sheffield wanted a new building.

Something awful occurred to him and he dropped his head into his hands, not caring that Ralph was still speaking. Maybe she knew all along. Maybe she didn't just walk in off the street because she needed a life outside her work. His hopes and dreams of a life with her turned to ashes. A woman who cared so little for the poor and the vulnerable had nothing in common with him. It made no sense to fall back on the defense of how wonderful the new mission would be, when the people here *now* would suffer. People like Savannah and her mother. And the employees. Marisol's face popped into his head and he groaned audibly.

"The staff. They can't wait around for the new building. They'll have to find other work."

Ralph nodded. "True. But you'll keep your position, and maybe the secretary, so that you can oversee the new project."

Grant felt sick. They were a dedicated crew. He couldn't imagine how it would be to break the news that their jobs were gone.

"Where is this new site?" He struggled to ask questions, to fight through the shock and disappointment.

"Out near Landry. Very nice views." The older man steepled his fingers.

"Landry...the neighborhood? Isn't that about five miles from here?"

He nodded. "Right. Not residential, of course, since city ordinances wouldn't allow it, but some strip malls and big-box stores."

Grant stood up and walked around the desk. He clenched his fists, fighting for control. "You're telling me the mission will close. Everyone will have to find new lodgings, won't finish their classes or training. My employees will lose their jobs. And the new site is near a strip mall in Landry? How will the inner-city home-less find their way out to Landry? On the bus? And how will they get to their jobs, and get their kids to school?"

Ralph held up his hands, eyes showing alarm. "Just hold on. You've got to look at the big picture, Grant. We can't turn this down because it's not the perfect loca-tion. A brand-new facility is something we've needed for years. That fire was long overdue, if you ask me. And I'm tired of hearing about how the mission is bad for the downtown area. This way, we're farther away from the fancy businesses and we have a great new lo-cation. Everybody is happy."

"No," Grant choked out. "Everybody is *not* happy. The people who need these services will suffer."

"We've got to do what's best in the long run." Ralph's black eyes turned serious, and he chose his words care-fully. "We would hate to lose you, Grant. But the board has made its decision. We're accepting the donor's land and his offer to build a new mission."

He shook his head, trying in vain to wrap his mind

around the past few hours. "Who is this donor, anyway?"

Ralph dropped his gaze. In the next half second of silence, Grant knew. Kurt Daniels had orchestrated another coup. He swore he would get Grant to take his money and he had succeeded. Could Calista have been in on this plan with his father, plotting and lying all along? He sat back against the edge of the desk, his hands limp at his sides.

"He wants to remain anonymous." Ralph had the decency to look ashamed.

"I'm sure he does," Grant murmured.

"He's not what you think, Grant. He's changed. He really thinks this will be good for the mission, and for you." His voice was quiet, as if he was worried Kurt Daniels would hear him. He stood up and headed for the door.

"I don't know what he is, honestly. But I do know that this is wrong on so many different levels." He felt his shoulders sag. He thought he'd gotten used to lies and betrayals, been hardened to them, but he must still have a soft spot because it felt as though someone had just kicked it.

"It's for the best. You'll see," he said, and with those words Ralph walked out the door.

The sharp trill of his office phone broke into Grant's shock. He moved to lift the receiver, and his greeting felt sluggish and awkward.

She could hear by his voice that he already knew, but she asked anyway. "Grant, have you seen the offer?"

There was a pause that was so long, she wondered if they'd been disconnected. "Yes."

Another beat of silence, then Calista rushed in to fill the void. "I've asked the board to wait a few days to make their decision, but it seems like the majority is in favor."

"I'm sure they are."

Calista chewed her lip and clutched the phone tighter. She had to make him understand. "At the Christmas party on Saturday, I think—"

She was interrupted by a sound that could only signal shock and disgust, something sharp and guttural. Then he said, as if the words were spilling out, "I may not have made this clear, but one thing I have had my fill of is lies. I've had a lifetime's worth, and I don't need any more. I'm not going to your Christmas party, Calista, because I avoid people who can't be honest. And don't try to say something like 'I didn't lie, I just didn't tell the whole truth' because we both know that's not true."

Calista's jaw had dropped after his first few words and her fingers had gone numb from gripping the phone. She swallowed. "Grant, I have a lot of faults, but dishonesty is not one of them."

"And how do I know for sure? Should I ask my father for a character reference?"

"Your—" Did he think she and Kurt Daniels were in league? She squeezed her eyes closed. There was no one to vouch for her; she had no advocates. "I don't know him. I'm as surprised as you are. I heard the news yesterday evening."

There was no response. She thought she heard him exhale.

"Anyway, I don't think I'll be up for a Christmas party this weekend. I have a lot to do."

Calista's throat closed shut and she struggled to take

a breath. She didn't care about the party, the dress, the elegant evening. If she hung up now, she might never see him again. He would always think she had schemed her way into owning the mission property.

"Grant, listen to me." Her voice shook on the last word and she stopped to swallow again. "Whatever you believe—about me and this deal and your father—just listen."

Silence. But there wasn't a click, either.

"This party will be full of people that I invited just for you to meet. The Genesis Drinks president will be there. And Terrence Brewer, the head of Alton Banking; and Jenn Blackrite, who runs Cimulus, the software giant; and the governor, Dennis Michael." She paused for a breath. He didn't interrupt. So maybe he was still listening. "Whatever you think—" she could hardly speak the words "—of me, I'm asking you to come meet these people. I think this is your best chance to save the mission. Your board is accepting the offer because of the fire. I'm almost sure of it."

"I don't see how it can possibly make that much difference." His tone was flat, colorless.

"You don't, but I do. I've seen how deep these corporate pockets can be. I know the kinds of donations they give. We're talking hundreds of thousands of dollars."

"Wouldn't it be better to approach their representatives, the traditional way? Nobody wants to be bothered at a party."

"Trust me, Grant. Just this once." Her heart was in her throat. "After the party, you can never speak to me again, if you want, but for the mission, I'm asking you…" She couldn't finish. The room blurred and Calista blinked furiously.

"Well, like you said at church, maybe I'm being too proud. I'm thinking of myself, and not the mission." He said it lightly, but his words cut her so sharply, Calista was surprised that she wasn't bleeding. He didn't want to be around her, it was clear.

"Right." She was proud the word came out clearly, not wavering or breathless.

"Then I'll see you Saturday. Can we meet there?"

He wanted to spend as little time as possible with her alone. Calista shrugged off the biting pain and agreed. As she hung up the phone, she dropped her face into her hands. Hot tears slipped between her fingers, and the grief she'd kept in check for the past several minutes spilled over her in waves. Yet again, in the end, all she had left was her job.

Lord, take this situation and everything in it. Help me to know what to do.

Grant stood on the steps of the Grant-Humphreys Mansion and tried to look pleasant. His face felt frozen, unyielding, but he forced the corners of his mouth into a smile. The elite of Denver business and society streamed out of luxury vehicles and up the steps, diamonds glittering in the darkness, white tuxedo fronts glowing. Golden light shone from the long window panes and off the oversize balconies. The sound of a string quartet and holiday cheer spilled out the door and mingled with the slam of car doors. He paced a few steps, from one giant pillar to the next, then checked his watch again. She was always early. Or so she said. He wasn't sure what to believe anymore.

The wide expanse of the stone steps had been cleared of the snow that fell earlier in the day. Tonight there would be more. Grant had always loved the snow, but now he felt empty, cold. That was about all he could manage and he hoped it was enough. God knew what he was feeling. He couldn't put any of the rest of it into words, anyway.

A silver car caught his eye and he straightened his shoulders. Calista got out, handed her keys to the valet and strode toward the front steps. He had told himself to be distant but friendly, focused on business. He was here for the mission. But one glimpse of her and his heart felt as though it was being squeezed in a steel trap. One with teeth. His mind seemed to take in every detail and catalog it for the future, without his permission.

Her eyes were darker, dramatically shadowed, and her lips were a shade lighter than her dress, a red that was purely Christmas. No plum or burgundy or demure wine color. The color reminded him of the very best Christmas memories he had. She was halfway up the steps, still focused on the front door, holding her ankle-length dress in one hand. A matching jacket covered her shoulders and her bright blond hair was up in a soft chignon, dotted with sparkling pins. On her jacket was a snowflake brooch that caught the light and shimmered against the soft skin of her neck. When she was just feet from him, she looked up, caught his gaze and tripped.

Chapter Fifteen

Calista rehearsed the words in her head, willing herself to remember. She had spent hours working on the right phrases, the right tones. He couldn't leave this party thinking she was a liar and a cheat. It felt as though her whole life depended on it.

She handed off her keys to the valet and started up the stone steps. The mansion looked as gorgeous as always, strong and sturdy, built to show the wealth and prosperity of turn-of-the-century Denver. Every time she visited, she felt another wave of awe. It looked like the party was in full swing and people milled everywhere. She glanced up at the balconies and noted the figures huddled in groups. It was a great party if people braved the freezing temperatures for a breather in the night air.

One hand went to her mama's pin on her jacket. It calmed her just a bit, and she whispered a prayer. *Please, Lord, be with us.*

She dodged a slow-moving couple and glanced up, one hand holding her dress so she didn't step on the hem. And she saw him just a foot away, standing cold and aloof in the shadow of a pillar. His handsome face bore some expression she couldn't define. His eyes were locked on hers. Tuxedos always made her feel as if the man was wearing a disguise, but he seemed achingly familiar. She dropped the fold of fabric in her hand to wave, and the next moment she was pitching forward. Strong hands gripped her elbows and he used the momentum to propel her clear of the last step. An abrupt stop, and she dragged in a breath, her heart pounding. They were only inches apart. His hands still gripping her arms, she couldn't seem to look away, even though his eyes had a hollow look to them that made her stomach clench.

"Well, that's what I get for being late." What a stupid thing to say, but for some reason it made him smile. A real smile that reached those bright blue eyes.

"Are you all right?"

"Of course, just not used to the long dress. And probably shouldn't be running in heels."

"I think that's a rule, isn't it?" He took her hand and tucked it into the curve of his arm.

"It can't be. Women run in heels all the time in the movies. Usually when they're dodging bombs or running from assassins."

He laughed a bit, a soft sound that made hope spring up in her chest. They were almost at the front door, crowds already visible inside.

"Grant, I'm glad you came. I really think this can work." So much for all the fancy phrases she was going to use. When she looked into his face, noted the set of his jaw and the line of his lips, she couldn't remember a thing she'd thought to say. Oh, well, it seemed to cover it.

His smile faded away and he nodded. "I hope you're right. You look beautiful. In case I don't tell you that when we get going inside."

Calista's heart jumped to her throat and she felt her cheeks burn. She wanted to be beautiful for him, wanted this party to be something special. If only they could fall into some other life, or start fresh. But that wasn't going to happen. They had people relying on them to keep the mission open. She swallowed. "Thank you. And you should wear a tux at least once a month. Just for fun." She gave him a saucy wink that had more confidence than she felt.

He snorted. "Don't get any ideas."

They stepped into the large ballroom and Grant could feel the gaze of every person there on him. The chatter of party guests grew quiet and eventually, it was nearly silent except for the string quartet. The marble floors and tall ceilings made the mournful tones echo. Calista glanced at him, her expression rueful. "Sorry, I tend to have that effect on parties. I suck the life right out of them."

He scanned the room, looking for familiar faces. Not a one. And the faces he saw didn't look exactly thrilled to see them.

"Come on." Calista held her head high, walking confidently toward a lanky gentleman with fine gray hair and a weak chin. As they crossed the room, the conversation seemed to pick up again, strand by strand, until the party was back in full swing.

"Brett, this is Grant Monohan, the director of the Downtown Denver Mission. Brett Caldwell, the head of our board of directors."

Grant reached out a hand, pasting a pleasant smile to his face. He could see the surprise flicker across Brett's face and wondered if the board even knew Calista volunteered at the mission.

"A pleasure, for sure. We're very happy with the mission's offer to sell. This will be a good move for all of us." Brett's tone was slightly condescending, as if he were thanking Grant for trading lunches.

"We'll see, Brett. Nothing has been decided yet." Calista's voice was light, but Grant felt her hand right on his arm. "Enjoy the party. We're off to make the rounds."

She guided him away, leaning her head toward his shoulder. He could smell a light floral perfume and something like vanilla. "Ignore him. He knows nothing is signed yet."

"And he also knows I can't force the board to do what I want."

She glanced up at him, her green eyes made deeper by the dramatic shadow. She reminded him of the old film stars, beautiful and elegant. He thought he would be happy to stare at her all night. Thankfully that wasn't an option. "Your snowflake pin is pretty. It looks like an antique."

She put a hand to the pin, touching it lightly with her fingers. A soft smile touched her lips. "It was my mother's. The only thing of hers that survived the fire. She loaned it to me for senior pictures...that day."

He turned her to face him, pausing in the middle of the crowd. "I didn't get a chance to tell you how sorry I am about your mother. And how very brave you were during the mission fire."

In an instant, she wasn't the CEO of a company that held its Christmas party in a mansion. She was a young girl, facing her fears. "I can't imagine the mission without Marisol."

He nodded. He couldn't imagine his *life* without Marisol. "Sometimes I think she holds the place together."

A woman approached them from the side, her dark hair dramatically streaked with white on one side. The gold column gown she wore showcased a lithe figure. Her eyes flitted from one to another, but her smile was bright. "Calista, dear! You've brought a date this year."

Calista introduced them, and he shook hands with Jenn Blackrite. He had always figured millionaires to be aloof, critical, like his father. But Jenn was witty and warm, asking questions about the mission and the fire.

"They're going to close if they can't raise the funds to repair the kitchen." Calista's words caught him by surprise. It was true. Mostly.

Jenn put a hand to her mouth, her large topaz ring winking in the light. "No! That can't happen. There are so many people who need the mission, especially now, in the wintertime."

"I agree. But what can they do?"

Jenn leaned forward, gripping Grant's arm. "We give to Universal Charity every year. This year we can give our donation to the mission. And more. We can't let it close."

Grant opened his mouth to thank her, when they were interrupted by a slim young woman. Jenn handed him her card, scribbling something on the back, with instructions to call on Monday. Then she walked away with the young woman, deep in conversation.

"See?" The glee in Calista's voice was infectious.

"But does she mean it? Or is it like 'let's do lunch' and then nothing ever happens?"

"Jenn has a great reputation and if she says she will, she will."

He couldn't help chuckling a bit. Was there hope after all?

"And there are so many more. Oh, Grant! I know this will work!" She fairly bounced on her toes, face alight.

"Where next? I feel like I should be using some sort of title for you, like 'Most Magnificent One.' You have a gift. I'm glad you use it for good and not evil." He was teasing, the success letting his words slip away without any thought.

Her eyes turned somber. "I haven't always. I made money to make money, with no purpose to it."

There was such a sadness in her tone, it was hard for him to resist reaching out and gathering her to him. He was barely aware of the guests milling around them. Her face was tilted up to him and he could see tiny flecks of gold in her green eyes. "That was then."

"And this is now." Her lips tugged up at the corners. "Let's get cracking, Mr. Director."

"I've got to take a break. My jaw hurts from smiling so much." Calista rubbed her cheeks and groaned. She almost wished she could go back to the days when she popped into a party for five minutes and then left.

"Agreed. I'm going to go over and drink the entire punch bowl."

Calista giggled, and then groaned again. "Please don't make me laugh. I don't think my face can take it."

"Knock, knock," he said, then broke off as she poked him in the side.

"Here, let's get some spiced cider and take it out on the balcony. I need some air."

Grant poured her a cup of the steaming, fragrant liquid and then took one for himself. She glanced at him, wondering if he was enjoying himself at all. He was certainly not as distant as he'd been on the phone.

The balcony was occupied with one other couple, an older man and woman holding hands, and they exchanged smiles. Grant led her to the edge and peered out into the night. "They said there would be more snow."

"Smells like it." Calista took a sip and let the spices tingle her tongue. She looked out into the darkness, struggling to find the right words. She knew better than to leave anything unsaid. This might be their only chance. "Thank you for coming tonight. I know the offer came as a shock."

"Calista." He set his hot cider on the balcony ledge and turned to her, expression all business. "I need to tell you something."

Her heart pounded in her chest and she searched for a clue in his face. Was this where he told her that he would never see her again? Is this the moment her heart would break?

She nodded. "Go ahead."

He looked out into the darkness, his profile half in shadow, and seemed to be having trouble finding the words. "I held the media announcement because I was receiving threatening letters. And it's true my father sent me checks that I never cashed."

Calista blinked, struggling to switch gears. After the fire, she wanted to hear the whole story. But this was an odd moment to tell it.

"There are rumors that my father's wealth is from illegal enterprises." He looked her in the eyes, gauging her reaction. "They're all true. So I refused to have any kind of relationship with him."

Calista nodded, but inside she was confused. Letters, money, broken laws. Was there anything here she didn't know or hadn't heard?

"When he showed up after the fire, he admitted he was the one sending the letters. Well, he was paying someone to do it."

She couldn't restrain a gasp. Her hand went to her throat, and she felt her eyes go wide with shock.

His face was rigid, eyes narrowed. "It's an ugly situation. And you deserve to know the truth."

"Oh, Grant. I'm so sorry." She reached out a hand and touched his arm. Her eyes started to burn and she blinked tears away. "You can't be held accountable for your father's deeds."

He let out a breath, his shoulders slumping. "But when image is everything, these things matter. I wanted you to know, probably should have told you sooner." He met her gaze. "You deserved the chance to step away from the situation, to consider your own reputation."

Calista wanted to deny it, but he was right. Sometimes image *was* everything. But she didn't care about image as much as she did a few months ago. Maybe that was a bad thing, but it didn't feel bad. It felt very, very good. She stepped closer, lifting her hand to his cheek, feeling the slight stubble on his jaw. His eyes were hot, searching her face. "I think my reputation can withstand a few rumors."

She felt his smile under her fingers, and he turned his head and pressed a kiss to the palm of her hand. "Let me know when it gets to be too much."

"I will." Her words were barely audible but his lips twitched moments before they met hers. Her lids drifted closed, reveling in the warmth of him, the familiar smell of aftershave and soap. One arm slipped around her waist and she let herself forget she was a CEO, forget that her life had been completely empty until a few months ago. She let herself be just a woman who was in love with a man. Something wet and cold touched her face and she opened her eyes with a gasp.

"It's snowing." She glanced up and grinned at the fat flakes falling thickly from the sky.

Grant's arms were still wrapped around her. The softness in his eyes made her breath catch. "This is the best Christmas ever." His voice was full of wonder.

She laughed, leaning back to look into his face. "I was just thinking the same thing."

He planted a kiss on her cheek and grabbed her hand. "What do you say we get back in there and raise some money?"

"Lead the way." She let him pull her back into the ballroom, heart filled with the sort of joy she had never had before.

Christmas Eve dawned bright and sunny, completely contrary to Calista's mood. After spending the night staring at the ceiling, she gave up at dawn and padded to the kitchen. Maybe making a few dozen sugar cookies would make it seem like Christmas. An hour later, her condominium smelled absolutely edible but she didn't feel an ounce of joy.

She checked her phone for messages for the tenth time that hour. No word from Grant since the party. She knew he was busy keeping the residents fed, but how hard was it to pick up the phone? Heck, he could even text a few lines. She would take anything at this point. She glared at the plate of perfect little cookies, trees and stars and bells with colored sprinkles. It had been shaping up to be the best Christmas in recent memory and now… Her chest tightened at the thought of spending Christmas without Grant. How many Christmas Days had she spent alone? But not like this, not missing someone so badly it felt as though a hole had been torn in her heart.

Calista straightened her shoulders. Maybe he was angry that VitaWow had turned down the mission's offer. Maybe he thought she had volunteered, trying to get inside information. Maybe he thought she'd started the fire. She just couldn't guess what was going through his mind. And if he wasn't going to tell her, there was no other choice but to go to the mission and ask.

She swung open the lobby door to the mission and strode inside.

"Hey, Lana, is Grant somewhere around here?"

Lana took several seconds to respond, her blue eyes wide. "Uh, he sure is. Let me call him out."

Calista put the cookies on the desktop. "Don't bother. I can go back, if he's not busy." Calista headed for the security door, waving away Lana's protests. "Have a cookie. They're fresh," she called and punched in the code with shaking fingers.

She was a modern woman. She knew that a little hand-holding and a couple of brief kisses didn't make a relationship. But that line he'd thrown out about how she was the only woman he was interested in right now? Somehow she had grabbed that one line and run with it. In her head they had been practically raising a brood of kids already. Until the fire, and the building offer. Calista gritted her teeth and tried to make her expression pleasant, when she felt only pain at how easily she had fallen in love with Grant. And how easily her heart was breaking. She should have known better. How many times had he said he was too busy for love? Five? Ten? And she had said the same thing.

But her doubts ran deeper than that. Calista paused outside his door and finally faced the possibility that Grant wasn't too busy to call. He knew who she was and how she spent her time. She poured all her energy into making money and selling a product that didn't really make anyone healthier. He would never want a woman like her. She closed her eyes and whispered a prayer. *Please give me strength to face him, Lord. I want to make sure he's okay and that Marisol is okay and the mission will go on. Then I can leave.*

She knocked loudly on his closed office door and waited for some kind of response. There was the muted sound of footsteps and the door swung inward, revealing the man who had changed everything about the way she saw the world.

"Come on in." His tone was subdued, and she caught a glimpse of dark shadows under his eyes before he turned away. His suit looked a little rumpled, as if he had slept at his desk. He definitely looked the worse for wear.

"I got worried. You haven't called me back." She wrapped her arms around her middle, feeling like she was trying to hold herself together. All her anger was turning to fear. He looked like a man who had lost everything.

"It's been pretty busy around here. You want to take off your coat?" He settled into his office chair and his gaze flicked past her. She saw how his usually freshly shaved jaw was rough with stubble.

Calista hesitated, then hung up her red wool coat on the hook. Clumps of fresh snow on the shoulders and hood were melting into nothingness. It was the same feeling she had in the pit of her stomach.

"Grant, are you okay? You look exhausted. And pale." She took a step forward, wishing she could take his face in her hands and wipe the frown from his brow.

"I'm fine." With those last words, he looked up at her. The expression made her breath catch in her throat. It was sadness, pity, resolve, pain. He shrugged, as if switching gears. "But your party plan worked. We've had half a million dollars in pledges already this week. The board agreed to reject the VitaWow offer. But when Ralph called over, he heard they had already voted against it. I'm glad your company decided it wasn't in its best interests to buy the mission site."

Calista frowned. They'd already been over this. "Grant, it was a great deal. No doubt about it. But what about the people here? What about the staff? They can't wait for some big complex to be built. Especially if it's way out of town."

His deep blue eyes settled on her, his gaze intense. "You're saying VitaWow board voted against acquiring the land because it would close the mission."

Calista paused and wished she could say the board was so compassionate. "No. I tried that argument. I also tried to say it would look bad for VitaWow to buy this place right after the fire. In the end I tried a little scare tactic."

"Which was?"

"I told them we couldn't afford to get tangled up with whatever struggle was happening between you and Kurt Daniels." She shrugged. "I don't know what convinced them, but I was praying my heart out the whole time."

Grant stood up and crossed the room in a few steps.

Calista felt her mouth drop open a little at the speed of his approach. His jaw was set; intensity radiated from him.

"That's what they told me. VitaWow backed out because nobody wants to be in the middle of the drama that is Kurt Daniels and his son. Reputations are valuable. Once tarnished, there's no restoring them. And what about you? Can you afford to get tangled up in this mess?"

Calista lifted her chin and said quietly, "I already am, aren't I?"

He stood inches away, expressions crossing his face faster than she could track them. "I'm sorry."

"Please, don't be…" And she meant to finish the sentence, to tell him how she understood what it was like to run from your past. How she wasn't sorry she came to the mission and met Marisol. How she'd learned to love something much bigger than herself for once. But there was a lump in her throat that made the words impossible.

He nodded and turned toward the window, his voice soft but steady. "I never should have gotten involved with you. It's not fair to drag anybody into my family's drama. But we haven't known each other very long and this city has a short memory. By next year, no one will even remember."

It was obvious he'd changed his mind about her. Them. Whatever they were. *No one will even remember.* He was going to forget her as soon as she was out of sight. She hauled in a breath and steeled herself to make a graceful exit.

"Grant, I want to thank you for letting me volunteer. I've learned so much about the needs of the people here. I've made friends…" Her voice trailed away into nothingness. How did you say goodbye when your heart was shattering?

He nodded, still not meeting her eyes. "Thank you, Calista. You're welcome back anytime."

She stood, not wanting to move away but not able to bridge the space between them. In the end, she slipped on her coat and walked out, wishing she was somewhere, anywhere, but in her own life.

As she pushed open the lobby door, Calista hoped her face showed calm, and not the raw pain that twisted through her.

Lana looked up from the desk and called out to her. "Come here, Calista."

It was the last thing in the world she wanted to do but she moved her leaden feet away from the front door and toward the desk. The Christmas tree winked and sparkled with colored lights. A group of kids gathered by the cafeteria doors, chattering and laughing.

Jose came over to the desk, watching Calista's face with a wary expression.

"Where are you going?" Lana seemed almost accusatory.

She coughed, trying to clear the lump from her throat. "I was going to head home."

"It's Christmas Eve and we're going to sing some carols with the kids. Savannah was asking for you yesterday."

How could she stay and sing carols when all her hopes were gone? She wanted to crawl into bed and never come out. "Thanks, but I need to go home."

"No, you should join us. It'll be fun." Jose nodded agreement.

"*Mija*, you are leaving?" Now Marisol had joined them, her dark eyes wide with surprise.

She could hardly lift her eyes. Of course they would all want her to stay and be festive. But she was barely keeping herself together for the few minutes it would take to get to her car. There was no way she could sing carols. "Yes, I need to go. I just stopped…to make sure everybody was okay."

"But everybody is not okay! Mr. Monohan is thinking that—and you are leaving without—and how will we—" Marisol broke down in tears at the last word. Her face crumpled with grief and her chin dropped to her chest as she began to sob noisily.

Calista felt her face go slack and she shot a glance at Lana, only to see the same shock on her face. Jose looked as if someone was pounding a nail through his hand.

"Don't cry, Mari. Don't cry. I'll fix this." Jose patted her awkwardly on the shoulder.

"No, it cannot be fixed! It is all ruined and now they will never—"

"No, Marisol, just wait. I can fix this." Jose grabbed Calista's arm and steered her back toward the office door.

"What are you doing?" she gasped in surprise.

"Fixing," he responded, his face set in a grim mask. He punched in the code and marched her back down the carpeted hallway to Grant's office. The door was open, just as Calista had left it.

"Mr. Monohan." Jose's tone brought Grant's head up with a snap. His eyes widened as he took in the scene before him: Jose gripping Calista's elbow, her expression probably furious and embarrassed.

"You need to know something." Jose paused, his chin jutting out. "Marisol is crying because Calista is leaving."

Grant studied his hands, jaw clenched. Finally, he said, "I don't understand. What does this have to do with me?"

Jose sighed. "You know what. If you want to be stubborn, then you go out and tell Marisol that you would rather break her heart than swallow your pride."

Calista felt anger boil up inside. Break Marisol's heart? What about hers? "Just wait a minute."

Jose turned and said fiercely, "No, you two wait a minute. We live in a place where dreams die, families are broken, kids are placed in foster care, sons are lost, parents leave. And you two are willing to let this good thing God has planned for you just…just fall apart because you're too proud to actually have a conversation."

Calista felt heat creep up her neck and into her face. *This good thing God has planned?* She shot a glance at Grant.

"So, you two stand here and think about it for a while. I'm going back out to see if I can get Marisol to stop crying so we can sing some Christmas carols." He said the last sentence in such a threatening tone that Calista almost burst out laughing at the incongruity. Jose was like a mother hen, scolding her chicks.

He turned and left the room, leaving Calista to stare after him, her mouth twitching.

The sound of a warm chuckle made her knees weak and she could hardly raise her eyes to meet Grant's gaze.

Chapter Sixteen

"Who knew Jose was so afraid of Marisol?" Grant asked, shaking his head.

"Or Marisol's tears." Calista closed her eyes briefly, as if gathering strength. "Look, Grant, she's a sweet woman but we can't let her expectations decide our futures."

Grant crossed the room and stood before her. He'd never felt more afraid, or more hopeful. He was jumping off the cliff and not even checking to see if there was a parachute. "I agree. It doesn't matter what Marisol thought was happening here. It doesn't matter what Jose will do to us if we don't make Marisol happy. What matters is you and me."

"Is there a you and me?" Her voice was almost all breath, her green eyes shining with tears.

"I want there to be. I know how awkward this is, with my father and the media—"

"I don't care. I love you."

Those sweet words coming from her mouth were more than he could bear. He opened his arms and she walked right into them, as if she had been made to live next to his heart. She smelled like warm cookies. Her voice was muffled as she spoke into his shirt. "He's right. I was too proud to come in here and ask to be part of your life."

He kissed her hair, her temple, feeling her arms wrap around his waist under his jacket. "You shouldn't have had to ask. I'm sorry, Calista. I was so sure you wouldn't want to be with a man like me."

She raised her head in surprise. "A man like you? You mean, a man who works at a homeless mission? Grant, the joy and purpose you have in your work has changed my life. I'm a different person because of you."

He searched her face, not able to believe that God could be so good to him. "I meant the situation with Kurt Daniels. We're trying to get to know each other. But he's got a serious past. Someday, there'll be a huge scandal. It will touch me, and this mission, just because we're related."

He watched her eyes narrow, appreciating his words. She said, "If God is with us, we'll be okay. And that future scandal? Bring it on."

A huge grin spread over his face and he shook his head. "I love you. You're scary sometimes, but I love you." And he dropped his head to hers, meeting her lips halfway. He lost himself in the joy of holding her close, of glimpsing a future he never could have imagined.

She broke off their kiss and tilted her head. "Listen," she whispered.

Out in the lobby the caroling had begun. The sweet sound of children's voices filtered through the office door and down the hallway, bringing a message of faith and hope.

He hated to let her go, but there would be time. Days

and weeks and years left to talk and revel in the blessings God had in store. "We'd better get out there and make sure Marisol hasn't flooded the lobby with tears."

She stood up on her tiptoes and feathered one last kiss on his lips. "Lead the way."

"That's what you said the first day we met. Do you remember?"

"Did I?" Her lips tilted up, eyes bright with love. "Well, I'm so glad you did. It's what you do best."

Live more abundantly. He paused, knowing that timing was everything. And he had a great feeling that it was the right time to say what was in his heart. "With you by my side, I'll lead even better. Will you marry me? Share your life with me? Be a part of this mission?"

A wonder that words so softly spoken could hold his entire future. "Yes, oh, yes."

He tugged her back into his arms, her tears blending into their kisses.

"But, Calista, I have to say something," he murmured as he trailed kisses along her cheek.

"Anything."

"You've got to give away that cat."

She pulled back from him, laughter creasing her face. "With pleasure."

Epilogue

"The photographer is wearing a path in the floor," Lissa said, popping her head into the room. "I don't think he's used to this kind of crowd." She slipped into the room and stood uncertainly behind Calista. "And you look totally gorgeous. In case no one has told you that."

"Tell him to keep his hat on." Marisol fussed with Calista's veil and frowned.

Calista met Lissa's gaze in the mirror and mouthed, "Thank you."

Jackie cleared her throat and stood up, smoothing down her elegant green satin dress. "I'm headed out. Lana's got all the groomsmen corralled." She waved her bouquet in the air and the scent of fresh baby roses filled the room. "Don't be late." She dropped a kiss on Calista's cheek.

"Never." If only she could get Marisol to stop fluffing her veil. The gauzy material was dotted with tiny freshwater pearls. It fell in stiff cascades down her back to her waist, accenting the simplicity of the satin bodice and cap sleeves.

"Mari," Calista whispered, gently catching the old woman's hand in hers. "It's not going to be a winter wedding if I wait any longer," she said, her tone teasing.

"Ah, *mija*!" Marisol shook her head forlornly. "I feel as if my children are growing up. But I suppose it is God's will. Just promise me that I can be *abuelita* to all your babies."

For the first time that day, Calista felt tears well up in her eyes. To be called *mija* with such fierce love, to be called family by this faithful woman, was almost too much. She rose swiftly, and reached out to hug Marisol tight, inhaling the familiar smell of chili powder and clean soap.

"Gracias, por todo," she whispered in her ear. Then with one final squeeze, she turned to the door.

"Are you ready?" Lissa bounced on her toes, the bridesmaid dress shimmering darkly with the movement. The sight of the young woman who preferred rips and tears in her clothes wearing something so girlie made Calista's heart swell with affection.

"Never been more ready," Calista said, taking a last sweeping glance around the old room. In all her daydreams she had never imagined prepping for her wedding in second-hand chairs, on ugly orange carpet, in front of a shadowy mirror. But how she had come to love this place and these people!

Marisol took a white handkerchief from her sleeve and waved it. "Now I'm ready."

Calista laughed out loud and took her arm. "Then let's go show them how it's done, Marisol."

Walking slowly to accommodate the older woman's halting steps, they moved to the entranceway as the music began. Lissa, Lana and Jackie progressed at a dignified pace, handsome escorts at their sides.

The change of music signaled the bride's approach and Calista smiled at the sedate notes of Pachelbel's *Canon in D.* Jorge lifted a hand in greeting, his head bobbing as he worked his magic with the stereo equipment. Grant was the one who'd asked him to play DJ for the day and Calista had half expected her walk down the aisle to be to a thumping hip-hop beat.

They stepped onto the green-carpeted aisle and Calista gasped at the transformation of the old cafeteria. A green velvet curtain blocked off the view of the kitchen construction. Trailing ivy and fairy lights lined the doors and the aisle. Tea lights and white satin bows decorated the sills along each frosty window, with generous boughs of holly every few feet. Her gaze swept the crowd, seeing so many friends and family. Her sister Elaine's husband stood near the back row, bouncing their baby boy as he fussed, smiling apologetically at the baby's contribution to the ceremony. Aliya, Josh and McKenzie grinned from the front row while little Savannah, pink sunglasses in place, waved like a metronome set on high.

At the very front stood Grant, impossibly handsome in a tuxedo, tiny white rose in his lapel. Eric stood a little to his left, red hair smoothed down for once. Elaine stood to the right of the minister. The two sisters locked eyes for a moment and Calista forced herself to glance away as her throat squeezed shut. The joy on Elaine's face spoke of healing and new beginnings, a family learning to love each other again.

The details of the room faded away as Calista looked into Grant's eyes. His face was alight with hope and the promise of years to love each other, of the family they wanted to make together. She wanted to sprint down the aisle but managed to keep a steady pace with Marisol.

With just a few more steps she stood at his side, unable to tear her gaze from his.

He leaned forward, dark hair falling over his forehead, and whispered in her ear, "I've decided to throw in a corner office to sweeten the deal. What do you say?"

She couldn't help laughing. "Just not the filing room?" she whispered back.

As they turned as one to face the minister, he spoke out of the corner of his mouth. "Nope. And it comes with some great art."

Calista blinked back sudden tears and gripped Grant's hand. God had moved heaven and earth, and the board of directors, to bring them to this point. She answered Grant's radiant smile with one of her own and knew that God's timing had never been more perfect.

* * * * *

Dear Reader,

Like most of this nation in the past few years, our family has walked the fine line of poverty through multiple job losses. Only by the grace of God have we never had to experience homelessness. Watching friends and family struggle through financial hardship, while witnessing the amazing generosity of others, encouraged me to examine my own opinions about poverty and the working poor.

Calista worked hard for everything she has and her success seems to be the American dream, right? But inside, she's lonely and unsure. When she searches for meaning in her life, her new faith nudges her toward a different kind of work. The people at the mission, especially the children, give her the family that she's been missing. But she sees the handsome director as impossibly perfect, just the way other people see her as CEO. It takes time for her to reach the man underneath, who struggles in his own way to find God's perfect will.

I love the verse where Jesus said He came so that we might have life and have it more abundantly. Sometimes God's idea of abundance isn't quite what we imagine it will be. Sometimes it takes a little reflection (or a lot) to see where He's handing out gifts in our lives. I'd love to hear about the gifts He's given you, even if they're not quite what you expected! You can snail mail me c/o Love Inspired Books, 195 Broadway, 24th floor, New York, New York, 10007, or through my website, virginiacarmichael.blogspot.com.

Virginia Carmichael

Questions for Discussion

1. Calista's father was cold and unloving toward her, but warm and friendly to others. How can hypocrisy do more damage than domestic violence? Do you think it's sometimes easier to be loving to strangers than to those whom we live with day in and day out?

2. Grant's father refused to acknowledge his son throughout his life, but then changes his mind. How did this affect Grant's ability to trust other people? Why would Grant agree with the phrase "love of money is the root of all evil"?

3. Calista is a powerful businesswoman who can make boardroom deals without breaking a sweat. Why is it so hard for her to walk into the mission and ask if she can help? Where would you be most out of your comfort zone and still be doing God's will?

4. Marisol has endured a terrible tragedy in her life, but she thinks that Grant has suffered more. How can a loved one dying be less painful than watching someone walk away? What is special about Marisol's ability to give advice and love to Grant and Calista?

5. Lana is a strong, capable woman but when Calista first meets her, she feels uncomfortable with her

unusual appearance. Would Lana ever have gotten a job as Calista's receptionist? Why or why not?

6. Grant gave Jose a job at the mission when he was still struggling to overcome his dependency issues. How is it easier for Grant to offer refuge and solace to Jose than someone like Calista?

7. Kurt Daniels wants to have a relationship with his son, after years of ignoring his existence. How does he ruin his chances of being a father, even in the end? Why would he think threats and money would buy him Grant's love?

8. Calista has the ability to make a lot of money, but realizes that she isn't as good at cultivating friendships or family connections. How does her growing faith change her view of success? How does God's unconditional love change the way she views people like Jose, Lana, Marisol or Savannah?

9. Most people would consider inheriting a huge fortune to be a good thing. Grant wants nothing to do with his father's fortune and Calista understands. How does her acceptance of his decisions help him to trust her? Could he have accepted the money with a clear conscience? When do the needs of others outweigh our own reservations?

10. Eric is Grant's best friend. What does his advice about "living life more abundantly" mean to Grant? What in your life is a perfect example of God wishing you life more abundant?

11. Most people would consider a CEO and a homeless-shelter director to be opposites. How are Calista and Grant a perfect match? How does Calista bring out the best in Grant's commitment to his residents? How does Grant encourage Calista to do what she's best at, including making money and business?

12. Grant makes a choice to accept Kurt Daniels's apology, and will make an effort to have some sort of relationship with him. How is it hardest to forgive those people who hurt us as children? Do you think Calista will reach out to her father in time? Should she?

WE HOPE YOU ENJOYED THESE TWO

LOVE INSPIRED®

BOOKS.

If you were **inspired** by these

uplifting, heartwarming

romances, be sure to look for

all six Love Inspired® books

every month.

Love Inspired®

www.LoveInspired.com

Love Inspired®

Save $1.00

on the purchase of any
Love Inspired® book.

Available wherever books are sold, including most bookstores, supermarkets, drugstores and discount stores.

Save $1.00

on the purchase of any Love Inspired® book.

Coupon valid until July 31, 2018.
Redeemable at participating retail outlets in the U.S. and Canada only.
Limit one coupon per customer.

52615199

5 65373 00076 2 (8100)0 12313

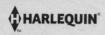

HARLEQUIN®

Save $1.00

on the purchase of any

Harlequin® series book.

Available wherever books are sold, including
most bookstores, supermarkets, drugstores
and discount stores.

Save $1.00

on the purchase of any Harlequin® series book.

Coupon valid until July 31, 2018.
Redeemable at participating retail outlets in the U.S. and Canada only.
Limit one coupon per customer.

52615203

5 65373 00076 2   (8100)0 12314

® and ™ are trademarks owned and used by the trademark owner and/or its licensee.

© 2018 Harlequin Enterprises Limited

HSCOUP0318

Get 2 Free Books,
<u>Plus</u> 2 Free Gifts—
just for trying the Reader Service!

Love Inspired®

Looking for inspiration in tales of hope, faith and heartfelt romance?

Check out **Love Inspired®** and **Love Inspired® Suspense** books!

New books available every month!

CONNECT WITH US AT:

Harlequin.com/Community

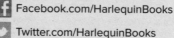 Facebook.com/HarlequinBooks

Twitter.com/HarlequinBooks

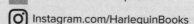 Instagram.com/HarlequinBooks

 Pinterest.com/HarlequinBooks

ReaderService.com

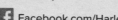

LIGENRE2018